THE BLACK
MOTH

THE BLACK MOTH

CAROLYNE TOPDJIAN

Copyright © 2023 by Carolyne Topdjian
Cover and jacket design by Mimi Bark

ISBN 978-1-957957-36-4
ISBN 978-1-957957-48-7
Library of Congress Control Number: available upon request

First hardcover edition October 2023 by Agora Books
An imprint of Polis Books, LLC
62 Ottowa Road S
Marlboro, NJ 07746
www.PolisBooks.com

Also by Carolyne Topdjian

The Hitman's Daughter

i. No Vacancies

Memories of your visit linger long after you've checked out of the hotel. No matter how quietly you tread, or how softly you whisper, these old walls have eyes, ears, and a belly of their own—gluttonous and insatiable. Over the years, Château du Ciel has sipped, swallowed, and soaked in your stories, one after the next, be they fresh or stale, salty or sweet: the slur of your wine-tipped tongue, the moan of your lover, the milk of your sex, and, above all else, the sweat of your nightmare. The walls record them all. Some memories merely graze like dust motes in shadows, unremarkable and microscopic. Others billow in waves, leaving behind a fermented stink like smoke rings in oakwood furniture. Then there are memories that slap, claw, tremor, and buck to be freed. Those are the ones that emit the darkest marks. And stains like that? Well, they'll never get out, no matter how bone-raw you scrub and scour. The past remains. Your secret seeps deeper into the foundation of the hotel, flavoring its marrow...even as its walls hunger to feed anew.

ii. Beneath the Veil

She processed it wrong—out of order: first the flick of the hit, fiery, stunning; then the shape of the gun. Its handler was like a lone actor on stage, stepping forward through shadows. Only this wasn't make-believe. On the contrary. The scream of her nerve endings was very real; so much so, it became muffled in translation, too overwhelming for her brain to translate. She flailed her hands to her wound, struggling to focus as, ahead, the barrel of the pistol floated in and out of her vision. Blood wept. She choked on a cry. Like angry storm clouds, pain gathered and swelled. It would break over her any second, scalding and agonizing. As soon as the shock wore thin, she'd be done for.

RUN! her father's voice bellowed in her ears. Except her muscles were brittle with exhaustion. Her bones felt twisted in their sockets, locked wrong like crooked hinges.

Gun still pointed, her enemy leered at her, a thrill pooling in their eyes. She barely registered their lopsided smile because...because...

She blinked, stumbled backward, and fell through the doorway into the vacant room. Her spine knocked against furniture. Gravity pulled.

Splayed on the floor, she gasped for breath as the world raced and slowed, a vortex sucking her under.

A trap. All along...waiting for me to...to...

Her vision blotted black as the door to the room creaked shut. Fire safety. They were weighted to close. To seal out danger.

But a second later, the door whined open again.

Leaden on the ground, she couldn't hit her attacker. She couldn't raise a fist or a heel or an elbow. She couldn't *see*. Her palms lay on her chest, drained of energy, and streaked her collar wet. For a delirious second, she imagined a dash of color like a silky red tie. Beneath her fingertips, her hammering pulse grew tired.

Footsteps vibrated—the weight of the enemy. She could feel their shadow slither over her skin like slick oil. Hovering. Watching. This entire time, they had been watching.

As her blood waned with her consciousness, her final sensation was familiar and comforting: cigarette smoke drifting off her attacker's clothes.

Part One
In Memoriam

To make the ghost speak, you must learn the language of death.

—SIGNS: A HANDBOOK FOR CLAIRVOYANCE

'Fore you pull the trigger, picture that third eye on the forehead. That's your target.

—CAIN FRANCIS, convicted hitman, in conversation with his daughter

ONE

They were close enough to see the points of the spires cresting the mountainous forest. Mave Michael Francis tilted her head for a better view out the taxi's rear window. *Home sweet home,* she thought with irony. Château du Ciel was said to float above the clouds—hence its name—but on this dusk, it seemed to loom atop the horizon. Like a shrine for the recently departed.

He's not dead. He's—

"Ain't it something?" the driver said, interrupting her thoughts. He watched her in his mirror. "Like a grand old hideaway in the middle of nowhere, huh. First time visiting the hotel?"

"Mm-hmm." She smiled tightly and leaned back in her seat to escape his view.

"Yeah, thought so. Don't get too many fares up here from the village."

She released a quiet breath. He'd bought her lie, had no clue who she was. Not yet. She adjusted her sunglasses to assure her anonymity. According to her father, her eyes were her tell, her weak spot. People noticed straight away, if only subconsciously. There was something off about her. Others (the few astute observers) immediately paid attention to her irises: one cerulean and the other bronze. Except Mave didn't care to be memorable. Least of all to strangers. She traced a strand on her wig and brushed its ends against her lips.

"You must've heard it's haunted, right?" the driver said, attempting small talk as he wound up the steep road, higher and higher. Soon, their ears would pop. "That why you visiting, for those ghost tours they've been advertising?"

"Mmm, and the view." Better to be mistaken for a superstitious tourist. One could never be too careful. She swallowed back her anxiety. This time would be different. Her month away, visiting her newfound aunt in Manhattan, had given her perspective. She'd begun meditating. Journaling. It helped. Even if the majority of her entries were lovesick letters. Aunt Parissa had suggested she try therapy, but Mave wasn't quite ready for that. She'd seen a shrink once, right after Cain's trial when her thoughts had been darkest. She'd lasted half a session. Never again.

Trust issues, darling, Aunt Parissa had remarked just last week, toasting her affectionately with her wine glass. *Runs in the family, you know.*

Ten minutes later, they passed through the gates of the property, onto the pebbled laneway. As they snaked around a fountain of angels that grew mold for wings, the driver hunkered forward for a better view. He whistled in awe as he pulled up to the hotel's entrance. Mave had forgotten how impressive the château's edifice could seem at a glance, even as the shadows fell. If anything, the darkness helped, soaking the stone walls in romance and soft streams of lamplight. Twenty-three stories high, nestled above the remote forests of western Colorado, one-hundred-year-old French architecture at its finest. From the outside, you could almost pretend that within the hotel, the hand-cut crystal chandeliers weren't housing more spiders than candles.

Mave tipped the driver and slipped out, eager to exit the cab's cloying scent of nicotine smothered in pine deodorant. As she waited for her suitcase amid a chorus of crickets, she bundled her scarf tighter around her neck. Nerves swilled in her stomach. Standing still was always the worst.

"Here you are, young lady," the driver said, wheeling her the suitcase and shutting the car's trunk. "Good luck with your ghost."

Mave stiffened. "Excuse me?"

"On the tour," he tossed over his shoulder, already climbing back into his cab.

"Oh, right. Thank you," she mumbled. She drew in a lungful of crisp mountain air, clearing away her jitters. She wouldn't let the comment of a stranger unravel her. She was strong, capable, a survivor. She was *alive*. Braced by the clean breeze, she strode through the château's ornamental doorway. Her momentum lasted all of five steps.

"Hello, welcome to..." The bell boy flinched and tripped over his greeting as he took her in. Her tailored suit. Spiked heels. Ruby lips and black bob. *Look the part*, Cain had always said. So much for going unnoticed.

He straightened his shoulders, avoiding her eyes though she still wore her sunglasses. "Uh, Ms. Fran-cis." His voice cracked. He cleared his throat and reached for her suitcase and handbag before she could protest. "Sorry, almost didn't recognize you. I'll have these delivered to your new suite. Immediately. Everything's ready. You want me to arrange early turn down service?"

Oh god. She held in a sigh and removed her sunglasses. "No need." She smiled brightly. "I'm not a guest, remember?" Yet neither shopgirl nor resident owner sounded right to her ears. If anything, she felt closer to a child playing dress-up in one of Cain's disguises.

"Oh. Yeah. Of course." He blinked. After an awkward pause, he whisked away her bags like a soldier on a mission. At least he hadn't saluted.

Mave resumed her path through the lobby. No guests. Plenty of dust. Even the weak lighting couldn't mask the desolation. *A seasonal slump*, she tried consoling herself. Her heels echoed on marble tile. She waved politely as she passed the check-in desk, experiencing a similar stiff reaction from the receptionist as the bell boy. She'd hoped the month away would help ease the tension. A new suit. A new season. In fact, a last-minute wedding was booked to mark the spring equinox. Though it was a goth-themed event—all black roses and pricking thorns —it was a hopeful sign nonetheless. Julián seemed optimistic.

During her stay in New York, Mave had held regular online meetings with the hotel's new director. She'd requested HR profiles on all personnel—had memorized every name and headshot, seeking hints to relate to them, any icebreaker no matter how superficial. In her presence, however, the staff were as nervous as always. Everyone except for Julián and—

"Mave Michael!" Bent over an appointment book, Bastian Toussaint straightened to his impressive height and sang, "Welcome back. How's my favorite shopgirl doing? Flight okay?"

As she reached his desk, a real smile tugged at her lips. The concierge had a way of doing that (never mind that she was likely the only shopgirl he knew). "Yes, thanks for asking. How's the fort holding up?"

"Good—even better now that you're back."

Mave's shoulders relaxed. She didn't have to try as hard with Bastian. "Heard my suite's ready," she said. "Any chance the key's here?"

"You bet." He dug into a drawer for the tasseled antique.

"And the security cameras?" Since she'd newly inherited the property, promoting her from unknown shopgirl to hotel owner, Julián had insisted she upgrade from her tiny room in the staff quarters. In truth, Mave had agreed for privacy over luxury. She'd chosen an old, defunct suite on the twenty-third floor. Based on the hotel's sprawling floorplan, her new residence checked off her requirements: close to the fire escape, far from the guestrooms, and clear sightlines to expose any visitors. As an added bonus, it featured a stained-glass skylight in its living room.

"Everything deactivated, just like you wanted," Bastian confirmed. "Zero cameras on that wing."

Excellent. She needed her space. No prying eyes. "And the wing opposite, 2301?"

"Uh-huh. Tech installed three cameras inside the grand penthouse yesterday morning. All's well."

She nodded. Her grandmother had been an eccentric, rich artist. Old money. Along with gifting Mave the hotel, Birdie had left behind sentimental paintings in her studio in the massive penthouse. Given the media's recent coverage of her death, Mave didn't trust someone wouldn't try to break in for a souvenir or two.

"Oh, and before I forget..." Bastian shuffled some papers aside and slid out a sheet for her. "Here's this week's schedule."

"Thanks. Did Julián give you the update, too?" she asked while perusing the itinerary. The last scheduled ghost tour was set to start in five minutes.

"Not yet, but he left a message. Let me guess: the wedding?"

"The one and only. Any chance you know a local lepidopterist?"

His mouth pulled into a frown. "A lep-what-now?"

"Yeah, I had to look it up, too. An insect expert. Or a bug farmer." She straightened the daily paper on the edge of his desk. The headline caught her eye: a string of residential break-ins in the village south of the hotel. "We need to get a hold of some black swallowtail butterflies," she said, her attention split as she scanned the article. At least the journalists had moved on from Birdie. And the fire at the hotel. "Like, *a lot* of black swallowtail butterflies."

"Ah, brother." He blew out his lips.

Mave quit reading and looked up. "I know. The bride is..." She drummed her nails on the desk, struggling for a polite description of their soon-to-be guest of honor: the heiress of a K-pop producer and real estate mogul.

"Nuts," Bastian filled in with an amused expression. "You must've heard about the velour curtains she's ordered: one hundred percent organic cotton, to be dyed a particular shade of carmine crimson."

"Mmm." She scrunched her nose. "And the pewter dinnerplates with matching goblets."

"Let's not forget the six-tiered black sponge, gluten-free, nut-free marzipan cake. You know Chef wants to strangle her, right? 'How can you make marzipan without almonds?'" he imitated with a growl.

A laugh rattled out with her breath.

"What does she need butterflies for?"

"Black butterflies," Mave reemphasized. "She wants us to convert the old greenhouse into a conservatory."

"I thought the wedding was booked in Queen's Hall for the whole run-down look. What did Julián call it—distressed décor?"

"Distressed" was another one of the hotel director's marketing spins for "ruined." Whereas the majority of the château needed a makeover to help showcase its deco design, Queen's Hall was in complete disrepair. "That's been switched for the reception afterwards," she clarified. "As of this morning, the ceremony has relocated to the greenhouse, and the place has to be full of black butterflies fluttering in candlelight during the vows."

"You serious? Has Bridezilla seen the greenhouse?"

"Apparently, Julián took photos on request and emailed her yesterday afternoon."

"With filters? It's a mess in there, way worse than Queen's Hall. Don't think anyone's used it since the nineties."

Her stomach did a flip. It'd been locked up for that long? Though she'd noted the glass building from afar, she hadn't searched its frozen interior. Vast as the grounds were, much of the hotel's property had been buried under snow since November of last year. But now with the thaw, it could be a good hiding spot for someone who didn't want to be found.

Absolutely not. Forget him. Fresh start, remember?

"Suppose cleaning it up is doable," Bastian muttered to himself, too distracted to notice her turn of thoughts. "It's going to take hundreds, maybe thousands of butterflies to fill that kind of space."

"Right," she said too cheerfully, "and we have less than two weeks to make it happen."

He stood a little taller. "I'll take care of it. Don't worry, I got you." Bastian knew how much they needed this wedding to happen without a hitch. Good word of mouth alone could secure more bookings and help pull them out of debt. But even as she reminded herself of her priority to save the hotel, the niggling feeling inside her chest persisted. Maybe she could do both. Maybe she could manage a high-stakes event *and* mend her secret heartache.

Learn to lie better, Cain whispered in her mind.

"Hey, before you take off to your new digs," Bastian said, "wanted to give you a heads-up about another VIP. He's checking in in a couple of days. Requested the presidential suite."

"Great. Anyone we know?"

"Matter of fact"—he bent closer, as if worried someone might over-hear them—"it's Dominic Grady."

Mave's brow peaked into her bangs. "As in...?"

He nodded. "Birdie's former art dealer. He mentioned he wanted to meet you to discuss business."

"Business?"

"Assuming it has something to do with your grandmother's art collection."

"Okay. Guess that makes sense." Though she had no interest in representation. Or in entertaining a man who'd had a brief yet scan-dalous affair with her mother a few years before Mave was born. If Cain ever found out... She worried her lip.

"Mave?"

"Huh? Oh, it's fine." She'd handle it. They weren't exactly in a posi-tion to turn down paying guests.

"Should I deliver him a gift basket?" Bastian asked.

"Sure." She frowned, diverted by the wall clock behind him. The second hand ticked sharply in her ears. She glanced down at the schedule again.

Bastian followed her gaze, seeming to read her mind along the way. "You want to check out the ghost tour, don't you?"

The opposite. She had no desire to encounter restless spirits; nor did she particularly care to partake in a romanticized ceremony that started in the château's infamously haunted library and concluded in its upper mezzanine with a tea leaf reading. The so-called ghost in her head was more than enough. But from early on, Cain had instilled in her a fight-er's work ethic. You couldn't block a hit you didn't see coming. You had to get in front of it. Control it. No procrastination—especially when it came to pain. Besides, the past three months had cycled plenty of whis-pers throughout these drafty hallways, and the staff would notice if she avoided the tour. She couldn't have more gossip.

A step ahead, the voice in her head growled in Cain's voice. *Show no weakness.*

She breathed out, wiped her sweaty palms on her hips, and flashed Bastian her one-hundred-watt smile. "Can hardly wait," she said.

Two

She slipped into the cavernous library and eased the French doors shut. They creaked anyway. Her pulse skittered. *It's just a library,* she chastised herself. She'd been here countless times. So why was she hesitating now? Because a glorified tour guide was going to force her to relive it all? To call upon the dead to rise? A shiver travelled her spine. Deep within the room, the murmur of conversation drifted, soft whispers buffeted by studded leather seats and towering rows of mahogany shelves.

Mave took a moment to soak in the library's scents of beeswax, ink, newsprint, wood polish. She rolled back her shoulders. *Right.* She'd win them over with charm, compliments. Volley back questions. The triple Ds, Cain called them: divert, deceive, and dominate. She snapped the elastic band on her wrist, gritted her teeth, and made her way past the dimly lit bookcases. The goal was to blend in, and she was already five minutes late.

Gracelyn's soft voice travelled across the room. "...du Ciel was built a century ago, with its newest renovation plans destroyed in a fire in the restricted underground tunnels directly beneath us."

Mave discreetly joined the rear of the group as a few guests looked down at their feet. Did they expect to find scorch marks on the Persian rug? In the wavering candlelight, she could almost imagine it herself.

The tapestry's ornate flowers seemed to wither and blacken in the shadows. Flames licked.

Holden.

She forced her gaze up before the memory could overtake her.

A middle-aged tourist in khakis waved to catch Gracelyn's attention. "Didn't some rich artist die in that fire? I saw it on *Evening Line.* Is her ghost here now? Do you feel her presence?"

The dozen or so visitors seemed to perk up awaiting Gracelyn's reply. A few readied their phones to record. They weren't here for the truth, Mave realized, remembering the death of her maternal grandmother. These curiosity seekers only sought to satisfy their already made-up minds. It's what they'd paid for: to have their skepticism confirmed, their imaginations spooked, their heavy hearts soothed. The dead walked among us. Or not. If only Mave could figure out that last bit. She rubbed the end of her nose and focused on Gracelyn.

The self-proclaimed fortune teller squinted into the dark corners, as if concentrating. Mave couldn't decide if she was legit or not. If anything, she looked like she'd raided a costume shop and was trying a little too hard: her grizzled hair tied back in a scarf; bangles tinkling on her forearms; a silk poncho draping her curves. Julián had brought her on a few weeks ago, along with a handful of hires for the hotel's supposed comeback. Turnover had been high after the fire, but Julián claimed they could spin the hotel's recent tragedies into a tourist attraction.

"Birdie Everhart did indeed pass away at the hotel, and I sense..." Gracelyn paused, drawing out the moment. "There *is* unusual energy in this library. But that's to be expected. The château has a long and rich history, dating back to 1921. As I'm sure you can imagine, that history has shaped the building's aura that we now feel—even before the tragic deaths of Birdie Everhart, Annabelle Leandro, and others, such as..."

Namedropping the body count. Mave had to hand it to her. She was good.

"What about the Spirit of Dead Poets?" another tourist broke in.

Hearing Holden's pseudonym, Mave stiffened.

"Perhaps," Gracelyn answered serenely. "But as I mentioned in our introductions, this isn't a séance." Her eyes caught on Mave. "And I'm not a medium."

Mave held in a curse and dropped her gaze. You'd think being five foot nothing would offer advantages like being hidden in a crowd. *I'm not a medium either!* she inwardly argued. She wasn't even a proper psychic, for god's sake, no matter what the staff were whispering behind her back. Yes, she had an extra sense, but it was more a practical skill for tracking lost, inanimate belongings. Like the key fob on the counter in the main lobby. At present, the portly tourist standing to her far-left was feeling in his pocket, realizing his car key wasn't there.

"Now, if I can direct your attention to the fireplace..." Gracelyn continued.

Mave quit listening as they shuffled closer to the black stone hearth. Would she ever get used to the loss of anonymity? Though it was merely the staff who noticed her—who treated her like an overnight celebrity—for a twenty-five-year-old woman who'd been raised by a hitman and trained to melt into walls, her out-in-the-open reputation was awkward at the best of times. It might even be funny if it weren't so troubling.

Whereas before she'd been left in relative peace in the hotel's basement boutique, the gift shop suddenly had a revolving door. Her opinion mattered, and what did she think: Were the candles too much? The dried amaranth? Did she approve of the old photographs arranged on the fireplace mantle just so? Would the revenue from the ghost tours be enough to cover the costs that the insurance couldn't? Should they prepare for layoffs? And finally—the most pressing of them all—would the hotel survive past the current fiscal year?

In truth, Mave didn't know. Her head was spinning from one too many worries. It wasn't like she had any experience in spearheading a business. Forget a six-hundred-thousand-square-foot formerly grand château with a tarnished name and growing debt. One could only pawn so many antiques. Mave needed a sustainable, long-term business plan.

The remainder of the tour was an unremarkable blur. Eventually, they wandered up the grand staircase to the mezzanine. The labyrinth-like halls were empty but for their little group. Mave pretended not to notice when they passed a corner with peeling wallpaper, a peacock's tail drooping on one side. Or when the vents wafted musty air. Or when the floors revealed scuffs and cracks. Ironically, the ghost tour merely highlighted her responsibility.

No more obsessing over the hotel's infamous Spirit of Dead Poets. It didn't matter that he had appeared and disappeared like smoke—had unraveled her deepest, darkest troubles and opened up to her in return. Their whirlwind encounter was done. Over. She would rip out those lovesick letters she'd journaled and throw them into the fireplace. On autopilot, Mave smiled and made small talk with a hipster couple visiting from Denver. The distraction worked. Until it was her turn for a reading.

As the rest of the group wandered to a makeshift counter to purchase loose-leaf teas and whatever potions Julián was pedaling this week, Mave stiffened on her bistro chair. Gracelyn approached her with a smile, crinkles framing her eyes. There was no way to bow out—not anymore. Mave licked her lips and blinked at the bottom of her drained cup where little dark brown leaves floated in wait. She wasn't entirely sure why she'd drunk the tea. This entire charade could have been avoided if she'd simply left the damned pot steeping—if she hadn't poured and pretended to ponder life while sipping, her mind in deep defense mode.

"So happy you made it," Gracelyn said, settling into the chair facing hers. She smelled pleasant, like freesia soap. "I'm excited to hear what you think. But first, let's have a look, shall we?"

"That's all right, really. There's no—"

"Oh, hush now, this is the fun bit," she said while helping herself to Mave's teacup. She slid it to the center of the table and placed the saucer on top. Her nails were neatly trimmed and unpolished. Worker's hands. Together, she lifted the saucer and cup in a quick, well-practiced flip, her bangles jingling in unison. She adjusted the base so that the handle faced Mave. "Now, think of a question, but don't say it out loud."

Mave nodded and simultaneously forbade her mind from thinking of Holden Frost—from all of the questions that had been burning inside her for three long months. This wasn't her fate, she insisted.

Gracelyn was an act. There was no reason for her blood to be pounding so sharply through her veins.

"Slowly," Gracelyn said, "using your left hand, spin your cup counterclockwise three times by its handle."

Mave swallowed and did as she was told. She rotated her fake fortune. One. Twice. Thrice. It seemed to take forever. Glass on glass squeaked mid-turns, causing the hair on the back of her neck to rise. She was tempted to inventory weapons to ease her tension—scalding hot water, a quick break of the Aqua Deco bottle by her elbow—but a full scan would be too obvious. She glanced up.

Gracelyn's expression seemed to have darkened, her penciled-in brows folded inwards. "Good," she said, although her tone didn't match the word. It sounded more like *get ready* to Mave's ears. "Now gently knock three times on the bottom, here." She indicated the center of the upended cup. Mave complied.

Tap.

Tap.

Tap.

Gracelyn lifted the teacup and peered within. She tilted the rim, then her head. She examined the inner pattern of leaves from every angle. Mave crossed her knees to keep them from jittering under the table. Was it her imagination, or was her reading taking twice as long as those of the guests? She was about to mutter an excuse to escape when Gracelyn softly cleared her throat.

"In your past, I see much travelling...unrest." Her pupils widened. "And there is a spider, symbolizing an unexpected gift, and"—her fingertip tracked paths from one clump of leaves to the next—"a lion. That's a sign of a protector. It watches over you. It leads to your present."

Surely, this was scripted, Mave suspected. Any semi-observant charlatan could recite mystical nonsense just vague enough to be accurate about something in your life. Like constantly moving from city to city during her childhood. Like inheriting the hotel and Cain always watching over her.

"There has been a sudden loss of someone you care for deeply." She slanted the cup for Mave to regard the inner patterns. "See here, this wreath on the right?"

"Mm-hmm," she hummed as her heart clamped. It was too close to the truth for comfort, even though all she saw amid the shadows was a spatter of dark leaves, crowded and fanned against the white porcelain like smashed ants.

"This wreath is very pronounced, and from it," Gracelyn continued, "you are now being pulled in more than one direction. This is your present. But your future, it forks here and..."

"And what?" she asked, her voice unintentionally wispy.

"There is a toad." Gracelyn frowned, seemingly displeased with whatever prophecy she was decoding. "And little worms. They stand at your crossroad."

"Okay." A little huff escaped her throat, not quite humor, not quite disbelief. The eeriest part was, she now thought she could see the worms. Like maggots. Squirming. Faceless. "What does that mean? A good gardening omen, I hope?"

"An unknown enemy," Gracelyn said, gravity pebbling her tone. "And those in the shadows, the worms, they seek to undermine you. You must be careful, Mave Michael." She leaned forward and entrapped Mave's wrist in her tight grasp, startling her. "These enemies are near."

THREE

The next morning, Mave marched to the rear of the property to meet the old groundskeeper. She'd detoured to the kitchens for coffee as an offering. As the nutty bouquet steamed from the takeout cup, she resisted stealing a sip and stifled a yawn. Then another. She'd slept poorly in her new suite. Though you'd think she'd be used to it by now—crashing in unfamiliar beds. Growing up, Cain had moved them around to evade notice, anywhere from seven to nine addresses a year. She'd coped by sneaking into her father's room in the late hours. She would curl up on his floor with her pillow and blanket, watching the steady rise and fall of his chest. Like waves in the ocean. But if she was being honest, it wasn't solely her strange surroundings that had kept her up last night.

Gracelyn's reading bothered her.

No secret enemies existed, she inwardly resolved. She would not be pulled in the wrong direction. "Moving on," she vowed under her breath.

Outside, drizzle peppered her cheeks and lashes. She squinted against the fluorescent clouds as her boots squelched in mud. The sky was a contradiction, turbulent and bright. In the distance, the greenhouse was backlit, its arched walls darkened by shadow. If the tall stalks were any indication, this section of property had been neglected for too long. They'd have to trim all the bracken and weeds along the way; maybe line the path with hurricane lanterns.

She reached the building's entrance and found Amos already there, scowling as he searched through his key ring. The hefty clip seemed as large and as noisy as one of Gracelyn's bangles.

"Morning," Mave announced, perkier than necessary.

The groundskeeper gave her a polite nod in reply. He finally located the correct key and pried it free from his crowded ring.

"How are you?" Mave tried again. "Thought you might like some coffee." She held up the cup.

Amos hesitated before accepting with a muted thank you. He was hard to read. Mave knew from his personnel file that the groundskeeper had been working at the hotel for the past eight years. He was sixty-one, though he could have passed anywhere from forty to seventy. His dark complexion was smooth but for his crow's feet, and his curly hair and beard were a timeless salt-and-pepper. "Here you go." He held out the key he'd separated. "Julián said you asked for a copy."

"I did. Perfect." Mave took the key with a smile, pretending not to notice that he'd yet to sip the coffee. She turned to the barred-up door and poked at its chain padlock. Not that it mattered. The entire lock was so rusted, it released with a squeal, and the chains rattled loose.

As Mave pulled on the door, Amos muttered, "Hold on." He unclipped a flashlight from his belt. "You'll be needing this," he said, gesturing toward the dark interior.

"Oh, right. Thanks." Mave switched on the flashlight and stepped inside with the groundskeeper on her heels.

Stale air and wood rot filled her sinuses. Her nose prickled. She wiped her face on the sleeve of her sweater, the wool rough against her cheek, and scanned her flashlight side to side. Amos stepped ahead of her with his own beam slicing the dark. He groaned audibly—or cursed. She couldn't blame him.

Tangles of dried ivy overran the floors and walls. The ceiling leaked, plinking puddles nearby. Based on first impressions alone, Bastian had been right. Nothing had lived inside this place for decades—nothing breathing, at least. A stab of disappointment shot through her chest.

Another dead end. Not that she'd truly believed she'd find Holden here. Her goal was to prepare for the wedding (or so she tried to convince herself).

"Do you know what they used to grow in here?" she asked.

"Before my time," Amos grunted while inspecting one of the leaks with his flashlight. "Staff shortages and cutbacks." He clucked his tongue. "This side of the gardens has been closed off forever."

"But don't guests wander and explore this way in the spring and summer?" Mave stepped over a broken terracotta pot and ventured deeper inside.

"We got signs to keep out," Amos said. "Folks usually steer back around to the front. And those the signs don't stop, the weeds and bugs normally take care of."

Mave surveyed her surroundings with a sense of unease. Rows of planters were caked with ossified perennials and yellowed mosses. A bench sat atop a ripped landscape cloth, the remains of a headless stone sculpture to its right, and a box of dust-ridden spray bottles to its left. It was easier to picture the greenhouse as once housing dark experiments than bright flora. The more she saw, the more her stomach soured.

She didn't like messes.

Amos tsked loudly. "Gonna be tough to make it in time for the wedding," he muttered, seeming to share her worries.

With black butterflies, no less. Her sigh was cut short by a crunch beneath the sole of her boot. Empty snail shells littered the gravel.

She knelt and swept them with her hands, needing to clean up something, no matter how insignificant. A piece jabbed her. "Ow." She inspected the mound of her palm and pulled out the sliver. "Any chance you see a broom?" she called to Amos. He was dragging in a ladder from beside the front entrance.

"Nah, but there oughta be a hose." He redirected his flashlight to guide her.

"Even better," Mave said, dusting her hands of dirt. "We can power wash the space."

She squinted in the direction he pointed and, sure enough, a hose took shape, tangled and crimped like molted snake skin. Mave crouched with her flashlight and followed the line. It led to the back corner of the greenhouse. More decay. More rust. A metal shelf was mounted beside a utility sink.

"Amos?" Wiping her fingers on her waist, she balanced her flashlight on the edge of the basin. "Think we can open and check these water lines asap?" She tried the faucet while he uttered a vague reply from atop his ladder, too preoccupied with assessing the ceiling.

Great. No shortage of damage. The metal handles stuck in her grip, stiffened from lack of use. "Come on," she said through gritted teeth. She jerked with force and bumped her flashlight, sending it clattering to the ground. She swore in the shadows and bent to retrieve it. And on the gravelly ground beneath the sink, streaks of blood lit up.

FOUR

Mud. It had to be dried mud. Except it wasn't. She knew it in her gut, even before she lowered her nose and breathed in the coppery residue. Old. But not that old—not enough for the dust to devour the stain. *Don't disturb a thing*, Cain cautioned. Mave checked over her shoulder, making sure Amos remained distracted on his ladder. She swallowed the knot in her throat and stooped to the ground.

Carefully with her flashlight, she tried to make sense of the markings. A drip here. A smear there. Nothing to suggest outright violence—not like when she'd been a girl and had discovered her father's hit in the bathtub, brains leaking—or on New Year's Eve when she'd walked in on her grandmother murdered in her penthouse. She shuddered and pushed those horrific memories away.

The gravel here seemed sprinkled and scored in parts, as if something—or someone—had been dragged next to the sink. *Maybe it's not even human blood*, she tried to appease herself. Or maybe another gardener had cut themselves on a tool or a branch. There were infinite possibilities. Only none were logical. Amos had said so himself. This greenhouse had been sealed up forever. The sink wasn't even operational. Anyone who worked the grounds would have known that. The rear gardens were overgrown, choked by weeds, and, up until recently, very much frozen. Who'd bled here? When? The answer came to her right as the mask materialized under the beam of her flashlight.

"You find it?" Amos said, directly over her shoulder.

Mave flinched and bumped her forehead on the bottom of the basin. She'd almost forgotten the groundskeeper was there. She stood and rubbed away the blunt pain. "Huh?"

"The hose." He shuffled back a few steps. "Thought I heard you call me."

"Oh, yeah. No, I...I did!" She prayed she didn't sound as manic as she felt. She leaned on the sink, her arms spread wide as if that might block his view of the ground. "Wondering if you could go and check on these water lines." She patted the basin. "We need them reopened. And also a broom. We need brooms."

Amos scowled again. She couldn't tell whether he was reacting to her orders, or if this was his normal go-to expression. "All right," he grunted. "I'll look for the shutoff valves, radio custodial, and be right back."

"Take your time." She smiled and waited until he'd disappeared from the greenhouse.

Mave ducked back down and stared. She hadn't dreamed it. Breath held, she reached forward slowly. Thickened cobwebs on the underside of the sink clung to her sleeves. Her focus remained on the mask.

In contrast to her fingers, browned in dirt, the disguise was pristine, its porcelain smooth like eggshell. Along its front, it featured an arched brow above a Roman nose with flared nostrils. To its left and right were an assemblage of eyes and mouths. She spun it in her hands, mesmerized by its surreal beauty, its symbolism. Three faces with a horseshoe cutout midway that, when worn, would expose a person's real mouth and chin. Holden's bearded jawline flashed in her memory. She closed her eyes, overwhelmed by the evidence she held.

This was his mask—the same one he'd worn the whole time they were sneaking around the hotel on New Year's Day. What did it mean? How had it ended up in the locked, decrepit greenhouse? That part made no sense. Unless...

Her eyes snapped open. The blood stains before her suddenly took on new meaning. The drip. The smear.

Mave rose for the nearest planter box and dragged it toward the sink. *Hide it. Before they come. Before they see.*

Whatever its meaning, no one else could know.

———

She paced in her bedroom, wearing down the already faded carpet. Yesterday, she'd been surprised to find the décor in her new suite was original to 1921: a creaky king-size bed curtained with chiffon, a lumpy shell-back sofa, a deco-print rug that gave her a headache if she studied it for longer than five seconds.

The wood boards underfoot groaned with her steps. She paused her pacing to check the mask was still on her pillow, as if it might disappear if she didn't confirm every five rounds of the room. She straightened it. The grotesque faces stared back at her. Guarded. Impenetrable like their owner. If only she could extract their secrets. She chewed on her thumbnail and turned to her journal at the foot of the mattress.

She flipped open to her letters. Unfinished. Undelivered. She wished she had someone to talk to about it. But Aunt Parissa was far away and their relationship was too new. Cain was in prison, overprotective and harsh. And when it came to the Spirit of Dead Poets, Bastian was horribly superstitious and apprehensive. He'd likely think Mave was cursed.

Maybe I am.

The next thing she knew, she'd abandoned her plans to burn the journal's pages and was scribbling everything she remembered about Holden Robert Frost—or *thought* she remembered.

They'd met on New Year's Day. He'd been a recluse who'd broken out of the social system. Unbeknownst to anyone, he'd lived in the boarded-up tunnels beneath the château. He spoke five languages and freelanced on the dark web as a translator. In fact, when she'd first begun working at the hotel, Holden had been contracted by Cain to spy on her. The more Mave wrote down, the more unbelievable the story seemed. Familiar doubts crept in.

Back in January, his name had slipped from her lips in front of police, and the sheriff had confirmed Holden had been a local from the village of Hazel Springs, a troubled boy with a juvie record—deceased for well over a decade. Mave drew a big question mark next to that so-called fact. She'd since gotten a hold of the public death records.

Holden Frost had officially died in 2006 in a suspected drowning in a reservoir. The details were lies edged with truths. But which was which? If he'd been alive for the past fifteen years, then who apart from her had seen him in person? Why did he solely exist on the dark web? Was his online persona even him—or an artificially intelligent bot that had fooled everyone, including Cain? Meanwhile, the staff at the château whispered of Holden's existence and thought him a ghost who haunted the library. The Spirit of Dead Poets. Goosebumps rose on her arms as her memories sharpened in a new light.

What if no one apart from her *had* seen Holden? They had always been alone—never in a room with a third party as witness. She shifted back to the mask on the pillow and ran a finger along its brow. He'd taken it off for her once, revealing the vulnerable and beautiful man beneath. All other times, he'd worn the mask to remain hidden—even on the night of the fire when he'd taken a bullet for her. It'd been the last time she'd seen him. He hadn't been around to shield her from the second gunshot.

She scratched her puckered scar under her shirt. The wound grew itchy whenever she focused on it—like at three a.m. while she lay awake in bed, wondering how any of it had happened, if she'd made up the strangest parts to placate herself. She'd bled a lot, had barely made it out of the tunnels alive. But what about him? Where were his charred bones? She shut her eyes and pushed the heels of her hands against her lids.

Not again.

She'd mentally replayed everything too many times to count: the fire, the shooting, the escape. She'd risked sneaking into the restricted tunnels, blackened in soot, searching, calling, desperate for answers.

There were none to be found. The greenhouse had proven no better. After Amos left, she'd wasted a good hour scouring the place, just as she had underground post-fire. But any signs of Holden's existence had vanished.

She opened her eyes and clapped the journal shut. Her jaw ticked. She stared at the wallpaper until its pattern danced in her vision. *Enough.* Yet a little voice sprouted in the back of her mind. It tugged, and it tickled, licking at her wounds. That mask. If Holden was alive, and if he wasn't at the hotel...

Another hiding spot beckoned—a dangerous one she hadn't entertained before now.

For good reason, M&M. No such thing as halfway, you understand me? Once you press go, there is no stopping yourself.

She thought about the lengths she would go to for closure, to prove to herself that Holden was neither dead, nor a figment of her imagination. She had to get ahead of the hit. Of the pain.

"No weakness," she breathed. But the fear of what she was about to do didn't release.

FIVE

You need to clean up some blood?

"Hmm?"

Bastian repeated himself. "You said you needed help with something?"

"I did. I mean, I do." She fiddled with a stack of business cards at the edge of his desk. She had to go through with this. She knew herself. If she didn't scratch this itch, it would grow worse.

"Oh boy, that bad, huh?" he said, catching on to her stress. "It's okay. I already got a lead on those black butterflies, so whatever Bridezilla's asked for, we'll make it happen. Go on."

"It's not for the wedding." She cleared her throat. "It's sort of...a personal favor."

"Ah." He smiled conspiratorially. "Got it. Won't say a word. What do you need?"

She imagined, as the concierge, he'd received his fair share of shady requests over the years. Private access to the pool, last-minute "massage" bookings, extravagant room service, or scandalous deliveries afterhours.

"Well..." She glanced around to make sure nobody was in proximity to eavesdrop. "I was wondering if there was a computer I could borrow. Maybe use exclusively? It has to be one close to the routers on the ground floor." Given the château's old concrete walls, the hotel's Wi-Fi was nearly nonexistent in the upper guest rooms. The lower level was no better for a signal, patchy and unreliable at the best of times.

Bastian threw her a curious look. "What do you mean? You can use the office computers anytime. Did you forget your login?"

"No, I don't want to—I mean, I can't use a computer that's also used by anyone else or tied to the hotel's network. What I'm doing has to be"—she lowered her voice—"untraceable." Cain had inadvertently taught her the basics. It's how he'd arranged his contracts for years: access with a VPN, decent security software, and a Tor browser. Surprisingly simple, when it came down to it.

"Untraceable. Okay, so you want to use a private window, clear your browser history?" Understandably, he seemed confused. She'd never before presented herself as technologically challenged.

"No. More than that. I'm talking about a private computer for a private *network*."

"Why do you...?" His smile fell as his eyes widened. "Mave, are you talking about the dark web? How do you even know how to—?"

Cain.

He must have read the answer in her face. "Jesus, are you in some kind of trouble? Has your father asked you to do something illegal?"

"What?" Cain was serving a double life sentence in a maximum-security prison. It was a reasonable assumption, she supposed, but that didn't make the world believing her father evil easier to navigate. "No. I'm doing some research—unrelated. I just can't say what it's for. It's, you know..." She traced her elastic bracelet, resisting the urge to snap it in front of him. "Private."

"Okay. And I'm not saying you have to tell me everything. But the dark web? It's called that for a reason, you get me?"

"I can handle it."

Bastian spoke in a hush. "That's what I'm afraid of. Mave, you know you're not alone, right? It's okay to let people in. We're here—I'm here. Shit, I know I sound like a meddling auntie, but I see you. These past few months, you've been carrying a lot. But a place like the dark web will only make whatever fix you need get worse. It's no better than dealing with the devil."

"Okay, you're right. *If* I were in trouble. Which I'm not." Obsessing over a mysterious recluse who might be a ghost didn't count as trouble, she silently insisted. "Promise. It's not illegal, and it's not about my father. There will be no trade with Satan." But even as she said it, her skin pricked in warning.

Devil doesn't need an invitation, M&M.

"I'll be careful," she said, struggling to convince herself as much as Bastian.

———

The château's spa was like a softly lit tomb. Navy canvas wallpaper absorbed the haze of pot lights. Eucalyptus laced the air. A lullaby of a pan flute with ocean waves floated from hidden speakers. Ironically, Mave didn't feel any sense of peace.

Bastian had set her up in an obsolete office turned storage closet behind the spa's reception desk and shut the door on his way out. Mave spun the lock on the knob, tucked the key into her pocket, and tried to make herself comfortable on a fold-up chair. A difficult task. She shifted her hips askew, unable to make room for her knees, which were pushed against a cardboard box full of lotions. Built-in shelves coupled with precarious wiring made it impossible to rearrange the computer table. The room was tiny. Unsure of its air circulation, she inhaled warily.

She turned to the cursor on the convex screen. No wonder no one used this computer. The PC looked ancient, and the hard drive made more noise than a sputtering car engine. Nevertheless, Bastian had assured her the router and modem had been refurbished and were up-to-date; its connection would hold. And it did.

Forty minutes later, she'd downloaded the necessary software to surf several questionable sites. Her fingers hovered unsteadily over the yellowed keys. It wasn't too late. She could still back out of this, find another way—a safer way. She chewed on her lip, allowing it to swell into a bruise. She knew of only one person who might have news about Holden Frost. He was part of a deep criminal network. He could at least confirm Holden wasn't a ghost—that she wasn't losing her mind. Except asking her father for any new intel was out of the question.

She'd spent the last four years avoiding Cain and had begun answering his postcards just this past winter. They'd traded no-nonsense updates about life. She'd mentioned her newfound role at the château. It was difficult to go from, *I approved my first purchase order today*, to, *Any news on that guy you hired to keep tabs on me, who you think double-crossed you and used me?* Cain was unforgiving. He kept score, an eye for an eye. He also knew her better than anyone. Not only would he see beneath her questions and dig out whatever feelings she wasn't ready to confess out loud, he'd scold her for letting down her guard. In the world of Cain Francis, emotional ties were a bad idea. Above all else, he'd made his views on Holden Frost clear: The Spirit of Dead Poets was nothing more than an opportunistic parasite who hid behind a mask and fed off others when they weren't looking. The hardest part was, her father wasn't entirely wrong.

Holden had been stealing from the hotel for most of his life, *and* he'd accept whatever translation contracts came his way through the dark web, no matter how immoral the client. Months earlier, Cain had minimally divulged that much to her.

Holden's employers and clients spanned borders, from small-time crooks to cutthroat gangsters. He had his fingers dipped into trouble of the worst kind. She knew this. His disappearance from her life was probably a blessing. Yet she also owed her life to him. And, if she was being truly honest, she was infatuated by him—his contradictions—even months after his brief entrance and exit from her life. When it came down to it, Holden got her unlike any man she'd ever met. Or kissed.

You couldn't kiss a ghost, she tried to rationalize, remembering that intense encounter, unless you were hallucinating.

She gave herself a small shake and typed in the dot-onion address. It had taken time to scour the lists of ever-changing website addresses, but she'd managed to locate a reliable marketplace with a forum one might go to for translation services.

Lurking through its pages offered no clues on Holden. Neither did its search engine. Her eyes were soon tired of scrolling through random vices for sale—everything from rare baseball cards (likely stolen) to prescription drugs (definitely illegal) to bottles of cyanide (highly lethal). Frustration fisted in her gut. She was out of leads and ideas. And yet the mask—the blood. If he'd survived, it was almost certain he'd make his way onto the darknet. This couldn't be another dead end. She wouldn't let it.

On a whim, she navigated to the market's discussion board and, before her fears could censor her, created a new thread. She titled it *Lost and Found* and hit enter.

With her bait sprinkled, she leaned back in her chair and tucked her hands under her thighs. Time moved slowly when you waited for the wolves.

————

That night, the mask under her pillow seemed to murmur in the dark, mocking her in Gracelyn's voice.

These enemies are near.

Her mind whirred restlessly over the tea leaf reading, the blood in the greenhouse, the discussion forum—turning and clicking, stuttering like the hard drive. How long until someone noticed her post? Would Holden see it—would he reply? She rubbed the scar on her ribs, tossed and turned. By three a.m., all hope of sleep was gone. Giving in to insomnia, Mave pulled on some sweats and slipped out of her suite.

The château's twisting hallways were especially eerie during the witching hour. A draft slithered up her shirt. She shivered and wrapped her arms around herself. It did nothing to stop the coldness from seeping into her skin. She scampered down the spiraling main staircase twenty flights, spinning and spinning. The answers weren't going to fall into her lap. She had to look for them, even if it meant searching those places more sinister than safe.

She used her master key and slipped into the spa. Inside, it was pitch black. She chided herself for not thinking to bring a flashlight, but kept the lights off. Risking attention on or off a security camera wasn't worth it. She carefully felt her way across the reception desk. It was too quiet, no New Age soundtrack playing to drown out the patter of her pulse. She paused, sensing another presence.

"Hello?" she whispered.

The rise and fall of her own breath was the only reply. Her nocturnal imagination was orchestrating scares, catalyzing her dread. God knew this old hotel wasn't short on inspiration. She suppressed the feeling and tiptoed into the storage closet.

She didn't bother locking the door this time, keeping it cracked open instead. Even then, the walls pressed inward. Her fear of tight spaces triggered. She sat on the chair, drew her knees to her chest, and worked to lengthen her breaths. The computer seemed to take forever to reboot and reload the dot-onion site. The processor's clicks were amplified in the silence. At least it wasn't pitch dark anymore. She peeled a cuticle as she waited, her skin tinted a sickly green from the glare of the monitor. When the discussion forum at last flickered on the screen, her shoulders slumped.

No reply had come. In fact, her thread had been buried by more recent conversations of illegal trades and deals. So much for the wolves circling. Her impatience rekindled. She gritted her teeth and created a newer post.

Posted by: Neat-Freak [now]

Re: Lost & Found, Poet's Mask

Are you missing a mask worn underground? If so, contact me. I have a good track record and point of view from above the clouds.

She refreshed the thread and re-read her hints about—

A creak sounded.

Mave spun around and stared at the doorway, the noise there and gone. The screen's greenish light glowed from her retinas. A draft grazed her cheek. It was impossible to make out anything beyond. Her paranoia again. She turned back to the computer to power it off and froze. That sense that someone else was present...

The closet door whipped shut.

SIX

She twisted and stared at the door. "Who's—?" Her voice caught. "Who's there?" she called, her tone betraying her fear. Her throat clenched. Her lungs stilled in anticipation, a pair of balloons about to burst. The draft moaned softly through the seams of the doorframe. The closet was suddenly no better than a cage. *Get out of here. Now.*

She ducked and rifled in the nearest storage box. Finding some massage stones, she grabbed two, snatched a towel from a shelf, and wrapped the stones to her knuckles. She stood shakily, knees bent, fist cocked, body slanted in defense. She half expected to be trapped inside, for the flimsy lock to be jammed—but the knob turned freely and the door swung outward.

She licked her lips and waited. Nothing happened. No one jumped out to attack her.

She crept into the spa's reception area, slowly inching her way past the desk, chair, counter, wall.

A whisper-like vibration travelled across the space. She froze. Her ears sharpened, honing in on the sound.

Not the draft—breathing. Someone else was here. In the spa's waiting lounge.

Her heart pounded, flushing her with adrenaline. Had she been followed inside, monitored while searching the dark web? Was it another one of Cain's cronies? Or Holden himself? She couldn't leave without checking. She gathered her courage and crept toward the sound. She was so focused on the foreign breathing that she didn't notice the foot stool in her path.

She smacked her shin and bit her tongue as the stool fell with a thud. A flashlight flickered on. Mave released a shriek in unison with a figure who'd risen from the couch. Her words expelled in a rushed breath: "Ohmygodyou—" She inhaled through her nose and fought to settle her nerves. It wasn't a thug or Holden, but a drowsy-looking young woman with blue hair and a hooped nose piercing. "Who—I'm sorry, who are you and what are you doing in here?"

The woman rubbed the sleep from her eyes and squinted back at her. "Shit, you're..." She groaned softly, apparently recognizing Mave—probably from some awful news report. *Hitman's daughter inherits soon-to-be bankrupt hotel.*

"I'm Katie," she said, her voice raspy, "Katie Bowers. The new yoga instructor. I work here."

"I didn't see you in our HR files." That blue hair—she'd remember.

"Um, today's my first day." She shifted her weight. "Well, yesterday now."

Mave dropped her gaze and noticed the crumpled bedsheet and pillow illuminated by the cellphone in Katie's hand.

Katie shuffled indecisively, apparently debating how to block her view. "Hang on, I know what you're thinking and I'm not—" She cursed softly and pinched her forehead. "Okay, maybe I am. But I can explain. I didn't plan to crash here. It just sorted of...happened."

Mave shook her head, still disoriented from the shock of finding another person in the spa. "I don't understand." She wandered to the nearest sofa chair and leaned on its arm, hoping to hide the tremor in her knees. "Didn't—?" She drew in a stabilizing breath. "Didn't Julián assign you a room in the staff quarters?"

"Um, no, yeah—I mean, he did." She nodded nervously, her blue hair curtaining one side of her face.

"Okay..."

"But I can't sleep there," she blurted before Mave could probe further. "Please don't think I'm ungrateful. It's amazing that this gig comes with a room. Seriously. It's just, the room is, like, cold and creepy. The vent does this weird moaning thing and I think..." She frowned and gripped her forehead again. "Sorry, forget it. It's probably my imagination—like a stupid childish nightmare or whatever."

"It's okay." Mave slid onto the sofa and released the stones from her knuckles. She finally felt bone-tired, yet was in no rush to return upstairs. "I get it. I've had my fair share of nightmares here. This place has a way of doing that."

"Oh." Katie lowered back onto her makeshift bed across from her. "Right—thank you. It's so freaky to try to sleep through the knocks."

"The knocks?"

She fiddled with a thread on the hem of her t-shirt. "Like I said, it's nothing." She didn't sound convinced. Her flashlight shifted, casting ghoulish shadows across her face. "Just my imagination, right? I keep hearing these strange knocks in the wall, like three echoing claps, and then..." She shook her head. "Forget it." She mumbled into her lap. "Can't believe this is your first impression of me. I sound crazy."

"Don't worry." Mave tried to console her. "This hotel tends to go bump in the night. Old floors and pipes and whatnot." She held back that echoing claps weren't exactly normal.

Katie shuddered.

"Why, what else did you hear?" Her heart maintained its staccato tempo as she waited for an answer.

Katie seemed to hug herself. For a moment, Mave thought she wouldn't respond. "Whispers," Katie confessed, her eyes rounded and rimmed pink. "I can't make out the words, but they keep coming, and I thought maybe if I came here"—she gestured at the cozy lounge— "they'd stop. Please don't fire me," she rasped. "I really need this job. I can't go back to LA."

"I'm not going to fire you."

"You're not?"

She shook her head.

Katie released a breath of relief. "Thank god. For a second there..."

She giggled and pressed on her heart, her shoulders slackening. "You really scared the shit out of me, you know? I thought you were the knocking ghost."

Mave glanced at a litter of crumpled tissues on the coffee table and floor. "You sure you're okay?"

"What?" She followed her gaze. "Oh, no, that's...dust allergies. Sorry." She gathered her tissues into a ball and stuffed them into her pocket. She cleared her throat. "Not to sound like a hypocrite, but do you always go creeping around the place at three a.m.?"

"No, I couldn't sleep either."

Katie's gums showed when she smiled. "Well, maybe it's fate. We can keep each other company for a bit. Here." She dug out a lighter and lit a pillar candle on the table.

It must have been the fatigue or the buffer of night or the unexpected comfort of bumping into someone else who was scared and vulnerable. Mave didn't believe Katie had dust allergies. She slouched deeper into her seat and drew up her feet.

"So. You really own this hotel?" Katie whispered.

"That's what they tell me. I'm still pinching myself."

"Hey, can I ask you something?"

Caution coiled in her stomach. She smiled tightly. "Sure."

Katie leaned forward. "Is it true you can tell people where to find their missing stuff?"

She nodded.

Katie relaxed back into her cushion and laced her fingers over her stomach. "Cool talent." Along the edge of her sleeve, a calligraphic tattoo was visible. Mave couldn't help but think of Holden's right arm, inked with verses by Whitman, Poe, Rumi, Plath, and, of course, Frost. She'd have to describe the tattoos in her journal later. "You know," Katie continued, "I have a cousin who can drink soup up her nose and then spit it back out through her mouth."

Mave blinked as Katie held her stare. It took a moment to process the absurdity of the comparison. As if on cue, Katie's lips twitched and, together, they sputtered laughter. No one had ever teased Mave about her sixth sense before. Something inside her chest loosened.

"So, LA, huh?" she said once their amusement had ebbed. "That's a long way from here. What made you move and take a job in the middle of nowhere?" *In a rundown haunted hotel, no less?*

"Heard stuff about the big fire and got curious," Katie replied, more or less confirming Mave's hunch about bad news travelling. "When I looked into this place, there was this job posting. It seemed sort of cool. I was looking for a fresh start for my yoga practice." She shrugged. "Guess I had something to prove to myself."

"And now that you're here, what do you think? Sort of a fixer-upper, huh?" They both glanced around the shadowy lounge.

"Yeah, it's like..." Katie cocked her head sideways, as if searching for another perspective. "I can almost feel the history soaked in these walls, you know?"

"You sound like our tour guide, Gracelyn."

"Oh, yeah," Katie snorted. "Now that you mention it, this is probably her fault. Earlier today, she mentioned some dead poet that hangs around the place. I didn't think much of it then, but now—clearly, it's freaked me out on some deeper level. I'm such a light-weight. Note to self: no more orientation from the local fortune teller."

Mave's pulse kicked at the mention of the rumor about Holden. She reached for a cushion and hugged it as if it could shield her from the pain. "What did Gracelyn say? About the dead poet, I mean..."

"That if you listened carefully, real late at night, you could hear him citing lines from Edgar Allan Poe."

"Why? Has she heard him recently?" Her attempt to sound nonchalant came out reedier than she intended.

Katie frowned. "Not sure. Think it was more, 'here's the scoop on the hotel.' Obviously why I'm hearing imaginary whispers in my room."

"Out of curiosity, which one did Julián set you up in?"

Her eyes flicked up as she recalled the number. "Room 508?" When she glanced back at Mave, her posture grew rigid. "Has something like this happened before? Is 508, like, one of these rooms where they found a maid butchered fifty years ago or something?"

"God, no." Mave tried and failed to smile again, drawing on all of

Cain's training to keep her outward appearance calm. Room 508 had been her old room.

After a beat, Katie gathered her hair into a blue pompom and massaged her crown. "Shit, I know. I sound nuts again. I swear, I sipped one too many teas from Gracelyn. What about you?"

"Hmm?"

"You said you couldn't sleep either?"

"Oh, right..." A loaded question if she'd ever heard one. Her stomach roiled and words crowded the tip of her tongue. How she wished to release them, seek friendly advice, empathy—to tell someone about Holden's disappearance and the mask. But she had to do this by herself. Alone. "It's, you know, stupid work stuff." Her reply sounded awkward and stiff, even to her own ears.

Katie threw her a curious look. "The wedding?" she tried.

"Exactly."

"The concierge, Bastian? Heard his briefing about it. It sounds exciting. I mean, I know I'll be working during the event, but it'll be nice to be around a celebration of love." Her gaze melted into a distant point. "Always dreamed of having a big wedding. Eternal vows. All my family there to witness. Mom walking me down the aisle."

Mave's chest tightened. Cain would never give her away. To anyone.

"You?" Katie's eyes were glassy and doll-like in the gleam of her flashlight.

Mave found herself tongue-tied. She realized she ought to say something normal, like, *I love weddings, too,* or, *Aren't they romantic?* The only problem was she had no experience whatsoever in sharing such sentiments and every line felt like rocks in her mouth.

"Right, sorry," Katie said with an embarrassed smile. "Well, I guess I'll just..." She pushed up and began to collect her pillow and sheet.

"No, wait. You don't have to leave on my account." She straightened too, wanting to rewind the conversation. "I mean, as long as it stays between us, you can hang out here afterhours. Just until you get used to the place. And you clean up before housekeeping arrives, of course."

"Of course." Katie smiled. "Hey, Bastian was right about you, you know."

"What do you mean?"

"You're a real good person, Mave. Thanks, for real."

She nodded and thought of the mask under her pillow—its owner doubling over, his chest blooming with blood. If she were actually a good person, she never would have let so many people get hurt.

SEVEN

You might say I'm biologically scarred and desensitized for sad stories. After all, my mother died giving birth to me in a four-poster bed on the ninth floor.

My unnamed father was already long buried. With no one to claim me, my grandfather took it upon himself to run a cold bath in the en suite to drown me. All in under an hour. Yeah, it's fucked up, but so is the world. And you wanna hear the saddest part? Most days, I can't even blame the bastard.

He was right. An orphan nobody wanted. A creepy little monster. The spirit lives on, they say, but let's be real. Parts of me have always been dead. Broken. At least, that's what I used to believe. Then you came along.

The first time I saw you, you were in black and white on the monitor. I thought you'd be the easiest coin I'd ever been asked to collect. Yeah. Hindsight's a bitch. Should've known trouble preferred a pretty face. How else could you have been allowed inside my library where the ghost cried loudest? Some days, the spirit was so shrill that even I avoided the place. Yet you —the new girl—you pranced in through those French doors and made yourself right at home with a book. You must've been worthy of something, possessed some kind of magic to be immune to the screams. But I couldn't imagine what. Only dirt I had: you were the unsuspecting mark of a ruthless killer. Cain Francis. Real shame, too, because even locked up, that name had reach, pull. The world wasn't as big as everyone imagined, and you didn't fuck with a hitman. Those boys were a different breed. And the first rule of working the dark? Know your devils.

His instructions were clear. Watch you from afar. Report back. Don't approach. Don't touch. Don't so much as inhale the air you breathe. But how could I resist when you fired all the synapses in my brain like that—a million and one questions, buzzing and throwing me for a loop? I'd been alone for a long time. It's how I preferred it. No people, no bullshit. Yet I'd forgotten these feelings: surprise, curiosity. Didn't hurt that you were easy on the eyes.

I dug around a little. Hardly took any effort. An article about the trial surfaced. You were her—the daughter, his very flesh and blood. I had to know more. Off-screen. I'd be dead quiet. No one would be the wiser.

So the next day, when you wandered inside the library, same time, same place, I was already there waiting for you, masked, shadow ringing my head like a broken halo. I stared, my eyes tracing what my hands couldn't. I'd never been contracted to spy on someone before, let alone an attractive woman. It might have given me pause, might have made me question what the fuck that made me—one of those depraved, desperate stalkers with mental hard-ons or dysfunctional dicks—but lucky for me, I'd never given a shit about labels.

You were alone, perfectly nestled in the studded wing chair, knees crossed and nibbling on your thumbnail as you read. I didn't have to check the title. I knew that classic cover from a distance. Mary Shelley Wollstonecraft. I found myself wondering, what else did you read? Any poetry? Shelley's husband? Did you like the English romantics? A perplexed focus lit your eyes. Those eyes.

I did a second take. And a third. Your thick-rimmed glasses did nothing to detract from your unique irises. Sky and earth. I peered through the lenses, into you, and it was like the ground dropped out from beneath me. You were different from the others who ran scared from the ghost. You were...

I blinked, gave myself a hard shake, and nearly collided into a bookshelf. I inwardly cursed as I regrouped. Lusting after a mark was a bad idea. And yet that was exactly what I was doing. I may not have realized *it then, but I was a goner. I sighed, and you shivered—wrapped your cardigan tighter over your chest. I stiffened. Did you feel me? Were you cold? It was always a few degrees too cool in the library. Ghosts did that— made the space inhospitable for the living.*

The following afternoon, I came early. I lit a fire to try to warm the place before your arrival. I knew when you'd get here to the minute. The second. It was always the same. You liked routine. I anticipated your visits, began looking forward to them. I tracked your activities on the monitors, logging mundane information to report back.

On Saturday you borrowed Orlando, *took it back to the gift shop to read under the counter when no one was around. On Sunday it was* Sula. *I thought I had you figured out, but then on Monday, you picked out* Cujo. *And so it went. For three months, you were a puzzle I was assembling from afar. Everything was fine until that morning on New Year's Day.*

I found you asleep in the tunnels, and you looked cold again.

EIGHT

She awoke with a jolt, breathing ragged, sheets tangled between her legs. Her face was hot. Something felt off. It took a second for her to recognize the pressure cupping her cheeks—framing her eyes. Her hands shot upward and ripped off the mask.

She stared at the idle, monstrous silhouette next to her on the bed, confusion lapping her thoughts. Faint moonlight sifted through the curtains, settling like dust over the mask.

God, how did I—?

She must have put it on in her sleep.

Exhaling an odd smokiness from the back of her throat, she sat up and reached for a glass of water on the nightstand, her grip unsteady. Her teeth tapped the rim. Water dribbled. An irrational fear skated under her skin. She swallowed back the lingering flavors of the dream—the mask. Wearing that thing, she had dreamt of Holden. Or imagined she *was* Holden, spying on herself in the library last October. It had felt so real, like an out-of-body experience or psychic connection. A shudder coursed through her.

No. She shook out her hair, as if batting away the thought. *I can't do that,* she assured herself. *I can't tap into people's thoughts or memories. It's just stress—my vivid imagination.* Twenty-four hours had passed since she'd revisited the darknet, then bumped into Katie. She hadn't slept properly on either night—not since her return to the château.

Still. She ran her tongue along her teeth, wiping away the taste of Holden's smoke.

No, she repeated more sternly. She refused to believe the dream could be anything more than a strange projection of her desire. She stood, wary to fall back asleep, and found a throw blanket that could double as a robe. Bundled in the soft knit, she wandered out from her suite.

The hallways were vacant and still, as if the walls themselves were holding their breath. Before long, she was back inside the locked-up spa, eager for another check-in of the darknet. Everything was under control, she told herself. Scary masks and surreal dreams couldn't hurt you. Reality could. She'd stick to her plan.

She'd continue handling the wedding prep by day, and searching for Holden by night. Good. Fine. She ignored the part about a lack of sleep. As it was, her management team was pulling sixteen-hour shifts. Mave wouldn't let them down. She had to keep Bridezilla happy—ensure the hotel didn't sink deeper under the red line.

Huddled on the fold-up chair in the closet, she gently tapped on the keyboard. Katie might be in the lounge next door, and she didn't care to wake her for a repeated scare. As the forum loaded, Mave perched her wrists and held her fingers ready, overzealous to refresh her post in the busy stream. The motherboard lagged, hummed, and rattled clicks. Mave yawed.

Wicked never sleeps.

At last, the discussion board flicked on the screen. Her fingers twitched and froze.

She blinked, unsure she was seeing straight. Unlike the night before, her post wasn't buried and forgotten. She had one reply. Unread. Her lungs swelled with air. She opened her thread and skimmed over the words.

Her stomach plummeted.

Posted by: Bek-187 [5 hours ago]
Re: Lost & Found, Poet's Mask

Seems we got mutual contacts.

Bad news: don't know where your freak is hiding.

Good news: do know where your daddy is trapped.

Go ahead, check your DM.

Questions crashed in her brain in time with her soaring pulse. Who was Bek-187? Did they know her real identity? *How?* What did they want from her? Alarm pounding the walls of her chest, she jerked the mouse to a little icon of an envelope lit in the corner of her screen.

Don't look, the voice in her head warned. It was a trap. A mistake—one she'd blindly walked into.

What did I tell you, huh? Cain barked. *Keep out of the dark fucking web! This is what happens when you don't follow the rules—when you listen to your goddamned heart before your head.*

"I didn't—" she whispered lamely. She had no good excuse for failing to notice the private chat feature on the forum. Had she seen it initially—had she been thinking clearly and not overwhelmed with longing on that first day—she might have disabled it out of caution.

One message awaited her. From Bek-187.

Find the SDP—dead or alive—or watch your daddy bleed into his early grave. Now. Ticktock. No cops allowed. Just you. I got a timer here and won't wait long.

📎 004327001.bmp

She didn't have to open the attachment. Its preview loaded in horizontal bars, pixel by pixel, from the top of the screen, working its way downward.

A murky, indistinct background. Poor lighting. Somewhere indoors? A wall. Then a shoulder materialized, a short-sleeve white t-shirt hugging a bicep, a shadowed neck, followed by a lined cheek. She narrowed her eyes, making out the lateral portrait. As the bone structure of the person took shape, she sucked in sharply and palmed her mouth to stifle a cry. It couldn't be him. Except...

She'd recognize his face anywhere—eyes shut, frowning even in sleep. She had sought comfort from that same face on many nights, studying its fine creases, its soft lashes and sandpaper jawline. Whenever hit with the nightmares or the disorientation—whenever she woke in yet another rental apartment and the butterflies swarmed her stomach with an onslaught of longing for place, for a real home.

Cain.

They'd gotten to her father.

He was asleep in his cot in his cell, seemingly unaware of being photographed. He looked more aged than she remembered, the past four years deepening the silver along his temples. More than anything else, though, he looked vulnerable.

Tears welled, blurring her vision. She wiped her eyes and re-read the words a few times before they sunk in. *Get a hold of yourself.* Her breath was too quick, a scraping inside her throat, her lungs. Her blood throbbed between her temples and a headache thickened and pressed against the backs of her eye sockets. Everything seemed dimmer. The monitor grew dull. The towels on the shelf greyed. In contrast, the motherboard's clicks stuttered louder and louder like demonic laughter —a blood-curdling curse.

Find the SDP—Holden's alias, the Spirit of Dead Poets. She'd assumed she'd been cryptic with her post. She'd used an anonymous handle, had omitted real facts, deliberately over-specifying select details while overgeneralizing others. But it hadn't been enough. Someone other than Holden had decoded her post. They knew about his exis-tence—his disappearance—and his connection to her. They were after his whereabouts. And whoever it was, they were threatening to kill her father for the information.

She fumbled to power off the computer as if it might make the threat disappear. It didn't. The deadly ultimatum merely heightened as the screen hissed asleep in a stipple of static. A sheet of dark descended. Impending doom expanded through her chest and bled outward into the night. She fumbled for her penlight and turned it on. Her eyes shot wide.

A foreign face reflected in the black monitor. "Back again?"

Mave must have jumped a full inch off her seat. "Katie," she breathed.

"Oh, whoops." Katie leaned against the doorframe, her head tilted as if too heavy for her neck to carry. "Was gonna knock. But then I thought of that dead poet in the walls. Why are you in the closet?"

How long had she been standing in the doorway, behind her? Had she spied the screen? Cain's photo?

Mave cleared her throat, her thoughts scrambled. "Office upstairs is too drafty. The spa calms me." She tried to make her voice sound normal, tried to clamp the panic flooding her lungs. "Still hearing strange noises?"

They were after Holden. In reach of her father. Who, who, who?

Katie flashed her a funny look. "You okay?"

"Sure, yeah." She stood abruptly, her chair scraping loudly against the floor. The backs of her knees bumped into a box. No space. No air. "Nighttime jitters. You know. Excuse me." She shuffled past, glimpsing Katie's gaping mouth in the corner of her vision. She couldn't possibly make small talk. She scampered out of the spa, head lowered, mind stumbling. What in god's name had she done?

You laid your bait, Cain's voice replied. *Played in the forbidden forest.*

Told you so, told you so, told you so.

The wolves had come, hadn't they? They'd answered. They'd bitten. And she wasn't anywhere near ready for the cut of their teeth.

———

Snapping out of her daze, she focused on the signage. The familiar gold numbers took shape.

508

Her former room. She was so preoccupied with stressing over the threat to Cain's life, she had spaced out. She must have strayed to the fifth floor reflexively, out of habit. Curiosity itched.

Licking her dry lips, she reached for the doorknob, her hand strangely stiff. She checked over both shoulders—left, right. The hallway tapered into shadows like an endless abyss. Veins pinched in her temples and her vision swayed. She blinked to clear her head. It was as if

Bek-187 was here at the château, crouched beyond her sightline, and at any moment, would swoop out of the darkness and catch her. Trap her.

Her hand flinched away from the knob. Her paranoia was nonsensical. She wasn't being watched. She was alone. The night shift was elsewhere on duty. Remaining personnel were fast asleep. And the restricted hallway that housed the staff quarters was empty.

So why am I still standing here? What the hell am I doing?

She regarded the mahogany woodgrain ahead of her, the panels pulsing red-black. As if in answer, the knocks came slow and solid, like a heavy palm thumping the wall on the other side. Hard. Intentional.

One.

Two.

Three.

Her breaths shortened, grew animated as she backed a small step away from the door. She'd left Katie in the spa. Room 508 was supposed to be vacant. So then who—*what*—had made that sound from the other side of the door?

Like three echoing claps.

Her imagination raced. She wouldn't hear Edgar Allen Poe—she wouldn't. She rubbed her ears, preemptively shushing the poems. Her blood thudded. She gripped her skeleton key tightly. In one fell swoop, she thrust it forward into the keyhole, spun the lock, and shoved the door open.

The room's shadows ballooned into the hallway where she stood. Mave took one step inside, then another. She blinked into darkness. At emptiness.

Nobody is here.

Her faith hardened halfway up her throat.

She didn't believe in the Spirit of Dead Poets. No matter how much her fear preached otherwise.

Part Two
Slip The Dark

Hallucination

hal·lu·ci·na·tion | \ hə-lü-sə-nā-shən

An olfactory, gustatory, auditory and/or visual sensation that is devoid of any tangible material stimulus and occurs only in one's mind. Commonly held to be symptoms of mental illness or psychedelic drugs, these sensations are in fact healthy, natural modes of communication for mediums.

—Glossary listing, SIGNS: A HANDBOOK FOR CLAIRVOYANCE

NINE

Her stomach grumbled, demanding lunch. She checked the time on her phone without breaking her stride. She'd been trekking down the side of the road for roughly an hour. It was good to get away from the hotel. A change of scenery, fresh air, avoiding the recently checked-in Dominick Grady. The art dealer had left her two messages already. A nuisance. She had bigger problems. Mave inhaled the scents of the thick, damp forest and focused on the birdsong. The elements would help cleanse her thoughts—no matter the sting of a blister forming on her heel or the itch of her braids beneath her long auburn wig. She shooed a swarm of gnats circling her crown, readjusted the back of her shoe, and together cursed and praised her inspiration.

The town's sheriff, pushing fifty, had done this exact hike back on New Year's Day. Morganson had also ventured in the opposite direction from the town to the château, uphill and in the middle of a blizzard. All Mave had to contend with now was a light fog sifting inward from the banking trees and obscuring her route fifty yards ahead. She wouldn't be bested, no matter how exhausting the hike.

Should have driven.

She shushed her moan. She didn't have a driver's license, though Cain had taught her how to drive a stick shift. (Midnight practices accelerating from zero to sixty on backroads and abandoned lots. Always a common, plain car. Nothing flashy.) Mave had made her decision by sunrise. She'd bend another "rule" despite the clawing doubts and whispers—Cain's motto boring a hole into the depths of her skull.

Never trust police.

Bek-187's near-identical stipulation echoed for supremacy: *No cops allowed.*

She'd dissected the threat versus the risk for hours, each word knifed into her memory and transcribed into her journal under her pillow. By seven a.m., sometime between guzzling her second café crema and unbundling the daily papers in the gift shop, she'd attempted to research "Bek" on the regular net, not ready to revisit dot-onion sites. The sole information she'd learned was that "187" was the common penal code for murder. And murderers didn't like cops. Cain sure hadn't. In turn, he'd raised her to be wary of all the players in law enforcement, from the rookies to the chiefs. If it wore a uniform and carried a badge, you ducked and steered clear. That simple. You didn't wait for it to draw its gun, and you certainly didn't stroll into town miles away to solicit its help. Except Mave had exhausted all other leads.

It wasn't as if she could warn Cain to watch his back without also confessing the trouble she'd unleashed. Bek-187 must have wagered as much. No. Confiding in her father would make matters worse, force the enemy's hand—or Cain's. That's all she needed: to be responsible for Cain adding to his body count, proactively shanking someone no matter how deplorable, because of *her*. She was pretty sure pleas of self-defence were null and void for contract killers. That left one card in her hand, yet to be played—the last hint into the supposed life and death of the Spirit of Dead Poets. Holden had a juvie record.

The sealed records were all Mave had to go on, and on an impending deadline.

Ticktock.

She dropped her head back to view the bloated clouds and exhaled. She'd be careful with her request, use her grief card if she had to. Morganson would not—could not under any circumstances—learn of her interaction on the darknet with Bek-187, or vice versa. She mentally recited how she'd spin it to the sheriff, the same phrasing she'd been obsessing over for the better part of her hike.

You remember after the fire, when you mentioned my friend who—

The sound of a vehicle approaching from behind interrupted her rehearsal. She turned her neck and squinted through plumes of fog kneading the cracked pavement.

Speak of the devil.

A police cruiser materialized and decelerated to a stop next to her. The window was rolled down, the officer's elbow leaning out like he was out on a joy ride. "Ms. Mave Michael Francis." The way he spoke her name with a pleasant drag stirred her memory. The hospital. Recovering after the fire. "Almost didn't recognize you. You look well."

It probably helped that she didn't have tubes up her nose. She tilted her head to get a better look at him and tried to recall the name of the young officer who'd taken her statement three months ago. His kind eyes took her in, no doubt scanning her for details. (Her cropped sweater, boyfriend jeans, and sneakers were chosen to be unmemorable, suitable for either fight or flight in a pinch.)

"You're a little far from the hotel for a stroll, no?"

She corked an irritated sigh before it could escape through her smiling lips. *What do you expect? He's a cop. Being nosy is an occupational hazard.* "I was actually headed to town to run an errand," she said. True enough. No reason to lay it on thick. Though her plan was to approach Morganson alone for help, news of her visit was bound to reach her squad sooner than later.

"By foot?" His brow hitched. "You'll be hiking through dusk. Wanna ride? I'm headed that way anyway—end of my shift."

Her blistered heel hissed yes even as her mind whispered caution. The single other occasion she'd been asked to ride in a police cruiser, she'd been brought in for questioning for her father's arrest.

"It's going to rain any minute," he added.

Her gaze followed the two fingers he'd pointed up like a gun. Sure enough, the clouds had congealed into a cinerous mass since he'd pulled up beside her. She wasn't yet used to the fickle wet season here. She didn't have an umbrella. Or a good excuse. "Okay," she said, her physical comfort winning over her mental misgivings.

He nodded and tapped his thumbs playfully along the steering wheel. She moved toward the rear door. "You can ride up front," he called out the window, surprising her.

Okay. The front. That was new.

She tried not to trip over her feet as she walked around the vehicle's hood to the passenger side. A few napkins and stir sticks were scattered on the seat. No partner, then. As she shrugged her backpack purse straps from her shoulders, he swept the spot clear and tossed the napkins onto a folded newspaper on the dashboard. She slid inside in silence. Lightning blinked in the distance, glinting from the windshield.

You shouldn't be in here.

He waited patiently until she fastened her seat belt before shifting into drive.

The cruiser's interior smelled faintly of his lemony-basil aftershave. As he accelerated down the mountain, she stole a glance at his profile. His features were atypical of good looks—pockmarked cheeks, a long nose that looked like it'd taken a hammer along its bridge. Yet somehow, all together, the unlikely combination worked. She lowered her lashes to view the nametag on his uniform.

"René Rawlings, at your service," he said, his eyes never leaving the road. "Though everyone calls me Ren. It's French," he clarified, dipping his chin slightly at the nametag. "In fact, my great-grandfather was the architect who designed the château way back when."

She blinked, thrown off from the script she was preparing in her head. "Wait, really? Wow. That's quite the family legacy."

"I'm happy it's in good hands now. Excited to see what you'll do with the place."

"Uh-huh." Nerves spun in her stomach. *Relax. It's not like you've run it into the ground. Yet.* She wiped her palms on her thighs and tried to convince herself she was sweating from the long trek. "Have you visited recently?" As soon as the question left her mouth, she mentally kicked herself. Of course he'd visited. He'd been part of the investigation into Birdie's death. "I meant..."

"No, it's okay." He smiled, laugh lines framing his square jaw. "I get it. Not really. I used to come by as a kid more often. Hung around the grounds. Had a lot of fun playing hide and seek in those twisted hallways."

"I bet." She tried to think of a normal follow-up question but her mind was too busy tamping her anxiety.

I voluntarily got into a police car. If only Cain could see me now.

She made a concerted effort not to ogle the dispatch radio, the siren controls, the computer on the center console—each detail making her uneasy. In the end, she fixed her stare ahead and imagined tidying the newspaper and napkins splayed on the dash.

"So where exactly are we headed?" he said, thankfully breaking the awkward silence.

"Oh, to the..." She hadn't thought this through. The corners of her lips strained. "Art shop," she said, the lie springing from her mouth.

His brow furrowed.

Shit. Did Hazel Springs even have an art shop? The château being an isolated, self-sufficient world—like a little island on a cloud—she'd only visited the town a handful of times to run errands. "Birdie left some canvases," she doubled down. "I promised to pick them up."

He flashed her a curious look before she remembered she hadn't brought a car. *Dammit.* She was out of practice.

"You mean the Evergreen Gallery on Main?" he said, mercifully not asking how she intended to transport these imaginary canvases.

"That's the one." She swallowed her next lie about a delivery before she could deepen the hole she was digging herself into. She'd now have to hang around the gallery to keep her story straight. Better yet, maybe she could text Morganson to meet her there instead of at the station. Neutral territory. Less people.

"And after?"

How do you carry canvases up a mountain! Are they miniature paintings? "I'm sorry?"

"When you're done..." His thumbs lightly drummed the steering wheel again. "Maybe I could swing back around, buy you lunch? You could tell me more about your plans for the château."

"Oh, I—" She hadn't seen that coming. Was he pumping her for information? Flirting with her? Both? She couldn't recall the last time she'd been asked out.

"You haven't eaten yet, have you?" he added, giving her an exit.

She wanted to take the compliment, believe he was interested in her for the right reasons, one of the good guys despite the uniform. Lord knew it'd been too long since she'd been on any sort of date. Her throat constricted, holding in a hiccup of laughter. Her. Dating a cop. Inspiration hit. Maybe she could work this to her advantage, improvise a better plan.

"No, I'd like that. Lunch sounds nice. Except, first..." Was she really going to do this? Raindrops pelted the windshield, bullets of water splattering on impact. "I have one other errand. In fact, maybe you could help me?" She tucked her long, wavy hair behind her ear, angled her body slightly, trying to get a better read on him. What role did he prefer, bold vixen, shy girl? She smiled softly.

He started the wipers and threw her a look too quick to read. "What do you have in mind?"

In for a penny, in for a pound. "Actually, I was hoping to get a hold of some old police records."

"Records, huh?" His expression piqued with interest. "How long ago are we talking?"

"This would have been the early 2000s."

"All right. That's around when they started archiving from hardcopy to digital. Did you try putting in a request through the online records office?"

"That's just it." She bit her lip. "These wouldn't be available to the public."

"How so?"

"See, the files I'm looking for, they're about an old friend—deceased. And he would have been young when he was arrested."

"Ah, you mean a minor?"

She nodded.

"That complicates things. Depends on the severity of the crime." *Crimes*, she silently corrected. Holden had been arrested more than once. "Assuming they haven't been erased already, afraid those records will be sealed and only available with a formal court order."

"Even if the person is no longer living?"

"Yeah, the privacy act—it's still protected by law."

Dammit. No amount of schmoozing an officer, no amount of role-playing or crying or seducing in this cruiser could produce approval from a judge. She curled a strand of hair around her finger and frowned at the cluttered dashboard. The now-familiar headline on the paper sharpened into focus. It'd been the same news each morning.

POLICE INVESTIGATE SPREE OF HOME BREAK-INS – NO ARRESTS.

A fresh idea sparked. It was definitely a gamble. If she wasn't careful, she could end up charged with attempted bribery of a public official. "How about if it was"—she drew a circle on her knee and peripherally noted the draw of his gaze—"an informal request."

His eyes flicked to her face. Warm. Curious.

"Say I could offer you a trade," she continued.

"I'm not sure I follow."

"When you investigated the fire at the hotel, you remember about my hunches with finding lost stuff? Not to brag, but I'm pretty good at it, so..." She slid the newspaper next to the radar on the center of the dash, and waited until he glanced down. "What if it was possible for me to help you track some of these stolen items from the break-ins, and in exchange, I just *happened* to browse some old police files? That would be mutually beneficial and harmless, right? Because my consultation for locating lost property would be entirely voluntary." She blinked, holding her eyes wide. "I'm a concerned citizen, that's all—a business owner. These robberies are plastered all over the headlines, and the last thing I want is to have my guests sipping their morning coffees, browsing the paper and feeling unsafe, worrying over their watches being stolen by a cat burglar nearby. Right?"

"And the juvie records?"

"Who said anything about juvie records? I mean, if I should accidentally see some paperwork lying around about my friend, it would be entirely unplanned and not shared and certainly not official. No, it would be a...a..."

"A happy coincidence?"

"Well, since you put it that way." She smiled, lips pouting ever so slightly. "I'm just saying, it could be the break in the case you've been looking for—bust this guy once and for all." Her heart beat forcefully in time with the windshield wipers. She was banking on a lot—him being young in the force, testosterone-fueled, hungry to impress and prove himself.

"You really think you can locate these stolen possessions?"

"Assuming their owners are willing to sit with me for a few minutes, share their thoughts on what went missing, then one hundred percent." More like ninety-five. Her sixth sense wasn't an exact science, but now wasn't the time to split hairs. "Please, Ren." She touched his arm lightly —the feather tap Cain called it. *Body over mind, M&M. People like to pretend it's the other way around, but they're wrong. We're animals first. Always.* "It would really mean a lot if you could help me with this tiny thing. Our secret. You won't regret it, I promise. Like I said, it's harmless."

Even as the corners of his mouth curled upwards, and she knew that she had him, the words left a bitter taste in her mouth. The thing about trouble was, it didn't stick to promises.

TEN

Hazel Springs was a small town having an identity crisis. On its main street, storefronts alternated between quaint, tacky, and commercial. The suburban homes yawned mediocre middle-America with the occasional flipped bungalow turned McMansion. As they drove through the streets, Mave couldn't picture the recluse she'd met in the hotel's tunnels being raised here. Holden had been in the foster care system for ten years before being declared dead by town officials. They'd never located a body. Something told Mave they hadn't bothered to look terribly hard.

As promised, Ren both dropped her off and picked her up at the gallery. He'd changed into his civilian clothes in the interim, making him less intimidating. Mave couldn't help it; at the sight of him holding his umbrella open in wait, a thrill zipped across her skin. *Animals first.* His hand rested on the small of her back as they made haste to get out of the downpour, puddles catching on their heels. They headed to a nearby diner on the block, and he held the door open for her.

The restaurant was half full. As they made their way to a booth in the back, several customers greeted Ren by name while throwing Mave nosy looks. She kept her gaze averted, glad she'd selected a long wig to curtain her face. If anyone recognized her as the recent owner of Château du Ciel, they weren't so bold as to mention it. After all, her grandmother Birdie had been a difficult woman, openly elitist and rich, disliked by nearly everyone she came across.

What Mave perceived as glares kept her on edge. In contrast, Ren seemed relaxed, his noticeably muscular arm resting across the back of the bench seat. They made small talk between stolen glances and coy smiles. She learned he had two bulldogs, Willie and Nelson, and he, in turn, listened to her love of gift shops, the one at the château in particular. No forbidden subjects were broached—like why a man of the law would want to associate with the daughter of a hitman.

Gathering her courage, she waited for the perky waiter to saunter away with their order and leaned forward with her chin propped on her knuckles. "So, about our secret exchange, these robberies, what should I know?"

He slid his elbows forward on the table, his shoulders hunching and filling her sightline. "Beyond what's already being printed in the paper? Not a whole lot. It's still an open investigation." His tone was nice to listen to, smooth and unhurried. She imagined all the confessions a voice like that could induce.

"So a mysterious cat burglar targeting local homes and leaving no crumbs behind. Is that it?"

"Yep."

"And you have no suspects? No unruly teenagers hanging around?"

He slid his jaw sideways in thought. "Not the rush job of a typical teen. Whoever this is, let's just say they know their way around locks. Unlikely a first-time felon."

"And they're not taking any cars?"

"No, ma'am. Only electronics. Almost exclusively computers, tablets, routers, and the like. And books."

She blinked as the waiter returned and set down their drinks. That was an odd plunder for a home invasion. She reached for her glass, working to keep her tone casual. "Books? Like rare, first editions, vintage collector's series?"

"No, that's the thing." He lowered his voice. "According to the homeowners, the books are the only items that have no real value. We haven't figured out the motive for why they'd be stolen. Other than maybe the perp likes to read."

She nearly choked on her club soda. Holden liked to read. *A lot.* She dabbed the napkin to her mouth, hiding her stunned reaction. She cleared her throat. "What about security systems? No alarms tripped, no smart monitoring or CCTV nearby?" She thought of the cameras around the hotel's property.

"Hazel Springs isn't like a metropolitan city. For the most part, it relies on the old neighborhood watch."

"And?"

"And a couple of folks reported something small buzzing high in the sky a few days before the break-ins began. We think the perp might be using a drone to scout. As for security systems, yeah, at least two of the homes had alarms. But like I said, this guy's probably a pro—knows how to avoid front doors and disarm systems, even smart ones. Which would explain all the stolen computer equipment. Could be a hacker we're dealing with. No forced entry. In and out. Just like a ghost."

The hair on her arms rose.

"Afraid we don't know more than that."

They leaned back in unison as the waiter dropped off a basket of condiments and left.

"How about your friend?" Ren asked.

"My fr—I'm sorry?" Her shoulders knotted, suppressing a shudder. She raised her glass to her mouth and sipped slowly to buy herself time. *Get it together*, Cain's voice warned.

"The one who passed away," he said. "Our exchange, remember?"

"Oh, yeah."

"You want to tell me whose files you're looking into?"

She crossed her legs tightly, kept her elbows close to her ribcage, as if she might fall apart otherwise. "Holden Frost." Her voice sounded wispy to her ears.

Surprise flickered in his eyes, so quickly she was unsure if she'd read it correctly. Yet again, her attempt to get closer to the truth had unearthed more questions than answers.

———

It felt surreal—the attraction and gentlemanly doting of a police officer. She hadn't a clue what to make of it. Maybe that's why she ended up in the Oasis Spa on her break. She told herself it was to check the darknet for updates—Bek-187 might have sent another DM—but really it was to bump into someone who might get it, a person who'd been raised normally, gone on normal dates with normal guys. Not that Mave had been on a date with Ren. Had she?

The reception desk was empty. Mave chewed on her lip and eyed the locked storage closet. Dread pooled in her gut and her feet cemented into blocks. She couldn't bring herself to look. Not yet. She would soon. *Soon*, she vowed. She swiveled toward the waiting lounge.

She fished through the complimentary juice bar, trying to refocus, pushing away that image of Cain lying helplessly in his cot. The photo suggested Bek-187 could be another inmate in the prison, in reach of her father. Or it could mean it was someone with contacts. The criminal world had arteries and veins running in and out of the system—an entire organism that fed into society and formed its ugly underbelly. Cain himself had demonstrated these ties when he'd contracted first Holden to spy on her, then a con named Stratis to smuggle her out of the hotel and into hiding. This was back when it'd seemed like she'd go down for Birdie's murder. Yet she'd refused to cooperate in her father's plan to live as a fugitive. She'd chosen to stay behind and prove her innocence to the sheriff. Her instincts—contrary to Cain's—had proven good. So that left her back at square one: Bek-187 could be virtually anyone.

"An unknown enemy," Gracelyn had prophesized.

Katie strolled in hugging two large vases arranged with black orchids. "Oh, hey!" She set one vase on the coffee table.

"Those are stunning," Mave remarked. "Samples for the wedding?"

"Uh-huh. Julián asked staff to come grab a couple. Have you seen them? They have three tables full in Queen's Hall, every black flower you could think of. Believe it or not, these beauties were the rejects."

That's right. Dammit. They were deep cleaning Queen's Hall today while simultaneously finalizing decorations for the reception. With all her worry over Bek-187, finding Holden, and her arrangement with Ren, she'd nearly forgotten she'd promised Julián she'd get a head start on the floor plan in the greenhouse. And she still had to check in with Amos about the leaks and with Bastian about the black swallowtails.

"Hey, about the other night"—Katie scrunched her nose—"wanted to say sorry for bumping into you like that. You seemed pretty spooked. Hope everything's cool."

"Yeah, of course." She kept quiet about the part where she'd heard three knocks outside her old room. A bubble of guilt formed in her chest. "It wasn't you. I—" Her mouth hung open, unable to eject even a sliver of her troubles.

No sharing, M&M, Cain whispered. *Not unless you want to give them a weapon to use against you.*

"Are you busy right now?" she blurted instead.

Katie's eyes widened in relief. "Please, god, tell me you've got a job for me that doesn't involve checking expiration dates on face serum and deleting my ex-boyfriend's texts."

Mave found herself amused by Katie's candor. Any other staff member would've pretended to be satisfied with the mundane duties and lull in guest services. Katie seemed to have no filter. "Follow me," Mave said. "I could really use a hand."

———

They brought LED lanterns. Even in daylight hours with the door propped open, a permanent filminess clung to the air in the greenhouse.

"So, you mentioned your ex earlier. I was wondering..." Mave steered her wheelbarrow to the pile of rot they'd deemed unsalvageable. "How do you know when a guy isn't just into you for, you know...?"

Katie paused her sweeping, a small hill of broken terracotta by her feet. "The sex?"

She'd been thinking more along the lines of status, intel, money, a sick dare by his buddies. Or maybe Ren was buttering her up before asking if she'd become an informant. She had a direct pipeline to Cain after all.

Katie leaned on her broom, hip cocked. "Hang on, we're not talking hypothetically, are we?" Whatever reaction she read on her face got her excited. "Oh, spill! Who is he?"

"It's nobody," Mave said, deliberately busying herself with another planter. "We had one lunch. Thing is, I'm not sure if he's using me or really likes me, you know?" That had been the magic with Holden. From the outset, he'd treated her differently than other men. He'd seen her for who she was underneath all her guises and layers. Beneath the neat and organized shop attendant, the psychic freak, the criminally trained girl or the long-lost heir to Birdie's estate, she'd been just Mave. Given his own social rebelliousness and secret home in the tunnels, she supposed her oddities had been both familiar and desirable to him. Throw in their crackling physical chemistry and—

"Well, you could always give him the old bra-drop test."

"Hmm?" She shook away the memory of Holden's hands sliding up her ribs. "What's that?"

"Okay, you ask him to come pick you up, right? And when you answer the door, you make sure you're wearing a tight shirt but no bra. Then you count the number of times his eyes look down versus up. If the ratio is more than fifty percent south, then he's only looking to get laid."

She couldn't help but snort. "Seriously, Katie? Is that scientific?"

Katie's crinkly laughter was infectious.

As their conversation derailed, a little weight lifted from Mave's shoulders. She could almost ignore the giant axe threatening to fall on Cain's neck—or the bad reviews that would pour in for the château if she didn't revamp this greenhouse in less than a fortnight. They chatted as they worked. The manual labor was invigorating, giving Mave the adrenaline she needed to stave off her fatigue. She discovered that, like her, Katie had moved around in her youth. She also had boy trouble, as she put it, and was hoping her leave of LA would improve her luck in romance. Katie seemed plugged into the hotel's rumor mill; she shared all sorts of updates about who was dating who among staff. Admittedly,

Mave found the idle gossip easy to listen to, especially since it was about someone other than herself.

"Think that's the last of it." Mave batted the dust from her gloves and tried to picture an aisle. They'd managed to shove most of the central planters to one side and organize another pile for disposal.

"Nice workout!" Katie shuffled over, fanning her shirt away from her skin. "We make a good team. What do you think? Is it doable?"

Mave raised her lantern from the ground and swung it outward, visualizing her plan through the gloom. "Think so. We could order a deep red runner to divide the bride's side from the groom's. Arrange wrought iron garden chairs in rows, standing candelabras and black lilies at the makeshift altar." She pointed to the opposite end of the green-house and avoided thinking of the sink in the corner—the hidden blood beneath. "And the black swallowtails could be released there, from behind the wedding party."

"Wow." Katie contemplated her tableau, peering into the faraway shadows. "Gotta say, that sounds amazing."

"Hang on." Mave wandered to a tangle of overgrown dried ivy in the corner and pulled a few stems loose. "What if we gathered and braided some of these upward, redirected them into a kind of trellis archway?"

Katie looked to the ceiling with her hands on her hips. "With string lights?"

"Mmm, I love that. But do you think they're too decayed?" She hesitated, picturing dead vermin hidden beneath the crawling vines.

"Only one way to find out." Katie shifted closer and tugged on a few additional stems. They were knotted into place, caught on some sort of metal ring.

"Here, let me help." Mave bent next to her and, together, they yanked. The release was sudden.

They fell back onto their behinds in a cloud of dust. Katie coughed and waved away the airborne dirt. Mave's eyes caught it first. She froze.

"Hey." Katie leaned forward. "Is that a...?"

Mave's heart pounded in her ears as she pushed onto her knees. She crawled closer and wiped the gravel and mulch clear from her discovery.

An underground hatch. She was glad Katie was here to confirm she wasn't dreaming it.

"Huh. Where do you think it leads?" Katie asked.

To the tunnels—giving Holden an exit from the fire. "Probably an old storage cellar."

"Should we check to see?" Her voice had dropped into a scratchy whisper, as if contracting Mave's anxiety.

Mave imagined lowering herself into the darkness, the walls closing in and choking her in soot. The doorway's iron handle might as well have been a coiled snake. "No," she breathed, "health and safety violations." She swept the tangles of ivy back into place and told Katie they were done for now.

ELEVEN

Breathing smoke into you, I'll always remember how you tasted... like all the odes to pleasure and pain housed together, flesh and soul rolling on your warm tongue. Your mouth crashed into mine and, just like that, we became one beautiful instrument, exhaling and inhaling in rhythm. I felt your blood spike through the dark. Your skin grew slick and your pupils bloomed out toward the smudge of your lashes. And I knew. I knew.

Whitman was right: "now I place my hand upon you, that you be my poem."

Couldn't allow myself to get that close again. Not unless I wanted to give myself up—no caution, no fear—lose the mask and lay naked at your ankles. What would you do with me, huh? The things, the things...

Jesus.

So goddammed fucking gone.

Sometimes, in the worst of the pain, I dream we're back there. You throw me down like you did when we snuck inside the offices. You press into me, all that soft power molding into my hard weakness. Would you scold me for not being who you want beneath all these fake faces? Would you cry for me? Pity me? Save me? You and I both know you're too good for me. Too good, too bad. Didn't care then and don't care now. Fuck the doorbells and the daddies. Fuck the flowers and the candies and all the world's plastic *expectations—they mean nothing for you and me. Why can't we? What's stopping us, huh? If I close my eyes, we can be anything we want, flip this hell into a heaven custom made for two.*

But then I remember what really happened in that fire. All the reasons and rules rush back. It's not enough. I'm not enough. Whitman was right about that too: "I should have made my way straight to you long ago… I should have chanted nothing but you."

Fucking freak, hush. I laugh. So hysterical.

Only a matter of time before my screams take over.

TWELVE

Huddled on the couch in the dark, she blinked up at the skylight in the sitting room and searched for the moon. The jewel tones of the stained glass crawled with shadow. She shivered. The mug of warm milk and honey in her grip did little to ease her shakiness. Her chill was too deep. How was this happening? *What* was happening? She'd never before experienced such lucid dreams.

Not dreams, her instinct whispered. *You're inside his head. Thinking his thoughts. Feeling his emotions.*

Those screams. He'd been hurt. But when? In the fire or afterwards? Was any of it accurate? Did it mean Holden was a ghost?

On both nights, she'd woken to find his mask on her face—evidence of strange sleep behavior. Parasomnia. She struggled to hang on to the details of the dream, but they were already melting back into her unconscious. Her vision pooled with unshed tears.

She pressed on her eyelids. The questions overwhelmed her. She'd only ever sensed a ghost once, last winter, and on that occasion, her ability to perceive the dead had been more of an uncanny accident. The ghost had been longing for a lost object, and Mave had picked up the frequency. But this thing with Holden...the connection felt different.

She needed insight—someone who could help her understand what was happening in her sleep. Gracelyn wasn't scheduled for another ghost tour until the day after, but Mave had already decided. On her next shift, she would go to the fortune teller. She would speak in hypotheticals. Seek guidance. Even if it meant consulting crystal balls.

———

Behind the gift shop counter, she scrolled through the hotel's budget on a tablet, half asleep, a bruise swelling in her chest. She tried to focus on the expenses, only to have her mind float back to the mask under her pillow. A lump grew in the back of her throat. At least she'd cried enough through the dark that she'd conked out and avoided any more scares in the spa. She rubbed her brow and released a sigh as the bells above the shop door jingled.

"That bad, huh?"

She straightened her shoulders and smoothed the lapels of her fitted suit jacket. *Worse, actually.* She knew who he was, even before he introduced himself.

"I'm Dom," he said with his hand outstretched. He looked the same as he did in Birdie's photo album—trim cut, cleft chin, disarming smile —classically handsome, only older. If anything, time had etched Dominick Grady's face with flattering furrows. His grip was cold. "A pleasure, Mave Michael. I've been eager to meet you." An Irish accent laced his baritone voice.

"Yes, I received your messages." *And avoided them.* "Sorry for not getting back to you sooner. Things have been a bit chaotic here this week." She waved at the boutique though it was painfully empty of customers.

His brow crested upward with casual intensity, like a movie star pondering life. "Well, I won't keep you long." He flashed his deep dimples and slid his hands inside his pockets. "As you know, I used to be your grandmother's agent and a friend of the family's."

A "friend." She returned his smile. "Of course, I've heard so much about you." Like how he'd also been Birdie's lover and had betrayed her by sleeping with Mave's mother. Though the affair had been kept hidden, according to Aunt Parissa, Birdie had fired and shunned him without so much as batting an eyelid.

They weighed one another for a beat. Mave got the distinct impression Dominick Grady was trying to peel back her skin and get inside her head. He cleared his throat and blinked, as if to reset his thoughts. "I hadn't realized how strongly you'd resemble your mother. A spitting image. You must get that a lot."

Her heart tightened. "How can I help you?" she said, hoping to avoid any awkward, if not depressing, musings over the past. Her mother was dead. The château's budget, meanwhile, was as leaky as the ceiling in the greenhouse and required her immediate attention.

"I heard Birdie left you her art collection."

"Mr. Grady—"

"Dom," he corrected.

"Dom"—she forced another smile—"please let me save you the trouble. My grandmother's estate is still legally under review due to her..." *Murder.*

"Unusual death?" he offered.

"Yes, exactly. And I'm still sorting through her belongings and artwork. Many of her paintings seem sentimental. I wouldn't feel right parting with them."

"Oh, I wouldn't dream of asking you to sell. I was thinking I might appraise a few pieces, maybe arrange a visit and walk-through of her studio upstairs. For old time's sake."

You're lying. The suspicion slashed into her thoughts as smoothly as his smile.

"Birdie was one of my first clients," he added. "I owe a lot to her and"—another flash of those dimples—"simply want to pay my respects. Speaking of which, I was wondering if I could meet you for lunch in a few hours in order to discuss—"

The doorway bells jingled, stopping him short.

Mave turned to greet the patron. "Ren!" Saved by the cop. *In uniform. On duty.* "Shoot, am I late already?" She made a show of checking the time on her tablet and groaned. "I'm so sorry, Dom," she said, refocusing on him, "but I'm tied up with back-to-back meetings. There's a big wedding booked and I'm..."

Dom held up a palm with a placating expression. "Please, no need. Maybe another time, then? Just think about it." He nodded goodbye and swept out of the shop.

"Who was that?" Ren asked after the door shut.

"No one. A guest."

His gaze paused over her hair. She reflexively touched a strand on her blonde pageboy wig. Had she anticipated his visit, she'd have worn the same auburn waves again. "I didn't expect to see you again so soon," she said.

"What can I say"—a hint of a smile teased his lips—"I'm a diligent guy when you give me a challenge." Whether he was implying the challenge was her or their arrangement hung in the air, unsettled. He held a large manila envelope, the edge of which he tapped playfully against his palm. She slid her nervous hands into her pant pockets and pushed her tongue against the backs of her teeth.

Don't ask. Don't tell. Wait for it.

A childhood memory unfurled, an exhausting jiu-jitsu lesson with her cheeks puffed and flushed, her back stuck with sweat against the mat. *"The more you show me how bad you want the prize,"* Cain said, *holding the doll out of reach, "the harder I'll make you work for it."*

Ren wandered through the boutique at a leisurely pace. "Can see why you love this place so much. It's like stepping into a time machine, a hundred years and counting." He tilted his head up, admiring the crystal chandelier. "A blast from the past each time I come back."

"Really? Hasn't it changed at all since you were a kid?"

"Not really, no. Though maybe..." He regarded her with his warm brown eyes. "Some views have improved," he said with a quiet smile. He paused next to a display of artisan jam jars, browsing labels, and laid the envelope on a vitrine.

Hasn't changed...a hundred years... Her thoughts splintered in another direction.

"So, meetings back-to-back, huh? What are the gift shop hours, anyway?"

"Hmm?" She tried not to stare at the envelope—the secrets on Holden they potentially held.

"You free to play hooky tomorrow evening?"

Her heart kicked. Why? Was he asking her out on another date?

She narrowed her eyes and pursed her mouth coyly, gathering confidence from her Heartbreaker Red lipstick shade. "That depends. What's happening tomorrow evening?"

He strolled closer until he stood across from her. He leaned his elbows on the counter and perused giftwrapped soap in a basket. She pretended not to notice he'd forgotten the envelope on the vitrine. "One of the homeowners agreed to a follow-up interview about her stolen property," he said in that smooth drawl of his. "I was hoping you could join us. As a concerned citizen, that is."

She could make out the early traces of his five o'clock shadow. "What time?" The question came out breathy. Her cheeks heated, betraying her emotion. She wasn't entirely sure what was provoking her the most: the file he was leaving her, the promise to meet later, or the forbidden attraction and temptation. He glanced up and their eyes locked.

"Eight."

"I think I can make that work."

"Excellent. I'll pick you up."

"Okay."

"You still have my number?"

"Mm-hmm."

"Good."

"Good."

"Like your hair, by the way. And the suit."

"Thanks."

"Makes you look taller."

"I'm wearing heels."

"That right?" He leaned his torso over the counter and peered down at her stiletto pumps. The scent of is lemony-basil aftershave brushed her face. "Indeed, ma'am, you are." He tilted back with a boyish grin as the bells above the door jingled and another person entered the shop.

"See you tomorrow evening, then."

Not a date, she inwardly repeated, trying and failing to cage the butterflies invading her stomach.

———

She had too many questions. Her brain cramped and her headache returned in full force. She found leftover coffee in a mug and downed two Advil. She stared at Holden's teenaged mugshot. She recognized the brooding, skinny boy in the grainy picture by his penetrating stare. He was beautiful even then, a high fashion photographer's ideal subject: sharp, hollowed-out cheekbones, surly mouth, long lashes, and dark eyes piercing the camera with their intensity.

Veined like the wings of a black moth, she thought, recalling those eyes up close. *Nothing like Ren's uncomplicated brown.* If she had to guess, she'd say he and Holden were roughly the same age. If young René Rawlings had visited the hotel all those years ago to play and explore—if his great-grandfather had designed the grand building, drawing Ren back to property over and again—what secrets did he know about the château? Had he encountered the Spirit of Dead Poets? Did he know of Holden Robert Frost beyond these juvie records?

The sealed files were sobering. She had expected Holden's rough childhood given his upbringing and underground lifestyle, but to say he'd been a troubled youth would be an understatement.

Beginning as early as age seven, he'd been arrested for shoplifting. By the time he hit twelve, he'd racked up numerous charges, including larceny, truancy, vandalism, curfew violations, incorrigibility. A few felonies were tossed in for good measure: theft of a car, theft of intellectual property—on and on it went. One charge in particular caught her attention.

Unlike Holden's other crimes, he'd been arrested only once for this, months before his suspected drowning. Assault. The altercation had been between Holden and someone named Vincent Lorde. Mave attempted to look him up on the gift shop's computer, but between the lower galleria's poor Wi-Fi connection and the never-ending personnel dropping in, a proper search seemed impossible. She had to scramble to hide the papers and her screen each time the door bells jingled.

First it had been the kitchen staff clearing away her morning hoard of cups and saucers; ever since her reading with Gracelyn, she'd been avoiding tea and slinging back espresso brews. Then it had been Julián popping in for an impromptu meeting to review wedding plans; they were accommodating an entire floor with black tulip bouquets and prepping over two hundred welcome baskets complete with licorice mints and black truffle macarons for the VIP guests—and what were her thoughts on a dark chocolate fountain and/or an aperitif bar in the lobby for when the wedding party arrived? Then catering stopped by; the shipment of kegs from the local brewery was delayed, and could she help track some missing crates of bourbon from last fall because the bride's favorite drink was a mint julep? Simultaneously, Ren's nostalgia for the property niggled at her thoughts, and she barely had a moment to follow up on her questions about the château's history and print off forms in the main office for later reading.

By four o'clock, she gave up trying to get any secret research done in the boutique. She closed up early and escaped to the cigar lounge upstairs. Surely, no one would bother her in the bar at this time of day.

Entering the empty lounge, she sighed with relief, greeted the bartender with an order for coffee, and hid herself in the furthest corner of the room. Frosted glass screens etched with art deco designs separated the curved booths. The seats were upholstered in worn teal leather and shaded drum chandeliers that reminded her of stacked top hats softly lit the room. A part of her was still in disbelief that all this faded luxury belonged to her. She repositioned the oil candle burner on her table and slipped out the files. Not a half hour later, she'd made a mental a to-do list, beginning with checking the dark web for—

"Whatcha reading?" Katie called, appearing at her table.

"Hmm?" She was already sliding the juvie records back into the envelope and bit down as the edge of a sheet sliced her thumb. "Oh, nothing. Some old invoices." She pinched the smarting papercut between her lips. "How'd you find me? Don't you have another hour left in your shift?" she said, hoping to divert Katie. She moved the envelope to her lap, out of sight, and inhaled a long breath through her nose.

"Julián put in a laundry order and I got sidetracked," she replied. Before Mave could ask with what, Katie pulled up a chair, peered across the room, and waved toward the bar. "Lawrence, could I get one of these, too?" She gestured at Mave's mug and beamed a smile. She had a way with people, Mave noticed; made everyone feel familiar. It was funny, she thought. Katie was her exact opposite, extroverted and free-spirited. Not uptight and closed off like her.

Katie spun back to her with a giant grin on her face. "So, heard you had a special visitor today," she said in stage whisper, "or should I say, an *officer*." She was practically bouncing in her seat.

Mave's brow rose. "What?"

"*You* what! I heard the maids talking in the dryer room. Apparently, he's quite the catch in these parts. Half of housekeeping is drooling over him in his tight little navy—"

"Okay!" Mave sputtered with a palm up. "You need to rewind a little."

"You were spotted together in the gift shop."

Katie made it sound like they were a celebrity couple caught canoodling. Great. Between the small town of Hazel Springs and the château's isolation, it seemed Mave's pretend love life was the most exciting news in the county.

"Please, Mave," she whined, "I'm dying for some vicarious living here. You have to give me something. Is this the guy you mentioned in the greenhouse? Did he ask you out on another date? Is he a good kisser?"

Mave leaned back in her chair to steady her slight dizziness. She hadn't kissed Ren. She'd kissed Holden. She wanted *Holden*.

"Uh-oh. What did I say?" Katie's expression folded into worry. "I put my foot in my mouth somehow, didn't I? I'm always doing that."

Mave tucked her lips under her teeth and gave a subtle shake of her head as footsteps approached. Lawrence came around the booth's partition.

"Hope everything is okay?" he asked too formally, as if Mave were a top food critic about to leave him a review.

"Uh-huh." Mave smiled.

He quickly cleared her empty coffee cup with a nervous rattle, wiped the table clean in front of Katie, and headed back behind the bar.

"Okay, what is it, then?" Katie asked gently, leaning forward. The light of the oil burner fluttered across her face. "Maybe I can help."

"It's just..." Mave stared at the flame. The envelope on her lap suddenly felt like a thousand-pound weight. Cain's schooling echoed between her ears, years of cautionary tales and warnings that amounted to one rule: *Don't let them in.* But maybe there was another way.

"It's not about the new guy exactly," she confessed in a hurried whispered. "There's someone else. Or, at least, there was. He's not around anymore and I..."

Careful, M&M.

Mave squeezed her thumb beneath the table, feeling the paper cut sting. "I miss him."

"You mean an ex-boyfriend?" Katie asked.

She nodded. Close enough.

"What happened?"

"He ghosted me," she improvised, feeling the cruelty of her double entendre.

Katie scowled. "Guys are such jerks," she muttered. Her nostrils flared as she grew taller in her seat. "Listen, Mave, you can't do this to yourself, okay? You can't dwell on him anymore. Uh-uh. No matter how much it hurts. He's bad news. Good riddance, right? It's over and you have to...to move on."

It was only then Mave noticed the purple circles lining Katie's eyes. "Hey, are you feeling o—?"

Katie's tears welled without warning. "*Shit.*"

Mave passed her a linen napkin. "This isn't just about me, is it?"

She wiped her eyes quickly, seeming embarrassed, and sagged

forward like all the energy had been sucked out of her. "Still haven't slept. And my ex in LA, he texted me last night."

And the night before, Mave wagered, recalling all the crumpled tissues when they first met inside the dark spa.

Katie shrugged. "It was an ugly split."

"Did you text him back?"

"Almost. I erased everything before I could hit send."

"And then you stayed up the rest of the night obsessing over the what-ifs?"

Head hanging, she sniffed and nervously spun the oil burner on the table. Her nails were bitten down to their beds. "I know what you're thinking, but it's not only him, it's..." She reached for Mave's hand and dropped her forehead to the table with a soft thump. "I think I may be going crazy," she said, hiding her face in the crook of her elbow.

Mave tried to relax her shoulders and stared at their connected hands—a lump of knuckles. "What? No, it's okay. Insomnia is..." *Normal.* She cleared her throat. "Did you try a good book before bed? Sometimes that helps me sleep." *But not since Holden*, she held back. No matter which novel she was holding, all the words on the page fluttered and rearranged themselves into his whispers, his tattoos—the poetry, the library—his mouth on hers.

Katie shook her head, her face still buried in her arm. "You don't understand. Last night, I tried to move back into my room," she mumbled. "Didn't go so well. I kept hearing these awful whispers, but this time, I could make out the words." She sniffed and peeked up at Mave, fresh dewiness filming her eyes. "See? I'm hallucinating voices. I told you I'm going crazy."

"No, it's stress," she tried to convince her. If only she believed the excuse herself. "Why, what—?" She swallowed. "What did the voices say?"

Katie lifted her head slowly and blinked at her. Her skin had paled. Her pupils were dilated and her mascara had smudged, flecking her cheekbones like Rorschach blots. "No eye may see," she whispered. "Again and again: *No eye may see.* What do you think it means?"

A hint of awareness fluttered in the back of Mave's mind, a detail too foggy to articulate. *No eye may see.* Where had she heard those words? She shook her head. "Noth—nothing. Just a bad dream, I'm sure." She offered her best *all is well* smile and glanced away to hide her real thoughts.

Bad dreams at Château du Ciel had ways of coming true.

THIRTEEN

Once the dayshift ended and the smattering of guests retired for the night, Mave slipped outside. She raised the neckline of her collar to keep warm. She'd had enough sense to change out of her pantsuit and stilettos, but not to wear a scarf. The shushing trees offered no buffer from the wind as she zigzagged through the overgrown gardens with her lantern. Though a few moths flickered against her light, most of the glow seemed swallowed by the dark. The crickets chirped loudly, their normally pleasant chorus abrasive this evening. She silenced those in her path with her rustling steps. Nettles scratched and pricked her ankles. *Too many weeds*, she thought. How would Amos clear them in time?

Later—you're not out here to worry over the landscaping.

She reached the greenhouse, released the chain padlock, and stepped into the shelter with her heart knocking against her ribcage. She pressed the door shut with her spine and glanced around nervously. More than ever, the space appeared condemned, crawling with nocturnal shadows and god knew what else. She set down her lantern and pulled out her gloves from her back pocket.

She worked quickly, relocating the ivies that covered the mysterious hatch they'd stumbled upon earlier. She had to confirm her hunch: Holden had escaped this way. He had survived the fire. She gathered together the ropy plants and turned her face away from the stink of sulfurous muck that released. She yanked and pinned the stubborn-most creepers beneath a stone cherub statue. With her fingers curled around the iron knob, she paused.

An irrational fear gripped her: she'd open the hatch and a swarm of bats would rush out and attack her. She closed her eyes and breathed out slowly for a count of ten. With the worst of her imagination harnessed, she tugged open the door.

Its wicked creak drove her shoulders upward like a knot around her neck. A hissing silence greeted her in place of any bats. She frowned. The light of her lantern was too weak to pierce the yawning black hole. She switched to her cellphone, tilted forward on her knees, and directed its flashlight within.

A narrow, steep staircase appeared. Her skin pricked with pins and needles. Where did the descent lead? To a secret entrance into the hotel's lower galleria? To the sealed-off train tunnels? A forgotten crypt? She checked over her shoulder, weighing the risk. The crickets droned outside the walls of the greenhouse. Her unease festered. No one knew she was here. She'd deliberately avoided the search earlier with Katie, in case she found more evidence of Holden.

I'll be in and out. I'll only go down the steps enough to see what's at the bottom.

Her claustrophobia was already at work, funneling anxiety upward through her chest, crowding her throat. Last winter, when she'd investigated mysterious things underground on her own, she'd discovered the bones of a murder victim. The memory flashed in her head like a warning. What if she found a body—*another* dead body—*Holden's* dead body?

No one's been murdered! she argued with herself. She snapped the elastic band on her wrist. *Holden's alive.* Now more than ever, she needed it to be true.

She shifted her weight, swung down her feet, and lowered herself the first few steps. Her breaths were frayed, as if she'd climbed up a hundred stairs as opposed to tiptoed down three. She peered up again, tempted to retreat back to the hotel, cozy up next to the fireplace in the lobby, and order a cup of hot milk with cinnamon from the kitchen—something to thaw her bloodstream.

Keep going, her stubbornness nagged. *The quicker you do this, the quicker you get the answers you need and return inside.* She plucked her elastic band once more, the sting helping to distract from her fear, and descended another ten steps into the musty sublevel. A mistake.

The slam of the hatch door above nearly caused her to stumble and go tumbling down the remainder of the flight. She jerked her phone's flashlight above and stared at the now-sealed exit.

No-no-no!

She scrambled up the stairs, hunched her neck and shoulders, and pushed. The door didn't budge. Not even a hair. She shoved and pounded with the side of her fist. "Hello!" she cried, her voice echoing shrilly in her ears. "*Hello*, is somebody up there? Please! I'm inside, I—" Her lungs stuttered. "*Let me—out! Hello?*" She tried to calm herself, to slow her racing heart enough to listen for movement above, but her own panic was too loud, whooshing through her veins in all directions, jamming her senses. She lifted her light to the underside of the hatch, desperately searching for an inner knob, a hidden release, anything—then remembered she had a phone.

She threw off her gloves and with a shaky finger, tapped on Bastian's number. *Yes. There.* He'd get her out. He'd come and find her in a minute or two, and together they'd have a good laugh about how she'd—

The beeps pierced through her false sense of relief like poison darts. She kept the phone to her ear regardless, in denial that no ring was coming—listening to the ragged sounds exiting her mouth—clutching her ribs with her other hand. Her stomach twisted with nausea. She lowered the cell at last and blinked at its screen.

NO SERVICE

Too quickly, her hand shot up to find a signal. The phone flew from her clammy grip and went skidding down the steps, taking her light with it.

Oh, Jesus. Oh, please. Let me out of here. Please-please-please. I can't breathe—I need my phone—I need—okay...okay...

Her throat ran dry. She curled and shoved her shoulder upward against the hatch one last time. Nothing happened beyond bruising herself. She scratched her fingers across the solid wood, catching splinters. However that opening had shut, whatever had trapped her down here, it was clear she'd have to find her way above ground through some alternate exit.

She skittered her palms against the cold, stony walls and felt her way down through the blackness. Her gasps of air grew shallower with each step lower, snipping her oxygen, sharpening this nightmare she'd found herself inside. It was like a blade stabbing her lungs, quicker and quicker. Dimmer and dimmer. When she next tried to snap her elastic bracelet, it broke from the force.

There was no escape from the dark.

FOURTEEN

The melancholic coos of a pigeon broke through her dream. As if doused with cold water, she awoke with a sharp intake of air. She blinked on her back, muscles stiff, and ran her tongue across her gritty teeth. She was at the bottom of the steep stairs. Milky daylight streamed in from above. She squinted up in disbelief at the hatch door, gaping wide—perfectly open, exactly as she'd left it. Even her phone was within reach. Its red case shone in her peripheral vision, less than a foot away on the ground.

She turned her head and snatched it up. Like a sick joke, it lit up, displaying its healthy battery life, clear network connection, not a scratch on its screen.

She rolled up slowly, swayed and gripped her pounding temples. She'd never before passed out from hyperventilation. (Granted, she'd been close once, stuck in a dumbwaiter, crammed on Holden's lap; but he'd kissed her and she'd snapped back to life like Snow White on amphetamines.) She tapped on the phone's flashlight and peered deeper into her surroundings, confirming what she'd suspected all along. The tunnels—Holden's exit. At least that's what the sublevel looked like. After last night, she wasn't about to risk a deeper exploration.

She lumbered up the steps, ignoring her aching head, and found the stone cherub she'd used to hold down the vines fallen and broken into pieces. Nothing else was disturbed. She closed the hatch and hid it beneath the ivies. It was as if her imprisonment had never happened. Her mind was already devising a plan to make up for lost hours, even as another part of her questioned how she'd ended up at the bottom of those stairs overnight. How had the door sealed? How had it reopened? Could it have been the wind, an animal, a ghost?

No.

She dug her knuckles into her forehead. Nothing made sense. She needed to speak with Gracelyn about her dreams and hauntings. She needed to understand what was happening—who was doing this to her.

An unknown enemy.

———

She barely gave Katie the opportunity to look up from the black orchids she was arranging in a vase. "Morning," Mave said, sweeping past the spa's reception desk without stopping. "Can you make sure no one disturbs me in here? I need to take care of some things —uninterrupted."

"Oh, yeah, sure."

Mave was already halfway through the closet's entrance. "Thank you," she called, pulling the door shut behind her. She spun around and glanced at the tight walls, the storage boxes and shelves. Almost immediately, her claustrophobia triggered. She shut her eyes and tried to regulate the rhythms of her body. She reminded herself this room was not the same as the sublevel she'd been trapped inside. She was free to leave. There was plenty of air. Channeling Cain like a method actor, Mave switched off her emotions, opened her eyes, and got down to business.

The equivalent of 411 on the dark web was far more detailed than she ever could have imagined—startlingly so. She stumbled on one site with a decade-plus stockpile of personal data harvested legally and redistributed illegally. Like scrolling through a black-market resume, she was able to read up on the victim listed in Holden's juvie file: Vincent Lorde of Hazel Springs. She found his date of birth, citizenship, his most recent phone number and address, his education, work and credit history, even his browsing habits. (Over the years, he'd subscribed to numerous live porn sites.) Save for his social security number, it was all listed at the click of a button—including the names of Vincent's former legal guardians in foster care.

So *that's* how their paths had crossed fifteen years ago. Vincent and Holden had likely been placed in the same home. She scribbled his contact details on hotel stationary, then did another search on Holden Frost from Hazel Springs.

Unsurprisingly, there was far less information on him than on Vincent—much of it duplicated from his death record. She tried Bek-187 next. Zero results loaded. Predictably. She hadn't really expected the pseudonym to reveal any information. After all, anonymity was the point of the dark web (even if she'd blown her own cover with Bek). She couldn't put it off any longer. With a wavering breath, she navigated to the marketplace.

Her post on the discussion board had no new activity. But she had two unread direct messages. With a hit of nausea spiking her stomach, she clicked on her inbox and read the two messages at once. They were brief.

10.

9.

A countdown. Her chest tightened. How could she be expected to track a ghost in under two weeks? She had to help Ren locate the stolen property, look into Vincent Lorde, oversee the wedding plans. *Right.* She had to save this hotel from sinking further into debt or she'd have no home left—and neither would Holden.

She typed her response in haste, the deep-set keys snapping under the pads of her fingers.

I need more time.

She stared at her demand, frustration and desperation mixing a curdled cocktail in her gut. A few beats passed and the ellipsis icon blinked on the message box. Her spine stiffened. Bek-187 was logged on and composing a reply. She forced loose her captured breath and worried a hangnail, nipping, waiting. Those three damned dots seemed to wink forever on the screen.

Finally, the message appeared.

Too bad for Daddy, then.

Mave's blood pounded in her ears. She pictured that photo of Cain asleep. It wasn't like her father to be caught off guard. But maybe prison had worn him down. Maybe he wasn't as strong as he'd once been. Serving multiple life sentences would take a toll; surviving day in and day out alongside some of the most dangerous, violent criminals in the country.

She chewed on her thumbnail, deliberating her next words.

Say I do what you ask, give you what you want. How do I know you won't hurt my father anyway to protect your back?

If at any point, Cain caught wind that she was being blackmailed—threatened in order to protect *his* life—he would send a message to his enemies and exact revenge. Might was right, especially in a maximum-security prison.

Bek-187 replied. **Unlike yours, my back is covered. I avoid unneces-sary messes. You of all people should get that, Neat-Freak.**

Who are you? she typed.

An impatient associate. 9.

Of Cain's? Of Holden's? **What do you want with SDP? How do you know who I am?**

No more questions. 9.

Give me more time.

But her demand seemed to fall on deaf ears. No more replies came.

———

Bridezilla was coming. Julián claimed he was having heart palpitations as he passed along the details. She'd requested Mave be present for the surprise visit. He needed her there. The *hotel* needed her. Even so, the meeting now felt trivial. Mave had graver worries than a spoiled diva to please—like nine short days to figure out how to save her father's life. Yet her plans to approach Gracelyn between tours and to investigate Vincent Lorde's workplace in Hazel Springs had to wait. Mave pocketed an emergency postcard to mail Cain. (How she'd ask him to call her without raising his suspicions was a problem for later.) She locked up the boutique and dashed upstairs to make herself presentable.

Channeling the vintage *Vogue* magazines she'd found in Birdie's penthouse, she selected a sleek dark brown wig, cat-eye fashion glasses, and heeled ankle boots to give herself a few extra inches. Forty minutes later, they were in Queen's Hall.

Julián had visible beads of sweat gathering atop his strained smile, and Mave was muttering all sorts of assurances and promises that in a little over a week, when the VIP guests checked in, everything would be ready and fabulous. It would be *the* wedding everyone would be talking about, sure to go viral. Yes, they had secured the black swallowtail butterflies, she confirmed, even as she inwardly kicked herself for forgetting to follow up with Bastian.

The smooth lies exited her mouth one after the other. To her own ears, she sounded like a seasoned politician, a confident stranger. It would be magical. Spectacular. However, what a shame they hadn't known earlier about her visit; they couldn't see the greenhouse in person today as they were doing light repairs on the ceiling, securing scaffolding. (Another issue she hadn't addressed with Amos: the damned leaks.) The *Farmers' Almanac* predicted showers the entire week of the wedding, so they planned to erect a tented pathway across the gardens, allowing guests to stay dry as they were ushered to and from the ceremony and reception in Queen's Hall.

The bride seemed satisfied with Mave's answers. All things considered, she added minor demands—extra hurricane lanterns, outdoor crystal chandeliers, a curtained archway at the altar, an aisle of rose petals on natural ground as opposed to a red carpet. *Oh*, and rotating ghost tours for all her guests, plus a midnight séance for the wedding party.

The latter was a promise made by Julián, despite Gracelyn's absence and lack of credentials. Mave had checked the schedule earlier. The fortune teller wasn't slated to work the event. She was one of the few residents from Hazel Springs contracted by the hotel and didn't keep a room in the staff quarters. What her plans were for the wedding day was anyone's guess. Nevertheless, anything the bride asked for, she and

Julián nodded and praised and added to their already overflowing to-do lists.

By the end of the meeting, Mave was inwardly simmering with irritation and her cheeks hurt from fake smiling. When the bride left, they both collapsed into chairs. Visible sweat stains darkened the pits of Julián's shirt. He proceeded to chomp through half a roll of antacids as they conducted a post-mortem of duties and responsibilities. She was only half attentive, her mind circling back to Cain, to Holden, to seeking out Gracelyn, and preparing for her consult on the robbery investigation. Yet before she knew it, the morning had become the afternoon, and she still hadn't addressed the hardest challenges that lay ahead of her. The most she'd accomplished was mailing her postcard to Cain with a two-word message: *Call me.*

Less was more when it came to her father.

By four o' clock, she'd postponed trying to find Gracelyn until tomorrow. *You're avoiding it on purpose,* a voice in the back of her mind chided. Katie caught her outside the kitchens, where Mave had been summoned to sign an emergency invoice for ridiculously overpriced foie gras. (Bridezilla's latest menu change, Chef had uttered amid curses.)

"There you are!" Katie approached her with a bright smile. "Need your help with—"

"Sorry, Katie," she said mid-stride. "Maybe you can ask Julián? I've got another wedding emergency." She pointed distractedly ahead of her. She still had to find Bastian about the butterflies and Amos about the leaks.

Katie skipped beside her and matched her hurried step. "Oh, I know. That's why I'm here. Julián's swamped, too. I approached him first and he mentioned you instead."

"He did?" Lord help her. What now?

"Yeah, so…"

"Just spit it out, please."

"You need to volunteer for the complimentary facial we'll be giving the VIP guests."

"The what?" She blinked and slowed her stride. "This really isn't a good time. I've got a boatload of things to prep before the end of today."

"That's just it. See, in reality, the timing's perfect. You need a quick pick-me-up treatment since...well..."

Mave cocked her brow. Since she'd passed out in an underground tunnel and looked like a rundown basket case?

Katie cleared her throat. "Since I need the training for when the guests arrive," she finished tactfully. "I'm officially certified in yoga, but still learning esthetics. *And* Olga is scheduled today, so she can show me how."

Olga, right. Mave recalled the second spa employee from the HR files.

"In that case, can't you just practice on Olga?"

Katie shook her head. "She has to show me. We need a volunteer to pose as the guest. Plus, I was thinking, we have these detox vanilla-avocado crème packs that are about to expire." Her face sparked with excitement at the idea.

Mave was skeptical. "Are you sure those crème packs shouldn't be served in the kitchen?"

"Come on, it'll be fun—relaxing! Pretty please? It'll make me feel better—a way to say thanks for being so welcoming. Everything will be super pro and efficient. You'll be in and out. Promise. Look, I even tied my hair back in a bun and everything!"

It was hard to refuse Katie when she seemed so eager to please. Or maybe Mave was more tired than she cared to admit.

The next thing she knew, she was lying half dressed atop a spa bed. A heated blanket warmed her chest, and a harp soundtrack streamed softly through hidden speakers. Admittedly, the treatment room's dim lights and aromatherapy were melting away some of Mave's stress—despite the thick crème the older esthetician, Olga, slathered on her skin. Mave's entire face felt like a mold of wet plaster.

Katie instructed Mave to close her eyes. "How's that?" she asked as the finishing touches were applied: cucumber slices on Mave's eyelids.

Mave didn't want to disappoint them. "Mmm, nice," she said.

Olga cleared her throat. She had barely spoken two words since

Mave had entered the spa and declared her participation. Would the veteran staff ever let down their guard around her? "The mask will take ten minutes to set," Olga said. "I'll come back then."

"Got it," Katie replied as the door softly clicked open and shut. "You should soon feel a warm, tingling sensation," Katie informed Mave, "a natural skin exfoliation and rejuvenation." It sounded like she was consulting the label. "Okay. Guess I'll go check if Olga needs any—"

"Wait." She reached out for Katie's wrist before she could leave. The last thing she wanted was to be left alone in this small dark room with her eyes closed. Aromatherapy or not, her thoughts were sure to take a turn for the worst and set off her claustrophobia. "Stay. Keep me company."

"Oh, sure." Katie seemed to settle herself on the stool beside her. "So, since we're giving you some glowing skin, any plans for the rest of the day? I mean, other than work?"

"Actually..." Consulting on a police investigation was still technically work, but Mave figured it counted as "going out." Her stomach did a strange little flip as she thought of Ren picking her up in a few hours. Even though it *wasn't* a date. "The new guy's coming by," she said in a near-whisper. "The officer. He's taking me to Hazel Springs this evening."

The stool creaked as Katie shifted her weight. "That's good, right? Aren't you into him, even a tiny bit?"

"I am, but..." Mave couldn't name it. Her feelings were jumbled when it came to René Rawlings. How much of it was genuine, and how much of it was a knee-jerk response to his flattery and attention? Or the thrill of defying the world's expectations? *Mave Michael Francis dating a police officer.* As if she was innocent. And blameless. As if she could finally shed herself of Cain's reputation. "I feel nervous. That's all," she said quietly.

"That's a good sign before a date. Don't worry."

"It's not a real date. I'm just helping him."

"What do you mean?"

She cleared her throat. "Well, it's sort of unofficial, but I'm consulting on the robbery investigation. You know all those break-ins in town? I'm helping track some of the stolen items."

"Oh my god, Mave, seriously? That's incredible! You can do that? Like, you're a police psychic?"

She didn't want to make a big deal out of it. "Something like that. But it's a one-time deal. As I said, unofficial. Actually, it's probably best if you didn't tell anyone else. It's not like I'm not going to crack the case or anything."

"Holy shit, this is exciting! And I bet he's using this as an excuse to spend more time with you. Okay, after we wash off the mask, I can do your makeup." She moved away slightly, and a cupboard whined open.

Katie's enthusiasm was encouraging. Mave smiled, allowing herself the fantasy for a moment: her and Ren. A small swirl of guilt spoiled her mood as Holden sprung into her thoughts.

"You feel the mask heating up, right?" Katie asked while shuffling and arranging products. Cellophane crinkled. "Isn't that crème pack the best ever?"

"Couldn't say," Mave mumbled. "Never had a facial before today."

"Really?"

She gave a slight nod, careful not to displace her cucumbers. "Didn't exactly lead a pampered life. Or a normal one."

"How so?" Katie asked, repositioning herself back on her stool.

It somehow felt easier to share parts of herself with her eyes closed. "My father was really strict. I didn't go out and do stuff like other girls."

"What about at school?"

"I was homeschooled. Had some tutors over the years, but we always moved before I could really make any friends." Her first kiss had been at fifteen with the son of one of the tutors. Cain must have gotten suspicious, or it might have been a coincidence, because they'd picked up and left town a few days later.

"For what it's worth, you didn't miss much." Katie voice dropped low with bitterness. "High school sucked. Lots of girls were mean. Guys, too."

"There are mean people everywhere." She couldn't help but remember how she'd been treated during Cain's trail—or afterward.

Even here at the château. Amos. Olga. All the dirty looks she'd endured from strangers judging her to be a lowlife contract killer like Cain. "I'm glad you're not one of them," Mave added, "the mean people." She inhaled deeply. She suddenly needed Katie to understand. "I didn't know. When I was a kid"—she swallowed—"what my father did for a living. Not until later on, and by then, well…" She'd never spoken about it to anyone before. Not even that awful therapist years ago. "I guess I was scared. It was too late to stop him."

"It's okay," Katie said, her tone strained, affected. Mave couldn't see her to gauge her reaction. "I would've been scared, too," she whispered.

Mave let out a small breath. At least she didn't sound repulsed. In fact, Katie surprised her by holding her hand and giving it a light squeeze.

"Hey, Mave?"

"Yeah?"

"I'm glad you're not mean, too. I'm glad I found you."

The knots in Mave's shoulders and neck loosened. The sincerity in Katie's voice was unmistakable.

"Okay, you have five more minutes before Olga returns and we wash this off," Katie said. "I'll go grab some heated towels. Hang tight. I'll be right back."

Mave stiffened like a corpse as Katie let go of her hand. The door clicked shut with her departure. The discomfort was immediate. Like someone had switched off the lights. *Relax*, she thought. She was being childish. Lights on or off, her eyes were closed and it didn't matter. She would enjoy herself like a normal person.

She wiggled lower into the curve of the spa bed and focused on the cool weight of the cucumbers on her eyelids, the harp's echo, the warm blanket tucked to her chest. It was fine. Katie and Olga would return any second. A bead of sweat traced the back of her neck. Mave shivered despite the blanket and adjusted herself lower.

What was taking so long? Hadn't five minutes passed? Her hands twitched, reflexively wishing to wipe away the blinding cucumbers and cement-like mask. She paused.

The door creaked open.

Mave let out a sigh. "Finally. For a second, I thought you'd gone in search of a real hot spring." She huffed a hollow laugh. Cracks formed on her cheeks. Why weren't they responding?

The harp plucked sweetly in her ears.

"Katie?" Mave's heart galloped inside her ribcage. "Olga? Are you —?" Her voice frayed. "Are you there?" she tried again.

Don't take off the mask, a little voice warned in her head. *Whatever you do, keep your eyes closed.* She inhaled sharply. Her nose had picked up the uncanny odor, understanding before her mind.

Plastic. Polyethylene.

Fumes crawled into the room, polluting the spa's lavender and eucalyptus aroma, turning the air into a resinous chemical bouquet.

No. No, this isn't happening.

But it was. The inexplicable odor. Her dreams. Those knocks the other night.

No eye may see.

Fear locked her arms and legs as the reek thickened. She'd encountered this type of spontaneous, insoluble scent before. Only then, it had been ashes. This plastic odor didn't belong. It was wrong. Her intuition screamed: she hadn't misheard. Someone was inside the room with her. Except it was neither Katie nor Olga who had entered.

Inches from Mave's body, a ghost hovered.

FIFTEEN

"What's wrong?" Katie paced inside and cleared the cucumbers from her eyelids.

Paralyzed with fright, Mave blinked as her vision readjusted to the faint stream of light. The sharp stench of plastic was already dissipating, leaving behind the spa's herbal fragrance. Mave's lungs continued to heave and catch. "I'm—" She shuddered and managed to sit up, struggling to gather her wits.

"Here, take this." Katie placed a hot towel on her temples. "It'll help."

"Did you see anything?" she breathed.

"What?

"Just now."

The creases in Katie's forehead deepened. "You mean your hyperventilating?"

No. Katie hadn't seen or smelled or heard anything. Of course.

"What's going on, Mave? Are you okay?"

Mave scoured her face with the towel, her mask chafing and crumbling. "It's nothing," she mumbled. "I'm claustrophobic and—"

"Oh god! You should have told me sooner." Katie fussed to help clear the mask from her cheeks and hairline. "We could have asked Olga to set us up somewhere more spacious, like inside your suite." She patted her with additional clean towels and pulled out a small battery-operated fan.

Grateful, Mave swallowed the fresh air. Yet the stink lingered in her memory. Who'd visited her? Why did a ghost haunt these walls?

As Katie turned to the cupboard for more supplies, Mave shut her eyes again. It was easier not to see, not to ask. Because the truth might hurt far worse. The truth might mean Holden had been here all along, as trapped as in her dreams.

———

For whatever reason, maybe her scare in the spa or Ren's easy smile, she was less nervous in the police cruiser this time around. Ren was good company, keeping her distracted for the entire drive down the mountain. They chatted about everything from the upcoming wedding at the château to the continuous rainfall that was dampening the softball season (Ren coached a "moms for cancer research" team on weekends). He didn't bring up the juvie file he'd slipped her, and Mave didn't know how to broach the taboo subject. It was a shady trade at the end of the day, no matter how seemingly innocent. Questions about his youth kept her on edge. Did he *know* Holden? Surely, he must have been curious about her supposed friendship with a local boy who'd drowned fifteen years ago. But when they crossed into town, the topic still hadn't come up. Rather, Ren briefed her on the burglary victim they were about to meet.

Her name was Mrs. Darlene Hess. A lifetime resident of Hazel Springs, she'd been away visiting her daughter in Boulder on the day of the burglary. When she'd returned home, she'd found her computer equipment and modest book collection missing. Nothing else had been disturbed. Ren also added that while Mrs. Hess had agreed to a follow-up interview, she'd been openly skeptic when he'd explained the nature of Mave's consultation.

It turned out Mrs. Hess was more than happy to state as much to her face. "I think this is a waste of time," she said after greeting her coolly at the front door. Ren had mentioned Mrs. Hess was in her sixties, though her leathery skin made her look older—markings of too much sun. Her hair was a helmet of faded corn-yellow, and she wore large red glasses that offset her fuchsia lipstick, some of which had feathered into the creases around her lips. Her dislike of Mave was physically palpable. Mave wondered what offended her the most: that she was the daughter of Cain or the granddaughter of Birdie. Neither her paternal nor maternal side would've won a popularity contest in Hazel Springs.

Toward Ren, however, Mrs. Hess's body language warmed considerably. She smiled with all her teeth showing, patted his arm, offered him (or them, it was hard to be sure as she had eyes only for Ren) a glass of iced tea. Mave frowned, feeling herself a third wheel despite her necessary attendance. With a quiet sigh, she took advantage of her temporary invisibility and clocked her surroundings.

Two windows, three doors, two lamps, one phone cord. Overall, the bungalow was tidy and well-kept; characteristics which, despite everything, made Mrs. Hess more amiable to her. As she half listened to the small talk between officer and homeowner, it occurred to her why Ren was so liked in the community (or as Katie had put it, "quite the catch in these parts"). He was the perfect combination of unthreatening and authoritative—the type of police hero you'd see in children's picture books, climbing neighborhood trees to rescue orphaned kittens.

But would he take a bullet for me to save me from a lunatic in a raging fire?

She resisted the urge to scratch her scar, her thoughts lingering on Holden's sacrifice. They settled in the small family room, Ren and Mave sharing the couch, and Mrs. Hess on the armchair. Ren pulled out his phone and offered Mave a list of items stolen from the home. Scrolling through it made her self-conscious.

Ren and Mrs. Hess were watching her, as if waiting for her mystical lead. She remembered the ghost tour, how Gracelyn had given a short speech beforehand and included participants in their tea leaf readings like a ceremony. Mave never performed such fanfare. If anything, her sixth sense was more of a quirk, an innate reflex; but the way Mrs. Hess was regarding her, perhaps a flourish or two would break the ice, authenticate her as a psychic consultant. *Play the part*, Cain whispered.

Mave passed Ren his phone back and suggested they begin with the books. She figured Mrs. Hess would have more sentimental attachment to a novel than a modem.

"They were mostly beach reads and bestsellers," Mrs. Hess said, "paperbacks I'd picked up over the years at checkout lines. I probably wouldn't have even noticed them missing if it weren't for the gaping hole there." She indicated the pine hutch adjacent where, indeed, an entire shelf stood empty.

"In that case," Mave said, "can you think of one book in particular that stuck with you, maybe a favorite from the bunch that was taken?"

"Suppose…" Her eyes drifted askew as she contemplated her answer. "All right," she said, redirecting her gaze at Mave, "I'm thinking of one." A faint challenge glinted through her lenses, as if the goal was for Mave to guess the novel's title.

She cleared her throat. "Mrs. Hess, you're going to have to tell me the exact book I'm looking for. The more information you give me about the missing item, the easier it is for me to sense where it's currently being kept."

She arched a brow. "Okay. In that case, it was *The Davinci Code*."

"In paperback?"

"Yes. I said so."

"And do you remember what was on the cover? Apart from the title and author's name."

"Well, it was a while ago now, but I believe it was red. With the Mona Lisa's eyes."

Ren was already pulling up an image on his phone. "Like this one here?"

She nodded. "That's it."

He tilted his phone toward Mave so she could reference the photo.

"Perfect, thank you, Mrs. Hess. That's very helpful. Now, last thing, I'm going to ask you to please concentrate on a memory of your novel. Maybe think of the time you first read it. Simply put yourself back in that place: where you were sitting, what hour of day it was, how the book made you feel, that sort of stuff. As long as you're thinking about the book, it'll guide me."

"How long will this take?" she asked with a frown, as if it were a taxing memory she was being asked to recall versus a simple, pleasant one.

"Hopefully, not long at all," Mave answered, sticking to her smile like it'd been glued to her jaw. She was as eager as anyone to have this little experiment be over.

"Fine," she said, still sounding skeptical. "I'll try."

"Excellent."

"Are you going to stare at me?"

"No, sorry." Mave turned and blinked at Ren. "I'll just be..." *Staring at him.*

He subtly checked a smile, a muscle in his jaw ticking. In fairness, he *had* warned her.

She tried to clear her mind and lowered her eyes. The gold badge over Ren's breast pocket seemed to point at her. If she leaned forward a little more, she could rest her cheek on it. She locked her hand on her knee, kept her heel grounded and stifled its need to bounce. Just as she was beginning to think facing Ren had been a bad idea, she caught a scent from Mrs. Hess.

Her eyelids fell and fluttered reflexively.

Dan Brown, The Davinci Code. She breathed in, anticipating the sweet, dry paper pulp, ink, and...

ASHES.

Her eyes snapped open as a cough erupted from her mouth.

"Mave?" Ren sat forward in alarm.

The burn was so strong, it filled her nostrils and coated the back of her throat. "Excu—" Unable to continue, she bent over into her elbow and coughed out the scent, rejecting it even as her eyes teared from the smoke—the knowledge.

Fire, burn, ashes.

Those books were gone, all of them seared into oblivion. *Like Holden,* an awful voice whispered. She shook her head and pressed down on her chest, regaining control of her lungs.

Ren touched her shoulder. "What just happened?" His brow

formed a slash, his normally kind eyes hooded in darkness. "What did you see?"

"Ashes," she admitted, too dazed to improvise a lie. "They're burned. The books. No trace of them. I'm sorry, I couldn't..." Her voice gave and she stared into her lap. What did it mean? That Holden was burning books? Or sending her a message from the afterlife?

No.

She sat up straighter and wiped the corners of her eyes.

Ren's hand fell away. "Mave, it's okay, you don't have to—"

"Let's try some of the computer equipment," she said, turning to Mrs. Hess. "The keyboard would be best."

"Why?" Mrs. Hess narrowed her eyes. "Thought you just said they're burned."

She wasn't used to helping doubters and critics. If it wasn't for finding Holden and her agreement with Ren, she would have abandoned this awful attempt from the get-go. "The books, yes, as for the rest, I'm not sure. I'm assuming you touched your keyboard regularly." She no longer bothered with her fake smile. "Think of it like a pair of shoes worn by you. The more you walk around in those shoes, the more they absorb the shapes of your feet." In this case, the keyboard might have absorbed the energy of Mrs. Hess's fingers.

"All right," Mrs. Hess said, "go on, then." She didn't ask her to turn away this time. With a slow nod, they concentrated in unison. Mave inhaled deeply.

The reading was faster. Cleaner. The keyboard was as obvious as her own hand fisted on her thigh. Her knuckles were white. She sat back and forced her body to relax.

"Did you pick up anything?" Ren said after a moment. "Ashes again?"

She shook her head and debated downplaying what she'd sensed. She needed more time to think this through.

"Mave? It's all right if you want to call it quits."

Damn him and his soothing drawl.

"There's a navy-blue blanket on the floor," she said without inflection. "Mrs. Hess's computer is there, next to a video game console. I think it's a bedroom somewhere, in a house. It's messy."

"Anything else?"

Yes. No! "Aspenhill and Park," she said, naming the street corner she'd been drawn to while tracking.

"Which house?" Ren asked.

She shook her head. She'd been unable to see any street numbers. "I don't know..." She swallowed, her pulse too quick and her mind struggling to find a way to help both Ren and Holden.

And Cain.

No such thing as good and bad people, M&M. Only less evil and more evil.

"But if we drove by the neighborhood," she proposed, "I might be able to recognize the home." She also might be able to head off Ren, somehow locate Holden—*if* it was Holden. And if it wasn't?

Then I'd be interfering with a police investigation and letting more evil escape. I'd be no better than a criminal myself.

Ren watched her with a sober look.

There he is, Cain growled, *the bastard with the badge. Simply a matter of time before—*

His phone buzzed. "Sorry," he said, distracted. He checked the number and concern flittered over his already grave face. "My brother. Excuse me, have to take this. *Hello...*" He rose from the couch and stepped away and through the kitchen doorway, out of earshot.

"Poor thing," Mrs. Hess muttered, gazing after him.

Mave wondered if she'd heard wrong. "What do you mean?"

She blinked, seemingly startled to find Mave still on her couch. "Not that it's any of your business, but his brother's sick. Been battling it for a while; needs a new kidney. Ren offered his, got tested and everything, but he's not a match."

He won't take a bullet but he'll donate his kidney, a voice mocked in her head.

Mrs. Hess tilted up her nose and looked away.

"You don't like me very much," Mave blurted, "do you?"

"Perceptive," she muttered.

"Do you mind if—what have I ever done to you?"

"He's not listening." Mrs. Hess indicated Ren with a nod of her head. "So you can drop the innocent act."

"Excuse me?"

"You and I both know you're not here to do me a favor." She smoothed the fabric on the arm of her chair. "That's right, I saw that look on your face just now, when you saw whatever it is you *think* you saw in your head."

"What—?"

"You're in this for yourself. Conning that nice young man with your charms." She didn't look at her as she spoke, as if it were beneath her. "I've met your kind before. Just like your grandma, your—" She snapped her teeth together, editing out what Mave could only think of as *father*. "Sitting high and mighty up in your château," she carried on, "uncaring of the people you hurt, so long as you get what you want."

"You know nothing about me."

"I know you've got more blood on your hands than a butcher after Sunday market. That's plenty enough."

"Everything okay in here?" Ren stood frowning at them from the kitchen doorway. How much had he overheard? "Darlene?" He glared. He'd heard enough, apparently.

"Well now, I was only—"

"Everything's fine." Mave got up. "Mrs. Hess and I are all done here." For once, she didn't give a damn if she was being rude. She marched to the door without saying goodbye.

———

Ren waited until they'd driven a few blocks before bringing it up. "I'm sorry for the way she treated you in there. Had I known she—"

"You have nothing to apologize for." She crossed her arms, unwilling to meet his eyes. "Believe or not, I'm used to it. With my past and all, that's not the first time that's happened." A lot worse had occurred, in fact—strangers spitting on her. That's partly why she'd gone into hiding after Cain's trial. But a lot had changed since then. *She'd* changed. She wouldn't be shamed for who she was. Not anymore.

"You mean people..."

"Judge me for the sins of my father. I'm over it. How far is Aspenhill and Park?" She turned and peered out the passenger side window.

Ren took the hint. "Not five minutes."

Neither of them brought up her father again. They didn't need to. Cain Francis remained the elephant in the car, handcuffed in the back seat and weighing them down.

SIXTEEN

Mave blinked at the welcome mat beneath her feet; a trail of paw prints framed the message, IT'S BASICALLY A ZOO IN HERE.

"You sure this is the house you sensed?" Ren asked, evidently reading her doubt and misattributing it.

She nodded. "I'm sure." The more she considered it, the weirder it seemed. Dead or alive, Holden would never hide out in a suburban home in the middle of Hazel Springs. For god's sake, there was a child's pink bike in the driveway, tassels on its handles. And at least two dogs were barking from inside to announce their arrival. "You know who lives here, right?" she asked, unsure why she was whispering as the porch light switched on.

Ren didn't get the chance to reply as the door swung open. A rangy, middle-aged man appeared wrangling his German Shepherd by its collar. A second dog emerged from behind the first with its tail wagging, a terrier mix, quick to sniff Ren's calves.

"Hey, Roxy." He bent to scratch the terrier behind its ears with familiarity. She recalled he had two dogs of his own. They were probably dog park buddies. "Sorry to stop by so late," Ren said. "Nate, this is Mave Michael. She's—"

"Oh, hi," the homeowner sang with a surprised smile. "You're the unlucky owner of the haunted hotel!" It wasn't exactly a compliment, but she'd take it over Mrs. Hess's disdain. Nate gave her hand a hearty pump. His Adam's apple was noticeably large, like he'd swallowed a walnut and it'd gotten stuck mid-throat. Ren turned his attention to the German Shepherd (named Diana after the princess, she learned).

As Roxy pattered over to sniff Mave next, Ren explained to Nate the reason for their visit. To his credit, he was quite tactful. Nate seemed both cooperative and stunned by the idea that, according to a psychic reading, anything stolen could be inside his home. He invited them in.

Mave considered Nate in his house slippers, his bottom lip hanging as he patted Diana to calm her. If he was a professional cat burglar, she thought, then she was Queen Elizabeth I. Had she wrongly tracked the scent of the computer equipment after all? But when Ren described the navy blanket and gaming console, something in Nate's expression shifted.

"Liam!" he called in a tone reserved for a child who might be in trouble. Liam was presumably elsewhere inside the house. "Can you come down here?"

A whiny voice replied something unintelligible through the walls.

"Downstairs, *now*," Nate ordered, startling Roxy and Diana into another barking spree.

A minute later and all four of them were standing with the excited dogs in the living room.

"I didn't steal anything," Liam said, his eyes shifting nervously from Ren to his father. He was a scrawny boy with dyed blond hair tied back in a ponytail. No more than fourteen or fifteen, Mave guessed, though he'd already inherited his father's height. Ren asked him a few standard questions about his possessions and whereabouts on the night of the robberies. Liam provided both reasonable and solid answers—alibis from basketball practice to movie night with his family.

"Okay, then," Nate exhaled. "Just like I thought, a misunderstanding. Psychic wires crossed, huh?" He wiggled his fingers mid-air like he was casting a spell, but the joke fell flat.

Ren offered no reply, distracted by Roxy, who was prodding him for more pets.

That's it? Mave thought, her back prickling. She'd misunderstood nothing. Mrs. Hess's stolen computer was upstairs, presumably in this boy's bedroom. Now that she was closer to the item, she could scent it from memory alone—one hundred percent certain. "You won't mind, then," she interrupted, smiling innocently, "if Officer Rawlings has a quick peek in your room? Just to clear the mix-up. I mean, it's obvious to me there's a computer up there similar to the one Mrs. Hess reported stolen. A quick check of the serial number should confirm I'm wrong."

Liam regarded her liked she'd sprouted a ribbed forehead and was speaking in Klingon.

Ren cocked his jaw. "Since it's your word against hers, afraid it's a fair request. I need to be thorough, eliminate any false leads." His unhurried drawl was like a relaxing song on the radio. "Won't take but a second and then I promise to get out of your hair. Nate, appreciate you being so cooperative with the investigation."

"Huh?" Liam breathed.

"I suppose, yeah, no problem," Nate said, scratching his head nervously. "We want this bastard caught as much as anyone."

Liam licked his lips. "Hang on, it's not—"

"Upstairs, second door on the left," Nate told Ren, ignoring his son's mumbles. "Watch you don't trip on the mess."

As Ren moved to climb up a flight, Liam noticeably twitched, his body parts flexing like they were experiencing a mild electric shock. "Wait!" he cried.

Ren paused with his hand on the banister, his brow raised.

"I didn't know they weren't his"—his chest was heaving—"I swear!"

Ren faced the boy with his hands on his hips. "Didn't know what was whose?" he asked gently.

Nate was staring dumbfounded at his son, his bottom lip hanging again like the spout of a teapot.

Liam proceeded to confess everything, speaking so quickly he nearly tripped over every other word. More than once, Ren had to ask him to slow down and take a breath. Though told out of order, they'd soon managed to piece together most of Liam's story.

Last Friday, he and a few friends met up in the parking lot of the local grocery store. Someone brought beer. There may have been weed and Molly, Liam admitted after Ren's sharp probing, but he swore not to have partaken in any drugs. When Liam excused himself to take a leak, he bumped into "some dude in a mask." Liam couldn't remember the type of mask the stranger wore, nor his clothing, nor how tall or short, Black or white, young or old he was—it was too frightening an experience. (Or as Ren delicately suggested, Liam was too intoxicated at the time.) He only recalled the masked man's voice: deep and intimidating. The guy asked him what type of cell phone he owned, and then he proceeded to offer Liam the computer equipment real cheap in exchange for his phone, a pack of cigarettes, and fifty bucks cash (which Liam brought with him for pitching in towards snacks, not drugs, he insisted). According to the boy, he was ripped off, the victim in the scenario, too petrified to refuse.

"He pressured me into it!" he pleaded, his voice cracking.

"You were drinking *and* smoking cigarettes?" Nate's eyes had rounded into flaming marbles. "You told me you lost your phone!"

"I swear, Dad, I didn't—piece of junk computer he sold me doesn't even work!"

"Goddammit, Liam! Some shady stranger comes to you in a parking lot..."

As father and son bickered over the incident with Ren mediating, Mave tuned out. She crossed her arms, shielding herself from a sudden chill. First the computer equipment and the books, now the mask and the cigarettes. It may have been the case that Liam was high—he could have hallucinated or mixed up the details—except there were one too many coincidences. Everything she'd learned about the investigation pointed to Holden Frost. And that presented another puzzle.

Why would Holden run the risk and burglarize Hazel Springs, a town full of people who both thought him dead and might recognize him? Why not return to the château and resume his secret life underground as a translator on the dark web? Was it because the tunnels were uninhabitable after the fire? Or because he was suffering shock or amnesia after getting shot? Her own bullet scar itched. Her heart fluttered uncomfortably. She glanced at Ren surreptitiously—his holstered gun. It wasn't just Bek-187 she had to worry about, she realized. It was connected: Holden's disappearance and the robberies. Perhaps even her recruitment into the investigation had been less voluntary and more manipulated. Somehow, she had to figure out how and why before the police did.

SEVENTEEN

She uttered an excuse to Julián about scouting a new supplier for the wedding and borrowed Bastian's SUV for the morning. It wasn't as plain as she would have liked, with a fancy spoiler and souped-up rims, but at least its all-wheel drive handled the narrow and twisty mountain roads well. Plus, its navigation system made locating Lorde's Auto Body in Hazel Springs foolproof. She parked half a block away from the garage to remain inconspicuous and trekked the remaining short distance. According to Cain, nothing burned a cover faster than a legit license plate.

As soon as she wandered into the open, messy shop, she recognized its business owner, Vincent Lorde. He was hanging around the back corner, past the gutted auto parts and a sedan hoisted on the car lift. He was a large man with a bald head and a goatee, in conversation with a skinny, beak-nosed colleague in matching coveralls. His photos on the dark web, profile pictures copied from aboveground social media accounts, made him look more fit. In real life, he was beefy and broad, pillowed in fat. He stood with one leg hitched on a tool bench, the buttons of his coveralls strained along his gut. Both mechanics stopped speaking when they noticed her approaching.

"Excuse me," she said, her voice raised so as to be heard over classic rock playing from a radio. She smiled and feigned disorientation. "Sorry to interrupt. Are either of you Vincent?"

He shifted forward, wiping his fingers on a rag. "You need a tune-up, sweetheart?" The heavy rasp of his voice made her want to clear her throat.

"My name's Kennedy," she said, ignoring his suggestive smirk. "I called earlier this week, left you a message about my visit? I'm researching a piece for the *Gazette* on missing foster kids." Of course she'd made no such call about no such article.

His face immediately fell. "Pete, do me favor," he said to the beak-nosed man, "go check in with Sharon, see if those parts on the eighteen Chevy are on their way."

Beak-nose threw her a prolonged stare before shuffling away into the shop's front office.

Vincent stepped forward into her personal space, obviously trying to intimidate her. *Poor jerk*, she thought. He'd inadvertently given her effortless options to defend herself. Nose. Throat. Solar plexus. One upward slam of her knee and down he'd go like his dirty rag.

"Listen, I don't know who sent you here," he said in his rough voice, "but you're wasting your time. I got no message, and I certainly got nothing to say about Pammy."

Pammy? "Oh, no." She smiled brightly. "I'm here looking into another case. Holden Frost? Didn't you two know each other?"

He blinked a moment, his lower jaw dropping back into a frown. "Frost ain't missing," he said, regathering his machismo. "He's dead. Like I said, you're wasting your time."

"Shoot, I came all this way. Promised my editor." She cocked her hip and looked down at her feet, as if in a jam and brainstorming (the latter not entirely untrue). "Maybe"—she glanced back up—"you could go on a little break, and I could buy you a coffee. We could chat a bit more?"

He spun back to his tool bench, losing interest and busying himself. "I got coffee."

"Right. Okay." *Think.* "How about a beer, then?" she tried. She never consumed alcohol—not since a drunk driver had killed her young mother—but desperate times...

He stopped handling his tools and tilted up his chin to reconsider her from beneath his hooded eyelids. She waited, unflinching, as his gaze slid down her body like recycled grease. "Prefer whiskey."

"Whiskey's my favorite," she said, shining her smile.

———

She made sure to pick a seat first, closest to the exit. The fact that they were the only customers in the dim, seedy pub at one o'clock on a Monday wasn't a good sign. Less witnesses. More trouble. It also didn't help that the elderly bartender who poured their whiskies barely made eye contact before lumbering away.

She slid her tumbler forward on its used cardboard coaster and looked away from visible smudges on the rim of the glass. Vincent had already taken a healthy gulp of his whiskey and was watching her with interest. She'd skipped lunch. She'd be lucky to last ten minutes sipping slowly before the tipsiness hit.

He didn't even try to hide his ogling, openly appraising her breasts. "So, the *Gazette*, huh?"

"Mm-hmm. From the Denver office," she added.

"How long you staying in town?"

She dunked her finger into her glass and picked at an ice cube. "Just passing through."

"Shame. You know"—he leaned forward, as if sharing a secret—"I like 'em petite, sweetheart."

He was toying with her. A power game. She knew the type. He had information she needed and was testing her boundaries. She'd driven miles to find him. What else would she give? How far was she willing to go for a glimpse into his past? She brought her glass to her lips and took her time pretending to sip, counting on the ice cubes to hide her fake swallow. She realized she ought to be more tactful, but on little sleep with this creep at this sticky table, her patience was running thin. She set down her glass. "Was Holden Frost your foster brother?"

He'd be lousy at poker. She could read his thoughts on his face, second-guessing his decision to agree to this chat.

"Now where'd you hear that shit? You been talking to that old cow over in CPS?"

Child Protective Services. *Who there would have dirt on you and why?* She shrugged a shoulder passively, trying to keep it light. "Did a bit of research. For my article. Your name and Holden's came up more than once."

"Sure, I had the shit luck to live with him for a short time, but Frost is no brother of mine."

"How long was a short time?"

He took another quick slug of his drink, seeming to need a pick-me-up or a distraction from their conversation. "Dunno, three months, maybe?"

"And then what happened?" She felt the furniture tremor in time with his helmet-sized knee bouncing under the table.

"Frost got booted for bad behavior, moved somewhere else. Good fucking riddance."

"Why? What happened?"

He scoffed and flashed his teeth in a quick grin. "He was a liar. Fucking psycho." He angled down his head to offer her a view of his scalp. He tapped on a long, jagged scar. "That's what."

"Holden did that to you?"

He straightened and pursed his lips, as if pleased with her shock. "Twenty-three stitches."

"How?"

"Caught me napping."

"What do you mean?"

"Listen, sweetheart"—he wiped the end of his nose with his knuckle and leaned forward again, talking down at her—"it was a long time ago. I don't remember the details, just that he was a little twerp who got what he deserved. That's what I goddammed mean."

"Are you referring to his drowning?"

He grimaced again. "Yeah, I'm *referring* to that." She didn't miss his hint of sarcasm. He sat back and glanced around, maybe to order another round from the bartender. The old man was nowhere in sight.

"That must have been quite the story back then," she continued, feeling her time running short. Hers wasn't the only patience being tested. "Local kid drowning in a small town like Hazel Springs."

He smirked and redirected his attention on her, his eyes hardened and humorless. "Not really, no. Shitty people get shitty endings."

"That's just it. There's not a whole lot reported on his death. Can you tell me how it happened?"

"Fuck if I know."

Too quick. He was lying. "But you must have heard *something*." She twirled the ice cubes in her drink playfully, tilted forward until she could inhale the whiskey in her glass, stale liquor and dried syrup on the table. Her stomach turned. "Come on now. Bit of gossip?"

He prodded his lower lip with his tongue, back and forth, contemplating her, gaze cycling from her blue iris to her brown one. "He stole a rowboat off the dock. Ugly storm rolled in and took care of the rest." He clucked his tongue in mock sympathy. "Guess he wasn't a good swimmer."

Learned to swim at an early age—it was one of the first things Holden had said to her when they'd met in the tunnels on New Year's Day. What was Vincent hiding? Why was he so threatened by the past? She frowned and pouted, debating whether or not to mention the assault from the juvie record. His scar was presumably a souvenir from the altercation. But her instincts swerved. "What about Holden and Pammy?"

He flinched. "What?"

She'd gambled right. His troubled expression spoke volumes. He wouldn't give her a straight answer, but that was okay. She was no longer after his words.

"When I first introduced myself"—her adrenaline rushed with the venom in his eyes—"you mentioned Pammy." All presumptions and right guesses.

Careful, M&M.

Skilled and quick as she was in one-on-one combat, Vincent was much bigger, heavier. With the bartender out of sight, they were alone. An industrial road. No one to hear her screams.

Always overestimate your opponent, Cain whispered.

"Another foster kid, right?" She kept her face mildly curious. Unlike him.

He sniffed and wiped his nose again. "My break's over, sweetheart." He made a show of slamming back the rest of his drink and stood.

She readied her fist on her lap, the other around her tumbler, squeezing. Her muscles coiled as her mind streamed the choreography, the number of strikes it would take to escape him should things turn ugly. Alcohol flung in the eyes. Glass smashed to the temple.

Never start it. Always finish it.

He hovered over her, his gut inches from her face. She could smell the motor oil and sweat wafting from his coveralls. "I'm sure you can see yourself out," he growled, voice like grinding rocks.

He bumped the back of her chair as he passed to leave, giving her a small jump. Her heart pounded. She gritted her teeth and listened to his heavy steps fade out the door. With a glance over her shoulder to make sure he was really gone, she blew out the breath she'd been holding.

She deflated in her seat and stared at her glass. Thinking, planning. The ice melted as her resolve hardened. She'd have to dig deeper into Vincent Lorde.

———

Later that evening, she returned to her tiny office in the spa's closet and expanded her search on the dark web. After a few random guesses and fails, she tried the combination "Pamela Lorde, Hazel Springs" and got a hit. *Pammy* had been in the foster system all right, born the same year as Holden, but that was it. Vincent's sister? There was no information on her as an adult. She'd probably changed her name. With no new leads, Mave navigated to her DMs on the marketplace. This time, she was mentally prepared, predicting the private message that awaited her from Bek-187.

8.

Eight days to find Holden or Cain would be murdered. Though it was too soon for her postcard to have reached him, she checked her phone for missed calls. If—*when*—Cain called, what could she even say that wouldn't send her father on a revenge killing spree? It wasn't like she could ask for a quick list of his enemies. Over the years, he'd accepted numerous contracts; had "taken care of" countless people for money. It would be impossible to infer whether Bek-187 was connected to one of Cain's past clients or victims. She sighed and sat there a good half hour, racking her brain, trying to figure out Bek-187's identity, how all these puzzle pieces she'd gathered fit together.

She'd tried comparing the unknowns in her journal to no avail. It merely highlighted the three players she'd uncovered: first Bek-187; then a local burglar; and now Vincent Lorde. Each had secrets. Each linked to Holden. But how exactly? Their motives, the glue that connected them, were still missing. Then there was Ren and his family ties to the hotel. And the uncanny scent of plastic in the spa or the strange knocks she'd heard coming from inside her old room—whispers reported by Katie. Not to mention she'd mysteriously gotten herself locked in the tunnels below the greenhouse overnight.

With nothing to lose, she typed Bek-187 her latest pressing question and hit send before she could overthink it: What do you want with the SDP? Maybe I can help, offer more. We could avoid this whole nasty mess.

She waited another few minutes in case Bek was logged on again. She wasn't likely to get a straight answer, but who knew, a reproach or a refusal might unconsciously slip her a hint. Her phone buzzed, giving her a start. *Right lead, wrong source*, she thought, seeing the sender's name lit up. She anxiously expanded the message and read it more than once, her stomach fluttering with unease.

Ren had set up another consultation with a homeowner in Hazel Springs for tomorrow evening. Mave texted him back. She'd be there. Even as she tried to assure herself she was making progress, well prepared and a step ahead of Ren in suspecting Holden's involvement, second thoughts about their arrangement crept into her mind.

Ren wasn't dumb. She'd all but flagged Holden by asking for his juvie file. How long until he put two and two together, questioned the suspected drowning from fifteen years ago, and tied the robberies to Holden?

Besides, something told Mave the next time she tracked the stolen property, it wouldn't lead to a detour. The masks and books, the knocks and ashes—*no eye may see*—seemingly disparate details all hinted at the same thing: Holden was closer than any of them suspected. Or dreamed.

EIGHTEEN

The first time I experienced the scent of my burning flesh, I was just a kid. I'd been in the home for maybe a month—not long enough to have made friends with its best exits and trickiest hiding spots—not long enough to learn that I was most vulnerable under its roof.

He was bigger than me, tough and set in his shoulders even then. I was quicker. He knew that. So he came at night while I slept unaware, unguarded. The pressure of his knees on my elbows penetrated my dream, but still, I didn't wake. No. It was the sear of the cigarette that got me.

You'd be surprised. The scent is pleasing, sweet and smoky like pig's meat on a barbeque. And the burn? Hmm, that's something else altogether. No other pain quite like it in your body. It's white-white. Blinding. Claps your teeth together. Gathers all the veins off your bones like little baby snakes hissing alive. Pissface motherfucker. Tell you what, you never forget that original burn. It's like your first kiss, a rite of passage. It gives you a secret saved for the little bit wiser and the whole lot viler; it says, more fire is coming. Maybe not today, not tomorrow, but you better believe me, that burn is sure to reignite bigger and brighter. Soon...soon.

There'll be nothing left other than the char of your dirty damned soul.

NINETEEN

The morning after, she wasn't sure if the slight tremble in her hands was from her double espresso on an empty stomach, or the shock still buzzing through her blood. Another restless night. Another uncanny dream. She was desperate to consult Gracelyn. Yet the sight of the fortune teller arranging her tea settings in the upper mezzanine made her palms sweat. What if Gracelyn read between the lines and resolved Mave was truly cursed or going mad? What if she foresaw omens even worse than her first reading?

"Ah, just the person I was hoping for," Gracelyn exclaimed, noticing her approach. She set down a stack of saucers on her catering cart and brushed her palms on her waist.

Mave's smile felt stiff. "You need me for something?"

"Yes. Julián suggested we sell souvenir spoons along with the teas for tour guests. Thought you might have some stock to spare."

"Sure. I'll check inventory in the gift shop."

"Wonderful." Gracelyn moved toward her catering cart and hesitated when Mave remained where she was. Hovering awkwardly. She checked her wrist watch, buried beneath her bangles. "The next tour is in forty minutes if you'd like to join the..."

She shook her head and cleared her throat. "No, thank you." She reached for a teacup to arrange a place setting on the nearest bistro table. "If you have a second, I was hoping to ask you a few questions."

Gracelyn resumed unstacking the saucers. "Questions?"

"About ghosts. Just curious," she added, hoping to check any rumors before they began, "even though you mentioned you weren't a medium, you seemed to know quite a bit during the tour."

China clinked. "That's right. I learned from my mother. Both she and my grandmother were talented mediums." A hint of pride laced her tone. "Though I didn't inherit their gifts, you might say I was exposed to the practice from a young age."

"So you believe in hauntings?"

"Mm-hmm."

"And what about this place? I mean, all these tourists keep asking you about ghosts. Do you think...?"

"That the château is haunted?" Gracelyn blinked. "Most likely, yes. To be honest, I'd be surprised if it wasn't. This hotel has seen its fair share of tragic deaths. Especially recently."

Mave pretended not to notice Gracelyn's pointed glance in her direction. She threaded her words with airy laughter, hoping to sound casual. "You make it sound like there's not just one, but *several* ghosts."

Gracelyn arranged linen napkins next to each setting. "Well, yes, that's not uncommon, you see. My mother used to tell me that once the energy of one ghost occupies a space, it often attracts more restless spirits, almost like a magnet. Same can be said about the presence of a medium herself."

"A medium? How so?"

"The way she used to explain it, both the medium and the site of a haunting are like a lighthouse—a familiar frequency that can help orient and draw troubled or wayward ghosts."

Mave didn't like the sound of that. "But having a medium present isn't required, per se, to make contact?"

"No. But it certainly can help to encourage communication."

"So how did it work for your mother and grandmother, their mediumship?" She gave up trying to appear useful and crossed her arms. "For example, did they ever mention getting readings during sleep?"

"Like in their dreams?" Gracelyn paused. "Why, all the time, but I'd say those were less readings and more friendly visits. That's actually not limited to mediums. Many people are greeted in their dreams by loved ones who've passed on. It's common, nothing to be afraid of. The more you open yourself up to those dreams, the more clearly they might express feelings of resolution and peace."

"But how can you tell the difference between a real visit versus a made-up one triggered by your own grief or stress? How can you prove it's genuine—for example, speak back to the spirit? Ask questions?"

Gracelyn frowned as she gave it some thought. "Thing is, we have less control in our unconscious state. What you're suggesting, the only real way to have that level of direct dialogue is through a séance."

"A séance," she repeated.

"Absolutely, they can be quite therapeutic and healing for those in the physical world *and* in the afterlife. Why, did you want to—?

"No," she said too sharply. "I was mostly asking for the guests—just curious," she said before remembering she'd already stated that. She promised something about delivering the spoons and left before Gracelyn could wonder anymore about her motives—or her mental dysfunction. Mave could hardly metabolize ghosts passively, let alone actively.

Under no circumstances was she participating in a séance.

———

Her second police consultation was with a woman named Sandy Browning. She was a robust, six-foot-tall former competitive archer with two chins, bleached curly hair buzzed close to her scalp, and a Jesus fish tattooed on her bicep—a good friend of Sheriff Morganson's, Ren mentioned. Mave immediately took a liking to her.

"Look at you, tiny thing!" Sandy told her at the door. She whisked her and Ren into her homey kitchen. The room smelled of vanilla and freshly brewed coffee. Sandy offered them each a mugful with a generous slice of lemon cake, despite their polite refusals. It was the warmest reception Mave had experienced in a long time—maybe ever.

A part of her was captivated by Sandy, her charisma and her surroundings; framed family photos, pet portraits, blooming plants, tea cozies, ceramic jars, a wooden rooster. Was this what normal people's kitchens looked like? She and Cain had only kept the bare necessities. Oven mitts scorched brown. Rubber gloves. Bleach. Every surface had been clean and clear of personal items, more like a hospital room than a family kitchen.

"I don't collect a whole lot of books," Sandy told them with her hands wrapped around her steaming mug, "tend to give most away. So the two missing stood out as weird, you know? I'd kept them because I loved them, figured I'd re-read them eventually." According to her report, along with her computer equipment and tablet, the thief had stolen a copy of *Becoming* by Michelle Obama and *The Heart of a Woman* by Maya Angelou. As Sandy described her possessions, she joked her burglar must have belonged to Oprah's book club and laughed heartily.

Mave smiled, then concentrated in tandem with her. She ignored Ren's quiet study of her face and leaned forward on the kitchen table, bracing herself for another encounter of suffocating ashes. But the debris of books never came. The cozy kitchen melted away, and another interior materialized.

Cold, dusty. Matted yellow carpet.

Sandy hadn't been lying about her fondness for her books. It took Mave barely any effort before their location crystallized in her mind. A bright red door. A street number and a faded American flag hanging out front. No ashes. Unlike with her first search, Sandy's books hadn't been destroyed in a fire.

"Any hunches?" Sandy asked. "Do you feel where they might be?"

"I'm not sure," she said softly, still somewhat stunned by what she'd sensed. Because she had to be certain. No mistakes. She took a long sip of her coffee to help cleanse her palette and re-centered herself. Ren remained unreadable, his silent scrutiny of her unbroken. Mave swallowed, uncrossed and crossed her legs, finding it difficult to find a comfortable position. "Let's try focusing on another item instead. You said your tablet was taken, too?"

Sandy nodded.

"Just like before, can you describe it, then think of it?"

She did so, and in no time, Mave was back in her vision, the same dark interior, the yellow carpet pile matted like old fleece. She shivered reflexively. It was all there. Sandy's tablet. The wires. The monitor. The books by Obama and Angelou...and a third title Mave had initially sensed in the periphery. *Not Sandy's.* Mave felt her eyes tightening, her expression creasing as she pulled the scent deeper, closer. Dust—so much dust. Her nose felt grated, raw, crawling with mites.

She sat back and expelled a wavering breath, diluting the psychic scent and vision. It was unmistakable even then.

The Collected Poems of Walt Whitman. Holden's favorite.

"Where are they?" Ren asked, finally breaking his silence. She blinked at him. He hadn't even bothered to question whether or not she'd picked up on anything useful. It was like he knew. He saw her gripping the answer tightly in her mind, afraid to let go. "Mave? Whatever you saw, it's okay. We'll get the guy."

"It's 417 Emmerson Street," she said. It was nowhere near close to the truth, but that didn't make it wrong. Vincent Lorde had secrets. And his address was fresh in her memory.

———

As Ren drove her to check out her bogus lead, the streets were quiet. A couple of dogwalkers waved at the passing cruiser. An elderly man squinted to identify Mave in the passenger seat. She turned her face away, feeling nauseated. She'd never deliberately interfered with a police investigation before—not like this.

Aiding and abetting bad guys, a contemptuous voice in her head whispered, *it's what you do best.*

I had no choice! she argued with herself. She couldn't chance giving up Holden to the police—not unless she wanted to betray him after he'd saved her life, and simultaneously prompt Bek-187 to kill Cain. Put on the spot, her sole option was to create a diversion.

"You all right?" Ren's eyes volleyed between her and the road. "You seemed a little pale doing your reading back there with Sandy."

"The predictions drain me sometimes," she said. It wasn't a complete lie, even if fatigue wasn't the real cause of her blood temperature dropping. She hoped he would pick up on the implications of *predictions*. Her readings weren't always spot on. She could make mistakes, get her senses and streets mixed up. And though she hadn't in this instance—she could as easily point to the location of Sandy's stolen copy of *Becoming* as she could her own nose on her face—Ren had to be led to think otherwise; at least until after she alone checked out the correct address. Then if Holden wasn't there, she'd somehow undo her little white lie.

Not so little.

"We're almost there," Ren said.

"Who lives at this place, anyway?" Though she knew the answer to that, too, she didn't have to feign her curiosity. Ever since he'd looked up the address in his computer, what she really wanted to ask was *any priors?*

"Guy by the name of Vincent Lorde."

"You think he might be the thief?"

"Not sure. Wouldn't peg him as a pro, but he does have an old rap sheet for minor offenses, plus a distinct, low voice like the one Liam described. Like a wrestler on steroids." He seemed to give it some thought. "He could be Liam's masked man from the parking lot, but not necessarily the mastermind behind the break-ins."

She hadn't even considered that angle. *Oh god. I've officially started a wild goose chase.* She tried deepening her breaths, but her queasiness continued. "You must know him, then," she said, mostly to distract herself.

"Sure. For years. Even went to the same high school." His mouth curved into a subtle smile in response to her look of surprise. "Small towns, remember?"

"So, what, you two had algebra together?" Given her homeschooling, she couldn't picture it: having a past with classmates, belonging to a social circle.

"No, I was actually in the same grade as his younger sister. Vin was a couple years ahead of me. Thankfully."

Pammy? She bit the inside of her cheek. *Too many links*, her mind warned. Between Vincent and the château alone, Ren had to have met Holden all those years ago. For god's sake, he'd practically spelled it out for her moments ago: *small towns*. She frowned. "Why thankfully?"

"Let's just say Vincent was a classic bully, even then."

"How about his sister, what was she like?" Technically, Pammy had nothing to do with their investigation. "Maybe they're working together?" she proposed, grasping at straws.

He hitched his brow. "Well now, that'd be a twist."

"Twist?"

"Pammy ran away sophomore year."

Oh. Huh. That would explain why her online search had revealed zero new information. "And no one's heard from her since?"

You're pushing it, M&M. Stop asking questions on Pammy, or he'll be on to you.

His expression grew thoughtful again, then sharpened.

"We're here," he said, pulling up to the curb outside a small bungalow. She couldn't tell if he was truly distracted or choosing to avoid giving an answer. "It's probably best you wait in the car this time 'round. Assuming you're right and Sandy's property is in Vin's possession, it might be another case of pawned items. But if not, Vin's not the type of man to go down quietly, if you know what I mean."

She nodded, more than happy to hunker down in the shadows. In fact, if he hadn't suggested it, she would have made an excuse to stay behind. Ren's door slammed shut and her stomach clenched. "Relax," she whispered to herself. She swallowed and scouted the property through the window.

Peeling paint on the shutters. Weeds on the lawn. Black pickup truck in the driveway. She couldn't help but imagine the disaster that might occur if Ren actually arrested Vincent. He'd be forced into the back seat of the cruiser. Her cover would be blown and her lies exposed. She stared out the windshield and took long breaths.

Ren had no cause for arrest. Sandy's stolen possessions were definitely *not* inside Vincent's home. That much she knew. Whether Vincent was dumb enough to offer another reason to end up in handcuffs...

She gnawed the inside of her cheek as Ren knocked on the door. No response came. Ren shifted sideways with his hands on his hips and peeked through the nearest window. Vincent had to be home. The lights were on inside. His truck was parked. Ren tried again, banging harder for a reply. He said something at the door, muffled in the distance. A moment later, the door opened a crack.

Mave thought she saw Vincent through the gap. He and Ren must have been conversing. She bit her nails as she waited. And waited. Why the delay? What were they saying? The door seemed to shut unexpectedly, causing Ren to flinch. He marched back to the car. The look on his face wasn't happy.

Sure enough, he uttered a curse as he got back into the driver's seat.

Mave slumped lower under the sudden glow of the car's interior light. She pretended to stretch her legs, hoping to come across as lounging and relaxed versus hiding and nervous. "What happened?"

"He played dumb. Refused to let me in for a look around. Can't say I'm surprised. Afraid I can't search the place without a warrant." He started the engine. "How sure are you Sandy's property is here at his place?"

"I could double-check," she replied uncommittedly, "maybe do another reading with Sandy in a day or two." As they pulled away, her skin broke with icy prickles. A reptilian instinct caused her to turn her neck and look back at the house.

Vincent was watching from the window, his hulking silhouette unmistakable. Even through the darkness, she could tell when their eyes caught. The rest she imagined, she told herself, still staring at the house as it receded into a speck. She hadn't seen Vincent's mouth moving. She hadn't read the two words shaped by his lips: *You're dead.* It was simply a symptom of her guilt.

TWENTY

Vincent couldn't have recognized her in the police cruiser. It had been dark. She'd switched to her auburn wig, different from when they'd met at the garage. Except the barbed doubt remained. *What if?*

Leaving it until tomorrow felt like a foolish gamble. Not only did she need to keep her lies straight, stay one step ahead of Ren and the police investigation, but Bek-187 was clocking her. Cain needed her. He'd want her to do the smart thing.

The criminal thing, her mind warned. *It's bad enough you lied to the police. Now you're going to break and enter into an innocent stranger's home. Whether or not you're caught—whether or not you find anything useful—is that what you really want?*

Yet here she was, back in Hazel Springs in the middle of night, mere hours after Ren had driven her back to the château. She felt like a dog chasing her tail. Unable to stop.

The house she'd sensed from Sandy's longing was located on the outskirts of town. She'd scouted it online: a two-story home with a flag mounted beside its red front door. She'd borrowed Bastian's SUV again and prayed the neighborhood watch didn't notice the vehicle. As an extra precaution, she parked along a poorly lit sideroad and made her way on foot.

She slouched with her head low, made sure her hair was tucked away in her ball cap. *I'm nobody*, she inwardly chanted with her steps, willing her disguise to work. She reloaded the map on her phone. The trek seemed longer in real life than on screen. She quickened her pace on an incline, just shy of a suspicious run.

She reached another dark road, no homes in sight. That should have been a good thing. It would lessen the odds of a nosy local peeking through their blinds as she strode by. But a feeling of being watched merely intensified in the isolation.

She pulled out her penlight. The damned crickets were droning loudly again and the overgrown grasses that lined the shoulder of the road hissed and swayed in the breeze. She glanced over her shoulder every so often, redirected her light. Weeds scarred the pavement. Specks of insects danced through her beam. She broke into a jog, feeling foolish —like a victim in a horror film willingly running toward danger as opposed to away from it. Her breath rushed in her lungs, her heart a skittish thrum keeping time with her feet.

Soon, a melodic echo of windchimes wavered in the breeze. She hurried toward the sound, faster and faster. At last, the silhouette of the house with the red door materialized. She slackened her pace to catch her breath.

With no visible neighbors, the property was buffeted by mature aspen trees, skeletal branches jutting at odd angles. Mave focused on her destination. The home's upper windows were like two black eyes gaping down at her. No vehicles or signs of life anywhere. Given what she'd sensed through her reading with Sandy, she'd expected as much. All that dust. She wrinkled her nose, recalling the deserted interior.

The ideal spot for a squatter. Someone who wants shelter and isolation from the rest of the town.

She switched off her penlight, crept to the red door, and removed gloves from her compact backpack. Her hands were sweaty. She rocked her weight back and forth on the balls of her feet, and checked over her shoulder again. What if Ren had misled her? What if CCTV cameras captured everything after all? She adjusted her ballcap lower.

Wary of the front door and tripping an alarm, she crossed to the window. She held her palms over the brim of her hat, blocking the outside. Nothing was visible within—not without shining her flashlight through the pane and potentially announcing her presence.

Not yet.

She skulked around the home in search of open windows or a rear entrance. If her instincts were correct, then the thief—maybe Holden himself—had been slipping into the home undetected some hidden way.

"No forced entry. In and out. Just like a ghost."

Despite her body's stiffness after her rough sleep, she climbed over the backyard fence with ease. Her adrenaline helped, flushing her veins so hot they felt cold, or so cold they felt hot—she couldn't distinguish anymore. Overgrown ferns encroached on flagstone steps, leading down a slope. The lower she crept, the clearer she heard the sound of creaking. A shiver travelled her spine. She scanned her penlight through the yard and paused over an old glider bench rocking in the breeze. Back and forth. Creaking as if a ghost were seated on it.

She shook off the eerie thought and returned her inspection to the house itself. Approximately halfway around, a back entrance appeared behind a tangle of rose bushes. Her nerves tingled.

Has to be the one. It had a small sash window—ample space for a hand to slip through and release the inner lock.

Remember what I taught you, Cain coached through her rapid heartbeats. *Shut off everything else and concentrate. Five points if you flip the latch without scratching the window. Ten points if you avoid cutting the weather stripping. And twenty if you do it in under a minute.*

No matter the flurry of fear in her bloodstream, it was just like one of her childhood lessons. She'd come prepared. She reached into her backpack, pulled out a flexible blade, and gripped her penlight between her teeth. She concentrated on her goal. She counted.

Five points...ten points...twenty, she mentally whispered, imagining her father's scrutiny.

Another thirty seconds, and she had the door ajar and her blade tucked away.

Flashlight outstretched, she took a big breath like someone about to dive underwater, and stepped into a small walkout basement.

Yellowed posters of flora and butterflies were taped to the wall and a top-loading washer was covered in a film of dust. She bit her lip and eased the door shut behind her. Her ears rang from the sudden silence. The sublevel was cold and damp—grey cinderblock walls, a low ceiling exposed with copper pipes. Another few steps inside and she froze.

Cigarette smoke. The skin on her arms and legs pebbled. She inhaled the tang cautiously.

When she'd first encountered Holden's hideout in the tunnels beneath the hotel, she'd smelled a similar smoke. *Could it be him?* Nothing made sense. She followed the scent, pulled it into her lungs, exactly like she had on New Year's Day.

It led to a set of floating stairs—no risers or railing. The door at the top for the main level was shut. She thought she heard a soft scuffle overhead. Then silence. Acid pooled in her stomach.

She climbed up slowly, her shoulder brushing the wall. The ground's drop beneath her lengthened. She told herself not to look but her eyes flicked down anyway. The paranoia that a monster below would reach through the steps and grab her ankle hastened her feet. She pushed through the door at the top of the stairs, her muscles tightening at the scrape of hinges.

She was inside a short hallway. Just beyond, a living room appeared. Vacant. The space was dusty and cool and, above all, familiar—like looking into a mirror from the wrong side of the glass.

She shuffled forward onto matted yellow carpet. She'd already visited this room in her mind. The stolen books and tablet she had tracked for Sandy should've been here—plus the collection of poems by Walt Whitman she'd sensed. Except a sweep of her penlight revealed nothing but more dust.

A few pieces of furniture were draped with mismatched floral sheets. Couch, table, floor lamp. An imposing brick fireplace stood on the opposite wall. That was it. While she normally found decluttered spaces soothing, in this case, it felt wrong. Too barren. No hiding spots, as if the room had been readied for someone to spy on her from any angle.

She frowned and wandered deeper inside, still detecting smoke through the dust. If anything, the scent was stronger here. Maybe it was seeping room to room through a vent, because it was clear somebody, somewhere was having a cigarette inside this seemingly empty house.

She approached the fireplace to make sure she wasn't mistaking the smoke for drifting ash. Her penlight cascaded over the remains of a fire —tattered mounds of white ash glowing blue in her beam. *Recently made?* She recalled the burned copy of *The Davinci Code* from her first attempt to track and shuddered.

She recanvased the room corner to corner, making sure she hadn't missed the stolen items in the dark. Hours earlier, she was positive everything had been here. It felt and looked exactly the same...save for the cigarette smoke. Had the thief moved the stash in the time it'd taken Mave to drive to the hotel and return to Hazel Springs? How else could she have seen the—

A floorboard above her head groaned. A sliver of alarm pierced her heart. She swung up her light as the sound continued. Footsteps. It was hard to be sure over the hammering of her pulse. She licked her lips, her mouth dry.

"Hel—hello?" she said, her voice brittle and weak. She no longer cared if she was giving up the element of surprise. Her fight or flight instinct warred with logic and her need to track, to seek, to find. Holden could be upstairs. This could all be over if she could only find him and *know.*

Or it could a stranger up there, her fear countered. *A thief. A killer. A monster.*

She inched her way into a second hallway. Its striped wallpaper gave her vertigo. She fluttered her lashes, batting away the feeling, and found a set of wide helical stairs. She pointed up her light and tilted her head to see past the stucco ceiling, viewing nothing beyond a half-dozen curved steps. "Hello," she tried again louder, "is anyone up there?"

She waited. Counted to ten.

A knock echoed from above. She recoiled with a sharp intake of air, unblinking at the ceiling. Before she could summon the courage to move, breathe, call out again, another knock reverberated from the upper floor. And a third.

She held her palm to her mouth and swallowed back the urge to scream. Three knocks—just like she'd heard outside her old room in the hotel's staff quarters. She stood with her flashlight trembling, her muscles flexed. Why would Holden do that? Was he trying to scare her away? Call her closer? *"Who's there?"* she demanded with a confidence she didn't feel.

She flinched again as music started playing—a slow, hollow-sounding jazz tune. It was specked with static, humming through the floors and walls above. As a woman's voice crooned the first lines of the verse, Mave felt herself terrified—mesmerized.

"I'll Be Seeing You." Billie Holiday.

She liked the song, occasionally played it in the gift shop during lulls. Her head told her to get the hell out of the house and as far away as possible. Yet her feet began to float up the stairs, following the music, its lament and promise: long-distance lovers would be reunited.

She stopped at the top of the stairs, afraid to go forward. Afraid to go backward. The scent of cigarette smoke thickened along the second-floor hallway. She could nearly see the white tendrils uncoiling in the dark, signaling her to come, follow. Five rooms had their doors shut. One door remained open: the room blaring the sweet romantic song. All sorts of possibilities and impossibilities tangled in her mind.

What if Holden couldn't speak or was injured? That blood she'd found under the sink in the greenhouse—his screams in her dream—what if he was communicating with her some other way to compensate for the loss of his voice? What if he was the squatter here? What if he'd anticipated her visit, had been sending her secret messages this entire time by stealing and making local headlines? What if he *had* come back to the hotel, had attempted to find her in her old room, but had left since she'd moved out and the tunnels were ruined?

She stood at the dark doorway, with no real recollection of ever having moved from the landing. The song rattled at full volume. She was tempted to cover her ears but kept her hands hovering at her sides, ready to defend against any sudden danger.

She crept over the threshold and tried the light switch on the wall. A lamp flashed white and blew its incandescent bulb, stinging her retinas and nerves in unison. Darkness resettled. She darted her penlight across the hardwood floors, up the hunter-green walls—a master bedroom from the looks of it, vacant as below despite the saturation of cigarette smoke. A large sleigh bed was illuminated, its mattress stripped, and a wooden dresser with no mirror. Atop the dresser, a turn table spun next to a single book. She edged forward.

Her breath hitched as she recognized the Walt Whitman title from her vision. She reached out to touch the canvas hardcover, brushing it, confirming it was really there. The snag of a sticker gave her pause.

Wrapping the spine was a label: WHITM - CHÂTEAU DU CIEL.

A knot tightened in her throat. *It's him. Has to be.*

The copy belonged to the hotel's library—*his* library. Holden. What was he trying to tell her? To return it there? Would he meet her back at the château? Her heart tripping, she slipped Whitman's hardcover into her backpack and watched the dizzying record a moment. Her hand shook as she lifted off the player's needle.

The music stopped, tearing into silence. Her ears rung, and a deeper underlayer of white noise pushed through.

Gushing. Water running through pipes.

She redirected her penlight to the sound and stared at the door to the en suite she'd mistaken for a closet on her first pass.

Inside. He's inside the bathroom, hope whispered. After all, *someone* was smoking. Someone had rehidden the stolen items in the empty house, played the record, and turned on the water.

As she neared the bathroom, the thrum from the shower sharpened. She toed the door open and, through a puff of humidity, crept onto the tiled floor.

The bathroom had a single sink vanity next to a toilet, and a tub with its nylon curtain drawn. The hot mist of the shower formed wafting clouds, dampening her skin. Even as she reached out to the little daisies on the opaque curtain, felt the streaming droplets through the cloth, a voice inside her asked why Holden would go to such trouble. Why would he be taking a shower in the dark? She held her breath, pulled back the curtain.

The tub and shower were empty.

A sour sensation released in her gut. Desperation clawed at her heart. *Where was he?*

Something wasn't right. She shut off the water, the faucet's handle stiff in her grip, and listened to her ragged breaths stab into the silence. She pushed her ballcap off her damp forehead, turned to survey the rest of the bathroom. Her eyes froze on the fogged-up mirror.

Above the vanity, her figure reflected through a veil of condensation alongside a message. Its block letters dripped, mocking and familiar, niggling her memory.

NO EYE MAY SEE.

As her chest heaved and her pulse pounded in alarm, she stepped up to the sink and gripped the counter for balance. Who'd written this? When? Unable to think straight, a scream ripped from her throat at the sight of a masked man behind her in the mirror. She spun around.

No one was there.

Enough.

With a surge of anger, she tore out of the bathroom, searching for them in vain, her penlight jerking here, there. They were playing with her, sending cryptic messages to scare her.

"Where are you!" she cried, her voice grating and bouncing off the walls of the empty bedroom. "Why are you doing this?" She stormed out into the hallway, her head dizzy. "You can't hide forever! I know you're here!"

But did she really? If they were here, whoever *they* were, then why did it feel like she was chasing her own shadow down the stairs? Through the dusty living room? Back into the walkout basement and into the rear garden? It was as if she were a wind-up toy fully strung and released, forcibly yanked and snapping to rejoin the rest of her body.

She stopped next to the glider bench and dug her fingers into her waist where a stitch had formed. The glider still creaked. Her lungs heaved. Her stomach turned.

"Jesus." She cupped her head, crouched over, and spit into the grass.

What the fuck are you doing, M&M? Cain barked. *No one but you was ever inside that house.*

Her heart was still punching as if to escape her chest, but the fresh air was sobering, the slow creaks of the bench now a reassuring rhythm to help calibrate her breathing. The answer surfaced like a sunrise in her mind, glowing brighter and hotter with each passing second. The cigarettes. The song. The message.

Cain was right. And Cain was wrong. This entire time, someone *had* been inside the house. The only problem was, she'd been chasing a ghost.

PART THREE
NO EYE MAY SEE

Ways of establishing communication with those in the afterlife are limitless. One's singular requirement is to possess an innate sensitivity for the transference of energy; a delicacy of sensation. Like a reflex, such sensation need not be practiced or voluntary. Indeed, historical reports show that, at times, ghosts have made mediums smell, taste, see, hear, and *feel* select stimuli. Simply put, we take what the spirit gives—no more, no less. The communication can be clear, while the message is not. Rather, we notice what the ghosts want us to notice, gleaning only that information which they allow for us to absorb.

—SIGNS: A HANDBOOK FOR CLAIRVOYANCE

TWENTY-ONE

You had me scrambled up from the moment I laid eyes on you. It's funny. They'd called me a lunatic for a while, but it wasn't until I met you that I finally felt like one. A no-holds-barred motherfucking freak, longing for the hitman's daughter.

I go back there: to the library. Your mouth on mine. How can a few minutes—hours, days—turn into a lifetime? Yet it did. You did. Is this what falling feels like?

Before you, I'd only ever known love for one person. But Rah was like my teacher/father/brother, my entire kin rolled into a single misunderstood mind. What I felt for the old man was rooted early, bone deep. He held me from infancy. Heard me crying. Recognized me, alienated and angry at the world that killed my parents. So he named me Holden after The Catcher in the Rye. Just Holden. No last name. That came later.

CPS caught wind of me. No paperwork or trace, they demanded to know who I was. So I told them: I was Robert Frost. Holden Robert Frost. Even then, I ran away—came home to Rah whenever I could. He raised me despite his unravelling health; became my anchor. Together, we were two kicked dogs who found shelter and warmth, who gave each other light —the purpose of a father and son stranded in the dark.

But you—what you make me think, feel, dream—it's not the same. You're like a shot of euphoria, pulling me up, up till I find myself flying *above the clouds, swimming in the constellations. Boundless, weightless. I have no real reference. Only verses and odes and songs written in the name of.*

I've read the dead poets over and again. You don't think I realize their warnings? I'm in over my head. I oughta forget the slide of your neck under my tongue, the clutch of your thighs around my waist. Except selflessness has never been my strong suit. I've never claimed to be anything besides a creep. Maybe that's why I wrote to Bek-187. Maybe that's why I told someone else about you. I needed you to be more than a dream. More than just in my fucked-up head.

Bek had been straight with me from the beginning—a surprisingly good listener when it came down to it. So, yeah, I talked. And Bek told me everything I wanted to hear: I needed to be patient; girls took longer to fall, especially the good ones; you and I would be together soon.

Goes to show. I was better off listening to the dead poets.

TWENTY-TWO

She sat cross-legged on her bed, massaging her aching head and gazing down at Holden's mask. Her journal lay on one side and Whitman's book of poetry on the other. After her fruitless search in the house with the red door, she'd returned to the château without any further trouble. That had come later. In her sleep.

Brief and upsetting though they were, her dreams had triggered insights. She'd donned the mask and conjured Holden—had seen the world through his eyes again. She supposed a part of her had expected another episode of parasomnia. But that didn't make the longing and pain she'd felt—*he'd* felt—any less potent. The dream's details were hazy, yet they struck her like a punch to the gut. How could she reach him? Help him?

No eye may see.

She lowered her hands and drummed her fingers on the two books —the collected poems and the journal where she'd scribbled the riddle with multiple question marks. The latter belonged to the former. She'd solved the source of the message while dreaming. Walt Whitman had originally penned the words. That's why they'd sounded so familiar when Katie mentioned the strange whispers from room 508.

"O, Death! a black and pierceless pall... No eye may see, no mind may grasp / That mystery of Fate." It was one of the many quotes tattooed in fine script along Holden's right arm. Rather than provide clarity, however, the revelation snagged another thorn in her mind.

O, Death! Was that what she'd seen in the mirror last night? It had been foggy *then*, literally and figuratively. Add the passage of time and another bad sleep, and her recollection seemed a lot like Liam's drug-induced description of the mystery man from the parking lot: suspiciously vague. She struggled to picture the reflection she'd seen. A man in a mask. *What mask?* she scolded herself. It had been a peripheral smear in the dark.

Frustrated and impatient for answers, she replaced everything beneath her pillow, carefully made her bed, and headed down to the spa. It was still early. She'd check the darknet before opening the gift shop. Hopefully, everything would be quiet downstairs. Julián wouldn't be pacing his office with updates. Dominick Grady wouldn't be stalking the boutique. (Last night, the art dealer had left her another message.) Mave got as far as the spa's reception doors and paused.

Katie was behind the desk, holding a newspaper aloft, shielding her face from view.

Still crashing here.

Mave wondered if she'd been too accommodating, letting her remain here night after night. She ought to have given her a forty-eight-hour deadline, especially with the computer she was covertly requiring so near.

Katie must have sensed her presence. She lowered the newspaper slightly, revealing her rounded eyes. "Hey, Mave, did you see this?" She shuddered the pages to indicate a scandal of sorts within.

"What's up?" Mave entered and leaned on the counter with one elbow. Below the desk and out of sight, she dug her nails into her palm. She was on edge for Bek's reply, but Katie would probably consider it suspicious if she darted straight to the closet for two mornings in a row. Her eyes fell on the headline at the same time as Katie summarized the breaking news carried over onto page four.

"Some old guy in Hazel Springs has gone missing after his house was burglarized a couple of nights ago."

"What?"

She passed the paper to Mave, who scanned it for details.

According to the article, seventy-one-year-old Gerald Lee Baker had been reported missing by a neighbor after Baker had repeatedly failed to answer his door and retrieve his garbage bins, which were knocked over by wildlife and forgotten at the curb. A portrait of Baker had been blown up on the front page. He looked intimidating despite his smile— or maybe because of it. His teeth were crooked. His jowls sagged. He had deep rings under both eyes. In contrast, his browbone and cheeks were sharp and defined, the skin pulled taut and darkened by liver spots.

The photo had been released by police and included a statement from Sheriff Morganson. She advised all residents of Hazel Springs to remain vigilant. While there was currently no evidence of foul play, police were concerned for Baker's safety. A possible connection between the man's absence and the recent string of home robberies was still under investigation, and anyone with information on either incident was encouraged to contact the department's non-emergency tip line.

"Like I didn't have enough to keep me up at night," Katie mumbled. She picked a withered petal from the arrangement of black orchids she'd set behind the desk. "This creep breaking into homes nearby. People going missing."

"I'm sure they're unrelated," Mave said, though she wasn't convinced after reading the article.

"You're probably right." Katie sighed and turned to her for reassurance. "It's not like they'd ever come here."

"Yeah, no." *They may already be here*, her paranoia prodded.

"Okay, speaking of my worries," Katie continued, "I'm glad you popped in. I already ran this by Gracelyn."

"Hmm?" She was only half listening, preoccupied with reviewing what she knew about the robberies in Hazel Springs.

"Here me out." She spread her fingers like she was about to dance a jazz number. "I think we should have a séance."

Mave blinked as her heart skipped a beat. Whatever she'd been expecting for Katie to say, that hadn't been it. "What? Why?" What had Gracelyn told her?

"Look, you've been super great, but we both know I can't hide in here forever. I have to move back to my room. These whispers and knocks, my imagination or not, I have to face them. I know, I know"—she waved dismissively—"you don't believe they're more than the old pipes groaning, and that's okay. That's what I'm hoping, too. So I figure, what's the harm? It'll be like swallowing a placebo pill. Gracelyn's all for it. We'll make contact with the spirit in my room and, at the very least, get a friendly ghost vibe. More than anything, it's about going through the motions to ease my mind and assure myself that I'm safe. Maybe it'll even be fun."

"Fun..." She cleared her throat. "Seems you have everything worked out. What do you need me for?"

"Thing is, it's not safe to have a séance with only two people. Gracelyn mentioned it during one of the tours. She insists on at least three participants. 'Living anchors to the present,' she calls them, and I'm seriously not comfortable blabbing all my superstitious baggage to anyone else."

"I don't know. I'm not really..."

"It'll be effortless—promise. Everything's arranged. Gracelyn's got her last tour booked at four today, so we can meet up right after you close the gift shop. You only need to be there in body. You can, like, meditate through the whole thing while Gracelyn takes the lead." She squeezed Mave's knuckles. "Pretty please?"

Mave looked down and wondered how long their hands had been joined, Katie's atop hers. She pictured a pink whelk in the ocean's depths. The hadal zone, it was termed.

"Okay," she whispered. "I guess it's no big deal." As she uttered the lie, she couldn't entirely articulate why she agreed. She must have known, though, deep down. That's why her nails left bruises in her palm—tiny pink sabers piercing her flesh.

It was a big deal. A very big deal.

———

Sitting alone on the twin bed in room 508 felt strange, like the months had rewound themselves and Mave had regressed into an insecure drifter hiding from the world. The familiar mustiness saturated the space. The same dim bulb buzzed overhead, making it feel like midnight no matter the hour. As she waited for Katie to come out of the room's tiny en suite, Mave hung her suit jacket on the bedpost and, not wanting to wrinkle the sheets, slid down to make herself comfortable on the floor. She rested her back against the bedframe, took off her pumps, and set them neatly aside.

Candlelight flickered and shadows danced on the walls. Mave had never been to a slumber party in her youth. She wondered if this was the type of thing girls did; gathered on the rug so that they could gossip, paint their toenails, and summon the dead with Ouija boards. She hugged her arms around her middle as the vent kicked in with a rattle and moan.

The spirit.

The same dark promise she'd been dismissing all day sent her stomach spinning. She tried convincing herself she'd come both to help Katie and to prove her own theory wrong. But what if it worked? What if the spirit showed itself and it was Holden? Could she ask him all the questions she longed to in her dreams? During sleep, she was voiceless—a passive eavesdropper into Holden's psyche. But here, fully awake and in control, she might directly address him as Gracelyn suggested. *If* he appeared. *If* he was a ghost. Too many ifs. She pushed out a heavy breath and surveyed Katie's things to distract herself.

Hairspray, jewelry, perfume bottles, and cosmetics were scattered on the dresser. A quilt was folded at the foot of the mattress. And a picture frame sat on the narrow nightstand. At least the room seemed personalized—that was more effort than Mave had put in when she'd resided here. A cellphone chimed behind her. She looked back and found an older device on the pillow. Katie's cell? Before she could stop herself, Mave was twisting around and reading the text on the screen.

Colin Wilde: ***Look in your heart, babe. You know I'm right. You're mine. You can't leave—can't make it without me. We belong...***

The preview cut off. Katie's ex, presumably. He sounded clingy or romantic. Maybe both. A cloud of envy swirled in Mave's chest. What she wouldn't give to get a lovesick text from—

At the sound of the faucet shutting off, Mave swiveled around with a pang of guilt. Katie emerged from the bathroom.

She seemed distracted, her smile forced. She was clearly nervous despite her earlier conviction that a séance might present the solution to her problem.

"You sure you want to do this?" Mave asked. A large part of her wished Katie would back out. Maybe Gracelyn wouldn't show.

Katie nodded. "Yeah, it's just this room. Jitters." She scooted down next to her. "Guess we should entertain ourselves. I mean, there are still a few minutes until Gracelyn arrives."

"Okay." Mave crossed her ankles and tried to think of a conversation topic. It felt like an invasion of privacy to bring up the text. She nodded at the framed photo. A young girl and a woman with a scarf tied to her head were posing in front of a birthday cake, the girl scooped under the woman's arm. "Is that you as a kid?" She already knew the answer given the girl's gummy smile. The woman was toasting the camera with her wine glass.

"Yep. Me and Mom." She made an expression Mave couldn't interpret.

Mave's envy thickened. Yet another thing she would never get: a happy photo of her and her mother. "In Los Angeles?"

Katie shook her head, seemingly lost in thought. "LA came after..." She reached forward and set the frame facedown. "Stupid. Shouldn't have unpacked that here."

Mave knew a thing or two about complicated family dynamics. "Why?" she asked gently, considering Katie in a new light. Perhaps she'd judged wrong, and they weren't so opposite after all.

She shrugged. "She's not around. Makes me miss her even more."

"I'm sorry."

Katie's cellphone chirped with another notification. She plucked it off her bed, then stiffened as she scanned the text. She shoved away her phone and folded her arms. "You ever feel like the people you think you know, like maybe even your entire life, aren't who they say they are?"

All too well. She nodded, uncertain where Katie was headed with this.

"Was it hard for you?" An intensity lit her eyes. "Making amends with the person in your head, your heart, and the one in real life?"

"Yeah." She swallowed.

"And your ex?" Katie whispered. "The one you were thinking about the other day? I mean, before things ended, did you ever wonder if he was, like, *the one?*"

In truth, she'd never stopped to consider it—had never had the luxury to daydream past her immediate troubles. "I'm not sure I really thought of us as long term," she answered honestly. "The time we had together, it was really fast and intense."

"Maybe it's better that way." Her eyes glistened. "Rip off the band-aid. Let it all fucking gush." She sighed. "Otherwise, you'd be like me, a slow bleeder. You know, the first time Colin and I broke up, I was only sixteen." She rested her cheek on the side of the mattress, her body facing Mave and curled into a fetal position.

"That's pretty young." At sixteen, she'd been watching *Glee* on a discolored motel television screen and trying to imagine what it would be like to attend a real-life prom.

"Yeah, I was devastated. I was convinced it was because I wasn't pretty enough, so you know what I did? I stayed out all night partying, dancing with skeezy guys and secretly crying in toilet stalls. Finally, I ended up at this twenty-four-hour pharmacy. It was, like, three in the morning or something. I was staring at these expensive beauty products, pining to look like the girls on the labels, all glossy and perfect. Except I didn't have any money on me, so in a moment of exhaustion and total stupidity, I tried to pocket a lipstick without paying. I still remember the name of the shade, Irresistibly Pink." She stuttered a dry laugh. "Like that could fix everything, mend my broken heart and make him want me again."

"Did it work?" she asked, genuinely curious.

"Never got a chance to test my pout. I got caught for shoplifting."

"Ouch." She grimaced.

"You can say that again. The pharmacy owner ended up being a total hard-ass. He'd gotten burned a bunch of times with kleptos in the store and got a real thrill out of busting teens. He called the cops to arrest me."

"What about your parents?"

She shook her head, her mouth set into a grim line. "They weren't around. Straight to police. In a lot of ways, I was lucky; the cop who showed up got one look at me and took pity. I must have reminded him of a pathetic little sister or something. He talked the owner out of pressing charges so long as I went to see a counselor. Guess it was pretty obvious I was messed up."

"So what happened?"

"I was forced into this bullshit youths for second chances program. By then I was back together with Colin. And you know what the counselor told me? She said I was using him, relying on his attention to address deeper unresolved issues. Apparently, what I was really looking for was parental love and security. She told me I suffered from a loss of control. And for years, I denied it even though it bugged me—it was always there in the back of my mind, what she said. I kept going back to my ex. I kept getting hurt." She wiped her eyes. "But no more. A few weeks ago, I realized what that counselor said was right. So I got as far away as possible. I *am* in control. I can do this. On my own. God, I'm sorry." She sniffed and swept her palms over her cheeks, suddenly self-aware she was crying. "Listen to me going on. First the ghost. Now this. You must think I'm a total basket case."

Mave opened and closed her mouth, stunned by her honesty. "No. I don't."

She found a tissue in her pocket. "I guess more than scared, I've been a bit lonely here. So, thanks."

"For what?"

She flashed her a weak smile. "For doing this." She waved at the candles. "For listening and dealing with my crap, even though we pretty much just met."

Mave took a deep breath, all at once wanting to reciprocate—to explain about Holden, how they'd met, how they'd lost one another in the fire. But before she could return any sentiment, Katie passed her her shoes.

"It's nearly time, we should go." She swept her blue hair over her shoulder and leaned down to blow out the candles.

Mave watched her in confusion. "What do you mean? Go where?"

"To the library. For the séance."

"But I thought we were having it here. To contact the spirit in your room."

"Oh, right. I thought so too at first. But then Gracelyn explained the library was the best spot. Something about a fertile ground, and..." She bit her lip and looked away. "And she may have recruited a couple of extra volunteers, too," she whispered. "But please, Mave, don't bail, okay? I need you there. I don't think"—she swallowed—"I don't think I can do this without you." The helplessness in her eyes stirred something deep in Mave's chest. She couldn't refuse.

"Of course," she breathed. "We'll get through it together."

———

"Mave Michael!" Gracelyn seemed surprised to see her accompanying Katie into the candlelit library. "I'm glad you came around to the idea. Just in time, too. Please, come join us." She extended a palm out in invitation. The other two participants were already inside, seated around a cherrywood pedestal table with a chessboard top. It was the only round piece of furniture in the library, a snug yet comfortable fit for five people. Mave waved awkwardly at Julián as he muttered about quality control and a trial run for the wedding guests. The other participant, a man with grey hair, had his back to Mave. While Julián fetched more seating, Mave wandered to the stranger's right. Except he wasn't a stranger.

She hesitated. Her stomach felt like a jar of spiders with its lid released. Dominic Grady nodded, a curl to his upper lip. Why was he here? Had he known in advance she'd attend?

Perhaps sensing her paranoia, Dom leaned sideways; he spoke to her in a musical whisper as if the library were full of patrons, keen for quiet.

"I heard rumors...of Birdie." Naturally. His guilty conscious must have prompted him here in hopes of making contact with her grandmother. A murder victim. A woman he'd wronged long ago. "Isn't that why you've come?" he asked, curiosity flickering in his pale eyes.

Mave nodded stiffly as Katie took a seat at the table. Mave was left with the last spot next to Dom.

"I confess," he added, staring at her with an intensity that heightened her discomfort, "this place, it's full of memories. I'd forgotten how disarming it can be."

Mave sat and scraped her chair forward.

Almost immediately, the energy in the room rippled—became charged. The others must have felt it too. No one spoke. Gracelyn's freesia perfume trailed her movements as she rearranged candles to her liking, her bangles jingling. Julián removed his glasses and wiped the lenses with the ends of his tie. Mave avoided looking at Dom. She bit the inside of her cheek. The library felt underheated, overcrowded with the five of them, like a bus shelter on a winter's night. She forbid her hand from snapping her elastic bracelet.

"So how does this work?" Katie asked, her voice reedy.

"Okay, I have a general idea of how to conduct this ceremony," Gracelyn said, "but I can't guarantee we'll be successful. As I explained earlier, I don't have any sixth sense to commune with the dead. But I'm familiar with the basics, and since at least one ghost has been known to occupy this library, odds are good the spirits are attracted to this specific room." When Julián made a face of skepticism, Gracelyn added, "Picture a sidewalk full of freshly fallen, knee-high snow. When a person cuts across, they leave footprints and flattened tracks, which invites others to follow in their same steps."

"The path of least resistance," Julián noted.

"Exactly," Gracelyn said. "Other spirits are likely to return here, following the same path until their message is clearly delivered."

"And then?" Mave asked.

Gracelyn was opposite her, between Katie and Julián. "And then you should get your peace of mind, dear. Most ghosts only want to have their voices heard. They mean us no harm."

Most. Not all, Mave noted while keeping mum.

Katie nodded, her face younger looking under the frail candlelight.

"Now, the most important thing to remember," Gracelyn continued, "is to breathe evenly and to stay relaxed, no matter the outcome. Let your body weigh itself into the floor as much as possible."

Julián rolled his shoulders and shifted in his seat, ever the good sport.

"It's also important to remain patient," Gracelyn said. "Sometimes, the spirits can be shy when called on directly." She instructed them to hold hands.

Mave wished she wasn't stuck next to Dom, but it was too late to find an excuse to switch spots. She reluctantly clasped his cool fingers. In contrast to his solid, confident grip, Katie's hand on her other side felt limp. Gracelyn talked them through a brief relaxation exercise. Rather than calm her, it made Mave self-conscious that her own breathing was too clipped compared to everyone else's—her palms slick between Dom's and Katie's dry ones.

Finally, Gracelyn closed her eyes, exhaled deeply, and frowned in concentration. Bathed in candlelight, the surrounding bookstacks seemed to tremor. "Spirits who wish to communicate," she said in a low and steady voice, "you are welcome here. We are in the library of Château du Ciel. We wish you no harm, just as you do not wish us any. This is a safe space; come now, and tell us your story."

For a minute, nothing seemed to happen. Mave listened to the hum of a nearby floor vent. She counted petals on Gracelyn's paisley print shirt. By the time she reached thirty-one, she was inadvertently thinking of Holden. It was as if the conscious part of her mind had gone dormant and the subconscious part had stirred awake. She intuitively willed him to come. Dared him to face her, one way or another.

You are welcome here.

The chandelier overhead seemed to shimmer brighter, fracturing into silken hairs of white. She wondered if she was simply focusing too hard, when the light noticeably flickered.

Katie's fingers tightened around hers.

"Yes," Gracelyn said. "Spirit, are you with us now?"

The chandelier flickered again, and Mave felt a rush of cold enter her lungs.

Polyethylene. She scented the plastic, just like she had in the spa.

"We hold love in our hearts," Gracelyn carried on, seemingly ignorant of anyone else's fears. "Let us hear you, see you."

A draft sprung from nowhere. The candle flames made ripping noises as they thrashed for survival.

Mave blinked at Gracelyn. The older woman's lips pursed; she remained focused and straining in effort. In contrast, Katie's jaw had fallen open. Dom looked pale. Only Julián seemed unshaken.

"Come now, in peace," Gracelyn said. "A safe place. Who do you wish to speak to?"

The candles extinguished at the same time as the chandelier did, clattering to black with an audible riot of crystals. Mave's lungs filled with the airborne plastic. Someone yelped in the darkness. Beside her, Katie had grown rigid. Mave passively heard Gracelyn's continuous drone of soothing instructions, Dom and Julián's nervous huffs of laughter.

Her focus pulled elsewhere—like a vacuum sucking a part of her mind. Her consciousness stretched, tore. Her eyes rolled forward and back. She felt the stopping of time, her pulse stuttering, her senses freezing in two places at once.

In the first place—the finite one—she was in the library of Château du Ciel. Gracelyn's voice chattered casually in the background, murky, as if Mave's head was being held underwater. They were no longer holding hands. That much she knew. And either Julián or Dom had flicked on a flashlight from a cellphone.

And in the other place—the unfathomable one—she was alone with a masked man stinking of plastic.

Right mask. Wrong man.

This wasn't Holden. Too stooped. Wrong scent. His clothes were disheveled, his head sprouting mussed patches of white hair. And through the U-shape cutout in the mask, his lips were tinted a pale blue. His chin quivered with a turkey wattle.

Mave drew on all her strength. She pretended like she wasn't staring at a stranger in the porcelain disguise currently under her pillow twenty-three flights up.

She didn't even have to ask. It was like he read her mind. He slowly raised his hands.

The moons of his cuticles were noticeably purple as he peeled off the mask. Mave felt her mouth gaping.

Apart from his discolored flesh, he looked the same. Intimidating. Terrifying. Or so she assumed. She'd never seen or met him in person—only recognized him from this morning, in print.

Gerald Lee Baker wasn't missing. He was here. And he was dead.

Who do you wish to speak to?, Gracelyn had asked mere seconds ago. The ghost seemed to convey his reply to Mave alone. He stood before her with his arm lifted and, accusingly, pointed straight at her chest.

Twenty-Three

"What—? Why—?" Her words formed a clot from her head to her mouth. "Why are you here?" she finally managed to wrestle out, pushing her voice to be heard on the other side. She was vaguely aware of the light chatter in the library. Katie's and Dom's voices in the background. Gracelyn's reply. A tinkling laugh. Mave sat petrified. No one else noticed. No one else *saw*. She was in two places at once.

Her question seemed to agitate and confuse the ghost. His lower jaw swayed unsteadily as his upper lip furled, revealing his crooked teeth. Mave realized a moment too late that he couldn't speak with normal sounds. She didn't have time to cover her ears.

His moan was high-pitched, ringing like the off-key whistles of a hundred brandy glasses at the precipice of shattering.

Her teeth ground together and her tendons flexed at the unnatural harmonic. "Please..." she begged, her eyes watering. But the folds in his brow deepened as he doubled his effort to communicate.

"Gerald Lee Baker wants his wallet back. Gerald Lee Baker wants his mouth back. You find things. You can find—"

She shook her head frantically. "No, no. Make it stop. I don't know what you—"

"Track it. Go on."

"Track what?"

"*MOTHERFUCKING THINGS!*"

The scent slammed into her without her consent. She was yanked upward, tracking, following, higher and higher at an alarming speed. Black stars swarmed her mind's eye.

A head rush. A familiar bedroom bled into focus. And its contents.

The force of her shock, her recognition of her surroundings, snapped the connection. She was thrust back into her physical body. Sweaty. Fleshy.

Any trace of Gerald Lee Baker's ghost and her hallucination were gone.

Her fingers snapped inward, nails scraping the table. She blinked. Her ears rung. She yawned her mouth open to erase the white noise, stupefied. An earthy-sweet scent of snuffed candles filled her nose. *Beeswax. Not plastic.*

"—replacement bulbs for the chandelier. Mave?" Katie called to her with a smile. "What are you waiting for? Aren't you coming?" She stood by the French doors, the hallway light spilling into the mouth of the darkened library.

Mave squinted at Katie. The others were no longer with them. What just happened to her? How much time had passed since they'd been seated together in the circle, holding hands?

A nonsensical sound exited her throat. She swallowed and tried again. "Come where?" she asked, her voice sunken behind the thud of her pulse. Her spine felt bruised against the chair's backrest.

Katie furrowed her brow while still smiling. "Uh, Earth to Mave, to the upper mezzanine? For the reading? Gracelyn's probably ready by now. Don't want the tea to get cold since the séance didn't work."

Only it did. But for Mave alone. She licked her lips. "I'm a bit tired," she said, hoping the shadows hid her disorientation. "You go on."

"You sure?"

She nodded, not trusting herself to speak again or to stand in front of Katie. Her joints felt slackened in their sockets, as if any pressure might cause them to dissemble. She'd rise and become a pile of bones, a gelatinous mound of skin and muscle on the floor.

Katie said something else she didn't register and waved. The library's French doors shut. In the sweep of darkness, Mave waited. When she was confident Katie's footsteps had faded from the corridor, she crawled off her chair, curled over the nearest wastebasket, and threw up the contents of her stomach.

———

She was unsure which prospect scared her more: that she'd hallucinated the entire thing and was certifiably mad, or that her metaphysical encounter with Gerald Lee Baker had been real. She ought to be happy, she told herself, struggling for a silver lining. Holden hadn't showed up during the séance. It was proof. He wasn't dead.

But even if Gerald Lee Baker had visited her just now *and* during her spa treatment the other day, what about Mave's dreams? The Walt Whitman book? Who or what was behind all the signs of Holden's haunting?

As she zigzagged up the emergency stairs, she refused the idea again and again. *I'm not a medium*, she repeated in her mind. And yet it had been Holden himself who had first suggested it last winter. He'd tried to convince her of her untapped gift after she'd unknowingly picked up a spirit's yearning for her lost letters from thirty years ago—and the spirit's lost bones hidden in the boarded-up train tunnels. That would make Mave's experience today her second instance of sensing the longings of the dead.

Third if you count Holden and his mask.

A shiver skated up her back. That first time, her latent ability had been triggered by her grandmother's murder. And now...

Another murder, her fear whispered.

She arrived at the twenty-third floor and approached her suite, trepidation and doubt racking her brain with each step. She paused before the door, the mahogany panels looming, the peephole teasing. *No eye may see.* Then she heard it.

The soft music.

The wistful crooning.

It was easier to identify this time. "I'll Be Seeing You," like in the abandoned home in Hazel Springs.

She blinked at the lock. It didn't appear tampered with. She took a deep breath and slipped her antique key inside. The tumblers turned and clicked. One little push and the door swung open.

The song swelled louder, unhindered—Billie Holiday's smooth, silky voice serenading her over the soft horns and tinkling piano. A greenish glow cascaded down from the skylight, swirls of dust lacing the air. No one was inside.

With a sinking in her gut, she entered the shadowy sitting room. Her footsteps creaked across the floor. She didn't bother switching off the stereo, her attention fixed on the bedroom: its door ajar; a slice of darkness.

Her hand reached out shakily for the knob. She shoved.

The stench of rot wafted out, turning her stomach. She'd been warned—had seen it already in her inner eye. Yet when she flicked on the bedside lamp, dread swallowed her anew and pierced her raw with needles.

Through the bed curtain, the silhouette of a figure was visible. No movement.

She inched forward and brushed aside the curtain. Slow. Ready. Not that it mattered. The dead couldn't hurt you the same way as the living.

He was slumped on his side in the middle of the mattress, his face turned away, one knee bent. Same mussed, stringy white hair. Same disheveled clothes.

"Hello?" she panted. "Mr. Bak-Baker?"

Her toe stubbed against a hard object. She blinked down. Wires stuck out from under the bed—the edge of a laptop, the modem shoved alongside everything. It was exactly as she'd sensed during the séance.

"Mr. Baker," she said, her voice shredded, an octave too high. "Wake up." *Please wake up, wake up. This is just a bad dream.*

("Track it. Go on... MOTHERFUCKING THINGS!")

Her hand shot out automatically, her mind screaming for her to stop, to turn and run.

Rather than stir him awake, her prodding caused his body to tip onto its back. She flinched back with a cry frozen in her throat. His stomach was bloated. His mouth jutted open like a wound, bluish lips torn over crooked teeth, jaw glistening with expelled liquids—and his bloodshot eyes gaped open in the holes of Holden's mask.

Without thinking, she lunged forward, knees clambering the bed, and ripped off the mask. She clutched it to her chest and held her forearm over her nose and mouth. Nausea fisted her stomach, pumping, pumping. Her bloodstream spiked. Billie Holiday sang airy and distant in her ears.

Gerald Lee Baker's rotting corpse lay in her bed.

She couldn't bear to look anymore. She had to leave. Vomit. Scream. Her mind raced. This was a crime scene. It would soon be crawling with police. The sheriff. Ren. What would they think? Do?

Missing person shows up dead in your bed, M&M. All those stolen items stashed in your private quarters—they're coming for you. Hard.

Her lungs hitched. One last thing. She had to check. To hide. To seek. It would be under the pillow, beneath his head.

She rolled her lips under her teeth and held her breath. Despite her recoiling senses, she crawled forward onto the king-size mattress. She averted her gaze from his face and jammed her hand under the pillow.

Sandwiched under the weight of his skull, her fingers clawed the journal and files and yanked them out. She searched deeper for the book of Whitman's poetry, unable to feel it. Where had it gone? She couldn't shake the urgency: those poems had been left for her for a reason, held secrets between their verses. Inches from the corpse, she desperately sipped air and gagged. And like a curse, or a blessing, her cell chose that moment to ring.

Forget the damned book!

Dry heaving, she scrambled off the bed and out of the room, awkwardly slamming the door behind her with her hands cradling her belongings.

Panic seared her nerve endings. She was lightheaded. The music blared. She stumbled to the wall and ripped out the stereo's electrical cord. In the flood of silence, the phone's shrill ring was like a razor slicing her ear canals.

She swayed toward the couch, one palm out, and finally managed to grab a hold of her cell. Its display glowed bright with the number. In her heart, in her gut, she knew—already anticipated this moment. She answered and pressed the phone to her ear. Hot. Gasping.

A recording played instructions.

Mave accepted the collect call. Cain Francis didn't like to be kept waiting.

TWENTY-FOUR

Once the line connected, there was no *hello, I miss you*. No pleasantries or sentiment. On a call with her father, Mave was standing in the center of a tornado, watching the world twist and unravel around her. She clung to the rules of her upbringing, their rigidity keeping her moored. Namely, rule number one: All feeling was to be suppressed or else used as a weapon. Emotions were a means to an end. Absolute black and white. Clinical interest to calculate and control. These were the go-to emotional frequencies and parental teachings of Cain Francis—instincts gifted to her for moments like this.

It didn't come as a surprise, then, that the first words to exit his mouth were a reminder of the automated message, "We're being recorded," followed by, "What do you want?" He knew something was wrong. She wouldn't have written and requested he call otherwise.

Her tongue froze up. She'd been expecting him to use a smuggled cellphone and hadn't accounted for the part about their conversation being monitored by authorities. "To hear your voice," she whispered lamely. Cain did this to her—made her regress into a lonely girl, obedient for his approval. She hated feeling this way—this lost.

"You need to stop seeing that pig," he said out of nowhere.

She pinched her brow, her brain requiring an extra beat to make the connection from pig to cop. "I'm not... How do you know about—?"

She snapped her teeth together before blurting out Ren's name. That would be handing Cain ammunition. Her heart pounded, adrenaline coursing from crisis to crisis. The realization that he was spying on her, *again*, settled over her. "Who do you have watching over me?" Reporting back like before. Could it be? "Holden? Is he here?" She couldn't censor the desperation in her tone. His huff indicated he noticed.

"I don't do second chances, M&M. Whatever hole or grave he's dug for himself, expect the bastard knows better than to be anywhere near you after the fire last winter. That what this call is about?"

She understood his intention was to warn her of Holden's duplicity, yet the reminder stung. As if she were the trouble, the problem. Too high maintenance. Holden would never come back because of *her*. "Then who?" she asked, her throat gravelly. "Who's your rat this time?" She no longer cared if the officials were recording their conversation and taking notes.

His sigh was a soft reprimand. "Still haven't learned, have you? Always asking the wrong questions."

"Learned what?"

"Your lesson, Mave Michael. Gotta keep up if you want to earn your way through life. Don't trust the pigs on the streets. Don't look for the rats in the tunnels. They run together. If you're wondering where the stink is coming from, the answer is always them. They're dirty, together."

She shook her head, struggling to disentangle his cautionary cipher. Who ran together? Who was dirty? Ren and Holden? What was he trying to say, that more than one person was Bek-187? She debated how much to ask without tipping her hand. A simple *have you noticed anyone lurking around you*, or, *watch your back when you sleep* wouldn't do with Cain. Truth be told, she'd had her fill of codes and games.

"Who's Bek?" she said, risking the name.

Did he leave a dead man in my bedroom? Did you? The suspicion fired without warning, a bullet puncturing her thoughts. Loud. Resounding.

What if this was Cain's doing? What if he was behind everything—

orchestrating the photograph in his cot, the thefts, Bek-187 on the darknet?

I'm always watching, M&M.

She'd disobeyed him by trusting Holden last winter. Could this be her father's twisted way of disciplining her? Did he want her to find Holden so he could hurt him in return?

Every action causes a reaction. Someone crosses you, they best be ready for a counterblow.

The silence that followed felt like a slow punishment. "Hello?" she said, unable to withstand it. "Are you still—?"

"You remember what I told you about the cat eating the canary?" he replied cryptically.

Because she sang too fucking loud, she inwardly finished, recalling the childhood lesson. Their call ended without any closure.

Cain Francis didn't do goodbyes.

TWENTY-FIVE

Mave flinched at the figure standing in the doorway.

"Sorry to—Gracelyn suggested I..." Katie's voice trailed off. She stood in the entrance of Mave's suite, her hair like a blue halo from the hallway light.

How long had she been there, listening in on her conversation with Cain?

"The door was open," Katie said, seeming to sense an excuse was needed. She shifted her weight from foot to foot. "What's wrong? Why are you holding that?"

Mave glanced down at Holden's mask, hugged to her chest. "I need it," she said. "To keep it safe."

"Safe from what?"

"The police."

"Why would—?"

"Gerald Lee Baker is here."

Katie's brow crumpled. "Who?"

"The missing man from Hazel Springs. He's in my bedroom." Her voice sounded hollow and calm. Too calm. She couldn't interpret Katie's reaction. Confusion? Disbelief? "He's dead," she added, "and I have to...to see security—call the sheriff." The words fell from her lips. She couldn't keep this horror to herself. Not anymore.

Katie's mouth opened and closed as she processed Mave's assertion. "Oh my god. You're serious?" Her eyes flicked to the bedroom door. "How did that old man end up—?"

Mave shook her head in a tremor. "I don't know. I don't understand what's going on. But I have to put these away." She hugged the mask tighter with her journal and files, as she thought aloud. "Before the police arrive and seal up my suite. Before they—" She glanced around, picturing it in her mind.

In a matter of hours, they would be combing through every inch of this space. They'd poke through everything, everywhere—inside her drawers, her bedding, her couch, behind the curtains, the paintings, the rugs. It was bad enough Whitman's book of poems was left behind. She'd be a fool to surrender her written memories and research on Holden, too. How would she explain to Morganson how she'd come to obtain the juvie file?

"Mave?"

She blinked at Katie. The implications settled over her bones, causing her to shudder. She swallowed. "Please, you can't tell anyone I'm moving these," she breathed, "okay? They have nothing to do with the missing man and they're important to me. Sentimental. But the police won't see it that way."

Because you're tampering with a crime scene. A potential murder invest—

"O-okay." Katie nodded. "Do you want to go back to my room? Leave them—"

"No, no, I don't want you to..." She thought better of the words *get in trouble*. "I know a better place," she said instead. "But I have to be quick. Can you get a radio and call Oren? He's the security guard on duty tonight," she said. "Use the second line. It's private. But don't say anything else, just—just tell him to meet me in the offices in ten minutes. Take the service elevator. It's fastest."

Though her eyes remained wide with shock, Katie didn't object. "What about you?"

She shook her head. "No elevators. I'll see you downstairs. We have to go. Now." With Katie's silent agreement, Mave steered her out, locked up, and headed to the stairs alone.

At some point, her body grew numb, detached from her mind, and signaled her brain on a need-to-know basis. It was the sole way to cope. Get through it. On the main floor, a member of housekeeping vacuumed the hallway. *Lis. Liv. Something one syllable.* Mave's memory was on hold, reserved for emergencies only. She couldn't draw up the employee's name. As she passed, her lips pulled into their rehearsed smile. Her hand lifted and performed its casual wave.

By the way, there's a dead body in my bed. Stolen property planted in my suite.

She hadn't wanted to believe it, but Gracelyn's reading of her tea leaves had been right. The enemies were close. And if she wanted to expose them, she had to remain calm. Be smart.

She'd call the police soon. Soon, she'd report the horrifying death and discovery no matter how harmful to her and the property's already questionable reputation—she would. But first, she had to shield and arm herself. Starting with a visit to the spa.

Mave slipped into the storage closet and shut the door behind her. In one fell swoop, she hid the mask, journal, and juvie file in the depths of a cardboard box full of tea tree oils. A few product labels fell loose in the shuffle. She did her best to rearrange the old stock, resealed the box, and shoved the entire carton against the back wall. Then, as an extra precaution, she lugged the computer's bulky hard drive atop the box.

On her way out, she triple-checked she'd locked the closet door.

You're burying evidence, an unwanted voice in her head reprimanded. *Those things were on the bed. With the corpse.* She tried to push the worry aside, yet it rebounded bigger, louder. *You're committing a crime. Another crime. Just like—*

She snapped her elastic band, wrist pink, jaw clenched. *Think!* she cried to herself. Who did this? It wasn't as if Gerald Lee Baker stole his own belongings. It wasn't as if he drove miles to the château, broke into her room, put on Holden's mask, died innocently on her bed, then returned in spirit form to order she track his things under her bed. And fingerprints on the mask might prove that, might unmask the thief, or the identity of Bek-187 or Cain's spy.

Or Holden.

Because who else knew of his love of Whitman's poetry? Who else chain-smoked, wore masks, hid in shadows, lived as a secret criminal? She dug her thumb into her brow, trying and failing to temper her headache, and hurried up the grand staircase to meet Katie and Oren in the hotelier offices. Halfway up, at the turn of the landing, she ran into Dominic Grady.

"Woah," he said, steadying her by her elbows. "Apologies, I didn't mean to startle you. I was just on my way down to the shop to—"

"It's closed," she interrupted, stepping back from his reach. "You've caught me at a bad time."

"Oh." He frowned. "Well, if you'll only give me a—"

"Perhaps you could visit with the concierge for assistance? Or the front desk? I'm sure they'll be happy to help you with anything you need to make your stay more comfortable." She smiled tightly and, before he could respond, stepped around him to resume her flight. VIP or not, he would have to wait, dammit.

She had to get to security asap—before Morganson—to make sure nothing implicated Holden. As it was, he was already on Ren's radar thanks to her request for the juvie file. Mave had to take more precaution. She'd call police *after* she reviewed the tapes. Outrun them. One up the dirty pigs. Some first impressions, you couldn't undo.

Get there first, M&M. Control it. Or else her enemies would. Including the one planted by Cain himself.

Someone was watching her and reporting back to him in prison. Who was it? If not Holden, who had Cain recruited to be his little spy this time around? She had no opportunity to mull it over as she knocked on security's door and strolled into the small office.

Katie and Oren were already inside. They both looked up at her, their faces pinched and awaiting her instructions. The room felt stifling with no windows or natural light. The fluorescent tubes hummed and tinted the air neon yellow. Oren was at the desk in front of the monitors, his hulking six-foot-six figure spilling over the edges of his seat.

"Hey, boss." He straightened, the chair groaning under his weight. Ever since New Year's Eve, when he'd been on orders to retain her for an arrest and she'd escaped him, the security guard seemed partly anxious, partly in awe whenever in her presence.

Mave threw Katie a private glance. *You tell him?*

Katie shook her head ever so slightly and shuffled behind Oren. She stood with her arms crossed. No point in alarming Oren prematurely. Soon, the entire hotel would be aware of the rotting corpse upstairs.

Mave rolled a seat next to them. She explained the surveillance she needed: anything from the emergency stairwells leading up to the top floor. She doubted a person could've lugged a dead body up the main elevators or central staircase unnoticed, light foot traffic or not. And the cameras that lined the hallway to her suite had been deactivated. On her orders.

Oren pulled forward his keyboard without questions, eager to please, and typed in the appropriate commands.

A moment later they were staring at snow on the screen.

Katie cursed softly behind them.

"Oren, what's this?" Worry bled in Mave's gut.

"Hang on." His brow cinched and his mouth twisted. He typed more commands. Nothing changed. Only snow appeared. He fast-forwarded the footage. "Weird. Looks like some sort of electrical interference. Must have taken out the cameras for a few hours."

"And you didn't notice the malfunction live, in real time?" She struggled to edit her tone, not come across as impatient, scolding. They were short-staffed as it was.

"I was doing rounds. And when I got back... Cameras are fine now —see?" He played a series of live clips. The upper lobby. The cigar lounge. The parking lot. "Seems like a glitch that fixed itself," he said. Everything was crystal clear—except from the time range when stolen property plus a dead, missing local had been brought onto the premises and dumped into her suite.

"Try it again," Mave said.

"Yeah, maybe it's like a bad Wi-Fi connection," Katie suggested.

Oren nervously rubbed his lip and rewound the footage. Snow reappeared.

How was this happening?

No forced entry—in and out—could be a hacker we're dealing with, Ren had informed her days ago. *Or a ghost,* Mave thought, remembering the séance, how the chandelier bulbs had blown around the same time. Could that be the source of the electrical interference?

"What's going on?" Oren finally asked. He looked to Mave. "What are you looking for?"

Mave was suddenly anxious to call Sheriff Morganson and have her investigate.

"A person moving a dead body," she said, registering the fear in Oren's eyes.

TWENTY-SIX

The sun glowed blood orange as it tucked itself behind the mountainous horizon. Mave stood still as Sheriff Morganson joined her on the penthouse terrace. She held the railing with both hands to avoid fidgeting. The investigation of her grandmother's murder had suggested the sheriff was a fair woman; she could be swayed to recognize the truth. But Morganson was also impossible to read and permanently intimidating. Stout. Short hair. Hawk-like gaze.

"Fresh air always helps," Morganson said. She inhaled deeply, her nostrils flaring. Mave assumed she meant to clear the stench of death. "Word has gotten out about your help finding the stolen property." She paused and looked at Mave. "First with Mrs. Hess, then with Sandy."

The acknowledgment gave her a slight start. "You found Sandy's things? At Vincent's?"

"Not quite," Morganson said, "but after your first lead proved right, we're taking your tip seriously, still working things out."

She interpreted that to mean they had yet to secure a search warrant. But what about the computer equipment beneath her bed?

"Look, I know we went over all of this," Morganson said, "but I need you to confirm a few more details. Now remind me, before you discovered the body you were...?"

"Participating in a séance." She tried not to fidget. "In the library in the lower galleria."

"Uh-huh. And you didn't drop by your suite for anything since this morning?"

"No. I was in the gift shop for most of the day."

"Who else has a key to your suite?"

She shook her head. "There are masters." Her throat ran dry. "Housekeeping, management. Even then, it wouldn't be hard to borrow or lift someone's copy." She kicked herself, admitting it aloud. She'd been so distracted. She should have changed her locks from day one.

"And the cameras were disabled because…?"

"I didn't—I mean, they weren't disabled *every*where. It was"—she struggled to find the right words, the innocent words—"some kind of malfunction with the system."

"Right. And your security guard, Oren, he'd have no reason to tamper with the hotel footage?"

"No."

"What about anyone else with access to the office?"

"No," she repeated.

"Any recent arguments? Maybe an employee you rubbed the wrong way?"

Based on the amount of cold shoulders she'd received, Mave had rubbed nearly all staff the wrong way, but she left that out. "No. No one."

"And you're absolutely sure the door to your suite was locked?"

"Yes."

"After what happened here a few months ago…" Morganson stared at her with a stern frown. "Seems like someone's going to an awful lot of trouble to send you a message. Now, assuming facts line up about a mystery intruder leaving you Baker's body, it might be the thief's pissed off with your recent consultations. Like I said, word has gotten out about your help on the burglary investigation. *Or* it might be another person trying to mess with you—someone with another motive all together."

Like uncovering the whereabouts of Holden Frost.

"But it has to be, right?" she said. "The thief? With the stuff left under my bed?"

"No doubt there's a connection," Morganson agreed. She stared out at the vista.

"But?"

Morganson's brow cocked. "But it could be an indirect link," she admitted, "maybe even a decoy. We aren't ruling out other potential suspects. Yet. Especially since the items in your suite aren't everything." She paused, as if debating how much to tell her. "There's still outstanding computer equipment missing, including Sandy's router. And the books."

Mave cleared her throat. "And what about Mr. Baker's body? Is it— I mean, did he...?"

"Too early to say with all the variables."

"But you must have a theory."

"I do. More than one, in fact. See, the perp either finished him off or found him already dead. Saw it as an opportunity. Made lemons into lemonade, so to speak. Seems unlikely given the timing. We won't know for sure if Mr. Baker died of natural causes until after the medical examiner's done. But in light of recent events—Mr. Baker being one of the robbery victims gone missing and all—we're now treating this as a homicide investigation."

She stiffened. "Until when?" She had hundreds of guests arriving in less than a week—a critical wedding to oversee.

"Until further evidence rules out otherwise."

Mave doubted such a conclusion could ever be reached. Baker wouldn't have transmitted from the afterlife unless something had gone terribly wrong during his passing. She knew this firsthand from Birdie's death. Murder was messy, left energy stains. Dirty karma.

"Even in your best-case scenario," Morganson said, interrupting her thoughts, "there's still the question of how Baker ended up here at the château." She left the comment hanging for a beat, as if giving Mave the opportunity to make some critical confession. When she didn't, the sheriff continued, "Everything is being documented as we speak. The body'll soon be moved to the morgue, but we'll need to keep any personnel or guests clear of the crime scene in the interim. Afraid that means you, too. You'll have to relocate to another suite without your personal belongings—at least temporarily."

"Sure, of course." She nodded with a pinched smile. "I'll cooperate in any way I can." *Save revealing the whole truth,* her inner voice scolded. She'd already lied to Morganson earlier, when she'd claimed she'd removed nothing from the bedroom. Absolutely nothing. "But I'm hoping..."

Morganson's blinked in interest.

"Is there any way to keep this on the downlow," she finished, "off Channel Six and the *Gazette*'s radar? The hotel is still trying to recoup after the losses from the fire. The last thing we need is more death and scandal tainting the property."

Morganson let out a slow breath. "I'll do my best, but..."

"But?"

She pointed over the railing. Mave leaned forward slightly and looked down twenty-three flights. She squinted through the gathering shadows and made out activity on the driveway below.

Parked at the hotel's entrance was a white van with a satellite dish and camera mounted to its roof.

"Small towns," Morganson added with a sympathetic sigh.

News of Baker's body had already leaked.

———

Her shower did little to wash away the rancid memories of Baker's ghost and corpse, the mask on his nightmarish face. She pulled on her black trousers and searched impatiently for a clean white blouse in Birdie's massive armoire, her adrenaline not yet expended. "Come on. Where is it?" she muttered. Though her suite was on the same floor, her grandmother's former penthouse was huge in comparison. The residence spanned over twelves rooms, including an art studio plus sitting lounge, a private chef's kitchen, three bedrooms, five washrooms, two walk-in closets, and a secret boudoir. She'd never felt entirely comfortable here —maybe because it reminded her of Birdie's murder. Mave was contemplating whether she'd been cursed to stumble upon dead bodies, when a loud knock on the outer studio doors startled her.

Morganson again? Who else knew she was hiding in here? Abandoning her search for a blouse, she threw on her fitted suit jacket over her bra, buttoning it on the go, and padded out to the penthouse's main double doors. She checked through the peephole. The prospect of having to face a reporter made her want to scream. The two-faced journalists during and after Cain's trial had left her weary for life. She pushed out her breath, unlocked the door, and peeked into the corridor.

"Ren," she said, not bothering to hide her surprise. "Sheriff Morganson already questioned me." Suspicions about Cain's new spy were still fresh in her mind. But her father would never trust a police officer enough to trade deals. Especially if he was a dirty cop.

Ren took off his hat and brushed the top of his head with his palm. His eyes lingered a moment too long on her lips before dipping to her chest. As if self-aware, he overcorrected his wandering eyes by settling on her jawline. Her naturally brown hair was cropped just over her chin. Mave tucked a damp strand behind her ear and hitched her brow. He held up a plastic bag in his other hand. "Morganson mentioned you might be needing a few of your personal items. I, uh"—he smiled boyishly—"volunteered to drop these off."

She opened the door wider and took the bag from him. Inside, her lace undergarments were carefully folded on top.

"These have all been"—he fiddled with the brim of his hat—"cleared."

"Thanks," she said, her neck warming. The murmur of another conversation drifted from down the hallway. More police? Or the press? She quickly grabbed his wrist and ushered him in, shutting and relocking the door behind him. "Sorry." She crossed her arms and held together her lapels. "It's just, I'm trying to—I'm avoiding the..." She stumbled over her words, nervous all over again. "Hiding for a bit," she said, settling on the simple truth. She set aside the bag for something to do, and fussed over straightening its handles.

"You don't have to explain. You've been through a lot today." He glanced away from her bare feet and looked around the studio. She'd cleaned up considerably since Birdie's death. The space was neatly furnished. Soft spotlights cascaded over paintings she'd hung, model busts displayed on plinths—a tribute gallery to her grandmother.

"Huh," Ren mused, admiring the nearest oil painting, "looks great in here."

She shrugged. "Had a lot of beautiful pieces to pick from." Undoubtedly, his last visit and impression of the penthouse—when she'd been recovering in the hospital and the studio had been a crime scene—must have seemed more morbid.

He cleared his throat. The silence was awkward. "Well, just wanted to make sure you're all right."

She nodded. "Thanks again."

"Sure." He spun his hat in his hands. She got the sense he wanted to say more, but he cocked his thumb over his shoulder. "Best be getting back." He turned to leave, and she trailed his steps. As he swung open the door, a flash blinded them both.

"Hi, we're looking for—"

Mave's stomach plummeted.

"Shit." He slammed the door shut.

She pressed on her eyelids. Reporters. More than one from the sounds of it. "They found me, didn't they?"

"Don't worry. I'll have them leave."

"Doesn't matter." She sighed, feeling deflated with what she had to face. Again. "They'll just return after you're gone. Stalk me outside the door until they get their stupid story and photo. Freedom of the press."

He furrowed his brow, as if picturing it. "In that case, why not leave them waiting and stuck out in that hallway for an extra-long time?"

"What do you mean?" She released a frail laugh. "Like never give them the satisfaction of leaving this room?"

A smug expression crossed his face. "Only in appearance. I know another way."

"Out from the penthouse?" She shook her head. "No, I've seen your great-grandfather's blueprints." She'd studied them at length since inheriting the property. "There is no other exit apart from those double doors."

"Who said everything is in the blueprints?"

Her eyes grew wide.

"How much you want to bet me I can get you out of here undetected?"

"Um, with that look you've got? Nothing."

"Come on." He offered his hand. Her gaze flicked to the door as someone knocked with vigor. It was all the motivation she needed. Despite the warning in her gut, she tentatively accepted Ren's hand. She had adrenaline left to burn, after all.

Without a word, he led her back through the sitting lounge and into the master bedroom, straight into the walk-in closet she'd been rummaging through. "You're telling me there's—"

"Yep. Hang on." He released her hand.

With a determined look, he began to inspect the four walls. "It's been years. Give me a sec." He opened a shuttered wardrobe and pushed aside garment bags she'd arranged in perfect rows. She was sentimental for reasons she couldn't articulate—wanting to hang on to her grandmother's clothing as if it would please Birdie in the afterlife. A penthouse kept like a time capsule.

"Ah, here it is."

"Here *what* is?"

His upper half had disappeared inside the wardrobe. "Scuttle hole," he replied while reaching upward.

She didn't like the sound of that. She shuffled beside him. They were shoulder to shoulder. His lemony-basil aftershave drifted in her direction, renewing the flutters in her stomach. She looked up.

Along the closet's ceiling was a seam with a wooden trim, leveled off and barely noticeable. An attic? Ren pounded with the side of his fist more than once, then cursed softly with his lashes fluttering as the scuttle hole loosened with a sprinkle of plaster.

She blinked. There it was. A way out.

From the looks of it, it was a crawl space intended for structural maintenance or insulation, but it obviously led elsewhere through the rafters. An escape route, like he'd promised. A shiver sliced her spine.

She clutched her collar together. His history and knowledge of the château's secrets—it reminded her too much of Holden.

He grinned as he batted the dust from his hair. "See? Just like when I was a kid."

"I'm sorry." She shook her head. "I can't."

"Sure you can. It's nothing. A short scoot through and you'll end up inside housekeeping's linen closet across the way. At least that's what used to be stored in there. Scout's honor." He held up two fingers. "We can slip out unnoticed, and those reporters won't have a clue you got out right under their noses." He looked smug again.

She backed up a step. "You don't understand. I can't. I won't." *Not with you.* She folded her arms and brushed her neck. "I'm claustrophobic."

"Oh." He suddenly seemed to notice her lack of enthusiasm. "Hey, okay. No problem. I didn't mean to..." His low drawl was extra soothing, perhaps to offset that her breathing had accelerated. "Here." He reached up to reseal the attic's entrance. She focused on his healthy biceps, how they flexed in the act. The distraction was welcome.

"Okay, forget that." He dusted his hands and shut the wardrobe. "I've got another idea to help you de-stress. My brother swears it's foolproof. This way."

Five minutes later, they were seated on the kitchen floor, their backs against the cupboards, with a tub of chocolate ice cream between them.

"Why the floor again?" she asked, amused.

"Cool tiles. Better posture. That's what André says—my brother," he added softly. His eyes glazed over in thought. "Honestly? I think it's because he's stuck in a bed and overheated with meds most of the time." He chuckled lightly, though the humor didn't reach his eyes. For a second she could see through the uniform, past the hero on duty.

"That's gotta be tough," she said. "How's he doing, anyway?"

A quiet sigh escaped him. Had she not been paying close attention, she would have missed it. "About as well as he can without a properly functioning kidney."

"And the donor lists?" She wanted to comfort him but wasn't entirely sure how. "Any hope?"

The corner of his mouth twitched in a failed smile. "Yeah, he's on a waitlist. Matches are tough to find, though. Hey, if you happen to know anyone young and healthy with A negative blood..." He huffed. "Kidding. Let's dig in." He lifted his spoon with a flourish, obviously wanting to change the subject and lighten the mood.

"You sure this hasn't expired?" She searched the tub's label. She hadn't exactly stocked the fridge or freezer since her grandmother's death.

He scooped out a generous amount. "Ice cream doesn't expire," he said, shoving the entire spoonful into his mouth. She looked up in time to catch the doubt on his face. "Mmm," he feigned, making her laugh. "Yeah, maybe we'll just..." He reclaimed the tub, put the lid back on, and rose to drink directly from the sink's faucet.

"You don't have to do this, you know."

He flicked his wet fingers playfully at her, and she waved away the sprinkle with an amused scoff. "Do what?" He grinned, resettling beside her. He wiped the water on his jaw with the backs of his knuckles.

"Try to cheer me up. Really, I'm fine." Even if she wasn't. Even if it felt nice to have someone notice her—want to spend time with her.

"Know you are." His smile softened. "But you wouldn't be in this position, having to hide in here, locked out of your own room, if you hadn't gone out of your way to help me relocate all that stolen property."

"Technically, Sandy's things are still MIA," she pointed out.

"Oh, don't you worry. We'll find them. And the bad guy, too. Only a matter of time."

She wanted to believe him. She wanted to buy into his confidence and story: he was an honest cop, uncorrupt and uninvolved with either Bek-187 or Holden or the thief turned likely murderer. There was nothing scary about the police officer who sat next to her. He was solid. Uncomplicated. Coached softball. Cared for his brother. Before she knew what she was doing, she was touching the gold badge on his chest. Her brow knit as she dragged her finger down the ridged metal. She swallowed.

Not so scary.

Maybe that's why she remained still as he leaned closer. Maybe that's why she shut her lashes and allowed his lips to graze hers—gently at first, as if prolonging the promise of pleasure, then fully, skillfully. His mouth worked over hers much like the drawl of his voice, with a simultaneous smoothness and depth that was easy to fall into. How simple it would be, she thought in a flurry of lust. She could grow to care for him—more than like him. He could rehabilitate her freak reputation, make her life feel normal, predictable. He angled her chin, cupped her neck. His other hand slipped lower. The butterflies in her stomach twisted.

Holden.

She couldn't help it. Eyes closed, she thought of him. His rough beard unlike Ren's patchy five o'clock shadow. Holden's hands coarser on her skin, mouth hungrier, smokier, the way he tasted like—

A loud, echoing thump caused them to jump apart. Like a muffled hammer falling on pipes.

Twice.

Again.

Three heavy knocks—a haunting weight from the other side of nowhere.

Ren blinked at the walls with a stunned expression, his breath quickened. She inched back on her heels, pulled together her gaping jacket to cover her bra, and touched her lips with trembling fingers. A hybrid of regret and confusion swarmed her chest.

He didn't notice, too distracted trying to pinpoint the source of their interruption. "I'll get rid of the damn reporters," he said, rising and rationalizing the impossible. He marched away.

She didn't bother to correct him. It wouldn't matter anyway. She alone understood the longings of the dead.

TWENTY-SEVEN

Not two hours after Ren escorted the nosy reporters off the property and back to Hazel Springs, more knocks came— these less ominous sounding and clearly originating from the penthouse doors. Mave's eyes flicked to the antique alabaster clock on the mantle. Ten p.m. She sighed and slipped on her stilettos, fully dressed and ready to face the inevitable.

Bad news never sleeps.

She mentally prepared her lines as she shuffled to the door. *We at Château du Ciel offer our deepest condolences to the family of Mr...* She answered with her plastic smile cocked and ready.

A short man with light brown skin, gold wire glasses, and a stretched face made longer by his pointed goatee stared back at her. He didn't return her smile. Nor did he carry a camera. No phone outstretched to catch her on record. Not even a notebook or a satchel. He wore a golf shirt, dark jeans, black running shoes, and spoke in a standard English accent. "You must be Mave Michael." It wasn't a question.

"And you are?"

He didn't so much as blink, his eyes like faded asphalt. "May I come in?"

She tilted her head. "I don't make a habit of letting strangers into my home in the middle of the night, so, no."

"Of course. We haven't met. But I'm a friend of your father's."

The temperature in the doorway seemed to drop ten degrees. Her shoulders tensed. "You must be mistaken. My father doesn't have any friends."

"No?" he asked, a simple one-word challenge.

No, Cain's voice warned in her mind. She narrowed her eyes, unsure whether to shut the door in his face and call security, or to switch tactics and pump him for more information. She was at a loss. Who was this man? What game was he playing? He seemed to sense she needed more to go on.

"He trusted me enough to get you out of the hotel on January second at zero hundred hours."

At midnight. New Year's Day. Her eyes widened. The con who'd been contracted by Cain back in January. She regarded him with newfound suspicion. If he was who he claimed, then back then, he'd been tasked with smuggling her out of the château and to a safehouse, all while hotel staff and guests were snowed in and under police orders to stay put. Except Mave had never shown up for her scheduled rendezvous to become a fugitive.

"You're Stratis," she said, catching on.

Still no blink. "Sometimes. To some people."

"And to others?" Was he saying he was Bek-187? Or another gun for hire like her father?

"I'm nobody," he replied. "I don't cause trouble. I clean trouble. Now may I come in? I prefer not to conduct business in front of cameras." He leaned subtly to indicate the closest one mounted to the hallway's ceiling.

Her heart clapped against her ribs. "Not sure you and I have any business." She paused, playing his aloof game, letting him wait. In the end, curiosity replaced her red flags. "You have five minutes. Hands where I can see them." Once he removed them from his pockets, she stepped back and allowed him to enter the studio.

As he shut the door behind him, she positioned herself at an angle.

Feet apart, elbows slightly bent at her sides. She cocked her chin, prompting him to speak.

"Cain sent me here."

"Why?" she said, even though she could guess the answer: their phone call.

"He's concerned about your welfare."

"I don't need his concern."

"Needs are seldom a factor in these equations."

"What equations?"

"The ones that pose a problem. The ones that require a hard solution. That's where I come in. Now, you go on and tell me everything that's happened, and I'll come up with that solution. It's what I do."

"You clean trouble," she said, repeating his job description. A criminal fix-it man.

A single nod was her only assurance to trust him. It was barely enough not to have him tossed from the building. A million and one misgivings fired in her mind. Exactly how long had he been here on the property? Was he Cain's spy? Was he telling the truth? Would he really take care of Bek-187, keep Cain safe, help her find Holden? But any potential answers kept rebounding to her earlier suspicion.

Cain could be Bek-187. Maybe this man was his lacky; the person who'd broken into her suite with Baker's body. He was clearly aware of the cameras. This visit could be a part of Cain's elaborate test—a way for him to control her life, even from behind bars. Lord knew her father had difficulty showing proper affection. By now she'd gotten used to it. Manipulative though they were, Cain's so-called lessons were his sole method of parenting.

She crossed her arms, no longer threatened—merely agitated. "Look, I'm not sure how much Cain's paid you for your little visit, but I'm afraid my problems aren't for sale. You'll just have to explain that to him. I'm fine. I don't require your services. Or his meddling."

He raised his palm and slowly pulled a business card from his breast pocket. "For your troubles," he said, "whenever you're ready." When she didn't move to accept it, he slid the card onto a plinth.

"I'll see myself out." With a farewell nod, he shuffled out the way he'd come, the door's musical creak announcing his departure. Mave quickly locked the door after him and snatched up his business card.

It listed a phone number. Nothing more. A nameless nobody like he claimed.

Teeth gritted, she stomped into the sitting room and headed to the secretary desk in the corner. She yanked on its sliders, lowered the polished tabletop, and searched its drawers, one after another. She found what she was looking for—a postcard of the château—and traded it for the business card. She shut the secretary with a huff. She might not have divulged much to Stratis, but she had a thought or two to share with her father. Beginning with what he could do with his spy.

———

She spun down the staircase in a blur. Intrusive thoughts swarmed and stung like wasps in her mind. *Baker's ghost. Baker's corpse. Bek-187. Cain. Stratis.* Staying in the penthouse, replaying everything nonstop was driving her mad. She wouldn't be kept prisoner in her own home. She needed to be free—to check the darknet, put her mental energy to better use.

But a quarter of an hour later, her research merely uncovered more upsetting news.

Locked inside the storage closet, Mave gripped the sides of her chair to avoid smashing the monitor to the floor. Bek-187 had not only ignored her last message for more time, they'd gone on the offense. There was no misinterpreting the reply. Bek was keeping tabs. Just like her father.

Uh-oh. You broke a rule. No cops, Neat-Freak. You get one last chance. Next time, the penalty will be more than time. It'll cost you Daddy's blood. Don't say I didn't warn you: 5.

Bek had attached another photo of Cain asleep. The same nightly shadows hardened the lines on her father's face, making him look grimmer, worn down by time—only in this latest image, he wasn't alone. The photographer had captured his own gloved hand, deliberately reaching into the frame. He held a shiv inches from Cain's throat.

Something about its handmade quality—its taped handle and dirtied, dull grey metal—made it look deadlier than any store-bought knife.

She put her head between her legs and counted to ten. Twenty. The blood rush helped. She had to figure this out. Bek-187. Holden. Her father. There had to be a clue somewhere she'd overlooked. What was she missing? Was Bek another inmate or a crooked guard, or simply someone with an inside man in the prison? Or was Cain staging his own threat? Without confiding in her father, how could she uncover Bek's identity? As she pushed up, her eyes fell on the box where she'd hidden her journal and the juvie file. *And Holden's mask.*

She could take Gracelyn's advice—give herself over to her dreams of Holden. She could stop fearing and resisting that connection. Another episode of parasomnia might uncover more of Holden's secrets—like his link to Bek-187. But the mere thought of wearing the mask again made her nauseated. She wasn't sure she could stomach it after finding it on Gerald Lee Baker's corpse. She lugged the hard drive off the box regardless, and dug past the tea tree oils.

Three-quarters of the way down the box, her anxiety bloomed and sprung shoots into the branches of her lungs. Deeper and deeper. Faster and faster. She gave up her strategic rifling and tossed out the oils.

Where were they? *Where—*

She stood and upended the entire box. Packets of oil scattered around her feet. All identical.

The mask. Her journal. Holden's juvie file. Everything she sought to hide was missing.

———

She sat in the hotelier offices with her heart pumping in her throat, reviewing the security footage with Oren. She noticed Dominic Grady wandering the lower galleria in the early evening and kept quiet (he was probably searching for her again); and shortly thereafter, an odd presence in the lobby.

"Stop it, right there," she instructed Oren. He froze the image.

"Who's that?" he asked.

"A boy from the village. His name is Liam."

"You know him?"

"Only by name," she replied vaguely. "Can we see where he goes?"

Oren continued the footage.

Liam was entering the hotel's main lobby, glancing up and around as if canvassing the space, but for what? He hitched his schoolbag on his shoulder and bounced on the balls of his feet as he wandered inside, past reception.

Mave chewed on her lip. The teenager from Hazel Springs who'd purchased Mrs. Hess's stolen computer—what business did he have here at the château, miles from his home? They noted the boy loitering along the corridor on the ground floor, perhaps headed to the grand staircase, when the recording blinked into snow. Again.

Another electrical glitch in the security system.

"No!" Mave cursed, unable to hold in her frustration. "How does this keep happening?" Oren seemed helpless as she ordered him to forward the footage. The effort was useless.

Nothing had been captured on tape from the hours leading up to Stratis's visit. Or from the timeframe when her secret belongings had gone missing from the spa. Mave wondered if that meant the two were related. Stratis may have stolen her stash after she'd refused his offer of help. But how could he have guessed her hiding spot? Each time she tried to make sense of it, the scenarios snagged and knotted—tightened into an ache in her skull.

Oren promised he would call an IT system electrician to look into their glitch first thing in the morning. She asked him to send a copy of today's tape to Morganson (perps were known to revisit their crime scenes), and to install a new, extra-secure lock on the spa's closet door. But it wasn't enough. She'd had her fill of games and manipulations.

Come morning, she was determined to reclaim control. Think like a wolf. Hunt like a wolf. Even if it meant becoming the criminal herself.

TWENTY-EIGHT

With no mask under her pillow to usurp her dreams, she fell into nightmares choreographed by her own mind. Cain's neck slit. Holden's body charred. Gerald Lee Baker lurking over her bed, wearing the three-faced mask, his bluish lips splitting to reveal his crooked teeth as he raised a Zippo lighter and set her bed curtains on fire.

It was no wonder she felt like a zombie come morning. She swept her palms along the sharp creases of her suit, and with an outward poise she didn't feel, headed down the winding grand staircase on a mission. She didn't need Cain's criminal fix-it man. She didn't need anyone. She'd handle this herself.

The halls of the lower galleria were cool, dark, and quiet as always—save for her heels, which clicked on the marble tiles and echoed her footfalls. She self-consciously lightened her step, and ran a mental inventory of complimentary keepsakes to offer the VIP wedding guests. She'd keep them pampered—herself distracted—a mundane task that could bring the solution of her deeper problems into focus.

She stepped over the morning delivery of bundled newspapers and entered the dark boutique. Her keys rattled. The bells above the door jingled. She bent to gather the newspapers, switched on the chandelier, and flinched.

Vincent Lorde was seated in the corner of the shop with his thick fingers laced over his stomach. His feet were propped on a vitrine.

Play dumb, Cain whispered.

"Excuse me, sir." She sounded winded.

He wore a trucker hat, the brim angled low over his eyes as if he'd settled down for a nap. For a second, she wondered if he might be asleep after all, until his voice struck her like a spray of gravel.

"Well, if it ain't Mave Michael Francis, up bright and early. Not that you could tell in this joint." He shoved up his hat and looked around. "Lit like a fuckin' dungeon," he mumbled.

"I'm sorry, how'd you get in here?"

"Door was unlocked. You know, you really should keep better security."

He was lying. She never would have left the boutique unlocked.

Unless I got so distracted with going to the séance yesterday that I absentmindedly forgot on my way out.

She slowly set the newspapers on the counter while keeping herself close to the door. "We actually don't open for another hour. If you'd like to come back then, I'd be happy to help you with—"

"Oh, I don't think so, sweetheart. Or do you prefer *Kennedy*?" He widened his eyes in mock surprise, baiting her for a reaction. She did her best to keep her face and tone neutral, her pulse shooting.

"I'm not sure I follow."

"Bullshit." He dropped his feet and rose.

She edged against the counter and leaned back casually with her elbows. The stapler was within reach.

He wagged a finger. "Had a feeling something was off about you when you came sniffing 'round, and not just because of your freak Siamese eyes." He gestured at his own face to indicate her dissimilar irises. She acted indifferent—wouldn't give him the pleasure of witnessing the sting of his insult.

"I admit, took me a day or two to figure it out." His coarse gaze coasted down and up her body. "Thing is, people in Hazel Springs, they like to talk a lot of shit, get up in other people's business. See, ever since you dropped by pretending to be from the *Gazette*, Rawlings, he's been following me around, asking too many questions. So I did a little asking of my own and, low and behold! Found out nobody named Kennedy works at the *Gazette*. Meanwhile, Mr. Boy Scout With A Badge has been hitting a new piece of ass, toting her all over town." He clicked his tongue. "Pretty little thing, too, according to Sharon down at the garage. Now, imagine my surprise when Sharon pulls up a picture on her phone from a goddamned news blog and tells me *this* is the girlfriend." He swept his hand up and down to indicate her with a derisive chuckle. "The owner of Château du Ciel!" He pronounced it in three syllables: *du-cee-el*. "And I think to myself, hang on now, I *know* that face. Except for the hair—that part's wrong, you see. Otherwise, she looks just like that nosy bitch who came around my garage a few days ago."

"I think you're mistaken."

He took his time, measuring her with his eyes narrowed. "Had a feeling you might say that. And crazy thing is, I thought so, too, at first. Even with the picture, it kept bugging me—made no sense. Why would Rawlings' new girlfriend be pretending to be somebody else? Why would she be digging into my past? So I decided, why the hell not? I'll drive up here and have a look for myself.

"I asked for you at the front desk, and they told me you kept an office in the gift shop downstairs. So then, here I come to wait, cuz, hey, maybe I got it wrong. Maybe you'll show up and, in person, you'll look nothing like that little wannabe reporter. And would you believe it, soon as I step inside and check out the place, I find this in a drawer under your counter." He held up a piece of paper.

She had to squint to see past the shadows. Her throat clenched.

Holden's mug shot. It must have slipped out from the juvie file unnoticed on that first day, when she'd been shuffling to hide the paperwork from visitors.

Careless. Stupid.

"Now go on." He stepped forward and leaned on another vitrine a few feet away, his biceps bulging like overinflated footballs. "Lie to me again...I dare you."

The way his veins popped on his arms, she worried the display case might shatter under his weight. She swallowed. "What do you want?"

"What I *want*, is for you to get your fucking cop boyfriend to stop tailing me."

"He's not my boyfriend."

"I don't give a shit what he is to you. Far as I'm concerned, you can call him your best bud or your body guard or label him whatever you please. What you can't do is fuck with me. You understand what I'm saying? I don't take kindly to lying bitches messing with my business."

"Why?" She played her hand. "Are you afraid everyone will find out what really happened to your sister, Pammy? That she ran away because of you?"

His jaw pushed forward and something shimmered in his eyes beneath the anger. Pain? Regret? "Better watch your mouth," he grumbled low from his chest, like a mountain lion giving a warning. "Dunno what game you think you're playing at, bringing up all this shit about my sister, but it's clear to me Rawlings's done a number on you. Got you all twisted with your panties in a bunch. You want the dirt? Wanna play reporter some more? Well, newsflash: you're in over your pretty little head. Got your facts wrong, you hear me? So I'm gonna say this once, and only once, cuz, shit, I dunno"—he crinkled his eyes, regarding her with a mixture of distaste and condescension—"Rawlings is a two-faced dirty fuck, and you look a bit pathetic, to be honest. So pay attention."

She ground her molars together, trying to ignore his tone—like she was a stray dog in need of his leftover scraps.

"Pammy ran away because of this fucking psycho you're so keen to research." He shook Holden's mug shot, hatred plain on his face. "He put all this garbage in her head about getting out, starting a new life for herself. *He's* to blame for what happened to Pammy. Not me. And you know what? Son of a bitch is lucky he's dead. Or I'd break his fucking neck myself." He crushed the mug shot into a ball in his fist and whipped it at her ankles.

She looked down but kept still, her heart pounding, her eyes frozen on the wadded paper. Let him think her petrified with fear. It wasn't wholly inaccurate. A part of her was terrified. And the other part—she tried to name what she felt.

Mad. Offended that he'd come here, into her home, her shop, sullied her happy place.

"That why you hate Holden so much?" she asked, her voice reedy. All at once, flashes of her masked dream came back. Younger Holden. The sting of the cigarette. She sucked in sharply. "You burned him," she whispered.

"Whadja say?" His eyes bugged wide as his shoulders flexed tighter. Her adrenaline rushed, his reaction equally satisfying and intimidating to behold.

"When you were kids in the foster home"—she shook her head in disgust—"you burned him with a cigarette in his sleep."

His smirk fell as he was taken aback, his face twitching in a series of conflicting expressions before folding inward. "Who the fuck—Rawlings tell you that shit?"

"Did you do the same to Pammy?"

He froze. Something in the air between them shifted.

Stop, Cain warned in her mind. *You're poking a bee's nest.*

She dropped her gaze, trying to dilute the confrontation. Too late. She felt him rather than saw him.

He lumbered toward her until the steel-toed tips of his work boots were in her line of vision. She couldn't help but cringe as his breath pulsed on her forehead, a sour mix of coffee and cigarettes. She told herself it was okay. She'd be all right. Even though he was a large man, he was a lot of bark—no bite. Yet. And he was also a typical male who saw her as a cowering young woman. So she let him get close. She could use that to her advantage, strike his weak spots before he could so much as lift a finger.

"Why the fuck you so interested in Pammy, huh?"

"I'm not," she said, somehow managing to keep the quiver in her gut from entering her tone. "I'm interested in the freak." She pinched her lips, held her breath, and looked up—allowed him to see the truth in her eyes. This had only ever been about Holden.

He sneered. "Whatever gets you off, sweetheart. But I got nothing more to say about that dead prick. So you better quit prying about him and my sister—*now*. I never wanna hear Pammy's name from your lips again. We understand each other?" He waited a beat to prolong his threat—to allow for it to settle into her bones.

She said nothing and flicked her eyes down again, keeping track of his limbs. He must have taken that as assent, because he kept going with his demands. "And while you're at it, get your boy Rawlings to back off. Else I'll come back. And next time, Mave Michael, I won't be so—"

He made the mistake of lifting his hand toward her face.

Whether he meant to brush a lock of her hair, grip her chin, or worse, she'd never find out.

TWENTY-NINE

Cain's *never let them touch you* rule took over. Speed over strength.

In one move, she slammed the stapler into his eye and rammed her knee into his groin.

He roared, buckled over while swatting the stapler stuck to his face. Before she could duck around him, down he went, taking her with him and shocking them both with the fall.

Her head and chest crushed under his hulking weight. Panic lanced her heart. She shoved an immovable wall, her nose and mouth gagged by muscle and fat. She tried to shimmy free her arms and legs, but he had her pinned—she couldn't breathe. A second more, and he grunted and shifted to retaliate—enough for her lungs to suck in his stink of sweat and for her limbs to release. She kicked off her heels, gaining better traction.

"Fucking bitch!" he snarled. Blood dripped from his pinched brow. He jerked to re-pin her by her wrists but managed to snag only one. She was a feral animal, twisting unpredictably to escape. He banged them into a table. Snow globes shattered. Faster. Smarter. She'd trained in mixed martial arts for years with Cain. Unless he leveraged his considerable body mass, she could get out.

She clawed his trachea and kneed him a second time—harder—the impact ripping her nails and bruising her quadricep. He released her with an unintelligible curse, doubled over. She rolled away, hardly feeling the glass that crunched into her flesh. She sprung to her feet, rushed to the door, and yanked, displacing the overhead bells. She raced down the vacant hall. She couldn't sense his pursuit but couldn't be sure either. A little further. A little more.

She waited until she reached the upper lobby before calling the police.

———

Without the panic threading her veins, her mistake crystalized. She hadn't been thinking straight. It had been a rash and careless decision to get Ren involved—one that threatened to get her caught in her own web of lies. Ren couldn't arrest Vincent, not without exposing her duplicity. Her only saving grace was the hotel's remote location. Mave had time to plan.

By the time Ren arrived, Vincent Lorde was long gone—where to, no one knew. The security cameras (no longer glitching) last recorded him stumbling through the conference wing and exiting the building from a side door.

"We really should get a medic to look at you," Ren said. He held his flashlight over her palm while she used tweezers to pull out the tiny shards of glass lodged in her skin.

"I'm fine," she said, "only surface cuts." She dropped a sliver into the kitchenette's sink. "Some antiseptic and I'll be as good as new. Just keep the light still, please." The staff lunch room had all of two lamps burning under forty watts each, drawing long shadows against its burgundy damask walls—better suited for employee naps than meal times.

"I know you say that, but, Mave..." He tilted his head, tried to catch her gaze. She pretended like she didn't notice, biting her lip in focus as she poked with the tweezers. He didn't relent. "Look, surface cuts or not, you need to press charges. Vin's committed more than one felony here—he broke in, attacked you."

Technically, she'd been the first to strike. And the second. Vincent hadn't done much more than accidentally topple onto her. As for breaking in, she was still fuzzy on the whole issue of the boutique's locked door.

"Victims in these types of assault..." His words trailed into a sigh. "What I'm trying to say is, it's normal if you're feeling—"

"I handled it," she cut him off. She was hardly a victim. Even if she was, she couldn't press charges. Morganson would book Vincent. He'd blab to the sheriff—to the reporters and god knew who else. He'd tell them all about her obsession with his former foster brother, Holden Frost. Too many of his answers would cast her under a suspicious light and lead Morganson back to her doorstep when she had a wedding to run and a ghost to locate. Not to mention the little part about her previous lie—that Sandy's stolen property was currently stashed inside Vincent's home. It had all blown up in her face. This was her own doing, the mess she'd made for herself.

"I handled it," she repeated under her breath.

"You did. That's not what I meant. It's just—Vin, I've known him a long time. He's more than an asshole with a chip on his shoulder. And he's smarter than he looks. If he comes around again, you don't engage. You turn, run if you have to, and you call me *immediately*."

She finally glanced up. "You make him sound really dangerous."

This time, he was the one to avert his gaze.

"Ren?"

He leaned forward on the tiled countertop and cursed under his breath. "I'm not supposed to say anything."

"About what?" she pressed.

"About the fact that he doesn't have an alibi for yesterday." He flicked his stare back to her, seemingly deciding to share parts of his investigation in confidence. "You didn't hear this from me," he said in a low voice, "but he was borderline hostile when we questioned him last night. And without the hotel's security tapes, we can't rule out he wasn't the one to dump Baker's body in your bedroom—especially when you find him here on the property, threatening you less than twenty-four hours later. I'm following up with your security, doing some routine interviews in case he was spotted yesterday by any of the hotel staff, but it doesn't look good. This is a big place. Lots of hallways and hiding spots."

"What about Liam?" she said, remembering the footage before the cameras cut out.

"Nathan's son, Liam?"

She nodded. "You mentioned the security tapes. Didn't you see him? I asked Oren to send Morganson the footage. Liam was here yesterday too. Skulking around."

"Yeah. Morganson already questioned him. Look, Liam's just a regular kid; he wouldn't leave a dead guy in your bedroom."

"Then what was he doing here?"

"Looking for a part-time job. Bastian confirmed he stopped by, asking about a dishwasher position in your kitchen. He's not who you need to be worrying about, Mave. It's Vin who's dangerous."

She shook her head. "What are you telling me? You think Vin is a killer?"

"Maybe. Maybe not. We can't prove anything. Yet. But it's clear he's trying to stir up shit for you, one way or another."

She glanced at the cuts on her hand and considered his warning, whether Vincent's visit could've been provoked by more than her lies. He'd certainly held on to his deep-seated hatred for Holden all these years. That was a big grudge to keep against a man who was supposedly dead. She struggled to guess the depths of his resentment. He hadn't even denied burning Holden with his cigarette. Come to think, he'd demanded to know if the source of her information was Ren.

She turned to him and blinked.

"What it is?" he asked, noticing her shift in worry. He placed a hand on her shoulder for comfort, but she tensed and suppressed a shiver.

Why would Vincent assume Ren might've told her Holden's secrets, unless...?

"When you were younger, in school together, did you know Vin burned other kids with cigarettes?" The question slipped from her lips before she could weigh its risk.

His expression darkened. He opened and closed his mouth, his thoughts unreadable. He drew back his hand and lifted his chin. His gaze sharpened.

Like a cop. Another mistake—she'd revealed too much.

"What's this about?" he said.

She was acutely aware that wasn't an answer.

Too late for second bets, M&M.

"That file you gave me. About my friend." She licked her lips, her mouth feeling like a dust bowl. "Did you know him?" In a way, it was a relief to finally get it out in the open, even if her heart had picked up its rhythm and the small of her back had pricked with sweat.

"You mean Holden Robert Frost." His drawl carried no inflection apart from its usual tranquil notes—no particular hatred or grief or fondness. She couldn't begin to dissect it.

She gave a subtle nod. "I read some more history on this place, found some old guest logs," she lied, struggling to keep control of the conversation before his suspicions kindled and caught fire. "I think he might have lived here. Or visited. For a bit."

"You're right."

About which part? she wanted to yell. She pinched her lips between her front teeth. It was better to wait, let the silence wear him down versus expose her desperation for clarity. As it was, her questions were marginally backfiring, revealing more of her secrets than his answers. Except he didn't elaborate. He merely interrogated her.

"Is that why you're so interested in what happened to him? You're digging into the hotel's history?"

She set aside the tweezers and crossed her arms. "Mm-hmm."

"He's not really your friend, is he? The Spirit of Dead Poets."

She froze. Her tongue felt stuck to the roof of her mouth. How did he know Holden's alias? Was he saying he was aware Holden worked illegally under the same name on the darknet? That he'd pretended to haunt the hotel for years?

"I wondered when you first asked about him," he said casually. Beneath his furrowed brow, his mouth slanted up slightly. "It's okay. I've seen what you can do."

"What I can do?" she repeated.

"Come on, Mave. Everyone knows this place is haunted. But I can't even begin to fathom what it's like to actually make contact."

"You mean..."

"With the ghost. I assume that's why you're digging into the story of Holden Frost."

It took her a second to process. He thought Holden was a real spirit. Because he'd drowned years ago. "Yeah. Of course." She tucked her hair behind her ears and cleared her throat. "Wasn't he the same age as—I mean, back then, when he was alive, wouldn't he and you have bumped into each other?" *Through Vincent. Or Pammy. At the château.*

"When we were kids, like eight or nine? Sure. I'd say we were even friends. Actually, he taught me a few of those hiding spots I was telling you about." He leaned his weight back onto the counter and crossed his ankles. The focus in his eyes melted in memory. "By the time we hit puberty, though, our lives had already taken different paths. Looked around for him when I visited in my early teens, but he was never in the usual spots." He shrugged. "Guess we'd grown too far apart. He learned to evade me and, eventually, I stopped looking and coming around all together."

"And then he drowned."

"Yeah. Damn shame. I remember feeling like I could have done something. Tried reaching out to him more."

"How do you mean?"

"Oh..." A confused look crossed his face. "I thought you'd heard—followed up on the drowning, too."

She had. She'd scoured every newspaper archive available in the county public library. During the timeframe of Holden's drowning, the most that had been printed was a passing line in the *Gazette*. She supposed a troubled boy's death hadn't exactly made for shocking headlines when there was neither a body washed up nor a family to mourn him.

She shook her head. "I don't understand. Was there some kind of foul play? With Vincent?"

"What? No, not at all. That's just it." His eyes grew distant, as if he were picturing the past all over again. "It was common knowledge in town, though I guess it was never official. He'd been too young at the time for a formal diagnosis. But you saw his rap sheet, all those arrests and red flags. He had early signs of antisocial personality disorder." He rubbed the back of his neck and blew out a heavy breath. "And that's only on the surface. No doubt the foster system was rough on him, fucked him up for good. Lots of kids get depressed, anxious, use self-harm as a cry for help. Except Holden was always more..." A hidden sentiment flickered in his eyes. "Extreme."

"Extreme how? What are you talking about?" A weight gathered in her chest. She didn't want the answer he was about to give.

"The drowning. He left behind a note. Dark stuff, poetry about death. Think he was quoting Walt Whitman." He blinked slowly, as if trying to clear the unpleasant memory. "Yeah, Holden Frost committed suicide."

———

Ren offered to stay the night. A security precaution, he suggested softly. But they both understood the subtext of his proposition. Even in another bedroom, on another floor, how long until he came knocking to check on her, and she gave in to her loneliness? Despite everything, the attraction between them remained. It would be all too easy to use him to shut off the twisted voices in her head, if only for one night...to escape.

But after their kiss, sleeping with him would be a terrible decision. Everything he'd revealed about the past, she didn't—couldn't fully trust him. Not so long as he was tangled in Holden's childhood and wore that badge. Somewhere along the way, a line had been crossed between the lawless and the lawful—between the lies and the truths. Whether that crossing had been committed by her or him was becoming increasingly difficult to gauge. It'd taken all her acting skills to convince him she was perfectly safe and to hide her paranoia as she turned him down. As soon as he left, she returned to the security office.

Oren must have been doing rounds. She locked herself inside and stared at the monitors without really seeing anything, the camera feeds flicking from hallway to hallway.

No eye may see. Walt Whitman's poem on death, the suicide note...

Her mind kept stumbling over Ren's claims.

According to the town of Hazel Springs, fifteen-year-old Holden Frost had committed suicide. *Or faked his own death.*

How much of Ren's version of the past was correct, and how much of it was twisted and exaggerated to fit a simple cover story? *Troubled foster kid drowns.* How she wished she could have drilled Ren for more details about the tunnels, Holden's foster care, his death. But at the end of the day, René Rawlings was an officer of the law. He couldn't help her, no matter how tempting his lips. And if she was being honest with herself, Cain's harsh judgement had infected her more than not.

What if it was a cover-up? What if Ren *knew* Holden had survived that supposed drowning years ago? He'd said so himself: they'd been friends. He might have been part of the ruse—made it seem like suicide. Her memory stirred. Fragments of her masked dreams sifted upward from her subconscious. Holden had told Bek-187 about her. They'd been friends.

Her eyes grew wide.

Was Ren that so-called friend? What if this entire time, he'd been aware of Holden's activity on the darknet, of his secret life as a criminal in the tunnels of the château? Or he'd been taking a cut to look the other way, and now that Holden was missing, he wanted him found in order to get more payments. Was that it? Or was her imagination running off with itself thanks to Cain?

If only she still had that horrible mask. Terrifying as it was, she could try to re-establish some sort of link to Holden's mind. There had to be a way to track it. The security feed blinked to the lower galleria. There was Oren, marching with a tool box to the Oasis Spa to install a new two-sided key bolt for the closet door. Watching him, an idea sparked.

She hurried out into the lobby and found Bastian sorting mail at the concierge's desk. She smiled brightly, hoping to dilute his concerned reaction. Ever since Baker's body had turned up in her suite, his face seemed permanently etched in worry.

"I'm fine," she said before he could fuss over her.

He didn't look convinced. "You always say that."

"Because it's true. Officer Rawlings is looking into it, and it's over. Everything's back to normal." She left out the bit about not pressing charges. "Anything for me?" she said, hoping to divert him back to his pile of mail.

Though she knew her last postcard couldn't have reached Cain yet, a sliver of dread still pierced her heart. Her father wasn't a man open to criticism from anyone, let alone his daughter.

"Just bills," Bastian said, sifting through the envelopes.

"Right." Debt she had to pay off by keeping the soon-to-arrive bride and her guests happy. No more dead bodies or sadistic bullies trespassing onto the property. "Speaking of bills, how are things going on your end with the wedding plans?"

Bastian sighed. "Glad you asked..." As he gave her his update, she was only half listening, too distracted by the anticipation of tracking. She found herself reflexively inhaling the metaphysical scents in the air —her inner eye already searching obsessively.

"...foam coolers for transporting them to the greenhouse. Their wings are super black. You think it'll work?"

"Hmm?" *Something about the lepidopterist's recommendations and the black butterflies,* her brain backfilled. "Oh. Yeah," she assured him, even though she understood nothing about shipping insects. "Sounds great."

He looked mildly relieved. "Anything else Bridezilla wants?"

"Not yet. But I was wondering about another thing. For me." She flashed another strained smile. "Any chance you have a copy of the key for the spa's closet where the old computer is stored?" She held back that the useless lock was currently being replaced by Oren. If Bastian was a second keyholder and his copy had been stolen, a small chance existed she could use her sixth sense to trace the key back to whomever had snatched her secret belongings from the box of oils—assuming that person still possessed the key. It was a lot of *ifs.*

"Just the one I already gave you," Bastian said. "Till recently, don't think anyone really bothered locking that closet. And with all the staff turnover"—he frowned—"safe bet any extra keys walked off or got misplaced."

Misplaced. Of course. That wasn't the issue, dammit. She needed an owner to track. Her shoulders slumped.

"Mave?" Bastian asked her. "You sure you're okay? You want me to call—?"

"No, it's nothing."

"Hey, I heard you had a séance the other night. Maybe Gracelyn can help," he suggested. "Do what you do to find lost stuff, but with her tea leaves."

Unlikely, but he may have been on to something. Mave checked the time on her phone. "Is Gracelyn here?" She should've memorized the daily schedule and inwardly scolded herself.

"Think she's finishing up with a tour in the mezzanine," he replied.

"In that case, can you radio her and ask her to meet me in the library? And I'll get a head start on setting up."

Gracelyn might not have been able to see into the past to point the finger at the thief. But Mave was willing to bet the ghost of Gerald Lee Baker sure could.

THIRTY

Mave lit the candles on the pedestal table.

"Thought you wanted another tea leaf reading," Gracelyn said, standing above her with a steaming kettle. "Another séance? To find a misplaced key?" Beside her, Katie looked equally dumbfounded. Mave had bumped into her on the way down to the library and asked her tag along without disclosing much.

"I figured we could, you know," Mave improvised, waving circles with her hands, "ease any negative juju or whatever. With the wedding coming up and all that's happened, I want to make sure the air is clear."

"Oh, well, I suppose..." Gracelyn seemed to reconsider her kettle. She set it on the fireplace mantel. "In that case, I should probably bring down some sage to burn, and that'll take—"

"*No*," Mave interrupted. Both Katie and Gracelyn stared at her. "I'd really prefer to give the séance another go."

"How come?" Katie absently picked at her chipped nail polish. "Last one didn't work."

Except it had. Even if she'd been the sole person with a mind freakish enough to sense Baker's ghost.

"Mave Michael," Gracelyn said, her face pleated in concern, "if you insist on a spur-of-the-moment ceremony, then candles aren't enough. We need a proper circle, more participants. That reminds me..." She dug into the handwoven hobo bag full of supplies she toted, and pulled out a weathered paperback. "Here. I found this in my drawer the other day and thought of you. It used to belong to my mother." She held it out for her.

Curious despite her impatience, Mave accepted and browsed the book's title: SIGNS: A HANDBOOK FOR CLAIRVOYANCE.

"You have a leaf through," Gracelyn suggested, "while I zip upstairs and see if I can round up a few tour stragglers to join us."

"Hang on," Mave said, "can't we just—?"

But Gracelyn was already on the move. "Won't be but a minute," she called over her shoulder. Her footsteps faded out the library's French doors.

"So..." Katie sat across from her and chewed on her fingernail. "Guess we wait, huh?"

Mave sighed. She didn't need a handbook. She didn't need a proper circle. In fact, just maybe... She wondered if her sixth sense alone, raw and underdeveloped, could be enough to re-attract Gerald Lee Baker's ghost. Gracelyn inadvertently implied it the other day: Mave was a lighthouse. The dead would come. She simply needed a little nudge in the right direction, and someone supportive to reorient her when she fell back to reality.

Someone like Katie.

"Here." Mave reached out to take her hands.

"Huh?" Katie blinked. "What are you doing? Gracelyn said to—"

"I'm too nervous to do this with strangers. It'll be fine. Between the two of us, we'll remember how this works. Just humor me. Please." She no longer cared if she sounded slightly manic. It only mattered that she uncover who'd been spying on her, who'd taken her secret belongings from a spot impossible to detect.

Who left me a rotting corpse in my bed.

They were connected. And Gerald Lee Baker would know his assailant.

Her insistence must have worked. Katie mumbled, "What the hell," with a shrug and clasped her hands fully to form a ring. Despite her apparent nonchalance, Katie's grip was rigid. Mave tried to slow her pounding pulse as they went through Gracelyn's rules from memory: both feet planted firmly on the ground, patience and centeredness. They even attempted the breathing exercises.

This time, Mave and Katie chanted the words of spiritual invitation together.

Almost immediately, a light wind brushed the nape of Mave's neck. It was so subtle, she thought she might have imagined it. She resisted the urge to scratch her neck and check over her shoulder. She kept still, concentrating. She repeated Gracelyn's welcome—an incantation of sorts: *Come. A safe place.* She pushed deeper, inwardly summoned him by name: *Gerald Lee Baker. Come.* The chandelier overhead stirred in the twirling draft, its crystal beads clinking. The room grew colder, darker. Mave saw her breath clouding a second before the wicks of the candles drowned in their wax. One by one, they extinguished with audible hisses that made her lungs tighten.

Her attempt to exhale long and slow released a stutter. Silence gathered. It ballooned in one space while Katie continued to chant in the other. The noise of reality gradually grew more and more smothered, negated by a hush like a gap, a fissure expanding. Here. There.

Mave felt her consciousness splintering in two. She tried not to fight it despite her blood thinning in alarm—her stomach tightening and twisting, smaller and smaller like a rag being wrenched. Her nose pricked like the onset of a sneeze that wouldn't release.

Plastic.

The ghost of Gerald Lee Baker manifested before her, shimmering like bitter heat off tar. As if he'd been around this entire time, waiting for her.

His skin appeared mottled, animated. Crawling with maggots. Her instinct was to scream and recoil and break the circle. Instead, she kept a clammy hold of Katie's hands...until everything dissolved except for the gore and anguish of the man wavering before her. A grievance. A haunting. This is what she'd asked for—willingly invited into her mind.

Her eyes teared. The after-world was a frozen void, an invisible and shuddering frequency of pain trapped inside the physical library of Château du Ciel. Yet on the outside, all was normal for Katie. Not a draft stirred. Not a person cried out in alarm. Mave knew her connection wouldn't last much longer. She squinted harder to see the ghost hovering in and out of her mind's eye.

Given the rabid energy he emitted, he seemed just as confused and agitated as before, uncontrollably craving his lost belongings: "*Where-where-where?*" It burned. Her lungs constricted and her sixth sense grated in pain—his longing insatiable and restless.

His stolen items, now miles away, sharpened in the darkness. Packaged and labelled in evidence bags. Boxed. Locked. But that's not what she needed. She tried bending her inner eye to her will, but it was no use. Her nose pricked with airborne plastic. Her focus kept retracting, whipping her attention back like the jerk of a leash; over and again to the police station in Hazel Springs.

His keyboard, mouse, modem.

She wasn't a proper medium, had no control. She only understood how to track the damned inanimate objects. It didn't matter that they were useless to her now. Her reflex governed itself.

"*No!*" Mave cried into the void, "*How did—?*"

She tasted wet polymer. Blood trickled in her sinuses. She choked through it—her itch, his pain.

"*Did...did someone do this to you?*"

His pink-marbled eyes sprung wide. He'd heard her through his longing.

All at once, a sack cinched over her face—nose, mouth, ears. Blackness. Bubbles. Polyethylene licks. She gagged. Struggled for air. Clawed at nothing. Her veins popped purple. Her lungs convulsed blue. And the answers materialized with a stabbing fire that ripped through her trachea and streaked down, down deep into her chest.

Gerald Lee Baker hooded with a plastic bag.

Dying of asphyxiation.

Never seeing his attacker—ever present and faceless.

He could tell her nothing. Gerald Lee Baker knew nothing. His murderer had sprung at him from behind.

THIRTY-ONE

The entire staff seemed to be on pins and needles as the cinerous clouds rolled in with the wedding party. Competing perfumes —Black Opium, Miss Dior, Chanel No.5—wet footprints, and luggage wheels streaked the lobby. Rivulets of rain veined the château's steep copper rooftops black, and drummed on its windows with an impatient crescendo. The bride had already checked into the honeymoon suite without incident, but Mave was far from in the clear. If anything, the disorder was merely being caressed and glossed over as it continued to simmer beneath the surface, like an ever-bulging boil dabbed with makeup and seconds from bursting.

While the weather forecast called for a washed-out weekend, Mave still hadn't addressed the dribbling leaks in the greenhouse with Amos. Maintenance was struggling to secure the corridor tents through the muddy gardens, and VIP guests were trickling in by the hour with requests for sold-out umbrellas and emergency dry cleaning. That wasn't all they wanted.

Could the temperature be lowered or raised? Could the pillows be softer or firmer? Julián fluttered through the lobby, overseeing the front desk, ensuring no guest left the lobby without a welcome black currant martini or black cherry shooter in hand. Guests loaded into the gilded elevator cars with their cocktails and red-stained lips, snapping selfies.

The château's art deco and romanticism were tempering any complaints. For now.

Mave watched them from the security monitors in the back offices. The occasional squeal of a reunion travelled through the walls and scraped her nerves. She made sure all the cameras were functional, debriefed with Oren, and headed to the greenhouse with a wheel of extension cords for the string lights—electrical that had yet to be checked for burnt fuses.

Everything was under control, she told herself. She was handling it. There was still time.

It was okay that Bridezilla had ordered custom haute goth uniforms for the staff working the wedding without consulting either her or Julián. It was okay that the shipment of black swallowtail butterflies would arrive at the eleventh hour. And that four guests were already whining about the mountain pollen and their dust allergies, and demanding air purifiers be delivered to their rooms while the black tulips be removed asap.

Entirely. Under. Control.

A few hours later, she was nearly done rearranging the last terracotta pots with Amos, her clothes damp from a mixture of rainwater and sweat, when her cellphone rang with an internal number.

Julián. She answered and listened to an update that made her heart stop: Rats. In the kitchen. The health code violation had been spotted and averted by the sous-chef. Only a few staff members knew about the disaster. *Contained*, Julián said, sounding exhausted. They had trapped the three vermin before any guest caught wind. The potentially contaminated food, meanwhile, had been thrown out, and the space sanitized. Even so, dread swirled in Mave's chest. What if they'd missed more rats, or droppings in the foie gras? Not five minutes after Julián's call, her ringtone gave her another start.

Dear god, what now?

A private number glowed on the display. She was tempted to decline.

"Hello?" she breathed, wiping her forehead.

"You alone?"

She stilled, immediately recognizing his growl—the same one she reflexively heard and used in her head. "Dad?"

"*Are* you alone?" he repeated with an edge.

She frowned. "Huh?" Amos had already left for another chore. "Yeah, why?" No collect call this time. He must have been using a smuggled cellphone, which also meant the prison authorities weren't monitoring their conversation.

"You're in trouble," he said, catching her off guard.

"I'm—?" She scanned her peripheries, momentarily alarmed, as if an attacker were hidden in the greenhouse. "What are you talking about? I'm fine." Her eyes fell on the vines covering the secret hatch. The two little scripted words, *I'm fine*, had never sounded more inappropriate. Cain must have thought so, too, because he called her out.

"If you think crying foul to a cop after some shit-for-brains local tries laying hands on you is *fine*, then you're worse off than I thought. You need to tell me what's going on. Now."

"How do you know about—?" She snapped her jaw shut, her temples throbbing. He was watching. Always watching. Her chest visibly rose and fell, irritation climbing with her pulse. If only it were that easy to defy him—trust him. Childhood insecurities flooded her mind. She dug her nails into her palm, refusing to regress. "So, what, we're back to me taking your orders like a good little girl? We're just going to ignore the fact that you're invading my privacy, *again?* Did you even read my last postcard?"

"Listen to me, Mave Michael. Very carefully. I never asked Stratis to pay you a visit."

Her throat constricted. "What?"

"Stratis. I haven't spoken to him since January."

"No, that's—" What was he suggesting? Was this another test? A lie? She paced to the corner and leaned on the old sink. "That's not right. He told me you and he were..." Her voice trailed off. She stared at her feet where she'd first seen the bloodstains.

Cain Francis has no friends, her instinct whispered.

"Told you we were what?" he barked. "Recite it exactly, word for word."

She swallowed thickly. "He said you were concerned about me, and he was there to...to..." *Fix my problems.*

"Goddammit. He's on another job." An unspoken threat threaded his words and triggered goosebumps on her arms. "What did you say to him?"

"What? Nothing!" She was still a step behind, struggling to untangle Cain's secrets from those of the fix-it man who'd showed up at the penthouse. "This makes no sense. Why would he—?" She shook her head. "No. *You're* his contact."

"Wrong. He's not working for me. Not this time."

"But someone else is. Who is it? Who do you have out here spying on me?" She wished she could see him, hit him, make him understand.

"You need to pay attention, M&M. My source isn't the issue."

"Of course it is! You expect me to trust you, but you can't extend that same trust to me! It's never been a two-way street with you."

"Don't confuse strategy with trust. It's for your own good."

"Prying into my life, sticking your nose where it doesn't belong isn't good. It never has been. It's underhanded—violating and demeaning. Even the fact that you're calling your lies a strategy tells me how messed up this is."

"I've never lied to you. Now we don't have a lot of time. You need to focus on—"

"No time, huh?" Something inside her snapped. His conditions sounded an awful lot like Bek-187's countdown. "Why can't you just admit it? You did this. You're withholding information, vital information." She scoffed, uncaring if she sounded petulant. If she couldn't level her frustration at Bek-187, Cain would have to do. "Why do I even bother? It's always the same with you! You never told me about my mother. My grandmother. Or Holden. Now this."

"What's *this?*" he hissed.

"Oh, no, I'm not falling for it. No more keeping me in the dark, do you understand me?" Her heart rammed in her ears. "Now I'm going to ask you one last time: who the hell is your spy?" She heard his even breaths, the wheels of his mind turning, calculating. For a second, she was almost hopeful.

"It's not up for discussion," he said.

"Then neither is my life."

"Don't be stupid, Mave Michael. You're letting your emotions—"

"Stop patronizing me! You don't get to tell me what I'm allowed to feel and not feel. This is exactly why I've avoided you for the past four years. You don't know how to stop, how to respect me or my choices. You think you're helping, but you're only making it worse!"

"You need to calm down. You don't realize what you're—"

She hung up on him and stared at the screen. Her jaw grinded and her hand shook. She'd never disobeyed him outright. She could hardly believe she'd cut him off mid-sentence. No doubt, he'd be seething at her insolence. *Good*, she thought, *let him have a taste of his own medicine.* "No more," she uttered. If her father couldn't be honest with her, learn to accept her boundaries, then they had no chance of moving forward.

When the phone buzzed a minute later with a private number, she ignored the ring and shut off her cell. Let him get her voicemail, she fumed. Let him be the helpless one in the dark.

———

Later that evening, after repeatedly directing guests during peak hours, signing impromptu invoices, tracking three lost room keys, and smoothing over a double booking, she finally checked her cellphone's notifications. She'd received two missed calls from a private number and one voicemail. Begrudgingly, she ignored the latter and waited until it was past midnight. She lay in the penthouse's guestroom, battling insomnia despite her physical exhaustion, until curiosity finally wore down her stubbornness.

She grabbed her phone off the nightstand and played the voice recording. Her heavy eyelids sprung wide. It wasn't from Cain. And it wasn't good news. Late night messages from unlisted numbers seldom were.

THIRTY-TWO

As rain dribbled over the edges of her umbrella and onto her rubber boots, Mave forbid her feet from reversing back to her car. "You sure he isn't home?" she said to Ren. Only Sheriff Morganson's SUV was parked in the driveway. But that meant nothing. It might have been a bluff, a pretense to falsely suggest he was elsewhere. Or he might have left his truck in his garage considering the continuous bad weather.

"Don't worry," Ren said. "With a possible homicide, Vin's too much of a coward." Earlier this morning, she'd called Ren in reply to his voicemail from the station, and he'd updated her on Baker's autopsy. The old man's death had been filed as undetermined. She refrained from blurting out that Baker had been murdered by asphyxiation with a plastic bag over his head. "Vin knows he's in hot water," Ren added. "He's probably skipped town for a few days. No one's seen or heard from him since he broke into your gift shop and threatened you." He marched ahead, obviously eager to raid the home.

Exactly! she wanted to say to him. Vincent had threatened her to get the cops *off* his back, not to have them barge into his home. Yet here they were, two days later with the sheriff already inside, conducting her official investigation.

What did you think would happen when you falsely accused him? she berated herself. *So he's a lifelong bully and jerk, that doesn't make him the professional thief. Or the killer.*

The authorities, however, clearly considered Vincent Lorde a menace to society. Though Mave hadn't pressed charges, in a small town like Hazel Springs, apparently mere claims of an alleged theft, assault, and breaking and entering had been enough to convince a judge to issue a warrant.

As Ren held the door open for her, she pretended to be busy shaking the water from her umbrella under the portico. "You go on. Be right there," she said. As soon as he disappeared and the door shut, she dropped her smile and rubbed her aching head.

Since hearing his voice message for her to join the search and continue consulting on the investigation, Mave couldn't decide if Ren's invitation was a good or bad sign. In fact, it'd been Morganson's idea. The sheriff had suggested Mave's psychic tracking might uncover any remaining stolen property with precision, just like she'd demonstrated with Mrs. Hess's computer. Mave was as good as any GPS or radar detector. Of course, she now saw the irony and scolded herself for her lack of useful foresight. Trust between her and the sheriff had been touch and go from the moment they'd met last winter. Who knew if Morganson really believed in her sixth sense, or if she was testing Mave's character.

Liar. Lawbreaker, an acidic voice inside her whispered. *You're the one who should be charged with theft and assault and breaking and—*

She wiped her feet on the coir mat with vigor. Ultimately, Vincent Lorde was a walking, talking threat to her—a threat she'd have *less* control over if she were absent when they rummaged through his home and came up empty-handed. At least this way, she could do damage control in real time. She already knew it wouldn't end well. It was just a matter of how badly—like losing control of a car on a slippery road. The trouble was already in motion, with no way to stop its momentum. You could only brace yourself and prepare for the hit.

She yanked open the door and stepped inside. Ren and Sheriff Morganson were speaking in hushed voices on the other side of a cramped and unattractive living room. Morganson greeted her with a brisk nod and held up her palm, ordering her to wait where she was.

Mave shifted uncomfortably. She couldn't hear everything over the pattering rain outside, but caught bits and pieces of their briefing. Something about a locksmith and Morganson being here for hours. She ordered Ren to go to the basement. Watching him be dismissed to another room, Mave felt her nerves prick.

"Thanks for coming," Morganson said.

"Sure. Anything to help." Mave smiled tightly and looked around. Vincent's décor was dated, with wall-to-wall '70s wood paneling. The dirty grey carpet might have been once green. "So," she said a little too loudly, "where do we start?"

Morganson pulled out a pair of gloves and approached her. "Put these on first," she said, her tone all business. As she went over procedures—noting not to touch anything more than once—Mave continued her visual inventory.

Despite having a large front window, the bungalow was extra gloomy and damp from the rain. It smelled mildly of rotten garbage. Nothing remarkable stood out. No family photos or creepy shrine of a younger runaway sister—at least, not in the front room. A chunky recliner sat across from of an oversized flat-screen TV; a table with an empty pizza box, crumbs, coffee rings, and beer bottle caps.

"You're timing is perfect," Morganson informed her as Mave slipped on the gloves. "We've actually just finished searching the place." She sounded casual, though something in her sharp gaze set Mave further on edge.

Anxious to break eye contact, Mave glanced down and readjusted her gloves. The sheriff had found absolutely nothing in Vincent's home, hadn't she? And now Mave was under extra scrutiny. "Vincent's not here, right?" she said, allowing worry to thin out her voice. Let Morganson think she was scared of him. Not her.

"He's not," the sheriff confirmed. "Looks like he might've taken off in a hurry, too. Left behind his razor and toothbrush in the bathroom. Food spoiling in the kitchen." That would explain the rotten smell,

Mave thought. Morganson cocked her head, staring at her too closely for comfort. "Convenient, I guess."

She cleared her throat. "How so?" *Convenient that he's not here to expose me as a fraud?*

Morganson frowned somewhat. "That's why you're here."

Mave rolled her lips under her teeth and played with a lock of hair behind her ear. *Quit fidgeting,* Cain cautioned in her mind.

"To do another psychic reading for the stolen goods," Morganson added when she offered no reply.

Oh. She nodded and ordered her shoulders to relax. "Mm-hmm." Her mouth pinched into another smile. *Relax, goddammit! You're acting guilty.* "Right," she said. Morganson didn't return her smile. It was one thing to mislead Ren—a man with an obvious attraction toward her—quite another to fool the sheriff.

"So," Morganson said, "in your first reading, what room did you say you saw Sandy's property?"

She hadn't. Her mouth felt dry. *Quick. Make something up,* her defenses cried. She crossed her arms and moved slowly about the room, staring at the walls like a secret door was hidden within one. "It wasn't like that," she said, figuring a half-truth would work better in this scenario. "Each reading is unique, and with Sandy's things, I didn't pick up on any clear room here."

"But you felt this house, this address," Morganson challenged. "Rawlings said you named it, right down to its street number."

"That's right." Her throat tightened.

"And now?"

"Now?" she repeated, her voice hitched in feigned confusion.

"Where do you feel Sandy's stolen property?" Morganson said.

"I feel..." She cleared her throat, closed her eyes, and counted to ten, pretending to track. She let out a huff of frustration. "I'm sorry." She shook her head.

"It's all right," Morganson said. "Take your time."

"Hey, Sheriff," Ren called from below. "Can you come down here a sec?"

"Maybe give yourself a minute to relax," Morganson advised with a stern look. She had undoubtedly noticed her nerves. "I'll be back in a moment." She turned and left for the basement, leaving Mave alone in the living room.

"Relax," Mave exhaled with a hand on her diaphragm. *Easier said than done.* She inched a few steps further inside. Confirming Morganson and her team were occupied in the basement running down from the kitchen, she wandered through the home's single hallway. The bungalow was small. It took less than a minute to orient herself to its remaining layout: one dingy bathroom with molded tiles and strewn towels; one cramped bedroom with walnut furniture and an aroma of sour sweat; and one smaller bedroom that had been converted into a gym/workroom.

Mave crossed her arms and stepped over a row of iron dumbbells. Through shadows, she peeked at Vin's junk, collected and mounted on the walls. A football jersey and flag, an unlit neon beer sign, a carved wooden fish, a garland of stuffed rabbits' feet. Drawn to a bookshelf, she clicked on her phone's flashlight and scanned plastic trophies, a stereo, water bottles, a teapot. She had a tough time picturing Vincent's thick fingers handling the delicate handle. She paused her inventory on the spines of three old yearbooks. With a quick glance over her shoulder to make sure no police had snuck up from the basement, she slipped out the edition marked 2006.

Hazel Springs High School. Home of the Hawks.

She flipped open the cover, perused a few scribbled signatures, year-end farewells and inside jokes, then leafed to the junior class. Vincent's photo was easy to spot. His head filled the entire frame of his portrait like an overinflated tire. He wasn't bald yet, no goatee, but he possessed the same thick neck. Beady eyes.

She flipped back to search the sophomore class and found René Rawlings. Though riddled with acne, his face was pleasant. Chiseled. With warm eyes and a lopsided grin. Light footsteps and chatter drifted from the kitchen. Time was up.

Mave made to shut the yearbook, when another name caught her eye. No photograph, just a listing to denote the student belonged to the same cohort and had been absent on picture day.

Holden Robert Frost.

With a sharp breath through her nose, she quickly snapped the cover closed, reached to the small of her back, and shoved the entire yearbook into her waistband. She was pulling the hem of her shirt over her hips when Morganson strode into the room.

"What are you doing in here?" she said.

"Having a look around," Mave replied, "for a reading, like you wanted. It helps sometimes. To change rooms."

"That right?"

Mave nodded in innocence. It was hard to tell whether Morganson bought her act.

"And?"

Mave furrowed her brow and looked around, as if surveying Vincent's clutter for the first time. "The stolen items...they're not here anymore. He must have moved them."

For a moment, Morganson said nothing, merely observed her with a curious gleam in her eye. "You sure?" she said, finally breaking the tense silence. "No new visions coming up?"

Mave ran her tongue along her teeth and shook her head. "Nope," she breathed, "nothing." Her gaze slid over Morganson's shoulder. Ren stood and watched them through the doorway, a silent sentry.

"I'm sorry," Mave added, staring at Ren, "if this was a waste of your time." He'd disclosed his friendship with Holden as a child; but he'd held back that they'd attended the same high school. *Why?* Why lead her to believe he'd lost all contact?

"No need to apologize," Morganson said. "We got more than enough on Lorde."

Her attention flicked back to the sheriff. Surely, she'd heard wrong. "You mean you found Sandy's computer?" She couldn't hide her surprise.

Morganson's shrewd gaze missed nothing. "Not that," she said, her brow cocked with undue interest in Mave's reaction. "A hidden safe. We managed to open it. Some interesting contents inside."

Ren smirked.

Mave's stomach tied itself into knots. All at once, she imagined

Holden's mask and her journal stashed in this awful house—all her secrets and wishes stupidly scribbled within like she was a twelve-year-old with her first diary. "Oh, wow." She used all her strength to stem the panic from her voice. "What was inside?" She crossed her arms and felt the yearbook tighten against her slick back. "I mean, if it's okay to ask."

Morganson took her time responding, her expression hard. "Drugs," she said, jarring Mave's bloodstream further with shock and relief. "Looks like Vincent has been stocking quite the illegal pharmacy here."

THIRTY-THREE

She took her time, pretending to browse overpriced cereals. The Main Street general store was across from the diner where, days ago, she'd had lunch with Ren. The handles of her shopping basket dug into her wrist. The discomfort was nothing compared to her impatience—growing like a rash, angry and red. She'd been wrong about Vincent's involvement. Yes, he was a shady creep who deserved jailtime, but not because of some long-awaited revenge on Holden Frost. Mave was starting to believe Vincent might truly believe Holden was dead, because it seemed his need for Ren to back off had neither to do with Bek-187's threat nor Gerald Lee Baker's murder. Vincent had other sins to hide. Which only made Mave all the more determined to uncover who *was* involved.

Who in Hazel Springs was invested in locating the Spirit of Dead Poets? Or in hurting her father in prison? After her frustrating conversation with Cain, the latter seemed the clearer threat to investigate. So here she was. Still in town for a last-minute rendezvous she'd set up.

She spun a candy rack, half regarding ingredients on packets. *Glucose syrup. Dextrose. Yellow 5.* The other half of her focus lay through the store's fogged-up windows. Her phone chimed in her pocket.

Bastian had sent her a thumbs-up in reply to her thanks. She released a quiet sigh, glad she'd recruited his help to retrieve the number from the penthouse, not trusting Julián's anxious energy. Earlier, the hotel director had messaged a string of texts about Bridezilla's demands for more candelabras breaking fire code. He'd hinted Mave was needed back at the château. But she had more urgent plans to oversee. Her trap was set. It was nearly time. The VIP guests would simply have to wait. Besides, she'd return in plenty of time for the rehearsal dinner. Any last-minute candles or rats or drama, she'd contend with then.

Mave checked the time. One more minute until her meeting.

Would he come? Would he predict she was scheming, spying from across the street?

Like father, like daughter.

She fixed her attention back through the window and idly spun the candy rack. Her stomach tightened in anticipation. Like a wolf. She wouldn't miss the prey.

———

She followed Stratis on foot, leaving a comfortable distance between them. Given she couldn't hide behind a wig and sunglasses in the downpour, she did the next best thing and lowered her umbrella over her head just shy of obscuring her vision. A few blocks away from the diner, Stratis slowed near a black Honda Civic, presumably his car. Mave was relieved to see it was an older model. Easier to break into. As he dug into his pocket for his key fob, she ducked behind a row of hedges and quickly sent him another text as his door locks beeped.

Sorry I'm late. At the diner now. Are you here? I can't see you.

She peeked around the branches and watched him read the message. He looked up and paused, his expression shadowed by the hood of his raincoat.

Come on, she thought. *You came all this way...*

A second later, he took the bait.

As his steps rustled past, splashing puddles, she edged around the hedges, making sure to remain out of sight. Once she was confident he was halfway back to the diner, she snuck to his car. The rain worked to her advantage; no one else roamed the street. She needed a reach tool, like a car antenna, but she was reluctant to vandalize.

She pulled out the screwdriver she'd purchased at the general store, and a moment later, was relieved to find her creative troubleshooting unnecessary. *Small towns*, she thought, pulling open the rear door Stratis hadn't bothered to relock.

She pocketed her screwdriver, climbed inside, and let out a slow breath. Her heart fluttered wildly as she made herself invisible on the floor of the backseat.

Patience, Cain whispered

Being a wolf required you wait.

———

Eventually—after she ignored his texts and stood him up—he returned to his car. No doubt, he was irritated and disgruntled with her manipulation. Mave was thankful when the engine started, its purr masking the rush of her breath.

They drove for hours. Side roads. Then the freeway. She'd powered off her phone, too afraid the glow of its screen might give her away. There was no way to track the time or their route. Rather, she lay perfectly still, curled on the floor behind the driver's seat. Had it not been for her adrenaline working overtime, the lull of the motor might have put her to sleep.

At last, he turned off the freeway and after more avenues, lights, and turns, they arrived at his destination. Given the healthy traffic and power lines she'd glimpsed, they had to be near a city. Maybe Denver.

She inwardly kicked herself for not considering the potential distance. Of course Stratis wouldn't be a resident of Hazel Springs. But how was she supposed to return to pick up Bastian's SUV, still parked near Vincent's home, and make it back to the hotel in time for the rehearsal dinner?

Worry about that later, she scolded herself.

She waited until Stratis exited his car. The sharp beep of the door locks sounded like a reward in a video game. *Level achieved*. Alone again, Mave sighed.

She unfolded and massaged her limbs. She'd never been more grateful for her small frame. (She couldn't imagine a giant like her security guard, Oren, crammed on the floor, lasting for the duration of that ride.) She turned on her phone to check its GPS, and got distracted by three new texts from Julián—the last of which detailed Bridezilla's demand for a minimum of three pennies, dated the year of her wedding, to be polished, then spray painted in black enamel, then supplied for each guest to make wishes in a nearby natural spring. With a suppressed groan, Mave manually popped the door lock and slipped outside.

She quietly clicked the rear door shut and surveyed her surroundings: a middle-class residential street. At the top of the driveway where they'd parked stood a two-story brick house. Stratis must have disappeared inside. Of all the possible roles of the fix-it conman who had shown up at her penthouse door, she hadn't considered suburban family man. The windows of the home were open, amplifying laughter and children's squeals from inside, clinks and water running, someone washing dishes.

Mave skulked around to the backyard, thinking she could get a glimpse through a window without alerting any neighbors. But the rear of the property wasn't empty.

Stratis stood on the lawn, absently pushing a young girl no more than four or five years old on a plastic swing set. His eyes were downcast, attention held on his phone.

Mave froze a little too late. The girl caught her trespassing. Even with baby fat, she had the same long face as her father. "Look, Daddy," she said, and pointed.

Stratis slowly drew his eyes away from his phone, perhaps expecting a bird or a rabbit. He gave a hard blink. When the swing rocked back to him for another push, he held onto its rope handles and eased it to a stop.

"Ella, I have to speak to this lady. Go wait inside."

"But, Daddy—"

"Inside," he repeated more sternly. "You can have some ice cream."

That seemed to do the trick. While still staring at Mave, Ella hopped off the swing and headed indoors. Mave and Stratis both waited until the patio door slid closed before acknowledging each other. She made the first move.

All subtlety thrown to the wind, she strode into the fenced yard and folded her arms over her chest.

Stratis frowned. "This is certainly a surprise, Mave Michael. Care to tell me what you're doing here?"

"I'm not going to tell you anything." She stopped a few feet away. The swing set stood between them.

Things get ugly, M&M, use the rope handle—wring it around his neck.

Stratis tilted his ear. "I don't follow. Especially after your last text..." He gestured with his phone. "Why request we meet at the diner, then not show up, then come all this way to my private home?"

"Like you did mine?" *Hypocritical bastard.* "Because you lied."

His brow peaked into his hairline. "I beg your pardon?"

"You lied," she repeated, annunciating the words more forcibly, "about who hired you. And before you say it's Cain again, please know that I spoke to my father, and he's less than pleased with whatever job you're working."

"Ah." He slid his hands in his pockets. "I see."

"Do you? Because I have a direct line to him on a smuggled burner." She held up her cellphone, emphasizing her bluff. "One text, and I can tell him to finish it."

He studied her carefully through his gold wire glasses. "Finish what?"

"The hit on you."

His face twitched. "Cain would never—"

"You really think that?" she interjected. "Obviously, you're nothing close to being his *friend*."

"May I ask for how long this has been going on?"

"What's that?"

"Well, last Cain and I spoke, you were refusing to respond to his letters. I wrongly assumed that was still the case."

His postcards, she nearly corrected him. Cain didn't write letters. He liked brevity. Efficiency. No point in sealing envelopes when the authorities might tear them open and read every line. Stratis was waiting for her reply, his expression too patient for her liking.

"We've been in touch since the fire at the château." She saw no harm in giving him a straight answer.

He gave a slow nod. "Of course."

"Of course, what? You didn't think I'd reach out to him? Find out you were working for someone else?" she spat. "Who is it, who hired you to pretend to fix my problems?"

"I was never pretending, and I'm afraid I'm not privy to—"

"Really?" She raised her phone again and made a show of hovering her finger over the make-believe number for Cain's burner. "Just one text," she said in a low voice. If he forced her hand, rather than alert Cain, she'd end up messaging Julián the word *Go*. Her mind was already prepping dialogue to keep up the ruse. Luckily, she didn't need it.

"It's not what you think."

"The name. Now."

"All right. Fair played," Stratis said. "Just put down your phone, please, and I'll share with you what I know about my client. As long as you agree to call off Cain."

Mave lowered her cell. "Speak, then."

"At present time," he said, "my client is known as Thom Stearns."

Something in the recesses of her subconscious stirred—a memory too faint to articulate. "What does that mean, *at present time*?" *Thom Stearns*, she mentally echoed. She didn't know any Thoms, and yet... "It's not his real name?"

"Correct."

Her pulse picked up its rhythm, anticipation flushing her with heat. "And does he have one—a real name—or another alias?" Her muscles flexed, readying, waiting for the blow that Stratis had been contracted by Bek-187.

"He does," he verified. She could sense the cogs of his mind turning —the pause painful to wait through. "But it's not the one you're thinking of," he finally added.

"How the hell would you know what I'm thinking?"

"Because, Mave Michael, I never lied about my skillset." A part pompous, part defensive smile curled his lips. "To solve problems, it's my job to know things, or, at least, to make educated guesses and calculate the odds. And I'd wager right now, there's a three to one chance you think Thom is someone from the darknet. But he's not *them*."

"Them *who*?" she said, her jaw tightening.

"Bek-187."

The ground thinned. She reached out her hand and gripped the swing set. Was this man the real thing, or an expert con?

"Thom goes by The Spirit of Dead Poets," Stratis continued, each word causing the spin in her head to worsen, "and if I'm not mistaken, I believe he adopted his latest pseudonym from a famous poet he admires."

Thom Stearns, Mave realized, finally placing its familiarity, too stunned to say it aloud. Holden's latest alias paid homage to T.S. Eliot.

PART FOUR
DEATH DO US PART

Do not fear the connection, however proceed with caution. Those who linger in the afterlife are no more or less dangerous than the living. Good and evil does not end with death. If anything, it is exacerbated.

—SIGNS: A HANDBOOK FOR CLAIRVOYANCE

THIRTY-FOUR

Thom Stearns—T.S. Eliot! That's what had been stirring in the back of her mind. Her brain digested the information swiftly, swallowing it whole like the starving. *How very like Holden.* It seemed too good to be true. As if Stratis was really a fix-it man—her very own fairy godfather with all the answers to the enigma that had been foiling her for weeks, months.

She blinked at him, struggling to gauge how much of his supposed frankness was real. How much of it was another ploy, another lie to throw her off course.

"I have nothing to gain by lying to you about this," he added, clearly picking up on her doubt. "Not with my life on the line. I have my own family. And my reputation to maintain."

"Reputation?"

"To clean up trouble, remember? That would hardly be the case if I were now leading you astray." He readjusted his glasses, handling the frame carefully on one side—so damned relaxed. "Keep in mind, Mave Michael, it was your father who initially brought me into the fold, trusted me to help you. While my contract may have changed hands, its intentions remain the same."

"To help me."

He nodded as she chewed on his claim, unable to deny it sounded half sane. He was right: Cain wouldn't have recruited an incompetent man to come to her aid. "Fine," she breathed. "Tell me everything. Start at the beginning. And don't leave anything out." She hoped her demand sounded less desperate and more foreboding—like Cain's quiet rasp.

"Perhaps you'd like to come inside first," he offered. "My wife makes a delicious Masala chai. It'll warm you right up."

Her eyes flicked down. It was only then she realized she was shivering.

———

The riddle of Holden Frost had been weighing on her heart for too long. Since her release from the hospital in January, she'd broken into the barred tunnels of the château. She'd frantically rummaged through the remains of the fire, searching for the bones the authorities might have missed—nauseated with dread. For months she'd been grappling with mental demons, doubt whispering to her that Holden was a ghost. But in her heart, she'd known. He'd always been alive.

All of it real.

She sat at the farm-style table in Stratis's colorful kitchen, a foreigner in an unknown world. Children's art was scattered on the fridge with magnets. Bowls of fruit, succulents, pots and jars of aromatic spices crowded the countertops. Sipping her tea (Stratis hadn't exaggerated the goodness of his wife's steep), Mave remained mesmerized as he filled her in on what had occurred in January. These were the pieces she'd missed while she'd been shot and unconscious, battling for her life in the hospital. And it turned out, Holden's story wasn't all that different from hers.

According to Stratis, he'd literally stumbled upon Holden months ago, thanks to Cain.

"Shortly after New Year's Day," he said, "when you didn't show up at midnight to meet me and escape the possibility of a murder charge, Cain reached out to me again. He ordered I return to the château one last time, with the goal to smuggle you out of the hotel by whatever means necessary."

"You mean forcibly," she clarified, realizing her father would have done just about anything to get her away from her enemies.

"Well"—a trace of a smile touched his lips—"I prefer a good sales pitch over aggression, but you get the gist." He crossed his legs and sipped his own tea before continuing. "When I arrived, it must have been the height of the fire in the tunnels. I saw black smoke billowing out, and after a failed tracking attempt, I began to think you were lost to the flames. I was readying to leave again, empty-handed, when I caught sight of a flashlight in the distance. I followed it, and found it was coming from an old greenhouse."

Holden. "He was really familiar with the hotel's underground short-cuts," she whispered, picturing it in her mind—Holden at the bottom of those steps where she'd found herself trapped mere days ago. "He would have managed to crawl out from the fire there," she speculated.

"That's right," Stratis said. "Mind you, at the time, I had no idea it was Thom and thought it might be *you*."

"So you broke inside the greenhouse to search."

He nodded. "And I came across Thom, masked on the ground, bleeding and burned. I dragged him to the sink for water but the pipes were shut off. He begged me not to go to the authorities—something about getting arrested, not trusting the system."

She leaned forward, literally on the edge of her seat. "And then what?"

He sighed. "I was already dreading your father's reaction when I left the hotel without you for a second time, so I took Thom for answers." He shrugged. "I imagined I might trade the information with Cain. I transported Thom somewhere safe where I managed to remove and clean the bullet he'd taken. I gave him some heavy painkillers, fluids to rehydrate. But beyond that, there wasn't a whole lot I could do. One side of his flank had some nasty burns that required a specialist. I convinced Thom that he needed to see a proper doctor or he'd likely get an infection that could lead to worse. In turn, he offered to pay me a generous sum of money for a new name."

"Fake ID?"

"Yes. And as part of the deal, he also asked that I drive him to a hospital in Denver, posing as his uncle. There, we used his new identity as Thom Stearns and checked him into the ER."

She shook her head. "Why bother posing as his uncle?"

"The morphine I'd given him left him at a disadvantage—coherent but somewhat..." He paused and searched for the word. "Intoxicated. On top of that, his stitched-up bullet wound could've raised questions. He needed a sober advocate at his side to help him neutralize the situation."

"You lied for him."

"I fixed his problem," he said, as if correcting her. "I spoke on his behalf, filled in the triage nurses and extinguished any suspicion of foul play."

"And his prognosis? What did the doctors say?"

"I departed shortly after his initial blood work results came in. He was already being treated for smoke inhalation, and from what I know, receiving additional fluid resuscitation and antibiotics to ward off infection."

"So his chances of recovery were good?"

"Save for a painful recovery and permanent scarring, I believe so, yes."

"But it's been months! Why hasn't he contacted me? Why not come back to the château, his home?"

"I can't say for certain, but I suspect he's still undergoing treatment. Perhaps skin grafts. The procedures would take time for scheduling and post-op." His tone softened in response to the worry on her face. "Repeated medical attention would make it hard for him to leave the city. Purely conjecture on my part, but the fire destroyed the home you mentioned, did it not?"

"Wait, you're making it sound like you don't know where he is anymore."

"That's correct. I don't."

"No, that's—" She shook her head. "You said he's your *current* client. If not, how did you end up at the château again? How do you know about Bek-187?"

"Ah, well..." He shifted and picked an invisible piece of lint off his knee. "Weeks ago, Thom contacted me again. He asked for my services to keep an eye out for him."

"Keep an eye out, how?"

He sighed softly, obviously uncomfortable with sharing the particulars of his contracts. "He pays me, and I report back on certain activities on the darknet."

She narrowed her eyes. "Activities like?"

"Mostly deals and trades. Translation requests."

"You're saying you saw the post I left on the marketplace, the message board." *And the reply from Bek-187.*

"I did. And when I shared the information with Thom, he paid me double my normal fee to help you."

"But then, you must have some way to reach him."

"I'm afraid since I left him in the capable hands of the hospital nurses and doctors, all our interactions have been through inbound calls initiated by Thom himself. Untraceable and private. There's no way for me to find him unless he wants to be found."

No one ever finds me unless I want them to. Holden's past words echoed in her memory.

"So he's using a burner phone to contact you," she thought aloud. "How often does he call?"

"He's never used a set schedule. He calls only when he wants something, which is sporadic—once a month, twice in one week—never a pattern."

"Okay, but you mentioned possible skin grafts. What about the hospital records?" Her words sped up, her goal both visible and out of reach. "They'd have an address or number on file for him, wouldn't they? I mean, even with his fake ID, wouldn't he still be checked into a facility, transferred to a burn clinic or someplace known?"

He frowned. "Perhaps. I've had no reason to keep tabs or follow up. Though I did retain a copy of his initial blood work."

"Can I see it?" She checked the sharpness in her tone. "Please."

He raised his brow. "Certainly. However, in return..."

She held her breath, her stomach fisting, resenting the conditions he'd stipulate.

Everything has a price, M&M, Cain growled in her mind. *No one helps you for free—least of all another con.*

"When you next speak with your father," Stratis said, a shrewdness in his gaze, "can I rely on you to relay our interactions in a positive light?"

She slowly exhaled. He was still afraid of Cain and his outside contacts—his deadly reach—and rightfully so. She nodded. "I promise."

"Very well. One moment." He pulled out his cell, tapped and scrolled until he'd found the hospital record in question. A second later her own phone pinged with a forwarded message. "I photographed it," he said as she scanned the image of the blood test on her screen. Most of it went over her head—medical jargon detailing levels of cells, calcium, protein, alkaline phosphatase.

"Now, Mave Michael." She stiffened and blinked up at him. He wasn't done with his conditions—would ask more of her. "With your father and Thom as my references, and our meeting here in my private home"—he smiled, doing nothing to reassure her—"I believe I've warranted my credentials. As you know, I'm aware of your initial correspondence with the individual who goes by Bek-187. And, before you ask, no, I don't know of his or her real identity. Nor had I heard the name Bek-187 prior to finding your post. However, if you could be so kind as to fill me in on the remainder of your exchange—those through your private messages to be exact—I'll be able to provide further assistance and, I'm sure, take this worry off your hands." He held her in his hard gaze and leaned back casually in his chair, fingers laced together on his lap.

This had been his objective all along—to fulfill his contract, together with ensuring his good standing with Cain. He was a professional. Calculating, like her father.

She lowered her eyes to her tea and spun her mug absently, taking her time to compose her reply. Yes, Stratis seemed well-informed and forthcoming. But she still didn't trust him, not when his motivations were obviously funded by his "client." Was it really Holden who had hired him? Her mind kept going back to Cain, his life tests. She'd been burned too many times by jumping too fast, putting her faith in the wrong people. And Stratis was clearly plugged into the criminal network. His offer sounded too good to be true. As an opportunist, he may have been improvising, bending the truth to fit his needs, like when he'd lied to her about being on a job for Cain...*if* he'd lied. It would be more prudent to bargain directly with her father for the truth, and to check Stratis's leads in the interim—further confirm his trustworthiness. Besides, relying on a stranger to take care of her problems left her feeling exposed. She wasn't ready to hand over that kind of control. She gathered her confidence and looked up.

Fastest way to get to know your opponent, Cain whispered, *is to play his game better.*

"Thank you for the information and the tea," she said with a smile. "But if you really want to help me and impress my father," she added, "then you'll do this one last thing..."

———

She had a lot of time to think as the taxi drove her back to the château. She had called the hospital. The patient Thom Stearns, who'd checked into the emergency room last January, had indeed been transferred to a burn clinic. With a forwarding number, Mave had next spoken to an administrator from the clinic and hit another roadblock.

While records showed a patient by the name of Thom Stearns admitted months ago, that same patient had left the clinic's care rather unexpectedly, mid-treatment. He'd never been formally discharged. The administrator had been unable to provide her with Mr. Stearns's contact details due to patient confidentiality rules but, perhaps taking pity after hearing Mave's repeated pleas as Holden's supposed wife and single mother of his children with overdue child support payments, she'd added in confidence that Mr. Stearns's file also contained a log of voicemails left by the clinic. He'd been unresponsive and had never called

them back, even though, according to the physician's notes, he was at
risk for repeated infections. Should Mave track him down, the administrator stressed she'd do well to encourage Thom to return for further
treatment.

As the taxi ride lulled her nerves, Mave slouched heavily, her body
blanketed by exhaustion. Whether going by Thom Stearns or Robert
Frost, it seemed any footprints left by Holden had yet again evaporated
into thin air.

Halfway to the château, the buzz of her cellphone broke into her
slumber. She blinked warily at the screen, readying for another stressful
update from Julián. But it wasn't him. The text was from Stratis. It took
her a second to process.

How?

She straightened and stared at the brief message, now fully awake;
the phone number from the confidential hospital records. Before she'd
left his home, Stratis had assured her that he had an insider. He'd get her
what she needed—it was only a matter of time. Even so, she hadn't
allowed herself to hope...until now.

Anxiety spiraled in her chest. Counting on the cab driver's igno-
rance, she went ahead and dialed the number, too eager to wait. Even
though the clinic's administrator had warned her Holden wouldn't pick
up, she still felt a spear of disappointment when an automated voice
messaging system played after four incredibly long, torturous rings.
With a hand on her stomach to steady herself, Mave left Holden a
message...maybe. Whether or not it was the correct number, whether or
not he'd actually receive it, was yet another unknown burning in
her gut.

Come back home.

Doubts circled like vultures, diving and picking at the remains of
her thoughts.

What if it was a trap? Stratis's information. The number. How
could she be certain she hadn't just left a message for Bek-187?

Stop it, she chastised herself. She'd drive herself mad, thinking like
this. Needing reassurance, she pulled up the photograph of Holden's
blood test as Thom Stearns and reviewed it more closely—his name, the

date and time. Her attention snagged on a detail she hadn't initially noticed. Holden's blood type.

"Huh." She raised the screen closer to her face and zoomed in on the fine print, making sure her eyes weren't playing tricks. A sourness bloomed in her core.

A negative. A rare blood type. Same as Ren's brother.

THIRTY-FIVE

The long cab ride back to the hotel allowed her to plan her next move.

Preparation is everything, M&M. They'll be bigger, stronger, ready to kill. But you can outwit them, mind over body. Three parts strategy, one part delivery.

It kept looping in her head, coiling in one direction, then the other like a restless snake: Holden's uncommon blood type was a match with Ren's brother. André Rawlings was in desperate need of a kidney donor. Time was short. Like the countdown Bek-187 had given her. *Ticktock.*

He knows. It's him.

Her enemy in plain sight. The bad man was the good guy. Bek-187 —René Rawlings. Could it be? But then why bother with the strange robberies in Hazel Springs? The burning of stolen books? And what about the murder of Gerald Lee Baker, the recurring song of Billie Holiday, or the eerie message left for her on the mirror?

No eye may see.

The suspicion gave her an idea, a way to go on the offense, stall and buy herself more time to figure things out.

Even though she hadn't uncovered Holden's present location—he might be long gone from the Denver area—she'd made progress on his recent whereabouts, which meant she'd *almost* met Bek-187's demands. The rules of the game were clear: *Find the SDP, dead or alive*, or else Cain would be murdered. Sharing what she'd learned about Holden's hospital stay wouldn't be enough. And if it was, if it led Bek to Holden, what good would that do? She'd essentially be trading one life for another. Because if Bek was Ren, that meant he wanted to poach his childhood friend's kidney to save his brother.

It was too outrageous.

Mave clenched her molars. She felt herself going in circles. There had to be a better way. A smarter way. She couldn't give in to the blackmail so easily.

When the taxi at last pulled up to the château's main entrance, two vehicles were parked ahead of them in the horseshoe-shaped lane—and one was Bastian's SUV.

Mr. Fix-it.

Stratis had held up his end of the bargain, and given the hour, Mave had no time to wonder how he'd managed to transport the vehicle with the key in her pocket. She hurried out of the taxi—rain threatening to soak her almost immediately—and zipped to Bastian's car. She retrieved Vincent's stolen yearbook from the trunk, then, mid-dash, relayed instructions to the valet to move the SUV to the staff lot.

Through the lobby doors, she shook the raindrops from her hair. A grand piano played in the distance. The wedding rehearsal was in less than twenty minutes, and the ground floor appeared busy with guests wandering. Mave would have been late for the walk-through, except Julián had already texted her to say the bride was experiencing some wardrobe emergency; they had bumped the rehearsal time. Thank god.

Mave hustled, doing her best to dodge any questions and avoiding the front desk staff altogether as she passed the reception area. Luckily, everyone seemed preoccupied as she swept through the hallways. For once, no one noticed her presence or stopped her with a problem to solve.

When she reached the Oasis Spa, the lights were off inside. Katie must have locked up and left for the evening, probably reassigned duties for the rehearsal by Julián. *Good.*

Mave slipped into the spa. Soaking in the darkness, she shot Julián a brief text that she'd made it. She'd meet him in the greenhouse soon. Silently praying for no additional updates of pre-wedding drama, she headed straight for the storage closet and used the new key Oren had given her. Once inside, she rebooted the old PC. It awakened bit by bit. The motherboard's slow ticks grated her nerves, and she drummed her fingers in an attempt to drown out the noise.

Come on already. She switched tactics and half-heartedly searched for her journal and Holden's mask again as she waited. The same end results thwarted her. They were gone. She returned to her seat with a huff and flipped to Holden Frost in Vincent's yearbook.

Absent. Invisible. She looked up and found André Rawlings in the senior class. He was thinner than Ren, sickly looking even then. His only resemblance to his younger brother was his eyes—a warmth and gentleness that made you think him a good person.

The desktop loaded on the computer screen, pulling her focus. Mave put away the yearbook and logged onto the dark web. She navigated to the marketplace, and clicked on her string of private messages from Bek-187. She wasn't entirely surprised to discover a new, if not final reminder.

Time's almost up. Did you find the SDP, or will you visit daddy in the prison cemetery?

Enough. She sucked in her cheeks and typed her reply in haste. It felt cathartic, pounding the keyboard, playing hardball and striking back. She was a fast learner, knew how to distort the facts into vague yet targeted threats. Sprinkle in a few wishful exaggerations, and she reassured herself her stall tactic was foolproof. Bek-187 would be an idiot to ignore her counter-threat. She hit enter.

New developments: I have what you want. And I know who you are. I have copies of the files. If you want your true face, name, and dirty business to remain private, I suggest you do what I say. Meet me online at midnight, here on the market's chat, and we can discuss some mutually beneficial revised terms for our deal. Only then will I tell you where to find the SDP.

It didn't give her tons of breathing room, but she had every intention to stall again at midnight, however long it took. She had to keep both Holden and Cain safe for another day or two. Her heart thumping with adrenaline, she shutdown the computer, relocked the closet, and headed to face her next dreaded problem: the wedding rehearsal in the leaky greenhouse.

As if mocking her along the way, thunder rumbled and flickered the lights.

THIRTY-SIX

Considering less than twenty-four hours ago, the garden path had been crawling with weeds and caked in mud, the staff had done a decent job creating a tented corridor. Gravel slowed her steps, a few pieces slipping into her shoes and nicking her feet; but more importantly, Mave remained dry as she travelled to the greenhouse. The wind, on the other hand, was a different beast.

She shivered as it whistled through the seams of the tent. Fabric snapped and yawned to her left and right. It felt as if someone were outside, trying to grab at her through the tent. Rain splattered against the canvas walls, exaggerating the storm's proportions. More than once, her eyes flicked up in worry—especially when the outdoor chandeliers they'd wired flickered and swayed. The hurricane lanterns fared no better. Several were already snuffed, while others fluttered wildly to remain lit. Mave hugged her arms around herself and picked up her pace.

She'd passed a few stragglers on their way to the rehearsal, however it seemed the majority of the VIP guests were already ahead, ready for the run-through to begin. *Shit*. She was late.

Mave scurried past the impressive doorstops, granite grotesques shipped in for the occasion. The bride spotted her tardy arrival from the altar and threw her a cutting glance.

"Sorry," she mouthed while sidestepping next to Bastian. Soft voices carried. Up front, the wedding party was being given instructions along with the string quartet: who would walk down the aisle in which order, according to what cue.

"Where's your custom uniform?" Bastian whispered. "I had it delivered to the penthouse."

She noticed Bastian's attire—a three-piece suit, all black save for its eggplant trim and satin detailing on an inner vest. It was double-breasted, with pewter buttons and a tail coat. He looked more like a sixteenth-century butler than a concierge. She caught sight of Julián deeper inside the greenhouse wearing a similar, over-the-top getup.

"Didn't get a chance to go upstairs yet," she whispered back. "What's the big deal? I'll just wear the stupid costume tomorrow night."

"Julián said he texted you. It's supposed to be a full dress rehearsal."

"But she's not even in her wedding gown." She indicated Bridezilla with a subtle arch of her brow.

"Staff only," Bastian qualified, speaking low and barely moving his lips. "She ordered I have a tailor ready for alterations in half an hour. She wants each fitting to be perfect."

How thoughtful, Mave inwardly griped while resisting rolling her eyes.

"Also, heads-up," Bastian breathed, "she's not impressed with your wishing pots."

Her gaze dropped to the nearest arrangement of black clay and smoked crystal pots. She'd strategically grouped them with Amos throughout the greenhouse. Ringed with various blooms in deep purples, she'd intended for them to function like mini fountains; when the guests arrived for the ceremony tomorrow, the ushers would instruct them to toss their black pennies and make wishes for the bride and groom. So what if the pots also worked to collect the rain water currently trickling in from several parts of the roof? It was original and memorable, dammit—part of the site's rustic charm.

As the string quartet headed to the corner where they'd arranged their instruments on stands, Mave and Bastian melted back and out of the way. The groom and best man took their place, and Bridezilla and the wedding party made their way to the entrance for the walk-through. Not one of them so much as glanced in their direction. Irritation swelled in Mave's chest. The countless hours she'd put in with her staff to transform this decrepit space into something magical felt dismissed. She took a moment to appreciate her own vision come to life. The black flora. The perfectly arranged rows of cast iron chairs, the rose petal aisle, the string lights and candelabras and stupid black butterflies soon to be released.

"These aren't swallowtails!" the bride said, as if on cue.

The string quartet began to play a familiar tune—not the wedding march, but "Paint it Black" by the Rolling Stones.

"I specifically ordered black swallowtails!" she continued in a loud whine. She was leaning down to peer into one of the many soft-shell cages currently being brought into the greenhouse. The oblivious delivery-man seemed to shrink away. "What the fuck are *these*?" she called after him. "These are not...!"

Mave looked to Bastian. His eyes had grown wide, taking in Bridezilla's reaction. "Ah, shit," he muttered.

"Bastian," she said in a stage whisper to be heard over the violins, "what's she talking about?"

"They're the black moths, remember? I told you about them."

"Huh?" She shook her head. "When?"

"After that goon broke into the gift shop." He waved a hand nervously and, clearly under stress, slipped into his Islander lilt. "You know, I explained to you how we couldn't get the butterflies, but could do moths instead. They're all black. Same look. Different bug." He blew out a breath and wiped his forehead. His eyes stayed glued on the drama building at the entranceway. "Knew it. Crazy, that one. My fault; I should've—"

"No." She touched his elbow. "Don't worry," she said with a nod. "I'll handle this." Her cheeks felt hot as she straightened her shoulders, smiled tightly, and strode over to address the bride amid her increasingly audible complaints.

Julián had already made his way over and was muttering apologies to Bridezilla; but rather than talk her down, his presence was merely giving her a soft target. "You're *sorry*?" she squealed. "Tomorrow is supposed to be my special day and you brought me disgusting moths."

Mave clasped her hands behind her back and dug her nails in her palms. *Control it.* The quartet had stopped playing. Everyone's attention seemed to be on the bride and her mini tantrum.

"Well, you see..." Julián mumbled.

"Ugh, and you." She rounded on Mave, acknowledging her at last, though for the wrong reasons. "You promised me everything would be perfect. How do you explain this?" She pointed at a cage with her sharply manicured black nail. Visible tears welled in her kohl-lined eyes. "This isn't perfect."

Mave gritted her teeth and cleared her throat. She stifled a sudden urge to either laugh or lunge at this woman and her ridiculous meltdown over such an insignificant detail. Forget that it was a near miracle Bastian had managed to find hundreds of black moths and have them express delivered in under a week. Of course, Bridezilla wouldn't see it that way. Mave was close to screaming herself. This wedding. This hotel. This entire upside-down life, groomed to please others and cater to their impossible demands: find Holden; uncover his past; save her father; keep her home; solve a murder; make this miserable bitch-bride happy because she couldn't have her pretty little black butterflies. It was one slap too many. She felt her smile cracking and made no attempt to mend it.

"You're right." She licked her lips. "It's not perfect. In fact, it's—"

A high-pitched scream ripped into the greenhouse. All heads turned to the entryway.

A young woman no more than sixteen stood with her face noticeably pale and contorted in horror.

"Matilda, for fuck's sake!" Bridezilla shouted, her tone a blend of irritation and worry. "What is it?"

The guest named Matilda blinked her wide eyes and pointed out into the tented corridor. Several guests and staff approached at once, along with Mave and Julián. Crowded together, there were audible gasps and a shared cringing at the sight.

A skinned and bloody goat's head was mounted on a stake, planted a few feet outside the greenhouse.

"Julián?" Mave whispered, but he merely shook his head with his mouth hanging open, as dumbfounded and repulsed as any of them. Who'd put this here? Mave looked around at the shocked faces. It could have been anyone. No cameras existed in either the tent or greenhouse to expose the culprit.

"What is god's name is—?" Bridezilla spun and hissed at Mave, "Is this your idea of a joke? First the moths, then sick sacrifices? I never asked for this! I never said *satanic*!" Her tears were finally streaming in full, trailing black ribbons down her cheeks.

"We'll have it removed at once," Julián said, though it was unclear whether Bridezilla heard him over her continued tirade.

Mave's phone rang, and she blinked, letting out a stream of air from her nose. She pulled out her cell, intending to mute the call, and frowned at the number on her display. She shook her head. "I—I have to take this."

"You *what*?" Bridezilla screeched.

Without a second thought, Mave wove through the wedding party and marched past the staked goat's head.

"Wait!" Bridezilla yelled after her. "Where do you think you're going? I'll make you regret..."

Mave ignored her rant. The itch to tell her where to shove her petty problems had already faded. She hurried out of earshot through the billowing tent, answering the call mid-stride—another collect call from the prison. Getting things cleared up with Cain was critical now that she'd left Bek-187 a counter-threat.

No more games or tests.

"Hello?" She stuffed a finger in her other ear to muffle the din of wind and rain against the tent. The storm had finally blown the electrical on the chandeliers, leaving only a few hurricane lanterns to mark her path. She strained to hear the automated prison operator. A click sounded, as if the line were being redirected.

"Hello?" a man's voice repeated. It wasn't a recording and it didn't belong to Cain.

Mave quickly checked she'd read the call display correctly. The penitentiary's name and number remained lit on her screen.

"Yes?" she said.

"Is this Mave Michael Francis?" the man asked.

"Speaking." She was walking quickly, nearly out of breath and halfway back to the building.

"My name is Samuel Habib. I'm the CO3, a counsellor assigned to your father's ward."

"Sorry, what's this about?"

"You're listed as the sole family member and emergency contact for Cain. Is this correct?" The dual formality and gentleness of his voice made her chest tighten.

"I'm—has something happened to him?" In four years, she'd never once received a call from an officer at the prison.

"I'm afraid I have some bad news." He cleared his throat softly. "There was an incident earlier this evening." Silence stretched as her mind worked to both block and interpret his meaning. "Ms. Francis, are you still there?"

"Yeah, um, yes. What"—she swallowed—"what kind of incident?" Her voice sounded thick, as if her throat was stuffed full of cotton. She wasn't sure if she'd spoken the question clearly, but he answered.

"There's no easy way to say this. Your father's been transferred to the medical ward."

"What?" She stumbled a step. "Why—what are you...?" Cain was hurt? She held her forehead, feeling her temples throb. "What's wrong with him?"

"I'm so sorry, Ms. Francis. I realize this must be a shock, but it's urgent. I'm not the doctor and wasn't forwarded the details of his chart, only the prognosis. His condition is critical. Most inmates who're admitted to..."

She slowed and leaned on a dusty credenza in the hallway, having no recollection of returning indoors.

"...unconscious...most likely to die in..." A distant part of her registered the counselor still speaking. "...that...contact immediately in case..." His voice wavered in and out of her hearing, competing with the rush of her blood. "...last wishes. Do you understand?"

"Yes." She understood perfectly.

She had refused Bek-187's demands—had threatened a hard criminal. And he'd retaliated. Because of her. This stranger on the phone was telling her Cain was moments from dying.

THIRTY-SEVEN

How could this have happened? *You did this! Your fault!* The scathing voices burned and stabbed at her mind. She hadn't revealed what she'd discovered about Holden—his new name, his last known location and phone number. She had it. She'd withheld it, risked countering Bek's deadline with demands of her own. But criminals had fragile egos. She knew this. They didn't like to be shown up by anyone, much less a young woman and daughter of an enemy. She wandered down the grand staircase, not even recognizing where her feet were carrying her until she was already there: the library.

Holden's library.

She frantically wiped the tears off her face and paced up and down an aisle of bookshelves, someplace she knew the security cameras couldn't reach. Between the dusty rows of stories—Austen, Woolf, Morrison, Christie—it was easier to think. The books made her feel closer to Holden. Even though he was elsewhere. Still hidden. The acute awareness tore into her heart.

She was alone. And Cain was hundreds of miles away in an ICU, unreachable, fading fast.

What have I done?

Her knees gave as the weight of her despair settled. She heaved on the ground and rocked forward. Her forehead met the end of a bookcase. She closed her eyes and welcomed the bruise—a too-brief distraction from her greater pain. She prayed, cried, screamed in her head: *You can't take him!* The only parent she'd ever known, though full of faults —she wasn't ready to say goodbye. Not like this.

She waited for Cain's rebuke to come, but suffocated by grief, her imagination of his voice remained silent. Maybe it would be like this forever. Muted. Hollow. No more advice. No more—

The chime of her phone made her jump in her skin. She blinked down reflexively at the noise and stared at the text from Julián, no longer seeing or caring. All her emotions were currently occupied. She had none left to spare on Bridezilla's meltdown. What was the point? According to Julián's urgent text, she was threatening to ruin the hotel with a lawsuit and was leaving them permanently scathing reviews with hundreds of influencers with whom she had personal sway thanks to her famous producer father. It meant nothing. Mave felt nothing. Not about the wedding.

Cain was dead. Dying. Gone. Leaving.

"Mave?" Katie's voice carried down the aisle, startling her anew. "Hey, there you are! What are you doing down—? Mave?" She approached her and knelt beside her, her brow furrowed in worry. She reached out and gently cupped her shoulder. The touch instantly warmed and surprised Mave, as if she'd forgotten the feel of another's hand. "Are you okay?" Katie asked. "Why are you crying?"

"I'm—" She wiped her face, but it was no use. New tears leaked to replace those she'd erased.

"What happened? You look heartbroken! Is it your ex again?"

Mave shook her head, her throat too swollen for words.

"The new guy?" Katie guessed. "Did he do something? You two break up?"

"No, he's—" Her voice hitched, and she pushed her palms to her chest to try to settle her lungs. "We were never together," she said, because it was easier in that moment. To pretend. To go along with the trivial misunderstanding of her pain. She accepted the tissue Katie was offering and blotted her eyes. "He's not a good guy," she rasped, not entirely certain if she meant Cain or Ren. Her feelings were mixed up, muddied.

"What do you mean?"

"He's a liar, like the rest of..." A new batch of tears welled.

"Shh, it can't be that bad. Everyone swears he's a gem. What did he lie about?"

About everything. About nothing. About being Bek. "He only wanted to hurt—" *Cain.* She shook her head again and buried her face in her hands.

"Hey, shh, come here." Katie pulled her into a hug.

Mave stiffened. Coldness stirred deep inside her. She couldn't remember ever being hugged by a friend. The thought was so depressing, she became overwhelmed all over again.

"What did he lie about?" Katie repeated.

"Doesn't matter," Mave sobbed. "Ren's just using me."

"Ren?" Katie tightened her hold. Mave could feel the sudden swell of her empathy—the transference of pain amplified through Katie's arms. It was as if Mave were made of glass. Katie took in everything: Heartbreak. Humiliation. Devastation. "Well, if that's true, then we'll forget all about *Ren*. He's a jerk. A nobody who doesn't deserve you. Shh...It's going to be okay," Katie whispered, her voice thick. "Boy trouble is the worst. But in the morning, you'll see, everything will seem better."

Mave couldn't bring herself to reveal that the boy was her father, and he wouldn't get better. He'd get worse. Much worse. He'd be dead and gone come morning.

———

She jostled awake, knees dropping from her chest. It took a moment to recall her surroundings: deep in the library's reading nook, nestled in her favorite wingback chair. Last autumn, she'd curled up in this exact spot during her breaks. She hadn't been speaking to Cain back then, or returning his mail. What she wouldn't give to rewind time. She rubbed her eyes, sore from crying, and peeled off a fox-fur throw. Katie probably blanketed her after Mave fell asleep, then left. It had to be late. A stillness clung to the air, a silence that only seemed to occur past—

Midnight!

She scrambled up and fumbled to find her phone. Where was it? She groped around the seat before spotting it on the ground next to her foot. She snatched it up. The time glowed one a.m.

No. NO.

She darted out from the library as fast as her legs would carry her. Her head pinched in pain with every step, but she couldn't stop—she wouldn't. She refused to accept she'd missed her meeting. She had to confront Bek-187 for what he'd done to Cain.

She reached the Oasis Spa and, in a rushed daze, staggered to the closet and fumbled with her keys until she managed to unlock the new bolt. After multiple attempts to steady her shaky grip, she flung open the door and stumbled inside. She powered on the computer. She typed and retyped her passwords, bit and ripped her cuticles as the agonizing minutes crawled and the darknet gurgled and loaded. Finally, she blinked at the community board on the marketplace, and clicked on her new notification. She'd received one private message.

Bad move. Not how this works. I keep my promises, and if you release my name to the public, I'll come and slit your pretty little throat next. Have a good sleep, Mave Michael. We're done.

It was timestamped well before midnight which meant...

"*No,*" she breathed, imagining Bek-187 typing this message, then another—giving the green light and setting into motion the hit on Cain. "NO!" she yelled. Her vision blurred as anger swelled and engulfed her from head to foot. She slapped the side of the monitor, causing it to flicker. Her palm stung.

The answering knock on the spa's outer doors nearly caused her to fall off her chair.

She stood spine straight, ears primed. Had Katie heard her? Or someone else? She wiped her face and tried to control her breath before turning to investigate.

Mave flinched.

Her visitor was already inside. He lurked at the closet door, watching her intently.

THIRTY-EIGHT

He stood with his hands on his hips, blocking her exit. He wore jeans. His t-shirt was untucked and highlighted his toned biceps. Casual, as if he'd just woken and thrown on his off-duty attire. He didn't appear to have his gun belt, but that didn't mean he wasn't carrying a weapon.

"How did you find me?"

"Checked with Oren on my way in," he said simply.

The security cameras.

"What"—her eyes flicked to his hands, expecting him to draw a hidden gun, but he didn't so much as twitch a finger—"what are you doing here?"

He titled his head, reflecting back her open suspicion. "I got your message to meet. Came as soon as I could. Even though I know it's too late."

"You. Got my message," she repeated, her brain filling in the details. *On the darknet. Bek-187. Too late.* Her mouth grew dry. Cain had already been fatally wounded for her mistake. His sadistic pride. "You're saying you..." She swallowed. "You're..."

He flexed his jaw. "I'm what, Mave? Fucking tired of this little game we're playing? Pissed off? Damn straight, I am. But I'm here anyway, even though I've been telling myself not to come for the past few hours.

Nearly turned the car around every half mile." He scoffed and scratched his bottom lip nervously. "Said I never should have trusted you," he mumbled.

"What are you talking about?" she breathed, her blood quickening. He'd been the one to start this. Not her.

"I'm talking about you and me. Your father. Your lies."

Her fists tightened. "Don't talk to me about my father."

"Why? Because you thought you could follow in his footsteps and pull a fast one on me, treat me like the town idiot? Admit it. This has always been about Holden, hasn't it? You're obsessed with him. From that day we met in the hospital months ago…"

"Get out of my way, Ren. You said so yourself. We're done. You *won*, okay?" Hearing it aloud, her stomach cramped as if churning poison.

"Won? Are you fucking kidding me right now?"

His continued act, his twisted affront, it was too much. The damage he'd done to her was cruel beyond words—asking her to choose between her father and Holden, leaving her to grieve in guilt for the remainder of her life, alone. It was all she could do to not leap forward and claw his face off with her bare hands.

"Isn't that why you really drove all this way in the middle of the night?" Her voice was like a shard of glass, slicing up her throat. "To see me defeated and confess my sins?" She held out her hands, wrists pointed out. "Well, congratulations. Okay? *Yes*. I lied. I have no idea what happened to Holden, where he ended up. You satisfied now with your sick demands? Or did you change your mind, and you're here to slit my throat after all?"

He frowned deeply, regarding her like she was unhinged. "Yeah, you can save me the theatrics. And you left out the part about posing as a fake journalist, then pretending to have a sixth sense to manipulate me into tailing a son of a bitch who happened to be Holden's foster brother years ago. That's right." He curled his lip. "I found Vincent. We had a nice little chat, getting caught up on recent events. He had a lot of interesting things to say about you."

"So, what, you're going to arrest me? You two are buddies now? Or has that always been the case? Years ago, you and Vincent." She reached for the yearbook and flung it at his knees.

He recoiled and looked down at his feet.

"Where'd you get that?"

She ignored his interrogation. "You're inside. You and Holden. In the same class. You knew him longer than childhood—much better than you let on."

"I already told you"—he glowered—"Holden and I were estranged then. He barely even showed up to school, and this has *nothing* to do with the past."

"Now who's the liar?"

"Look..." He pinched his forehead like she was giving him a headache. Her knees twitched. She wanted to dive around him, but he refocused on her too quickly. "Holden convinced Pammy to run away; that's why Vincent still hates Holden all these years later. And you know what? Vin's right." His eyes glistened with venom, losing all trace of their usual warmth. At last, the monster unmasked. "You're acting like Holden was a saint, but the truth is, he was a fucking creep. A vindictive shit-disturber who bailed on everyone and everything—including his own life. Maybe he finally realized it, and that's why he killed himself a few months after Pammy disappeared."

She shook her head. "You're twisting everything around. I don't want to hear anymore. Not after what you've done."

"What *I've* done?" He looked scandalized again, like she was stabbing a knife at him and crying foul at the same time. He couldn't possibly be comparing the suffering of his brother from natural causes to murdering Cain. As if it were Mave's fault that his twisted plan to illegally steal a kidney from an involuntary donor had failed. "You're the one who's pretending to be someone she's not," he spat, "acting the victim when you're really as coldblooded as your—"

Mave couldn't say exactly when she hurtled the heavy monitor toward him, only that she'd reached her limit.

He hollered in pain as it landed on his foot, his eyes stunned wide. They'd both tripped, him forward, her sideways. He scrambled and grabbed her ankle but she had far too much training, adrenaline and anger burning inside her. All those mornings she and Cain had sparred on the mat in their latest living-room-turned-gym—they'd practiced each maneuver tirelessly, again and again: locks on the hip, thigh, knee, calf, ankle.

What do you do if he comes at you this way, M&M? Or the other way? He'll be heavier. You need to be faster. Sharper. You understand? Like a sliver of soap at the bottom of the tub.

Teeth, nails, elbows, she gave it her all—starting with her heel, striking him square in his nose. Even though he deserved it, the crunch of bone on cartilage made her wince. She tasted blood on her tongue—had bitten herself from the hit. She turned away before seeing the damage done to his face. Head wounds always gushed the worst.

Free of his grip, she jerked away on all fours, desperate to escape before he potentially pulled a knife or gun. Ren merely rocked and moaned in pain as she hurled herself shoulders-first out from the closet. Hands flailing, she slammed the door shut and scrambled for her keys.

"Maaave," he groaned from inside. "What the FUCK!"

She jammed in the key. Hearing the click of the bolt, she let out a wavering breath. Oren, god bless him, had installed a double-cylinder deadbolt. A key was needed from either side to disengage the lock. The only way Ren was getting out of that closet was either with her cooperation, or that of a locksmith or firefighter to axe their way in. No doubt he had his cellphone, but it would be hours before help could arrive from Hazel Springs. Forget that it was the dead of night in the middle of a thunderstorm that would slow even the sturdiest SUV up the slippery mountain road. Her lungs emptied themselves of their sour panic and, for a moment, she merely slumped against the wall. It was over. She'd caught Bek-187. The enemy was trapped.

She flinched anyway as the door rattled. He punched it next, the vibration travelling through her flexed legs and spine. But the lock held.

"Mave, let me out," he said after a beat, too calm, reverting back to his smooth tenor—or trying. He sounded markedly stuffed up with his nose broken.

"No," she breathed.

"We can get you help," he said. "I won't press charges. Just let me out."

"What are you—?" Her mouth hung agape. "*No.*"

"Please. Let's talk about this some more. Calmly. Work something out."

"Work *what* out? Some insane plan B for your revenge fantasy to find your brother a miracle kidney? You're a *murderer!*" She waited for his reply, but he said nothing. She heard him shuffling, a soft grunt, then nothing. Her body temperature dropped. His silence was worse than his gaslighting. She stood up and stared at the door. Why wasn't he answering?

"I found out about their blood types matching," she whispered, needing to kill the quiet pressing against her skull. "They're both A negative. Holden. Your brother."

Her mind raced in various directions at once. What was he planning, doing? What could he use from the storage boxes? Why was he acting as if she had been the one to commit a heinous crime? Why bother travelling up here to confront her, simply to continue to lie about his motives? She staggered a step and leaned on the back counter. She wished she had x-ray vision, a secret way to see him through the wall. Her eyes swept across the space—scanning as Cain had taught her —and stopped on the black orchids. The flowers were oddly placed, shoved off-center against the back counter.

It's not right. They should be displayed up on the reception desk, visible for everyone.

Following her instinct, she slid them aside and inhaled sharply. A peephole. Someone had been watching her, keeping tabs. The notion that Katie might be spying on her for Cain suddenly knifed into her thoughts, making her lightheaded. When she lowered her eye to view inside the closet, she was awarded a perfect view of Ren and the computer. She also saw why he was no longer responding.

He had returned the monitor upright and was currently seated on the metal chair, a pile of blood-stained towels at his feet. Acid burned through her veins with the realization. She hadn't logged out. Ren was on the darknet.

THIRTY-NINE

She rapped on the door to room 508 and crossed her arms, impatiently waiting, worrying, fuming. If Katie was inside, she wasn't answering. She knocked again. If she wasn't in the spa and she wasn't in her room, then where the hell was she at this late hour? Mave was almost afraid to know the answer. Her dread was momentarily interrupted by her phone buzzing with a notification. Then another. Her lungs swelling, she pulled out her cell and saw a series of new texts from Ren.

Look, there's been some kind of massive misunderstanding. Heard what you said about my brother, and just so you know: 1. I had no idea about their blood types matching.

2. A potential donor is a lot more complicated than matching blood types.

3. Even if your suspicions were true, Holden is DEAD. You're talking about him like he's alive!

???

What the fuck is really going on, Mave? I saw your inbox. Talk to me.

She didn't answer, too many doubts clawing her mind, shredding her ability to understand what was happening. What if she'd been wrong about Ren and he wasn't Bek-187? But then why had he—?

Her phone buzzed with another text from him.

FUCKING HELL. THIS IS BULLSHIT!!! LET ME OUT!!!

She inhaled through her nose, utterly exhausted from his games. ***Just answer me this***, she wrote back, ***are you Bek-187?***

The ellipses icon showed he was typing. She chewed on her lip as she stared at the three little dots blinking. What was taking him so long? It was a simple question. Seconds ticked. Her imagination twisted. She readied herself for whatever longwinded excuse he was busy composing. But when his text buzzed on the screen, it was a single word rather than a paragraph.

NO.

She swallowed and fired off another question. ***Then why did you show up to meet me tonight?***

Surely, that couldn't have been a coincidence.

This time, his reply was quick. ***BECAUSE YOU BEGGED ME TO COME IN YOUR TEXT!!!***

Her brain felt like it was imploding as she struggled to piece together his replies and sift out the truth from the lies.

What text? she wrote back with trembling thumbs. ***I never sent you one.***

She scrolled up to re-read their earlier correspondence as confirmation and blinked in disbelief. There *were* no earlier texts from Ren. None. No mention of setting up a meeting with Sandy to track her stolen belongings. No back-and-forth about him being outside to pick her up for their appointment with Mrs. Hess. Where had they gone? She closed her messages and reopened them, hoping to retrieve the lost texts, but her screen refreshed with the identical results. All her previous messages to and from Ren had been mysteriously deleted. Her phone chimed again.

Then what do you call this? he wrote. A screen shot from his cell directly followed.

She tapped to enlarge the image and read the words that, for all intents and purposes, seemed to be written by her, timestamped from a few hours ago.

Something really bad has happened. I need you to come up

here to meet me. Please be quick!! I can't ask anyone else for help.
Don't tell anyone, but it's an emergency!!!

Her chest tightened with understanding before her mind—resisting, rejecting. She'd been passed out in the library when this supposedly panicked text from her to Ren had been delivered. When someone else wrote it, posing as her. When someone else sent it, counting on it to lead her to mistake Ren for Bek-187. Then that same someone deleted Ren's replies and all her correspondence to clean up their dirty work.

She ignored the next pleading text from Ren, her thoughts spinning.

Katie had been with her. Inside the library. The spa. Day and night. Every time, in the perfect position to keep an eye on her. Could she be more than Cain's spy? She pulled out her phone, her heart drumming wildly, and composed a brief text to Julián. She'd set things straight. Prove Ren was a twisted liar.

Just wondering, did Katie specifically ask to stay in room 508, or did you assign it to her randomly?

Julián may have been asleep, but given their stressful day battling Bridezilla, it was unlikely. Sure enough, she hit send and received his reply almost immediately.

Who's Katie?

Mave's pulse skipped a beat. There had to be a simple explanation. Julián was tired, had forgotten an employee's name. She licked her dry lips and typed. *The new yoga instructor. The one with the blue hair who works in the spa.*

The ellipsis icon blinked and a second later, Julián's reply appeared.

You must mean Olga. She's the only part-timer for the spa. But her hair isn't blue.

Mave's stomach twisted and her heart squeezed upward, into her throat. *Then at the séance we performed the other day,* she typed shakily, *who was the young woman seated between Gracelyn and me? With the blue hair?*

Julián swiftly replied in three back-to-back texts. *Unsure who you mean. You were the one seated next to Gracelyn.*

With Dominick Grady. Then me. No woman with blue hair was there.

Why, everything okay? Where are you?? Did you see my other texts about—

She stopped reading. Stopped breathing. She lowered her phone and stared at the door ahead of her. Her old room. Katie's new room. Mave pulled out her master key and dragged a sip of musty air into her lungs. She slid her key into the lock and spun the bolt with a sonorous clack.

When the door creaked open, she saw the space clearly for the first time.

It was empty. The mattress stripped. Unoccupied. As if no one had been assigned the room for months.

———

The hotelier offices and security room were empty. The nightshift guard must have been doing rounds. Mave kept the overhead lights off, feeling safer in the dark. She helped herself to a staff computer and scoured the HR files. Julián had spoken the truth. Nobody by the name of Katie or Kaitlyn or Katherine had ever been hired on at Château du Ciel. Mave swiveled to the security monitors. She'd seen Oren run the commands enough times to figure out how to load the footage she needed.

Ready, M&M?

Her throat swelled.

Compartmentalize. Control it: Emotion off. Focus on.

Her heart pounded. She felt closer to Cain than ever before—determined to see this through to the end. Mave played the recording.

She watched herself, mere hours ago, inconsolable and fleeing down the grand staircase. She entered the library. Alone.

In the footage, Mave wiped away her tears. She disappeared between the bookstacks. The recording rippled and cleared. Nothing else seemed to happen in the library—not until fifteen minutes later. She emerged from behind the bookshelves. Her shoulders slumped. She was still alone, wiping tears from her face. The video exposed the truth she'd been unable to see before now.

Apart from Mave, not a person had entered the library.

As the recording continued, the monitor showed Mave mumbling a few words to herself. She dragged her feet to the wingback chair in the corner of the library. She collapsed into the seat and gradually nodded off. Exhausted with grief. Oblivious due to inexperience with her gift, her stress, her need to save the hotel and Holden and Cain. But the answer had been in front of her the entire time, hadn't it?

Katie the blue-haired yoga instructor; Katie from LA; Katie who was seeking a fresh start, away from her ex-boyfriend; Katie who understood Mave's heartbreak; Katie who was afraid the château was haunted...she was nowhere to be seen on the security footage. Because she'd never physically existed to begin with.

Solely in my vision. My sixth sense. Making me see what she needed me to experience—to understand.

No eye may see.

Mave shivered and trembled. The realization that Katie was a ghost threatened to overwhelm her mind, her heart, everything she'd believed —its very implication...

Mave could sense far more than lost, inanimate objects. She could sense lost souls.

A psychic. A medium with an uncontrollable, natural talent to seek, find—attract. *A lighthouse.* She'd been neither willing nor able to recognize it. Until now.

Under scrutiny, the truth stood out like the black orchids in the spa, off-center, out of place: how she'd found Katie late at night, right after she'd discovered Holden's mask and begun to entertain seriously the idea of the afterlife.

No such thing as coincidence, M&M.

Katie had arrived at the hotel. Something about Mave's search for Holden had attracted her, because...because...

Who are you? Why are you really here?

The riddle peeled itself apart in layers.

Perhaps the staff had been wary around Mave not simply because she was the daughter of a hitman, but because they unconsciously sensed it, too; Mave had a shadow. Katie's presence was off-putting. In the cigar lounge, when the skittish bartender addressed only Mave and never delivered Katie the coffee she'd ordered; or during her facial, when

Olga was curt while applying the mask and instinctively working around Katie; or at the first séance, when Katie's interactions had been one-sided. Gracelyn, Dominick, Julián, they had each ignored her despite her efforts to engage in conversation. No one but Mave had responded or reacted to Katie's presence. And that could only mean...

Katie didn't know.

However she had died, whatever her link to Mave's search for Holden, the young woman haunting the château believed herself alive.

PART FIVE
AMONG THE FLUTTERING
BLACK MOTHS

Countless firsthand reports indicate that the passing of the spirit into the afterlife is not a predefined, standardized experience. It can be a peaceful transition for some, while for others, it is difficult, fraught with turmoil and heartache. Indeed, throughout the history of time, the inevitability of mortality has plagued humanity. *Death* has never been an easy outcome to accept—least of all for the deceased.

—SIGNS: A HANDBOOK FOR CLAIRVOYANCE

FORTY

Floorboards creaked in the outer office. Footsteps approached. A muffled voice followed. Mave turned off the security footage and pricked up her ears.

Not the night guard.

A woman was speaking, but too low for her to make out. The hair on the back of Mave's neck stood on end as another voice drifted—distinctly deep and marbled. She recognized it.

HIDE.

Her head turned left, then right. The room was too small, windowless, minimal furniture but for the desk. Crawling beneath it would be too obvious. She stared wide-eyed as the voices approached the door to the security room.

How do you become invisible! Cain hollered. Someone knocked on the door.

Go where nobody looks. It was the first rule of hiding. *Up.*

Mave moved on instinct. In one swooping motion, she found the perfect spot next to a vertical duct. She pressed her hands firmly against the wall, kicked up her feet to the wall opposite to suspend herself like a bridge, and spider-crawled up the narrow, recessed nook.

The knob spun and the door moaned as it swung inward. A flashlight slashed the dark, stealing Mave's breath. Her spine clapped against the ceiling.

"*A toad...little worms... These enemies are near.*"

Gracelyn walked in mid-speech: "...need to stop it," she hissed. "I did *not* sign up for this. I feel sick, Vincent. I think I'm going to be sick." She crossed her arms and curled forward onto her stomach.

"Take it easy, Gracie. Already told you, I got everything under control." He eased the door shut behind him, his wide bulk blocking the exit like a mound of sandbags.

"You say that now, but you saw that last message she sent!" She hugged herself tighter. "If she knows who you are, then who's to say she hasn't figured out the rest? Who's to say she's not on to me, too?"

"Look, you need to calm the fuck down," he growled. "The bitch was bluffing."

"Then why go to all that trouble?" Gracelyn's voice wavered. "Why pretend to kill off her father in some bogus call? If he were to find out you faked his murder—a *hitman*—Jesus, Mother Mary, I feel sick."

Mave's heart rose into her throat. She grinded her teeth together, muffling her gasp or cry or scream. Faked? Cain was *alive*?

"I'm being thorough, playing it out," Vin said. "And if you wanna avoid getting caught, then shut up and let me fucking focus."

He lumbered past Gracelyn and sat on the desk chair Mave had been using mere seconds ago. "Huh, look here," he said, leaning back with a smug expression. "Seat's even warm, which means that moron just left for his rounds. We got plenty of time to erase your little shenanigans."

Gracelyn's attention volleyed between Vincent and the door, her foot tapping.

"*My* shenanigans? You were in police custody this afternoon! How was I supposed to know what deals you were cutting? If it wasn't for my improvisation, finding that journal, sending that text to plant doubts in her head about Rawlings, she'd be calling him for real with an entirely different—"

"For fuck's sake, what part of *bluffing* don't you get? Now hold that flashlight still."

Gracelyn huffed through her nose. "Fine. Just hurry up. The

wedding tours have been cancelled and I'm not even supposed to be here, remember?"

Vincent clacked a series of commands on the keyboard, seemingly familiar with the hotel's operating system. In no time, he'd loaded the same recording of Mave from earlier in the night, grieving Cain in the library—except he forwarded the footage an hour ahead.

On the monitor, Mave was still passed out on the wingback chair in the corner. A shadow hovered over her. A second later, Gracelyn appeared on screen. Like a trained pickpocket, she eased the cellphone free from Mave's side. She tapped the screen awake, hovered it over Mave for facial recognition, then busied herself.

Gracelyn texted Ren.

Gracelyn begged for him to come.

Gracelyn deleted his replies.

Mave's skin crawled.

Seemingly satisfied Ren had given up responding and taken the bait, Gracelyn set Mave's phone on the floor next to her and paused. She regarded Mave asleep. She briefly exited the camera's frame, then reappeared with the fur blanket. She draped it over Mave.

"Look at you," Vin rasped. "Fussing over that little bitch like a mother with a sick kid. You're too soft, Gracie. First disobeying my orders with the hatch, now this."

"You're the sick one," Gracelyn muttered.

"What's that now?" Vin snapped.

She shook her head and swallowed. "Nothing. Just please. Be quick. I have a bad feeling..." She glanced back at the door with a deep frown.

After a tense beat, Vincent resumed typing.

"You sure you know what you're doing?" Gracelyn whispered.

"Ye of little fucking faith." He sneered. "Always underestimating me like the rest of 'em." He hit one last button with flourish and leaned back as the footage flickered to snow. "See? This system's a joke compared to some others I've cracked."

"Fine. But that's it. No more. I've done more than my share to pay you back for what my son owes you. Okay? I'm out."

"Are you now?" He typed additional commands, and the cameras' live feed streamed on the monitors. "Last I recall, Gracie, your boy was on a weekly prescription. Nasty habits ain't cheap."

"We *agreed*. He's getting clean now! And I've risked enough." She clutched her neck, absently rubbing her collar. "That disgusting goat's head you had me stake just about got me busted."

"What can I say"—Vin shrugged—"I got inspired by that kid's revenge job, dumping the rats in the kitchen." He snickered, as if remembering. He'd seen it. He'd cleared the security footage, after all.

Liam, Mave caught on as her blood ran cold. The teen's visit the other day for a supposed job as a dishwasher. With his backpack. He must have smuggled in and released those three rats to get back at her after she'd exposed his lies to his father.

"What are you still doing?" Gracelyn hissed.

"She's not in the library anymore." He grunted. "Where the fuck'd she go?"

"Doesn't matter! We have to get out of here. The guard could come back any second." She tilted her attention to the door.

Vincent scoffed. "I'll handle the guard."

Gracelyn flinched. "What does that mean? You need to stop talking like that. It's bad enough what you did to poor Gerald." She shut her eyes and cringed.

Mave's stomach sunk hearing her confirm it. Vin had murdered Gerald Lee Baker. Her muscles tightened and strained.

"Why do you keep bringing that up, huh?" He scowled as he searched the live feed from hallway to hallway. "Told you that was self-defence. Besides, you were the one who let me into her room. Gerald wasn't so *poor* then, was he?"

"What else was I supposed to do when you call me up with another ultimatum?" She shuddered.

"Listen, it's done. No one can trace shit back to us."

"No, there is no us, Vincent, because I didn't kill anyone."

He suddenly stood to his full height and stared her down. Gracelyn shrunk back against the door and looked at her feet. "You need to watch yourself. *We* did what we had to. You get me?" When she didn't reply, he stepped forward and pinched her chin, forcing her to gaze up at him. "I said," he overenunciated, "do you get me?"

Gracelyn gave a strained nod.

"Good." He patted her cheek and turned back to the monitors. Gracelyn's shoulders heaved with her breath. "Now," Vin growled, "since you're so worried about saving your ass, why don't you stop clucking in my ear and get the fuck out of here?" Somehow, he made the invitation sound like a threat.

"And my son,"—she swallowed—"we're done?" She shifted her weight from one foot to the other.

Vin turned and looked at her directly. "For now."

The fear in Gracelyn's eyes was visible even through the thick shadows.

FORTY-ONE

The door creaked shut with Gracelyn's departure. Mave fixed her attention on Vin. Alone.

He scanned the rooms and halls flashing on the monitors' live feed. *Searching for me.*

Mave remained frozen, her breathing shallow, praying the duct's recess was enough to shield her—praying the hissing vent would smother the loud thumps of her heart.

He tinkered with camera controls, scratched his bald head, and, finally, turned off the monitors. He pulled out his phone. What was he doing? How long would he stay here? Mave couldn't keep herself wedged to the ceiling indefinitely. An ache built in her arms.

Her eyes flicked down. The exit was close. If only she could drop down and slip out without being spotted or having the door creak. She didn't have all the answers, but she'd heard enough. With Gracelyn as his accomplice, Vin was Bek-187—the thief, the blackmailer, the liar, Gerald Lee Baker's murderer. Ren had been right. All these years, Vin hated Holden for driving Pammy away. He'd do anything to get even. She stifled a shiver.

Mave pictured herself rushing to Ren in the spa. She'd apologize, explain everything, and Vin and Gracelyn could be arrested on the spot. Vin rose at last, stretched his arms with a sigh, and headed to the door. He paused with his hand on the knob and checked over his shoulder.

Don't look up. Don't look up.

He scoffed, as is finding something amusing, then turned and left.

Mave exhaled as his large figure disappeared past the doorframe. The door whined as it closed. Finally. She shifted her weight to relieve the ache in her arms. But as she dipped her hip, her cellphone slipped from her pocket.

NO!

In a matter of a seconds, the phone fell on its corner, skittered sideways, and ended up in the center of the room with an audible clap.

The door pushed open again and Vin stomped through. One sweep of his flashlight and he spotted the phone.

Mave stiffened in place, palms sweaty and arms quivering to remain wedged.

He stood there a beat, gazing at her phone. With his face pinched in part suspicion, part confusion, he snatched up the cell and examined its neutral case, its screen. Her wallpaper was set to the manufacturer default, offering no hint of her identity. He looked to the desk, as if expecting to spot a domino effect. How else could a phone be tossed across a seemingly vacant room?

Don't look up. Nobody looks up.

Mave trembled and chewed on the inside of her cheek.

He prowled three hundred and sixty degrees around the small room, scanning each corner with his flashlight. The scent of smoke drifted with his movements.

Ashes. The burned books.

He ducked and checked under the desk. Seeing nothing beyond dust bunnies and wires, he let out a sharp huff and straightened. He glanced down at her phone again and the knot in his brow tightened. As if in reply, her cell chose that moment to buzz with a notification. Vin blinked at the screen, previewing a text she'd received. His jaw fell open.

Another update from Julián? *Or Ren.* That shocked expression he wore—Ren must have sent her another pleading text.

Her mind and body raced in opposite directions—fight or flight?

Seemingly incapable of settling on either one, she kept her elbows and knees locked, hands and feet planted. Her joints tremored. She had to hold out a little longer. Another minute, another second.

Vin's face seemed to redden in the shadows. He abruptly spun and stormed out of the office. It happened so quickly, Mave remained frozen, fraught with dread as she processed his reaction.

Exactly what message had he read on her phone? Was he going to find Ren locked in the spa closet for himself? What if he hurt him? She listened for any sounds of life from the hallway. Hearing none, she gasped with minor relief and additional unease. Whatever Vin had seen —wherever he was headed—he'd set off in an awful hurry.

Not over, M&M. Go.

She slunk down from the ceiling and shook out her joints. With no time to waste, she swung open the door and jumped in her skin.

The sound came first—a whipping pop—a painful punch in her neck, hot. Hotter.

The sight of the gun's barrel materialized in her vision.

Her legs jammed. She barely registered his lopsided smile because...because...

She blinked and fell back into the office with a broken grunt, her hands flailing toward her neck. Her spine collided into something hard. The desk. Gravity pulled.

Splayed on the floor, the world raced and slowed, a spiraling vortex sucking her under.

He was waiting for me to...to...

Her vision faded to black as the door creaked shut.

A second later, it whined open again.

FORTY-TWO

M ust be drunk on morphine again. Dreaming. Half gone, fucking high on life. Or maybe I finally did it, lit myself up for good. Damn nurse is always yelling at me about it—won't shut up, that one: No smoking! No playing with your lighter in bed!

But that's alright. Better to float dead in the sky than flare alive on the ground.

And this time, it isn't just because I can feel you with me, but...

"I—I see you, Mave." God, you're beautiful. In my mask, your eyes are framed like two jewels. Sea and earth. Infinity. This time—this dream—I never want to wake.

"Holden?"

At the sound of my name on your lips, I sigh. My lungs drain their smoke, my head bows, drawn to you like the moon to the sun. My skin grows restless, pushes past the numbness and drugs for your touch. It's like you feel it, too. The pull.

Your hand drifts toward me like a feather. I hold my breath.

You trace my old scar in my brow. Heat ignites on my face, flows down the stem of my tongue, all the way down my throat till it bursts in my core.

Wake up.

I've never felt more alive than I do now.

"What is this?" you say.

I swallow thickly. "You tell me. You're the one channeling me."

"Channeling?"

"Don't stop." I sigh and lean into your touch. Hungry, thirsty, burning on and on without release. "Please, I...I need you."

"Am I...?" You blink at me, as if not believing your eyes. "Are we alive?"

A short breath escapes me. "Define alive."

"I'm serious."

So am I. "Depends on the day."

"Holden, please stop." An emotion I can't read flutters in the depths of your eyes. You pull away. "No more games."

Games? I think of the last reports of you running around with Rawlings. RAWLINGS. I curl my fingers, knuckles sore. I crave another smoke. I'm feverish. I want to hit something. Smash his motherfucking face. Life's never been fair, so why should any of us bother to play fair, right? "I don't know what you want me to say." My heart flutters in pain, a broken wing inside my chest. It's lame and piercing. "I'm not the one looking for one man while running into the arms of another." It occurs to me I sound like a jealous asshole because that's what I am.

"What?" You frown as if you're trying to read my thoughts, your mouth held in that little O shape that drives me crazy.

"That what you like?" I keep going. God help me, I keep going. "Boy Scouts with good haircuts and shiny badges?" It's fine. Pammy liked him, too. All the girls did. I just thought you'd be different.

"That was never—how do you know about...?" Your mouth pouts again, and I want to kiss you so hard, it'll make me bleed all over again.

"Did Stratis tell you?" you ask.

I give a small nod and recognize the sting in your eyes.

"If that's true"—your voice hitches and I hate myself, want to take it all back—"if you care so much, then why haven't you come back?"

"You think this is easy for me?" I can hardly think straight. I want you so bad. Even if you're faraway, or I'm broken, or it'll kill me. "You think I want this?"

"Want what?"

You have the same hunger—I can read it in the way your gaze roams over me, taking in my lips, my neck, my shoulders. You don't seem to notice the burn.

"Are you afraid?" *I say, daring you.* "You think I'm going to dissolve into smoke if you push too hard?

"Holden, I don't understand what this is." *Your chest heaves.* "What's happening to me—to us?"

"Simple." *I feel the fire building low in my gut—the good kind. I want it. I fuel it. It overrides everything else until I can smell the flora and salt of your skin inches away.* "My longing. It's so strong, you can sense it. Taste it. I want you to find what's mine."

"Your mask." *You blink in understanding.* "You lost it."

"Not just my mask. My home. You. Me. All of it." *Not dead. It's so fucking intense.* "You're channeling me through it."

That little fold between your brow buckles. "Your mask?"

"Think it's a coincidence that you found it? That you're sleeping with it over and over again?"

"But what about now?"

"You're wearing it."

A ripple of surprise widens your eyes.

"Go on, check for yourself."

You raise your hands to your face and run your fingers along the porcelain bone.

There it is. You feel it now, Mave? "Pretty sure you can reach me through it," *I add.*

"But how?" *You shake your head.* "Before, I was dreaming..."

I shrug and catch your gaze. "Doesn't matter what you call it."

"But how can I speak to you now? How am I here? In your dream—or mine?" *You reach for your temples, disoriented, before remembering my mask is still there.* "No. This can't be real. There has to be rules, order to the tracking."

"Why are you so hung up on rules? What are you so goddammed afraid of?"

"I'm not afraid."

"Yeah? You sure?" *If I have to prove to you it's real, so be it. I'm ready to bleed. In fact, it'll be my motherfucking pleasure.*

I edge closer and slide my hands around your waist. "You feel this?" *Because I do. I close my eyes, overwhelmed by the rush.*

I sense your answer in the race of your pulse, the heat of your breath. I pull you flush against my body. "How 'bout now? You feel this?"

"Holden."

It's the way you say it—summon it. I come undone.

I kiss you like the first time. The last time. Harder. Faster. I feel my stitches tear but I don't care. Raw. Honey. Fuck. Your mouth is like a lifeline. I need...I need...

You break away, your eyes mirroring my ache and wonder.

"'Love is a smoke,'" *I quote Shakespeare against your skin, trace your swollen lip with my thumb,* "'made with the fume of sighs.' Now do you understand? Do you see? The answers you've been chasing, they've been inside you this whole time."

Use your gift. Deep down you know how. It's no different than how your heart pumps or your lungs flow.

You exhale and nod.

"Show me," *you say.* "I'm ready now. I need to know how it happened."

"Anything," *I whisper.* "Just stay with me here a little longer."

I press my lips to yours. I burn hotter, brighter. Together, we melt deeper into the dream.

FORTY-THREE

September, 2006

In the small town of Hazel Springs, the first party of the school year always held the most promise—better than any homecoming or prom, winter formal or chaperoned event. September's rager could make you or break you. Excitement and nerves swirled in preparation. Rumors rippled and circulated, twirling like the crisp leaves in the autumn breeze. Seniors scored kegs and collected cash orders. Juniors prepped playlists, subwoofers, and portable speakers. All week, they whispered in class and passed each other notes. Rides and curfews, cover stories and lies were carefully arranged, traded, and bargained for with various currencies: stolen vodka coolers and cigarettes, weed and hash.

On the night of the party, mud-crusted four-by-fours parked next to shiny sedans borrowed for the night; humble bicycles for the less fortunate. It didn't matter *how* they got there. Only that they came, got noticed. Veni, vidi, vici. Of these aspirations, Holden Frost felt nothing but derision. More than anything, he despised this annual ritual. Apart from reeking of hormones and insecurities, cheap perfume and bug spray, the outdoor party was a one-night-only pomp and status marker —a stamp of belonging that would validate his asshole peers throughout the rest of their school year. The sole reason Holden bothered to show was because Vincent Lorde made him.

And Pammy. Her freckles...

Earlier that day, Vincent made Holden an offer he couldn't refuse. A badly disguised threat, in truth, but Vin being Vin—a year and a half older and already filled out like an ox—he liked to play the good gangster on occasion. Holden's options were either to earn Vin's favor by acting as Pammy's designated driver—making sure she and her fairweather friend June safely got to and from the party—*or* Holden could have his balls kicked in while he slept under their shared roof. Vin didn't give a shit if it meant Holden had to jack the neighbor's rusted Chevy Impala to transport Pammy and June. What wheels he chose were his own business. *Just don't get fucking caught* was Vin's only stipulation.

Holden considered telling Vin to fuck right off—no matter the size of his foster brother's fists. But just last week, he'd made a promise to Rah: no more fights. So here he was. At a social gathering. The single person within a five-mile radius who could pass a breathalyzer test. (Too bad he didn't also have a driver's licence and a legally obtained vehicle.) *Christ.* It was torture.

Though Vincent was also in attendance, he couldn't escort Pammy himself. For one, Vin was far from sober. By eight p.m., his drunk bellow and bark could be heard rattling the nearest tree trunks. And two, having his little sister tag along cramped his style. Vin ignored Pammy in public. As always. She wasn't exactly in a position to help his social standing.

Holden liked Pammy, but even he could see she tried too hard. She clung—be it to other girls who manipulated her for their own gain, or to the boys with the cleanest cuts who humored her in hopes of scoring an easy blowjob. Holden tried not to listen to the cruel gossip. But he wasn't deaf. Pammy, on the other hand, seemed to live with her head in the clouds.

She pretended there was good in everyone. Even him. So Holden played along. He didn't have the heart to tell her she was naïve. And dead wrong. Not everyone had good in them. He wondered if Pammy truly believed in people's innate kindness, or if it was just a con to compensate for her mother. At least the reason Holden was stuck in the system was because his folks were buried six feet under. Pammy, though... The entire town knew Chandra Lorde's pathetic story: single mom and alcoholic battling cancer, hooked on painkillers, deemed unfit by the court to care for her own kids. Hence Holden's latest involuntary lodgings with Pammy and Vin, living in a foster home of a retired daycare worker named Tina. He wished Rah would take him back. The château was his home, its dark, underground tunnels the single place he ever felt anything remotely close to normal. But during Holden's most recent visit, Rah was scribbling nonsense on the walls and smelled of week-old piss. Holden sighed.

It was now past midnight. He'd run out of cigarettes. He last noticed Vin playing beer pong with his fellow goons next to the bonfire. Pammy and June, who ditched him as soon as he parked the car, he'd lost track of hours ago. Holden was tired. There was only so much people-watching he could endure amid sneers and snickers aimed at his back—wannabes judging him a freak. Meanwhile, they were the ones dancing with uncoordinated limbs on puke-laced soil. *Fucking jerks.*

As Justin Timberlake sang of bringing sexy back, Holden wandered deeper into the forest—far enough to ignore the thud of the bass, lewd shouts, and laughter. He was skinny and wiry, skilled at climbing trees to impressive heights. After pointing his flashlight upward to make sure no surprise nests or creatures awaited him above, he scaled a mature pine and made himself comfortable inside its curved bough. He pulled out a beaten-up paperback from his jacket pocket and settled back to escape. To numb the pounding hunger of his head and his stomach and his dick.

Or he tried.

Footsteps and giggles drifted his way. A loud shush. Another giggle. And then...

Fucking hell. Of all the trees in all the forests.

From the base of the pine's trunk, the smacking lips and slobbery moans were impossible to tune out. Holden switched off his flashlight and pinched the bridge of his nose. He placed bets in his head. How long would this take? Thirty seconds? Thirty minutes? If he pointed down his flashlight and shouted, would they bother to stop? Or go away? Or goddamn *notice*? He angled his head for a peek through the branches.

The dark made it hard to see. And whether that was good or bad was up for debate. Their moaning had found a rhythm. What Holden's eyes couldn't make out in the shadows, his mind filled in under the glaring lights of his imagination—with or without his permission. But then a breathy name ruined the fantasy.

"*Ren...mmm.* Wait."

René fucking Rawlings. Of course it was Mr. Golden Hero banging his girlfriend. Who else?

"Just...come on..." Clothes rustled.

"Wait."

"Gotta condom..."

Holden's fists tightened. Ren with his winning smile and his winning arm. Star pitcher of the school's baseball team. His ERA and broad chest made up for his bad acne. The girls pined after Ren. Including Pammy. She'd confessed as much on the car ride over. It was all her and June could talk about. *Ren this*, and, *Ren that*. Holden just about vomited in his mouth. The way Pammy described him, it was obvious she'd held this crush for a while, years maybe. Forget that Ren barely acknowledged her existence. Holden had kept quiet.

He knew the bad guys in town. And he knew Ren's dirty little secret —including the real reason why he was so good on the mound. So unbeatable. The creeps in juvie gossiped, too. Holden remembered back to when Ren was as scrawny as he was, when he would come to the hotel and seek out Holden through the vents. And now?

Holden crawled the vents alone.

"Does this mean...?" his girlfriend exhaled.

"Yeah, yeah..." Ren grunted.

"You want me?"

"Yeah."

"Not her?"

More moans.

"Then say it," she breathed. "Say my name." Her voice was pitched and drawn out, sticky like burnt sugar. "I wanna...hear you...say it."

Ren did. More than once. And it was the wrong name. One Holden didn't want to hear.

His muscles bunched so tight, they felt as if they might snap off his bones. The worst of it was, deep down, in the pit of his sour stomach, Holden knew it wasn't over. Not even close. More blows were coming. It was one of the first things this ugly, forsaken world had taught him. Pain was patient.

The darkness took its time to bleed out in full glory.

———

Holden's attendance record was worse than any other student in Hazel Springs. He did or did not show up to class. On those days when he bothered to "make an effort," as his youth care worker called it, it certainly wasn't because the law mandated he attend. No. The law and its requirements were a joke to him. Rather, Holden had come to learn from a young age that Rah, even if partially incoherent, schooled him far better than any so-called teacher in the shithole of public education.

Rah was the smartest man Holden had ever met. Unbeknownst to anyone, he patiently and passionately tutored Holden in languages, biology, astronomy, world history, and, most notably, classical literature. Rah—who secretly raised Holden as a baby until he was no longer capable—even went as far as to name him after J.D. Salinger's rebellious hero. Of course, Holden didn't share any of this with his disgruntled and underpaid youth care worker. Instead, he chose to join his classroom peers (whom he considered a herd of dumb sheep) whenever the need arose; a dirty little reflex that whispered, *Go on, make the assholes squirm.* For that reason, Holden was present on Monday morning after the big party. Not because of Pammy. That was just bad luck.

Holden spotted her in the hallway by Ren's locker. Since driving her and June home yesterday morning, Holden hadn't spoken to Pammy.

He'd heard all he needed to in the stolen Impala before dropping them off and ditching the ride.

Ren is dumping his girlfriend.

Ren and her are a thing now.

Ren uses his tongue when he kisses like he—

The first bell rung shrilly in his ears. A crescendo of chatter filled the hall. Sheep shuffled. In no rush, Holden leaned against the cinderblock wall and crossed his arms. From the looks of others who were either openly staring or stealing glances, tilting their heads or dragging their heels to get to class, Holden wasn't the only one who'd noticed Pammy's stiff posture—or how Ren pretended she was invisible. Ren jammed a textbook in his backpack in silence.

"You promised," Pammy hissed, her voice rising despite her clenched jaw. She apparently realized her audience and was trying to remain discreet. Too late. The fickle sheep watched. Ren reached into his locker, unresponsive; didn't even turn his head in her direction.

In an alternate world, one where he wasn't a villain, Holden pictured himself grabbing Pammy by her shoulders. *You're too good for him.* He lit a cigarette and pulled a drag, uncaring of teachers who might poke their heads out to check for stragglers in the hallway. *Come and catch me if you can. Dickwads.*

"Ren," Pammy said, a note of desperation pinching her tone, "at the party...you promised me..."

Holden's stomach turned. The echo returned, mocked him—their fucking at the base of the pine tree, Pammy's neediness, Ren's lies. His cigarette trembled between his fingertips.

Too good for him.

Ren still didn't answer her. But one of his shitface buddies did. Perhaps bored of waiting for Ren to either man up or hurry the fuck up, he stepped in closer. "Hey, Pammy," he said with a lecherous grin. When she glanced his way, he pantomimed with his tongue and fist pumping out one side of his cheek. Laughter rippled from onlookers. Someone playfully slapped Shitface on the shoulder. The crowd was only starting to warm up.

Baa, baa, black sheep. Holden bided his time, his cigarette fraying ash.

Ren finally bothered to look at Pammy. He wore his frown like a confused and conflicted professional hero. He lowered his head, as if needing to bow to reach her. "You okay?" he said. His eyes were so damn warm.

Holden felt it in his gut. So did Pammy.

Her mouth twisted to hold it in as her tears welled up amid more snickers.

No two words had ever held more pity in the whole entire universe. It was worse than Ren's silence. Worse than if he had told her to stop stalking him, gaslighted her, called her the dirty names the others did behind her back. But that came after. By next week, even June would join the sick chorus. *Baa, baa.*

Pammy's breaths shortened. Her shoulders deflated and curled inward. She opened her mouth and was cut off by the second bell. Ren's girlfriend appeared around the corner. She sauntered over, oblivious, and brushed past Pammy. As Pammy stumbled backward into the lockers, Girlfriend didn't miss a step. She sidled up next to Ren, tossed her hair, and wrapped her skinny arm around his hip in possession. "You ready?"

Mouths hung open, drooling in anticipation.

Holden, Ren, Pammy, the entire hallway—they kept still as she arched her perfect breasts into his perfect ribs. They were made from the same plastic mold. Ren nodded. It was all the encouragement Girlfriend needed. She leaned in and branded him with her lips.

Shitface whooped and told them to get a room. The audience thinned, disappearing through doorways. Pammy never stood a chance. Maybe she finally saw what the rest of them did. That had been the point of the September rager, after all. She'd been ranked. Her stamp had dried its ink.

Pamela Lorde is good for a drunken fuck on the side.

Her tears broke. She wiped them in vain and wandered away, unseen by the one person whose attention she craved most. Holden stayed where he was. He took a deep drag of his cigarette, held it in. He waited.

Ren was in motion, crossing Holden's little patch of space. He must have felt his hard stare because he slowed. The clique was oblivious, chatting and distracted.

A calling. It happened quickly.

Ren slid his brown gaze to Holden's black one. They snapped together like two magnets. Holden exhaled expertly, smoke streaming from his lungs into Ren's face with an unmistakable challenge.

Ren's lashes fluttered, his nostrils flared, and a vein ticked in his jaw.

The fun and games had only just begun.

———

All it took was an anonymous tip to the principal. Holden attended school for this sole purpose: to pay them back for all the times they'd hurt him. And now Pammy. So bye-bye, golden glow.

By fourth period, they'd searched Ren's locker and found the drugs. The rest was mere procedure. Pissing in a cup. Getting kicked off the team for the entire season. And a permanent note in his school record. It worked. The herd was abuzz with a fresher, juicier scandal. Pammy's humiliation was forgotten and replaced with Ren's shame. Turned out, everyone's favorite pitcher was a big fat liar. And once the first domino fell...

Ren's girlfriend dumped him. The town's dreams of making the regionals were ruined. And Ren's big, bright future was flushed into darkness.

Play-by-plays and rumors spawned and replicated like bacteria in heat. Public health pamphlets were distributed in gym class. The guidance counselor explained a future scholarship wasn't completely off the table, but Ren would have to work doubly hard to make up for the violation. Steroids weren't taken lightly by college recruiters.

But really, all the herd cared about was who.

Who ratted out René Rawlings and destroyed his reputation?

———

Before the sear, his smooth drawl drifted into Holden's dream: "Know it was you, chain-smoking *freak*. Maybe this'll teach you to mind your own fucking business."

He was shocked from a deep sleep. For a moment, there was only pain. And then...

Holden wasn't sure if it was before or after the cigarette burn sprung tears in his eyes, but he felt it either way. A shift in energy. He blinked his vision clear, peered through the shadows to orient himself. The crickets chirped through the open window. In some distant part of his brain, he realized Ren must have slipped in that way. But his attention was torn. Ren was still seated on him, crushing his abdomen with his weight. And the skin on his shoulder was blistering where Ren got him—got him bad. Ren must have noticed it too.

Still straddling him in a wrestler's hold, the rage in Ren's face melted into something else—an emotion unreadable to Holden. Maybe it was fascination. Or shock. They were both breathing hard. Ren tossed away the cigarette like it was burning him instead. Holden tried to buck him off with a grunt, but this goaded Ren. He dug his knees into Holden's elbows, doubled his hold, and pinned him harder. He was too heavy—too strong for Holden.

"Get off me," Holden said in a guttural growl. "Get the fuck off, you *sick* motherfuck—"

Ren jostled him by his wrists and thrust him deeper into the mattress until Holden could feel each coil digging into his spine. "Shut up," Ren said with a flash of anger resurfacing. His eyes glistened with heat as they searched Holden's face. "*You're* the sick one," he said. "Not me."

Something about Ren's expression, like a blink of recognition— Holden started to laugh. Ren was a psycho. Breaking into homes. Burning him with a cigarette. It was like looking into a mirror.

"I said *shut up*, freak." Ren rattled him again, and Holden laughed harder. Ren was forced to shift his weight to apply more pressure. "I hate you," he grunted. "*Hate* you." Their knees kicked and their hips clapped. Holden almost got free. Almost.

It was unclear who started it, but Holden was pretty sure it was Ren trying to get him to stop laughing.

His mouth was hard and hungry and mad. Later, he'd recall Pammy's description of Ren's kiss. But this was not the same—teeth and tongue and heat. It was over before it'd begun.

Ren tore himself off, wiping his mouth with his wrist. He tripped, knocked over items on the nightstand along the way—ashtray, paperbacks. He fled out the window before Holden could pull in his first lungful of unrestricted air.

Holden was left panting on his mattress, sweat-covered and throbbing in various body parts. He listened to the crickets' chirrup through the window. Ren wouldn't come back. He was sure of it.

A line had been crossed. And there was no turning back.

———

Vincent shoved him, and Holden went flying into the kitchen table. Glasses clattered and smashed. A chair toppled onto him. More than the bruises of his collision, his chest hurt from Vin's thrust—like two scalding irons had branded his lungs. He pushed off the chair and assessed the situation.

It was late afternoon. Just the two of them. Their foster parent, Tina, wasn't home yet. This was bad. He could see it written on Vin's face. He was fuming mad, beyond reason. Likely drunk enough to heighten his rage, but not so much as to slow him down. Holden's eyes flicked to the doorway. Almost immediately, Vincent stepped in the way, blocking the exit. He growled low and mean, "You ain't going no—"

Holden scrambled on all fours to get away as Vin stomped toward him for round two.

"You little shit! You helped her!"

Holden crawled under the table. Vin's reach was too long. He grabbed Holden by his calf, swung him out and flung him across the linoleum floor toward the corner. Holden's breath cut off as he struck the wall with the force of a canon. Vin staggered and leaned down, his feet planted like stumps. "I found out!" he cried in his face, his breath reeking. "You gave her the fake fucking ID."

Holden squirmed to get away, but Vin lodged one massive boot in the hollow of his stomach. He grimaced in pain. He was no more than a worm in an elephant's path. If Vin were to apply his full weight, he'd crush him in half. "I didn't...know," he gasped, "she'd use it...to run away." Acid seared his throat. He now wished he'd said no to Pammy when she'd asked him. It'd been over a month. No word. She had simply disappeared overnight, into thin air.

"What name did you give her?" Vin barked.

"She picked it...not me. I swear, I—"

"What name?" Vin said, pushing deeper. Holden gagged as he gripped and shoved at Vin's ankle, an unmovable piston. He felt the boot tread imprinting on the underside of his stomach, his kidneys screaming like they might rupture from pressure. Vin eased his step just enough so that Holden could speak. "I said, what—?"

"Kat—Katie," he stuttered. "She wanted...to be Katie. Now let me up."

"Let you up?" Vincent knelt forward, digging and digging with his foot, knee, thigh. He grabbed Holden by the collar. Holden tasted blood and vomit in his mouth. "You're the reason my kid sister's missing, you little—" The pain shot into his bowels and back, took over. His vision began to blacken. He clawed outward. A glass bottle glanced his fingers, fallen from the table. Before Holden knew what he was doing, he broke the bottle by its neck and struck Vincent square in the skull.

Vincent hollered.

Blood gushed.

The weight released.

And a woman screamed.

Their foster parent Tina had come home.

———

Though Tina only witnessed the end of their fight—painting Holden as the violent, out-of-control aggressor—they were forced into a truce for the sake of avoiding any further mediation or, god forbid, group therapy. Turned out, he and Vin (when sober) had more in common than not. They both missed Pammy. They both resented life. And they both had people writing them off as useless. The world looked at Vin and saw a dumb meathead. Holden saw a loud opportunist, one who drank too much and used his size to his advantage, sure, but contrary to first impressions, Vincent Lorde was anything but dumb.

They sat together on the hood of the car, sharing a smoke. A stolen beer sat between them. Vincent would likely end up following in his mother's drunken footsteps, but Holden kept this to himself.

Vincent scratched his jagged scar, bright pink on his head, and gazed up at the winter sky. His breath clouded. "You sure it was Katie she used?"

Holden nodded. "Katie Bowers."

Vin grunted. "Mom's maiden name." Holden knew for a fact Vin had been searching for a while. He seemed forever glued to the computer, scouring websites and news articles for his sister. But in truth, she could have been anywhere. New York, Chicago, Vegas. The cities were too big to track her. Assuming she was still alive.

"Think she had the right idea?" Vin said. "Getting out of this shit town?"

Holden took a drag, remembering her freckles. "Yeah. Maybe she did. Must be nice to disappear."

Vin gave him a sidelong glance. "What the fuck's keeping you?" He swigged his beer and went back to gazing at the clouds. "Not like you got any ties here. Even Tina gave you the boot. Shit, you had the perfect out."

Holden kept quiet about Rah. Truth was, he empathized with Pammy and Vin more than either one of them knew. It wasn't easy to watch a parent struggling with sickness. Disease. Last few months, Rah's illness had progressed. Holden would be surprised if he lasted the year. His chest felt heavy. He shrugged. "Couldn't go to a city. Don't like people. At least here, I know the dicks by name. Can beat them at their own game."

Vin chuckled. "Like you did Rawlings? You know, you ain't half

bad, Frost. I'm starting to think I like how your freak mind works."
They were silent a moment before Vin added, "There are better places
to play the game, though; places to get a serious win *and* disappear."

Holden raised a brow. "Like where?"

"You heard of the darknet?" Vin leaned back on his elbows and
flicked his cigarette. The hood dipped with his weight. "You could be
anonymous. Live a double life, online and in town."

Holden watched a crow beat its wings in the sky. "What if I was just
online?"

"How do you mean?"

"What if I did more than run away from this town. What if I died?"

"Jesus..." For a moment, Vincent looked stunned. Then his face
broke into a broad smile. "Know what? Between your freak brains and
my job hookups, we might be able help each other out."

FORTY-FOUR

Water plinked. Something briefly fluttered against the seams of her lips, the column of her throat—there and gone like a whisper.

She moaned, too hot, too cold, covered in sweat. Her tongue was thick and heavy, throbbing in time with her heartbeats. She'd bitten it badly, but couldn't remember when. When had she bitten her tongue? She struggled to clear her mind, but the sound of water dripping distracted her. It was familiar. And Billie Holiday. The jazz standard drifted softly in the distance. Mave knew the song. A lover's promise. Pining for her lost love.

"I'll Be Seeing You."

The verses rang in her ears. Hollow.

She blinked in the darkness and rolled her heavy head. The last dreamlike traces of Holden's smoke melted from her tongue, leaving behind a bitter aftertaste. She pulled off the mask, unclear how she'd obtained it while unconscious.

Where am I?

She pushed up from the ground and a new sound—an odd clinking —filled her chest with dread. Before she could fully process it, her gaze was drawn to movement.

Insects. Moths. They were everywhere, their black wings dancing through the shadows. The pieces came together.

She was in the greenhouse. And around her ankle, a thick chain lay coiled. *Clinking.* She drew up her knee and found herself shackled to the sink in the corner.

No.

She thrashed her foot, sending sharp pains shooting through her hip, spine, neck.

Her neck.

The rest of her memory came flooding back: the security office, Gracelyn and Vincent, opening the door to flee and—

Her hands fluttered to her throat where she'd been shot. It wasn't an open wound, but a scabbed, tender lump. She hissed in pain as she gently pushed on it. Her gland was swollen. Reflexively, she reached down to her pocket for her cellphone—she needed to call an ambulance, the police, anyone. Except she didn't have her phone. Vin did. Vin had shot her.

She traced her fingers to her neck again, assessing the piercing pain. It hadn't been caused by a bullet.

A tranquillizer dart, Cain's voice noted in her mind. Vin must have shot her with a strong sedative, put her to sleep like a wild animal. That would explain her grogginess and disorientation. Her thirst. How much time had passed? How long had she been locked up in here? It seemed to be night. *Another* night, her gut told her. She was so thirsty. At least twenty-four hours must have passed since the wedding day. Surely a colleague should have discovered her by now—Amos, Julián? Yet the greenhouse was abandoned.

All the candles had been removed. The aisle of rose petals, scattered by foot traffic, had wilted. An unplugged string of lights dangled from a broken trellis. The chairs she'd painstakingly arranged into neat rows were now haphazardly stacked. Forgotten storage, shoved away and locked up. The wedding had been cancelled. Someone must have released all the moths. And someone had put Billie Holiday on loop on a portable speaker nearby. They were re-staging it, the haunting, mocking her even now. Vincent. *Katie.*

All at once, the details of her dream flooded into her consciousness. Holden's memories: how Ren had been the one to burn Holden; how Vincent had helped Holden stage his drowning; how Pammy had run away after Ren's rejection; how she'd reinvented herself as Katie.

And then what? Did Vin know his sister was dead, that her ghost lingered?

No time for that, M&M. You have to get out of here. You have to drink something.

She cradled her empty stomach, her thirst clawing inside her throat. Her eyes fell on the wishing pots she'd arranged with such care, now overflowing with rainwater. The collected liquid looked more like black ink in the night. The wreaths she'd designed around the pots were gone. The entire greenhouse smelled of rotted earth. But none of that mattered.

She dragged her upper body toward the nearest arrangement, past the edge of what had once been the altar. Her leg held. She grunted, jerking to an involuntary halt. Bound to the sink with a six-foot radius, she couldn't get close enough. Desperation lanced her ribs. She gritted her teeth, readjusted her angle, and strained one arm forward. She willed her bones to grow, for her stiff shoulders to loosen. Her hands spread wide. She reached and reached until her middle finger grazed a terracotta rim.

She wiggled and inched the pot closer. The ends of her nails clawed and scraped, again and again. Moths fluttered in her vision, attracted to her heat, her sweat. The pot tipped.

No!

She sagged on the ground, her energy spent as the water soaked into dirty gravel. She wasn't above sucking rocks, but one more pot remained in sight. With a deep breath, she tried again.

She was gentler this time. More patient. Her persistence paid off as the second pot eased close enough to pinch with her thumb.

With a wave of relief, she carefully pulled it forward and rocked upward. She drank greedily, urgently, her thirst insatiable. Cold water dribbled from her jaw. It hardly mattered that the water tasted like soil and dust and moss. She dropped the empty pot and fell on her side, heaving.

Her belly full and sloshing with a mild cramp, she wiped her chin on her wrist and tried to control her diaphragm.

Breathe. Calm down.

THINK. You have to get out of here. Find help.

Her stomach and lungs somewhat settled, she hauled herself into a seated position. Her joints were sore. Every part of her was sore. She yanked on the chain, testing its strength. It rattled and held. She blinked to clear her eyes of dust and crawled closer to the sink. The links were secured to a sturdy pipe beneath the basin, impossible to release by sheer strength.

She bent her leg and inspected the cuff locked on her ankle. Steel. Basic lock. Picking it might take too long and she didn't have a pin. She flinched as a moth coasted across her wrist, her nerve endings over-sensitized. She needed bolt cutters. Maybe a pair lay forgotten on the shelves next to the sink. She crawled toward them to investigate, when the music stopped mid-verse.

Mave froze, her breaths amplified in the silence. Her skin stippled with pins and needles.

"Who's there?" she rasped, feeling herself watched.

An owl hooted in the distance. Her eyes instinctively flicked to the moths fluttering in and out of her vision. The wishing pots plinked like leaky faucets. Yet she sensed it. She was no longer alone. "*Who's there?*" she tried again.

A lantern turned on like a bluish fog. "It's me." Katie emerged from the shadows.

Mave squinted from the light.

A moment later, Katie's eyes widened on her pale face. She hurried next to her and crouched down. "Are you okay?" She looked around, as if disoriented, her pupils unnaturally dilated into the whites of her eyes. "What are you doing in here?"

Mave stared at her, still struggling to wrap her head around everything. Perhaps it was the way the lantern glared from her sallow skin;

Mave noticed now. Her youthfulness trapped in time. The dusting of freckles. Recent conversations echoed in her thoughts.

"These whispers and knocks, my imagination or not, I have to face them."

"Was it hard for you? Making amends with the person in your head, your heart, and the one in real life?"

"Ghosts only want to have their voices heard. They mean us no harm."

Mave didn't know how or why, but Katie was the key. If she wanted to escape these binds, to expose Vincent, then she couldn't run from her gift anymore. She had to help Katie understand her death. Holden had assured her it was as innate as breathing, except...

"What is it, Mave? Why are you looking at me like that?"

"It's just..." Her voice shredded. "I'm really happy to s-see you, that's all." She wouldn't be afraid. Not anymore. "Katie, this is really important. What day is it?"

"Sunday morning," she replied, distracted by the flitter of moths. "I don't like this place at night," she added softly.

Mave had guessed right. She'd been knocked out for an entire day. "And do you know why anyone else hasn't come by here? Found me?"

Her brow knit. "What do you mean? You sent a text, told Julián it was too much—you were taking some time off. Getting away after the wedding got cancelled. Right?"

Her heart dropped. *Vincent* had sent that text. No one would come. They wouldn't search for her if she wasn't missing.

"Katie, we're friends?"

Katie nodded, wide-eyed.

"See, I'm in a bit of trouble and I think"—she swallowed—"I think we can help each other."

"What is it, Mave? You're sorta starting to scare me." She sat beside her, seeming not to notice Mave's chain, and pulled her knees to her chest.

Selective vision and hearing. A passage she'd briefly browsed in that handbook on ghosts crystallized in her thoughts. *They glean only what they want.*

"It might be," Mave agreed, "a bit scary. But you have to trust me.

When we first met, you said you wanted to face your fears—for a fresh start." *Like breathing.* She could do this. "I promise, I'll be with you. We'll get through it together. Just like—like when you asked me to come to the séance. You remember, in the library? We held hands?"

"Yeah," she sighed. "You were so great to try more than once. But it never worked. I still hear the knocks." Her expression fell as she hugged her knees. Mave could sense her helplessness. She was lost. Mave could track her, bring her back to herself.

"I know how now," she whispered. At least enough to *try.* "Tell me, before LA, where did you live?"

Storm clouds flashed in the voids of her eyes. "I don't want to remember that."

"Please, Katie. How about your mother? The one in the picture frame in your room."

"Mom?"

"Uh-huh." Mave smiled. "She wore a pretty scarf on her head." *From battling cancer.* "You were celebrating your birthday. Then what happened?"

Her tears fell quietly, without warning. She shook her head. "She died."

"I'm so sorry," she said, pushing to be heard past the knot in her throat. Grief swelled in her heart. "My mom died when I was young, too."

Katie rested her head on her knees. "I wasn't there. It was after I left for LA and someone..." Her frown deepened, slicing her features in shadows. "Someone sent me an anonymous email. About my mom's funeral. I couldn't *not* return. But then..."

Holden, Mave surmised. He must have eventually tracked her down.

A little moan escaped Katie. She began to rock.

Mave reached out her hand, offering her a conduit for her pain, her suffering. "It's okay. You can show me," she said, "and you won't have to feel it all by yourself. Not anymore."

Katie sniffed and regarded Mave's open palm. Her teardrops fell rhythmically like the rainwater. "You won't leave me," she whispered, "you promise?"

"Promise," she said. "I'll be right here. I won't let go until you ask me to. I know it hurts, but we have to do this. It's the only way to stop the whispers. And the bad people. You know them, don't you? The mean ones, like the person who hurt you."

Katie inhaled sharply.

She scented her recognition before anything else.

The stench in the greenhouse thickened. Not ashes from burning. Not plastic from suffocating. But rotted earth from...

The horror of Katie's passing hovered between them, emanating its reek. Mave's stomach turned and her fingers trembled. But she kept her palm extended.

Without a word, Katie slid her hand into Mave's. She squeezed tight. And the right side of her face shredded into blood and bone.

———

"You just waltz back in here after five fucking years!" Vincent shouted in her face. His breath was moist on her forehead, sweetly ripe with whiskey. The evening crickets had grown quiet. In the hush, the cemetery felt frozen. Hopeless. No amount of praying or lamenting could fix this broken world. Katie wiped her tears. Her face felt swollen from crying.

She croaked, "I'm sorry, I—"

"No. Uh-uh. You don't get to stand here on this grave on today of all days and be fucking *sorry*." He pointed at their mother's headstone. CHANDRA BOWERS LORDE. LOVING MOTHER. "You don't get to cry your crocodile tears, you hear me? You broke Mom's heart. You did this! You're just a selfish bitch who—"

Katie sobbed and slapped at his face with both hands. He grabbed her by her wrists. "Truth hurts, doesn't it, baby sis?"

"You hypocrite!" she spat. He let go of her wrists but didn't move back. Their chests heaved—his barreled out, hers caved in. She lifted her chin, meeting his bloodshot gaze. "Oh, I heard all about your rap sheet. You've been keeping busy these past few years, huh? Drunk driving, bar fights, dealing drugs. How many times did she have to bail you out, Vin? You don't think that hurt her, too?"

His face rippled in a series of competing emotions. "That's done. I'm out."

"You're on *parole*. Not the same thing. And if you're so done, then what was all that stuff I saw on your computer earlier, huh?"

His eyes bulged out. "The fuck you say?"

She crossed her arms. She wouldn't cower to him. Not anymore. She was too heartbroken, too mad. At him. At herself. How had this happened? Where was her big brother? The one who used to give her piggyback rides and let her crawl into his bed during thunderstorms? "You're doing something shady again." Her head ached, stuffed up from nonstop weeping. She wiped her nose on her sleeve.

"That's bullshit."

"With the Spirit of Dead Poets," she said. "I know what I saw, Vinnie. You two are scheming, some illegal business. Bootlegs?"

His jaw thrust out and his fists tightened at his sides. "Swear to god, you better stop running that goddammed mouth of yours before I—"

"You'll nothing, because if you do, then you'll be back in jail. Now where is he?"

"Who?"

"Holden Frost."

His nostrils flared. "Dunno what the fuck you're talking about." His upper lip always twitched when he lied.

Katie sighed. "Really? We have to do this? Because no one else would be signing off messages with poetry, and you and I both know it. *No eye may see*?"

"What the fuck you want from me, Pammy, huh? Why did you really come back?"

"I just want to say goodbye, okay? Is that so bad?"

"So say bye, then, and be done. What's that got to do with my life? You want me to say it's okay? You need my blessing, hugs and kisses or some shit? That it?"

"No." *Yes.* "Please, Vinnie..."

He pouted, softening the edges in his face.

"I'm tired of fighting with you," she admitted. "Do you really not care? Or miss me? Not even a little?"

His lips pinched tight. He avoided her gaze, staring at the headstone. Stubborn as always.

"Fine," she huffed. "Just take me to Holden. I wanna see him."

He scowled. "Why?"

"Because he was the only person in this entire shit town who was ever nice to me. *Always*," she added when he started to turn that particular shade of pink that only came when he was offended. "Even at school. And like I said, now that I'm here, I wanna set things straight. Thank him."

"And then what?" He tried to hide it, but she could see the hurt in his face. "You'll leave again? Turn your back on me, on your family?"

Her shoulders slumped and her tears streamed anew. She loved him. She did. But it wasn't enough. Since learning of their mother's death, the guilt had eaten away anything left inside her. She had left once. And she'd leave again. Vin didn't understand. This town was poison. Breathing its air made her sick. And now that she'd returned, she was both gasping for life and drained of it. "We all did what we had to," she said, her voice wispy, "to survive. You, me. Mom."

Vin sneered. She could almost hear his thoughts aloud: *Mom didn't survive.* She was dead. But he didn't say it. He didn't protest. Instead, he stared at her from beneath his heavy eyelids. She liked it better when he was yelling. "Come on, then," he finally growled. "Let's get this little reunion over with."

Katie hesitated as he marched away. Something in his calm demeanor was unsettling, like the eye of a storm. A sense of false relief sat heavy in her chest. But there was no choice, no other way to escape the deluge than to go through it.

She followed Vin to his truck

———

It wasn't over. Their resentment and bitterness merely rose with the altitude, winding and climbing, higher and tighter up the mountain road. Katie told herself not to dish it back. But Vin made it so easy, so tempting. He baited her over and over again, pushing the same sore buttons. And the worst part was, the stabbing pain in her heart meant she agreed with her brother.

He was right. He was right. He was right.

She'd bailed. She'd made their mother's addiction one million times harder—an impossible battle. Chemo had been a walk in the park compared to losing a daughter. Katie had left *him* to pick up the pieces of their dying mother. *Him* with all the hospice bills and the unimaginable grief and the goddammed funeral arrangements. Finally, she could endure no more of his judgment and superiority. Rage was a living, breathing contagion. The air inside the truck was acidic with it, cutting through the stink of booze and cigarettes. Katie screamed the words so loud that the windows rattled. She couldn't help it. They had been sitting on her tongue for too long.

You're nothing. A failure. A drunk. Just like mom.

Vin hollered something intelligible, his spittle striking her temple. He took his foot off the gas and spun the truck around. She jerked sideways into the passenger door. He was petty like that. He wouldn't give her what she wanted now, no matter how big or small. With the vehicle reversed, he sped back down, *down* to that awful, toxic town. Like a metaphor. You could try to leave, but really, the cesspool would suck you back in. He knew it, too. He mumbled promises: she'd never get out, not really. She belonged to the town, would be trapped there forever. Veins popped on his forehead. He looked crazed yet smug. He thought he had won. But no. Katie wouldn't return. Never again.

She grabbed the wheel. He slammed the brakes. And the world spun upside down.

———

When Vin cried, it was loud and ugly. His nose turned bright pink, his eyes became veined marbles, and his lips puffed out and sputtered. Katie wanted him to stop. But instead, her big brother howled her name. "Pammy, Pammy, please, oh god, nonono, Pammy..."

He did this so many times, she could no longer recognize his words.

Who was Pammy? She felt nothing and everything. The way he knelt beside her and peeled her off the cold, cracked blacktop. The way he cradled her roughly, flooding her with familiar smells: sweat, motor oil, whiskey, and musk. He slurred he was sorry. He didn't mean it. He sobbed and garbled regret, his throat clogged with tears.

Didn't mean what? she wanted to ask. *What happened?* Except she couldn't form the sounds. The questions dripped and dribbled away. He brushed slivers of glass off her cheeks. His fingers drew back slick—bright red like her eyesight, her hearing.

"We can't stay here," he said. "We can't... I can't..." His words faded into his choppy breaths. He ceased crying. His muscles froze up, as if bracing another shock. Then his eyes widened. They darted back and forth. The smashed truck. Her. The empty road.

He swore.

He licked his lips and heaved her up. "*Shouldna come back,*" he mumbled.

He moved swiftly and deftly despite his heft. He crossed past the curb, into the brush, and laid her in a nest of scratchy weeds. He lumbered away, out of sight. Cicadas buzzed sharply in her ears. Then he returned. This time, he avoided looking at her. He slung her over his meaty shoulder with one hand. She was leaking. Cold. No more than a wet sack of bones. Shards fell from her hair—a trail of little diamonds in stalks of dandelion. He marched...and marched.

Pine needles pricked. Branches snapped. Every now and again, low grunts and growls travelled through his chest. He was an animal in the wood. He belonged here; moved on instinct.

They passed the knotted stumps and roots of countless trees. The forest grew dense and humid. Like a fog, it swallowed her vision. She lost track of where she was or how she got here. She rocked with his footsteps even when he set her down. He tried to lean her against a trunk, but parts of her were misshapen and wouldn't obey. Clotted hairs stuck to her face. She wished to wipe them away. She longed to *see*. He abandoned his attempt to prop her and, instead, carved symbols into the bark above her shoulder. She couldn't make sense of them.

PKL.

He traded his pocket knife for his shovel. Turned away. He grunted as he dug. It didn't take long.

In one efficient maneuver, he pulled her by her ankles and rolled her into the shallow hole. The dirt was pebbled, basalt and petrichor on her tongue. It filled her up but left her empty. And trapped.

The earth held her. She was its prisoner. She wanted to go home. She wanted her mother. But it was so dark and heavy and hard. Too hard.

The thump of his spade rattled overheard, clapping through her skull. Her muscles spasmed into a fist. Her hand flinched in reply.

One. Two. Three. The knocks of her knuckles echoed long after he'd left.

FORTY-FIVE

Her lashes fluttered. She lay on the gravel in the greenhouse, her body shivering. Moths dancing. Katie was gone. Billie Holiday looped absently in her hearing. The pots she'd emptied were upright, brimming with drips. It was as if her moment with Katie had reversed itself. As if...

Pamela Lorde's broken bones flashed in her mind. The blood-spattered windshield. Vin's horrifying secret. Mave's stomach turned.

She pushed upright and crawled to the shelves in the corner, chains clinking. Her hands fumbled over random tools: rusted spray nozzles, trowels, weeders, sieves, tillers. No cutters or shears of any kind appeared. But landscape pins did.

She plucked one and felt its tip in the dark. It seemed just thin and strong enough to serve as a pick. She bent her foot at the ankle, brushed off the dirt, and inserted the pin into the keyhole. With a deep breath, she steadied her grip and manipulated the pin. Cain had taught her long ago, picking locks took patience and focus. And luck. She'd practiced on handcuffs countless times; she assured herself this wasn't much different.

It took five pins in total. She bent them and warped them and pried them, one after the next. Billie Holiday serenaded her again and again. Until the lock finally clicked free.

She inhaled sharply, her lungs filling with relief. But before she could unclip and remove the cuff from her ankle, something in the near distance caught her attention.

Which part of her registered his presence was unclear. Maybe it was her hearing, her sense of smell, or some innate reptilian radar. Mave blinked upward and searched for him through shadow.

The closest stack of chairs was over ten feet away. There was nowhere to duck, nothing to hide behind. Discarding her pin, her hand reflexively fisted gravel, readying to fling it in his face. She stood slowly, her feet spread for balance.

"Morning, Neat-Freak," he growled over the music.

Her eyes flicked to the direction of his voice. He emerged from a cloud of darkness. He wore a mask and carried a lantern—like the one Katie had held. The moths flittered at his wrists, the glass, the white of his mask. Mave could remember it now in the fogged-up bathroom mirror of the vacation home. He'd probably worn the same disguise while intimidating Liam into selling him his cellphone and cigarettes. It was scowling. But that was all it had in common with Holden's mask. Vin's covered his entire face and looked like a bearded monster from a Greek tragedy.

"Why the theatrics?" she croaked. He had her cornered. And he wasn't close enough to blind with dirt. Not yet.

"Come on, where's the love?" he said, tilting his head. "Heard you got off on guys in masks." When she didn't give him the satisfaction of a response, he lifted it off to reveal his smirk. His brow was scabbed where she'd struck him with the stapler days earlier. "To be honest," he grunted, "dunno how the freak always wears one." He wiped the sweat from his face and tossed the mask aside. "But seems it got you to *believe* now, didn't it? A little extra motivation—burnt books, cigarette smoke, a romantic song—to set the mood and keep you hooked." He waved, indicating Billie Holiday on loop.

"You were there," she realized. "You left me that book of Whitman's poems, broke into homes to make me think Holden was around?"

He grimaced playfully with a nod, clearly proud of his mischief.

"And the photos of Cain?" she asked, her voice like sandpaper. She already knew the answer. "Fakes?"

"What can I say? Folks underestimate me. I'm more than a grease monkey, sweetheart. Got all *kinds* of hidden talents."

She sucked in her cheeks, tasting bile. He'd doctored them. Cain had never been in danger. "What about the three knocks?"

His obnoxious grin faltered. "What knocks?"

Of your sister batting the earth ten years ago. So he didn't know of Katie's haunting, of her pain and grievance in the afterlife. Perhaps he was in as deep a denial as his sister, erasing that night he'd driven drunk and killed her. Mave had to be careful, patient like picking a lock.

"What do you want?" she said.

"Thought we had that covered." He placed his hand on his belt. An object protruded from his right hip. The hilt of his gun. "I want the freak."

"And I'm your bait?"

"Bingo. You're catching on."

"But why? What do you want with Holden so badly?"

Keep him talking, M&M. A little closer. Let him reach you.

Vin frowned as if reminded of something upsetting. "Passwords is what. The freak changed 'em all before he disappeared months ago."

"Passwords," she repeated.

"That's right. We got shared business accounts. Or, at least, we did."

"Then why not just hack in? Isn't that what you do? How you got past all those home security systems in Hazel Springs? Or how you messed with the camera feeds here?"

He scoffed. "You serious? This hotel's system is fucking child's play, same with local monitoring. Darknet is different. Untraceable. You can't hack what you can't find."

"What do you need these passwords for? Money? I can give you the—"

"Oh, we're beyond money," he said.

"Then what?"

He blinked, as if debating how much to say. "Intel."

"What kind of intel?" she pressed. "On who?"

He narrowed his eyes. "Why would I share that with the likes of you?"

Mave shrugged and crouched down, feigning exhaustion. Her blood beat pure adrenaline. She pretended to have an itch and casually scratched her calf, her ankle. "I've got nowhere to go, no one to talk to," she said, hoping to distract him with his own narcissism. She saw it in the curl of his lip, the puff of his chest. Men like Vincent Lorde had complexes, liked to brag. "Humor me."

"Humor, huh?"

"You mentioned talents. How did you get involved in this business?" *In what?* This had to be about more than just bootlegs.

"Actually"—he blinked into the distance—"it was thanks to my sister."

Mave paused.

"She ran away," he said in a low monotone. "I started spending more and more time online looking for her. High and low. Near and far. I got hooked. Wasn't easy on me, you see, on my..." He trailed off. He knuckled his goatee as his face twitched with memory.

His mother, Mave imagined. He was remembering Chandra Lorde. That much had been clear in Katie's confessional. Her disappearance had permanently broken the financial and emotional cracks in their family.

"Searching for her took me down some pretty deep rabbit holes," Vin admitted. "I learned some tricks along the way, and low and behold"—he smirked again, shutting down his regrets—"turns out I like operating in Wonderland."

"But now, these passwords..." If only he'd move forward another few steps, close enough for her to fling the gravel and buy herself seconds. If she tried to unclasp her ankle and run now, he was sure to block her. And after he'd tackled her in the gift shop, Mave wasn't confident she could take him, not with his massive weight or her current grogginess. She licked her lips. "You're in a jam. Must be to go to all this trouble. Gerald Lee Baker?"

Anger flashed in his eyes, same as it had in the offices with Gracelyn.

He didn't like to be reminded of his sins. "Back luck. Old man wasn't supposed to be home."

"And what if Holden doesn't have these passwords you so badly need? What if he won't give them? Then what? Am I supposed to stay locked up in here forever?"

"Nah, not forever." He placed the lantern on the ground, moths trailing his movements. "Told you from day one," he said. The resolve in his glare made her veins ice over. "I got a timer and won't wait long."

Ticktock. It had been his first message as Bek-187.

"Read your journal by the way," he said casually, as if discussing the weather. He pulled the moleskin notebook out from his back and tossed it toward her. "You should know, sweetheart, deep down, I wanted you two lovebirds to make it. Really, I did. But truth is..." He pulled out his gun. "Life's a bitch. It don't do happy endings."

Her eyes widened. She recognized immediately. It wasn't the pistol he'd held in the offices, which meant—

Not a tranquillizer.

"What—?" Mave's throat tightened. "What do you plan to do with me, then?"

He aimed the gun at her. "Get up," he said, his teeth gritted.

"Wait. Please." Her mind raced. "I don't feel well," she gasped. "You have to unchain me from the—"

He fired without warning. The impact made her recoil sideways. She hit the ground, hands covering her head. Her lungs heaved. As the dust settled, she yawned to ease the ringing in her ears and flinched upright. Nothing bled. She seemed unharmed. The shackle was still wrapped to her ankle. But its connecting chain had broken off.

"Said get up," Vin repeated. The rumble of his voice penetrated her bones. She had to do something—delay him. "It's too dark," she croaked. "I-I can't see straight."

Careful, M&M. His finger is back on the trigger. And his aim is too good.

His eyes were dilated, his focus glued to her like black lasers. He jerked his chin. "Move over here." He stepped back, keeping her within range as an easy target, while cutting off any exit or opportunity for her to physically strike him. With or without the gun trained on her, she still couldn't reach him. "Slowly," he commanded. "Take the lantern. That's it," he mumbled, watching her shuffle to obey. "Pick it up. Good. Keep moving." He waved the muzzle to guide her.

She paused, desperately scanning for any cover, any weapon or decoy.

"*Now.*" In two big steps, he'd reached her and dug the tip of the pistol into her spine.

She tightened her grip on the lantern, her breath ragged. Her brain scrambled. She could see no option but to do as he ordered. "Wh-where?" She extended the lantern in the direction he was indicating.

"*Wh-where?*" He mimicked. "To the fucking hatch leading underground. Or did you forget where I locked you up last time?" The flinch of her shoulders betrayed her shock. It must have pleased him. His tone returned to mocking. "That's right, sweetheart. I did it once, and I'll do it again. Only this time, Gracelyn won't be out here to feel sorry for you and open the door. In fact, I left you a little surprise. Once you get down there, give that dead cow my regards, would you?"

She inhaled sharply. "You...?"

"Go on." He prodded her forward. "See for yourself."

The first kill is the hardest. But the second or the third...it's survival, M&M.

Vin murdered them all—Pammy, Gerald Lee Baker, Gracelyn. And she'd be next.

"You don't have to do this," she said as she staggered to her execution spot. "Holden will come, he will. If you'll just wait a little longer, he'll—"

"Quit talking."

"Wait. I can help," she rasped in one breath, "I know what happened all those years ago, how much it hurt to lose your sister."

"Leave my sister outta this," he warned, slow and steady, crystallizing ice through her veins, "and shut your goddammed mouth. Or I'll shoot it off."

Mave pinched her lips together. Her jaw clenched as tears gathered in her eyes. Another ten steps and the hatch came into view. It lay open in wait—a boxed hole like a coffin. *No.* This wasn't her ending. Holden, Pammy, the car crash, the accident, their dreams and memories flooded her mind. Mave closed her eyes, finally understanding. It no longer mattered which direction she moved. Or how much combat training or criminal insight Cain had passed on to her.

I'm a medium.

She drew in her breath and called on the dead. Calm blanketed her heart.

"I'm still here. I won't leave you."

"The fuck you...?" Vin mumbled. The nudge of his gun eased in her spine and they slowed to a stop. The music had shut off, amplifying their breaths over drips of rainwater.

"Together. Let me help you," Mave swore. With everything inside her, she opened herself in invitation. The stink of earthen decay gathered in her nose, mouth, throat, lungs. And another uncanny scent... sharp, resinous plastic.

Gerald Lee Baker manifested first.

He stood to her left. His withered skin hung and glistened, a putrid canvas of pleats on bone. Matted ochers and pansy purples; spoiled peaches and blotted creams; dried veins coursing over greyish lesions and gaps and boils and slits. Hair like white floss stood on his maggot-infested skull. And his jaw slackened and formed a gaping wound in his face.

The moths flocked to him, filling him, shaping him.

Vin's words fell hard on her neck. "The fuck is happening? What is that thing?" He felt it. Saw it. He had to.

"Gerald Lee Baker," she whispered. "He's here." The old man's pearly eyes rolled to Vincent. He raised one knobby finger and pointed at his killer. Rage wafted. "He wants his stolen things back," Mave whispered. *His life.*

But the hollow figure to their right called more urgently. Darker and older in shape, her grievance tremored thickly, saturating all sensation.

"Pammy," Mave sighed. "You see it now, don't you? How it ends? You're—"

She sucked in the moths, filling her mouth with their serrated black wings.

MavePammyKatie. Together.

Her throat scorched.

Loam and mold and clay coated her tongue, teeth, gums. She swallowed a paste of rot and saliva, tears streaming. "Your sister has a message for you," she told him, her voice garbled and her eyelids fluttering. The gun in her back tremored.

"Stop it," he breathed. "You fucking witch, whatever you're doing, you—"

"She says she forgives you for burying her alive."

"*What?*"

"She was bleeding heavily, injured and broken from the crash. When you carried her into the forest, her heart was still beating. Faint and seeping. And you buried her alive, under that old pine tree"—she choked on bloodied mud—"you carved her initials to mark her grave: PKL. Pamela Kathryn Lorde."

"I said that's—"

Vin shoved her with the gun. Mave tottered to regain her footing. The release registered: the gun no longer pressed into her flesh. In his shock to silence her, end the horror of his sins, he made the same mistake as in the gift shop. He reached out to grab her, to redirect her into the hole before likely shooting her underground to hide his dirty work.

Mave's equilibrium wasn't fully restored, but her reflexes were. She didn't think about it. As soon as his fingers dug into her shoulder, she swung the lantern up into his face. The gun fired aimlessly as he hollered and lurched sideways. His lips furled back. "Fucking—"

Another bullet blasted with a spark.

Mave's hearing rang. She couldn't tell if she'd been struck. Adrenaline took over.

She kicked him in a single swift motion, snapping her foot out for maximum power. She'd been aiming above his navel, hoping to wind him long enough to grab the gun while he was disoriented and gagging. But not feeling one hundred percent, she missed.

Her strike connected beneath his hip. Pain shot through her foot. She remembered too late the broken shackle was still bound to her ankle, yet it fortified her hit like a punch with brass knuckles.

Vin's jaw snapped wide as the gun flew from his grasp. He reared back in a half spin. The rest was too quick to process.

The rush of the swarming insects. The hatch. The fall. The blow.

Vin was there. And Vin was gone.

Later, Mave would only remember select details: how Gerald Lee Baker's ghost had laughed along the way. How Vin's chin had dipped against his sternum at an odd angle. How the drips from the leaky ceiling echoed into a flooded pot. And the crack.

Even through the ringing, she heard the crisp break of his vertebrae. Hours later, Sheriff Morganson would ask her repeatedly about the underground steps, how he'd tumbled down them, and Mave would merely shake her head.

It was the sound of that fracture that stayed with her. It played back in her dreams with Katie's ghost, Katie's eyes.

Pamela Kathryn Lorde stood over the hatch and gazed down at her brother's broken body.

FORTY-SIX

One Month Later

T he clock glowed three a.m. Tomorrow was a big day for the hotel. A good night's rest was in order, yet Mave remained wide awake. She slid the handbook onto the nightstand, overtop her journal, and lay back on her bed.

She stared at the ceiling in the dark. Mave had read *Signs* cover to cover more than once, and each time, her feelings about the fortune teller were mixed. Gracelyn had been trying to save her addict son from Vincent. Mave now understood—the entire town knew thanks to the local news. Gracelyn had stolen a master key and uniform from house-keeping. Security footage showed her slipping into the spa more than once, undetected, presumably to spy and steal Mave's things from the box of tea tree oils. Not that Mave shared that with police. It was a moot point. Gracelyn was dead. And Mave had simply been collateral damage. Still, she had a sense that through all those warnings—the prophecy, her tea leaf reading, the handbook—Gracelyn had been conflicted and trying to alert Mave. She'd helped her by releasing the hatch door. She'd given her honest advice about channeling the dead.

Her brooding was interrupted by the buzz of her cellphone. Mave squinted at the bright screen. *Unlisted.* A week earlier, she'd mailed Cain a postcard. It seemed he'd gotten his hands on another smuggled line for their chat. She answered and welcomed his terse greeting.

"Tell me. Start at the beginning."

Without need of small talk or segues, she got straight to the point. She told him how Holden had saved her life in the fire, about going on the darknet, seeking information on his whereabouts, and how Bek-187 had responded with a threat on his life. When she was done explaining, Cain remained silent. She expected he wouldn't be pleased with her actions. She held her breath, awaiting his judgment.

"Dad, you still there?"

"Are you okay?" His voice sounded deeper than normal. It caught her off guard. Those three little words were rare for her father to say.

"Yeah, I mean"—she shoved down a sudden knot of emotion—"I'm fine."

"Because if he so much as touched a hair on your—"

"Dad, I swear, I'm fine. He can't hurt me anymore. I handled it."

Vincent had survived that awful night. And he'd been hooked to ventilators in intensive care ever since. The accidental bullet he'd taken to his foot had been minor, but the fracture to his vertebrae... Doctors said he would never move again. Or wake up.

A vegetable for life.

"Good," Cain grunted, as if hearing the prognosis aloud. "Then we understand each other. He came after you. You got him to back off. You did your part. Now let me do mine."

"No, you don't have to—"

"He disrespected me, Mave Michael."

"So you're going after him, lying helpless in a hospital bed, to protect your pride?" She knew it was useless to argue with him when he got like this. His mind would be set.

"Wrong. It's not about my pride. It's about your safety. Survival of the fittest, M&M. It always has been. You're my daughter. And you nearly died trying to protect me from this fool. It should've been the other way around. And it will."

Regret wasn't in her father's emotional bandwidth. "What do you mean?"

"I mean you. And me. You didn't ask for my help when you

should've because you were too stubborn, too mad I didn't give you the name of my source at the hotel."

She scoffed. "It's more complicated than that, and you know it."

"Is it? It's an ugly world out there, and if you're going to survive it, you have to trust me."

"Dad, forget it. It's over. That's all I ever wanted. For no one to get hurt. To be free of this."

"Wrong again, M&M. You won't ever be free."

"Why the hell not?" But deep down, she already understood. Her father was a deadly criminal, imprisoned or not. Other Bek-187s would be out there.

"If they did it once," he said, his low rasp drawing goosebumps on her arms, "they'll do it again. But I can make them think twice about trying. Make it easier for you to rely on me."

"Rely on you how?"

"The person I had reporting back to me about your activities—my spy, as you like to call him—was Dominic Grady."

Her mouth slackened.

"He's in the system," he added pragmatically, "owed me a favor."

"Dominic," she repeated. The same Dominic who was a New York City art dealer, who, unbeknownst to Cain, had secretly slept with her mother years ago, and who had held her hand during a séance.

"After everything that happened last winter with—" He paused, omitting Holden's name, perhaps wary to remind her he was still missing. "Dominic had his uses," he finished.

Mave pinched the bridge of her nose, needing more time to process her frustration. At least this explained Dom's continuous lurking and requests to spend time with her. "Okay, well, I can't say that I'm happy or approve, and I already know you won't listen to me when I tell you to *stop* getting people to spy on me, but..." She released a pent-up breath. "Thanks. For telling me. And I'll need you to be up front with me from now on, okay? No more secrets, right?"

"So long as you're safe," he said, unclear if was agreeing to it all or in part.

It wasn't perfect, Mave thought, her eyelids heavy. But it was a start.

———

The following night, the hotel's bustle and buzz coursed through her like a drug. Addictive, nourishing. Finding a rare reprieve from her evening duties, Mave stepped out the main lobby doors. She wandered past the angel fountain where guests smoked cigars and chatted. Tipsy laughter drifted in the breeze. Mave found a parked limousine and perched on its bumper.

After the disaster of that weekend in March, ironically, it was the media's attention and vetting of her psychic talent that had brought the bride back around—"attention" being the operative word. Bridezilla called Julián the day after news broke of Vincent's arrest. She commended Mave for her unique assistance with the investigation and gave them an ultimatum: either they refunded her and each one of her guests for her spoiled weekend, including all extraneous wedding fees, *or* they offered her an exchange: a perfect postponed wedding in April with complimentary suites. When she hinted of a lawsuit over the goat's head, Julián caved, though he managed to talk her down to half-price room charges and an exclusive séance for her wedding party alone, led by the château's medium, Mave Michael Francis.

Mave tried not to worry about it. She turned her face into the moonlight and inhaled deeply. The nightscape offered a distinct comfort. Blooms of lilac and hyacinths filled her. She could almost ignore the pinch of her uniform's corset—but not the shape of the cruiser pulling up the driveway in her peripheral vision.

A moment later, the car door shut. His boots crunched over gravel.

Ren joined her and eased his weight onto the shiny limo. He held the manila envelope for her, but made no gesture to pass it along. Not yet. He looked forward, avoiding her gaze. His nose, though healed, was still crooked from her kick. A souvenir of their last encounter.

"Ren..." Her voice cracked. "You didn't have to come tonight. We could've done this over—"

"Thought you'd want to know," he said, crossing his arms, "forensics came back on Pammy's remains. Vin's been charged with three counts of murder. For his sister, Baker, and Gracelyn. Not that he'll ever wake to see a trial."

The journalists had been running stories all month: Vincent Lorde was a monster. The formerly incarcerated drug dealer had successfully orchestrated multiple home invasions in Hazel Springs, including one botched attempt that resulted in the death of Gerald Lee Baker. He'd gone on to shoot dead his accomplice, Gracelyn da Silva, after their arrangement had gone south. And most scandalous of all, a decade earlier, he'd murdered his younger sister Pamela Lorde. After years of scarce leads, police had unearthed Pamela's bones from deep within the mountain forest, solving the case of the missing young woman—all thanks to a local psychic, Mave Michael Francis.

Mave pushed back her shoulders and sighed. She wasn't sure how to feel about the media's new take, but at least she was finally more than a hitman's daughter. "Morganson told me," she said. "She called earlier and asked if I'd be interested in consulting on another case. I told her I'd think about it."

He wouldn't look at her. She cleared her throat. "Ren, I've been meaning to tell you, sorry for..." She indicated his nose. "Does it still hurt?"

"Nah." He inclined his head, searching the stars. "You? Heard you did physio for your ankle."

She rolled her foot in her stiletto. Her ankle remained scarred from the shackle and her strike. "I'm all right." She absently traced the phantom wound on her neck. Some nights, she still felt it—the bite and sink of the tranquillizer. Ren noticed.

He cursed under his breath and scrubbed his hand down his face. "If I'd known, Mave... Just wish you'd given me more of a chance."

"Me too." She smiled weakly. "I wasn't fair. I shouldn't have—I mean, you've probably figured I have a lot going on in my life right now, stuff I need to sort out before I get into any kind of..."

He finally looked into her eyes, searching each of her irises in turn. "Holden Frost?" She could read it now, that ripple of emotion in his features: longing. Remorse. The boy he'd kissed fifteen years ago in a fit of wanton anger and desire had vanished—but only in body.

She bit her lip and nodded. "You were right. About me being haunted."

"You mean he's really—?"

"Gone." It was the only truth that mattered. She wrapped her arms around her middle. "But this place..." She shrugged. "It has a way of keeping memories alive."

"And all that stuff on the darknet?"

"It was stupid of me." She brushed a strand of hair from her mouth and stared into her lap. "But it's over. You don't have to worry about that."

"Thing is, I don't know what's better." His smooth drawl tempted her to lean her head on his shoulder. She resisted. "Forget I ever saw anything," he continued, "or ask you if you need more help. Is your father...?"

"He had nothing to do with this. He's fine." *A survivor. Like me.* She picked at the ends of her corset's laces. "You were right about Vin's insane grudge," she said, oversimplifying the truth. "Guess it was easier to blame Holden's memory for Pammy than to face his own terrible actions. But Holden's not coming back, no matter how many threats or strange dreams this place gives me." It was one version of events. Accurate enough. After everything that had happened, her heart was more tired than hopeful.

"Hey, Mave?"

When she blinked up at him, he surprised her by leaning down. His lips were soft, pleasing, brushing hers with what could have been. "I'm sorry, too," he said, pulling away with his lashes lowered. "You ever get tired of chasing your ghosts, you give me a call." He slid her the envelope, pushed off the limo, and left her alone with her thoughts.

Once he'd driven away and out of sight, Mave opened the envelope.

Inside was his signed endorsement of her application with the county. Family documents further detailing the property's history. The legacy of his great-grandfather. All that research she'd done into his family line and the château had planted the idea in her head. The century-old architectural design, the hotel's local thumbprint, it was eligible for heritage designation. And with Ren's help, in roughly one month, Château du Ciel would be protected by law. The building would be impossible to demolish or replace, with or without steady revenue.

"Mave?"

She turned to Bastian's call.

He held open the lobby door. "It's time," he informed her.

She slipped the papers into the envelope, nodded with a smile, and turned back inside for the midnight vows.

———

The ceremony in Queen's Hall was darkly magical: fluttering oil lamps in arched ruins, iron pillars capped with grotesques, garlands of burgundy dahlias. The string quartet played a rendition of "Kiss From a Rose" by Seal. Even the groom in his tailored tux with satin lapels looked stunning, and, of course, Bridezilla in a custom-made violet organza gown, crowned with thorny black roses. Before long, the vows were over and the wedding party was strutting back down the aisle to "Just Like Heaven" by The Cure under a barrage of mulberry petals and camera flashes.

The two hundred and sixty-one guests gathered their belongings and filed into the grand ballroom. They oohed and aahed over the black champagne fountain, snapping selfies. Catering service began: Périgord truffle canapes, Gascony foie gras, Beluga caviar. Any indulgence the bride dreamed of, the staff perfected into reality. From the crushed velour and sable furs, to the lace gloves and patent leather, each detail appeared flawless.

Mave's cellphone buzzed. She glanced down at Bastian's message: a panoramic photo of the library. His thumbs-up followed. Everything was ready downstairs for her final check. Mave enlarged the photo. The table and chairs had been arranged across from the black stone hearth. The fire snapped and crackled. Over the mantle, the keepsakes hung as per her request: portraits of the dead...and a three-faced porcelain mask.

Mave replied she'd be down in a minute. She placed a hand on her abdomen, settling the nerves in her stomach. With a final scan of the chattering guests toasting and sipping from their pewter goblets, she left the extravagance of the reception in Julián's capable hands.

Inside the library, she thanked Bastian for overseeing the setup. The black calla lilies. Wrought-iron candelabras. Smoke of sage, clove, frank-incense.

It was perfect.

"You're gonna do great." Bastian gave her a warm smile. "Scare the ancestral shit outta that diva." He winked with his trademark hearty chuckle, and left her in good spirits to ready herself. The ritual required quiet, focus. She'd arrived early just in case—a full hour before Bastian would return with the select group from the wedding party in tow.

Savoring the solitude, she wandered to the fireplace. Heady incense and wood smoke steeped in her throat. She wiped the sweat from the back of her neck. She hadn't taken the warmer spring temperatures into account. Or perhaps a part of her was still anxious. She glanced up from the fire, seeking comfort from her keepsakes, and blinked.

For a moment, her heart merely stopped.

Holden's mask no longer hung next to the portraits. In its place, a blank notecard was pierced on the nail. Her mouth fell ajar. A prank? Did someone swipe the disguise in the time since Bastian had taken the photo and she'd come downstairs?

Mave pulled loose the stationary and flipped over the card. The message was brief.

Meet me in the penthouse.

Her chest rose and fell in uneven waves. The bold handwriting resembled Holden's. Was this real? When had he left this? She looked down the nearest aisle of bookshelves, left and right. The library was vacant of all noise and commotion. Not a soul in sight. And yet...the unsigned invitation.

With a trembling hand, she lifted the note to her nose and drew in its scent. It was unmistakable. Holden's cigarettes saturated the card-stock. Hope fluttered, warring with fear. She tried tracking the mask with her sixth sense but didn't get much more than a blurry read. It was nearby. And dark.

Upstairs.

Mave dropped everything and dashed to the twenty-third floor. Uncaring of pretenses or reputations—of Cain's warnings firing off in her head about traps and tricks and dangers designed in the name of foolish love—her blind trust strengthened with each step closer to the penthouse. Cons and lies be damned. A piece of her heart was missing. And she had every intention of reclaiming what belonged to her.

Her legs burned. She panted from the run, from the promise uttered to her so many months ago.

"Home. I always came back."

She fumbled and dropped her keys at the penthouse doors. With a curse, she managed to reclaim the right key. She flicked the deadbolt, flung open the door, and darted into the studio.

Empty.

"Holden!" Her voice bounced from the walls. She made for the next room, drunk on faith, nearly knocking over a plinth. A little rational thought slipped through the crashing currents of her yearning: the penthouse was locked and monitored with cameras, how would he get past?

Not bothering to check the sitting room or its many nooks and connecting doors, she darted deeper into the suite, to the master bedroom's walk-in closet—the one Ren had shown her. Ren had learned from *him*, after all. Holden had taught him the secret ways to slip in and out, unnoticed through the walls.

She rushed inside just as he was pushing out of the wardrobe.

Her breath caught.

There he was. After all these months. Whole. Alive. He swept crumbs of plaster from his wavy hair, bleached and overgrown with dark roots. In the cutout of his mask, his beard was shorter. As his dark eyes fell on her, a swell of emotion clouded her vision. She wiped her tears with the heels of her hands, trying to assess each part of him. He wore a skin-toned compression vest, a pair of hospital pants tied low on his corded waist.

"I dreamed of you," he said, sounding winded. "You were wearing my mask." Neither one of them moved, as if afraid the moment could end before it'd begun. Their chests heaved in unison and their eyes locked and pulled with need.

"I-I can't believe—" She swallowed the lump in throat. "You're..."

"I know." He blinked, matching her stunned expression. "I'd say I came as soon as I could, except I'm not sure if I'm really home or having another one. A dream. You look...you look..." He inhaled deeply as his gaze travelled down her black corset, hips, thighs.

"Holden?" She had to know.

Is this real?

She took a step forward and reached out cautiously, both desperate to touch him and nervous he might dissolve into smoke if she did. He fixed his stare to her mouth and waited, his thick lashes lowered and his breath wavering.

She unmasked him, dropped the disguise. She cupped his hollow cheek, and he swore. The spark between them rushed. Shocking. Heating. Igniting them whole.

He fell to his knees and buried his face in her waist. His warm breath pushed through the fabric of her dress, tickling her scar. She wanted to laugh and cry. She curled over him and inhaled his smoky hair. He moaned something into her stomach, sending tremors through her navel. A thousand tiny black moths fluttered over her skin.

He'd come back to her.

She kissed the top of his head, the side of his temple, his earlobe, his jawline. Found herself on her knees, too, wrapped in his arms and molded to his lips. He tasted like she remembered, like amber whiskey, oak and cinnamon and citrus. They swayed, losing balance, pushing, pulling—not enough. They tipped into the wardrobe and rattled hangers. She didn't want the kiss to end. But as she slid her hand up the side of his chest, he tipped his head away with a hiss.

She pulled back. "You're hurt."

"I'm okay."

"Show me."

"It's nothing," he gasped, "just some—"

"Show me," she repeated more anxiously.

"Okay." His lips curled up. He trailed his fingers down her throat to the top of her corset. "But only if you promise to keep parts of this outfit on as you nurse me back to health."

"Holden."

"Think we may need a bed."

"I'm serious."

"So, no to the sponge bath?"

"I swear, I'm this close to—"

He kissed her again and she couldn't help herself. She no longer remembered what they'd been arguing about.

————

They lay together on the velvet divan in the sitting lounge, curves to edges, their legs draped over top one another. He settled his head on her breast and played with the laces on her uniform. She brushed his hair, wound a lock around her finger, unable to stop touching him. She wasn't ready to give up this relief, this joy, no matter how fleeting. But she had to know.

"Vincent?" she whispered, almost hoping he wouldn't catch the question.

His fingers faltered on her laces. She thought he might not answer, or worse, shut down completely. But then he spoke.

"Stratis left me a message." He resumed his casual inventory of her corset. "Vin died earlier this afternoon."

Cain.

Mave closed her eyes, needing more time to process her feelings. "Are you—I mean, was he your friend?" she said. A pang of unease swept through her.

"Not sure I'd use that word." His voice stretched lazily, but she caught the edge beneath his tone. "More like...an associate."

That was the same description Bek-187 had given: an impatient associate.

She borrowed Cain's words from last night. "Tell me. Start at the beginning."

Without letting her go, Holden shifted upward so that their faces were level. His dark eyes were animated. "Two things you need to know about Vincent: he made a living as a low-level gangster and had delusions of grandeur. Years ago, when I first began working the darknet, we started a bootleg business—Hollywood movies."

"You translated films for him?"

He nodded. "We had a steady thing going. Bans on Hollywood productions in certain Arab and Asian countries made for good business on the black market. But then he branched out on his own. Wanted more and more money. Got involved with drug trafficking. Pretty sure he opened his garage to launder money for others. Heard he made some promises to the cartel he couldn't keep. They threatened to take him out."

"He mentioned you two had shared accounts, passwords."

He shook his head. "Never shared. Vin only knew I had connections. With his own bridges burned, he was desperate for a way back in. He probably wanted to steal my accounts, pose as me to stir more deals and record dirt, try to flip the tables on the guys after him. Like I said, delusions of grandeur."

"And when you disappeared after the fire?"

"For a short while, I was in a coma. Then drugged up as they performed surgeries on me—skin grafts."

"The burn clinic," she whispered. The one he'd been transferred to after the hospital in Denver.

He nodded. "I didn't realize until too late, Vin's been looking to find me for months."

"On the darknet."

"Yeah. He saw your post, probably figured he had nothing to lose. Would hardly take him any effort to doctor some photos of your father, make it look like he was really in reach of hurting him." He propped his head in his hand, his brow folded inward. She tried to rub away the crease of worry, but he grasped her hand and kissed her fingers.

"Soon as I heard he'd contacted you," he said, "I asked Stratis to come help you. I figured Vin would be up to some trouble, but I didn't realize just how stupid he'd be. Dangling your father as bait like that..." He sighed. "And then I had another bad spell, caught an infection and couldn't think straight with the drugs pumping through my system. I had no idea what you were going through. I should've reached out sooner. But I wasn't sure. The fire destroyed the tunnels, and the last time we spoke, you were so upset. I didn't know if you'd ever want to—"

"Holden, I'm—"

"This is all my fault."

"No." She held his face in her palms. "No," she repeated. "It was a huge misunderstanding. Everything that happened last winter. And afterwards." She exhaled the pain and regrets. "None of that matters anymore. You're here. You're alive. And I never got to tell you..."

He searched her eyes. "Tell me what?"

"Thank you for saving my life," she whispered, "in the fire."

"Always." He laced their fingers together. Electricity streamed between them.

An urgent knocking interrupted the moment. The studio doors. Bastian's voice carried from the hallway. "Mave, you in there? You okay?"

She cursed softly. In her hurry, she'd left her phone and radio in the library. She pushed up and fought a head rush. "What time is it?"

Holden lounged lazily with his arm tucked behind his head. "Two in the morning maybe?" He watched her curse some more and scramble to find her heels.

"There's something I have to go do, but—" She turned and stared at him, her heart knocking too fast against her ribcage.

He reached for her hand and squeezed, his eyelids heavy. "I'm here. Promise: as long as you want me, Mave, I won't leave."

Trust. He belonged with her. Together.

She nodded and leaned down, brushing the words against his lips. "Welcome home, Holden Frost."

————

If Holden could see the wedding party gathering in the library—*his* library—he'd likely wish himself into a real ghost just to terrorize them for an emergency evacuation. But now wasn't the time to think of Holden Frost's territorial instincts. Or his mouth on hers.

Mave sighed through her nose and held out her candelabra like a flashlight. As the giddy guests clad in platform boots and haute goth shuffled to take their seats at the round table, a newfound faith batted inside her chest. Everything was in order. She was ready. She held dripping candlewax away from a passing groomsman in a frilly shirt and surveyed the excited faces around her. Kohl-lined eyes everywhere. Raven tattoos. Black-polish manicures. And beneath the dark coats of makeup and glamor, the singular need and longing. They each wanted it. A comfort once held, now lost. A sign that, in the end, the pain of life and death led to something more.

This was Mave's calling.

Bastian mumbled *excuse me* to a bridesmaid and requested she shut off her phone. The social media influencer grumbled yet complied. Between Mave's no-recording policy and the basement's poor Wi-Fi, trying to document the library's romanticism was a wasted effort.

Once everyone in the wedding party found their seats, Mave smiled brightly in her red lipstick and joined them. She set her candelabra on the table. Silence settled over the room. Twelve pairs of eyes fell on her: the flickering main event. The medium.

"Please hold hands," she said, offering hers to the bride and groom to her left and right.

She sensed the circle solidify. It flowed through her palms and coursed through her arms, shoulders, spine, as clear and cleansing as saltwater in the ocean's deep. Mave closed eyes and saw. "Now, let's begin..."

Acknowledgments

The Black Moth has been a labor of love from start to finish. Thank you to Ann Leslie Tuttle for her expertise and support, and for always pushing me to write the best story I can. I'm super grateful to have you in my corner! Thank you to Chantelle Aimée Osman for her enthusiasm for this series, and for guiding and inspiring my plot in its early stages. Thank you to Jason Pinter and the team at Agora/Polis Books for seeing this novel through to the finish line, making sure it lands on bookshelves coast to coast. It's truly a dream come true, and I pinch myself daily.

I couldn't have completed *The Black Moth* without the help of my talented friends and critique partners. Thank you to the wonderful Sarah Robertson, Kristen Kolynchuk, Anne Stubert, Malia Márquez, and Karen Winn for reading pieces of my messy drafts. Chapter by chapter, you cheered me on and helped me stay the course.

Huge thanks to the fab readers, bloggers, podcasters, and librarians for selecting and/or recommending *The Hitman's Daughter + The Black Moth*. It means so much to me! Likewise, thank you to my writing comrades and communities at Crime Writers of Canada, Sisters in Crime, HWA, SF Canada, ITW, 22 Debuts, IALA, and Pitch Wars. I feel lucky to write cross-genre for the opportunity to "hang out" with all you talented and cool people.

A heartfelt thank you to my amazing family and friends, near and far, for their steadfast love and support. A writer's life is a lonely one full of overwhelming rejection, and your belief in me pulls me out from the dark and into the light - xo!